Stephen King

AMERICA'S BEST-LOVED

BOOGEYMAN

The most haunted of houses is the human mind.

—Patrick McGrath

Stephen King

AMERICA'S BEST-LOVED
BOOGEYMAN

George Beahm

Andrews McMeel
Publishing

Kansas City

www.andrewsmcmeel.com

98 99 00 01 02 EBA 10 9 8 7 6 5 4 3 2 1

This book was not authorized by Stephen King, his staff, or his publishers.

Library of Congress Cataloging-in-Publication Data
Beahm, George W.
Stephen King : America's Best-Loved Boogeyman
/ George Beahm.
p. cm.
Includes bibliographical references (p.   ).
ISBN 0-8362-5427-9
1. King, Stephen, 1947- —Criticism and interpretation.
2. Horror tales, American—History and criticism. I. Title.
PS3561.I483Z54 1998
813'.54—dc21   98-5322
CIP

Attention: Schools and Businesses

Andrews McMeel books are available at quantity discounts
with bulk purchase for educational, business, or sales promotional use.
For information, please write to: Special Sales Department,
Andrews McMeel Publishing, 4520 Main Street,
Kansas City, Missouri 64111.

for Colleen

BEYOND FEAR

by Stephen J. Spignesi

Men fear death as children fear to go in the dark; and as that natural
fear in children is increased with tales, so is the other.

Francis Bacon, "Of Death"

NORMAN VINCENT PEALE once wrote, "Fear can affect us early in life
. . . fear is strong."

The ability to cause fear brings with it a certain power; a kind of exqui-
site control over a person that is unlike the authority that money, class status, or even love can wield.

It is a measure of Stephen King's masterful prowess in this area that of
the many books written about him and his fiction, several of them have the
word "fear" in their title, including *Faces of Fear, Feast of Fear, Reign of Fear,
Kingdom of Fear, Landscape of Fear,* and *Fear Itself.*

What, specifically, is it that Stephen King makes us fear when we read
his books and stories?

Why, what else, but death?

Some of the most terrifying moments in King's fiction are about death.
King's most well-drawn characters—Mother Abagail, Ben Hanscom, Paul
Sheldon—are all shown the face of death and it is then that they become the
most human.

And yet, any serious reader of Stephen King will realize that King's fiction deliberately and regularly moves beyond fear; that the best of his work
addresses complex issues of morality and conscience; of love and lust; of

childhood and adult disillusionment; of the existence (or chimera) of God; and even such hot button topics as euthanasia, abortion, racial tension, and spousal abuse.

What this all means is that Stephen King wears a coat with many pockets—but to many who know him only by his "America's Boogeyman" persona (and the dozens of movies made from his works do not help to dispel such an image), those pockets are hidden and therefore invisible. Sadly, these are the people who will never be able to enjoy the many delights concealed in those pockets: One must reach into a pocket to discover what is inside it, right?

There are moments of great pathos and high drama in Stephen King's fiction.

In his 1998 novel *Bag of Bones* (his first with Simon & Schuster), for instance, King tells a story of racial horror that had such a profound impact on the people involved that the echoes of the incident survived even death, affecting the lives of people who weren't even born when the atrocities took place.

In *Rose Madder*, King takes us inside the mind of a battered wife, showing us—with painstaking clarity and a visceral specificity—her fear and emotional torment; helping us truly to understand what it means to be married to a sadistic abuser. King makes us cringe from Rose's pain—while telling us one hell of a good story at the same time.

In King's award-winning short story "The Reach," he tells the story of Stella Flanders's transcendant walk to her death, and in so doing, achieves a level of style and narrative excellence that stands equal with the best American writing of this century.

And in King's brilliant 1994 tale, "The Man in the Black Suit"—a short story that won the 1994 World Fantasy Award for Best Short Fiction and the 1994 O. Henry Award for Best American Short Story—King adds his own contribution to that genre of American stories in which Satan himself pays some hapless human a visit. The awards for this story were justified. "The Man in the Black Suit" is as good—if not better—than anything Nathaniel Hawthorne ever wrote and it is further evidence that a century from now—when we're all tooling around in flying cars and everything is voice-activated and computer-controlled, Stephen King's stories will still be read and enjoyed.

Foreword

I know, from endless direct experience, that a person who actually writes for a living . . . and clearly does well financially at it . . . is an object of curiosity to many—an exotic creature, not quite respectable, but very interesting. I'm buttonholed about it every time I appear in public—which used to be fun but has grown to be a nuisance.

—Robert A. Heinlein, *Grumbles from the Grave*

Everyone who works in the domain of fiction is a little crazy. The problem is to render this craziness interesting.

—Francois Truffaut

George Beahm, the author of the book you now hold in your hands, and I, your intrepid emcee, toil in a strange land, this Land of the King.

We both share a passion for the work of Stephen King, that's a given. But we also have in common an unquenchable desire to, first, know all we can about the terrain of this land; and, second, to then write down everything we learn.

Thus, we have the revised and updated edition of George's literary biography of Stephen King.

George tells me that even though the starting point for this new book was his original *The Stephen King Story*, he essentially threw out the majority of that earlier work and started over with this new Life of the King. It is a testament to King's prolific output and varied and spirited endeavors that since the publication of the first edition of *The Stephen King Story* in 1991, there is enough new information to paint a fresh portrait of this man known throughout the world as the Lion of Literary Dread.

It is well known that Stephen King feels that the scores of books about him are unnecessary. (We are all very familiar with his oft-repeated maxim, "It is the tale, not he who tells it.") King sincerely believes that his stories should be enough for his fans. In a letter, King once told me that he often found himself in the position of being "less than thrilled to be on the market again not as a writer with a book but as the subject of a book—a commodity to be pawed over like used goods at a church rummage sale."

King's fans unquestionably feel otherwise.

King's 1997 appearance on *60 Minutes* garnered strong ratings because his fans are interested in him as a person—not just as a writer. This is the bane of being rich and famous, I suppose, but is probably a small price to pay for being blessed with the artistic ability and power to touch so many people in so many ways with your work.

In this new book about King, George Beahm looks at the life of one of the twentieth century's most prolific—and important—writers. George takes us on a journey from King's boyhood years traveling around the Midwest with his single mom; to his formative years growing up in the small town of Durham, Maine; and through his high school and college years. He details King's first big score—the paperback sale of *Carrie*—and meticulously chronicles the rise of a literary figure who would ultimately become his own genre—"Stephen King."

In his massive bibliography of King's work, *The Work of Stephen King*, King scholar Dr. Michael Collings quotes writer Algis Budrys discussing this very unique development: "I think [Stephen King has] founded his own genre—and has been followed into it by scores of other writers. . . . "

Quick . . . how many other American writers can you name who are credited with creating their own literary genre?

There are countless writers known for working within a specific genre: Edgar Allan Poe for mysteries; William Faulkner for the Southern gothic; Sylvia Plath for self-contemplative poetry of alienation; Mark Twain for the humorous novel.

But Stephen King created his own hybrid of literary genres (the genre of "Stephen King") when he began writing, smoothly assimilating into one seamless (and occasionally indefinable) genre the trappings and characteristics of several narrative styles, including fantasy, horror, westerns, the coming-of-age tale, science fiction, crime fiction, epic poetry, the quest novel, and contemporary mainstream fiction.

In 1986, during an interview with *Time* magazine, King was asked his opinion of his own novels. His response? "The literary equivalent of a Big Mac and a large fries from McDonald's."

This from the man who wrote *The Shining*, *'Salem's Lot*, *It*, *Misery*, the Dark Tower series, "The Body," "The Reach," and countless other works that stand tall as superb and powerful examples of contemporary twentieth-century horror and dark fantasy writing.

Foreword

And yet Stephen King himself compares his novels (even his wonderful and timeless works like *The Shining* and *It*) to vapid, less-than-gourmet quality, eminently forgettable fast food.

There are those of us who do not agree with King on this point.

I am one of them.

And so is George Beahm.

And thus, George's new book.

May it enhance your reading and add to your enjoyment of Stephen King's tales.

And may it also take you beyond fear . . . to that world hidden somewhere deep in an inside pocket.

It is there, you know: All you have to do is go look for it. And George's book is a terrific place to begin your search.

Stephen J. Spignesi
December 1997
New Haven, Connecticut

THE LIONIZED KING

by George Beahm

EVERY YEAR IN November, book publishers around the world gather in Frankfurt, Germany, to get a preview of the big books for sale, most of them from the United States. In contrast to previous years, however, 1997's offerings seemed pretty ordinary—business as usual—until rumors began to fly that Stephen King, after two decades with NAL, was shopping around *Bag of Bones*, his latest novel.

The rumors, as it turned out, were founded in truth. King was splitting from NAL in a very publicized divorce, to the chagrin of the publishing industry and King himself, engineered by King's agent and manager, Arthur B. Greene.

King, however, was nowhere to be found. In fact, he was halfway around the world, out of touch, unavailable for comment, just as he wished.

A winter of King's discontent, the best-selling author looking for a new home was getting a reception from other publishers fit for a king—for *the* Stephen King, who got $2,500 for *Carrie* in 1974 and was now asking $17 million for *Bag of Bones*.

King, who started out as a writer, then became a major figure in popular culture, inevitably became a celebrity. The average guy on the street, when pigeonholed, will probably not have read any of King's books, though he might have seen a movie or two, but he will know the household name—Stephen King.

The Stephen King Phenomenon, as Michael Collings termed it, is unique among his fellow scriveners. The other best-selling storytellers—Tom Clancy, Michael Crichton, John Grisham, Patricia Cornwell, Dean Koontz, and Anne Rice, to name a few—have sold millions of copies of their books, and their reputations rest largely on their annual blockbusters.

King not only sells millions of books and belongs in that rank but he belongs in another rank, as well: a prolific *writer*. Working steadily, four hours a day, King creates a torrent of words—letters to the local newspaper, op-ed pieces, poetry, nonfiction in all lengths, screenplays, short stories, novellas, and, of course, monstrous-sized novels that make his publishers and his readers happy, while distressing some of his book critics, particularly those who have literary airs and look down at King, whom they perceive as a horror writer, the print equivalent of Jordy Verrill (a Maine hayseed portrayed by King in *Creepshow*).

King, back in his college days, decided the distinction between popular and literary fiction was arbitrary and consciously set out to bridge that gap.

For years, the literary cognoscenti have overlooked the fact that well-regarded academicians, gathering for the Literature of the Fantastic conferences, read papers on King's fiction, taking it seriously.

In recent years, however, the critical perception has shifted ever so slightly: King not only was the subject of a weekend seminar at his alma mater, where critical papers were delivered, but he started appearing regularly in the august pages of *The New Yorker* magazine, premiering with a long essay, "Head Down," selected for inclusion in an anthology of best sports writing that year; and, more recently, "The Man in the Black Suit," which not only won an award inside the fantasy field but, more significantly, *outside* it: The story took first place in the *Prize Stories 1996: The O. Henry Awards*, beating out a thousand other eligible stories, including the usual bumper crop of fiction by literary writers, some of whom were likely self-righteously pissed that King—vocal in his condemnation of the literary establishment—had even made an appearance in the book.

King, not his critics, has a right to be upset. His name is often used—misused, actually—as an example of a writer whose work can't be good because he's popular. (King, who has categorically stated that he thinks he'll never win a National Book Award, decided that a few years ago, in the company of other best-selling popular writers, he'd make an appearance at one of their award ceremonies; so he bought a table and invited his friend John Grisham and others who joined him in a show of protest, probably to the horror of the other attendees. This was *their* party, the literary writers probably sneered, and how *dare* these, these popular novelists make a mockery of our awards ceremony! Do they think *they* are going to win anything here? Not bloody likely!)

In the end, all that matters is the writing—a fact that some of the literary critics conveniently overlook, as they dismiss him.

In the end, it gets down to what King puts on paper. The fans, the adulation, the articles and books written about him, the interviews and endless profiles, the media attention, the cult of the celebrity—none of that matters. Only the words matter; the rest is eyewash.

On April 16, 1997, at Princeton University, one of its professors—who, not coincidentally, happens to be in the first rank of American literary writers—introduced King at a public talk. She said:

> Like all great writers of Gothic horror, King is both a storyteller and
> an inventor of startling images and metaphors, which linger long in
> the memory and would seem to spring from a collective unconscious
> and thoroughly domestic American soil. His fellow writers admire
> him for his commitment to the craft of fiction and the generosity of
> his involvement in the literary community.

The speaker who introduced him was Joyce Carol Oates, a writer and academic who, in my opinion, deserves a nomination, if not the office, of First Lady of Literary Fiction.

What, then, does it say when she endorses King and sings his praises? Does it mean she's lost all control of her critical faculties?

It means, in short, *pay attention!* There's something here, folks. Look past the boogeyman's fright mask and dig deeper, and you'll see stories like "The Body" and "Rita Hayworth and Shawshank Redemption," "The Reach," "The Woman in the Room," "The Last Rung on the Ladder," *Misery*, *The Green Mile*, and "The Man in the Black Suit."

King can write.

As King told *Fangoria* magazine, "People don't read me because they want horror. They read me because they like Stephen King. I've come to that conclusion over the years. . . . I think they come back for the voice, more than anything else."

That voice sounds out loud and clear, speaking to millions of readers and, through his movies, many millions more. King, who celebrated his fiftieth birthday on September 21, 1997, can look back and take pride in his still-growing body of work, which, when taken together, gives a unique view of contemporary America in a way that is refreshingly original and compulsively readable. Let the future decide King's place in Maine literature or American literature.

One of my beefs about "revised" books is that, far too often, the revision is minor, consisting of an additional chapter tacked on to the end of the existing edition. It saves money and time, but it's not exactly truth in advertising.

So here's what you need to know about *this* book: My goal is to write a literary biography in an accessible style. King has often stated that he feels the work's what's important, not the person, but the truth is that *both* are important and integral in any discussion of the literary body.

My readers who have dutifully bought *The Stephen King Companion* (both editions) and *The Stephen King Story* will find this book to be a straightforward accounting of King's life and work, with an emphasis on the written work, though some of the movies warrant attention.

Eschewing the popular convention of providing "juice," the tasty nuggets of gossip, innuendo, and half-baked truths and rumors that have come to be associated with unauthorized books, I have almost exclusively used public sources, drawing from King in print. King may be a public figure, but he's entitled to his privacy: I would not poke around his personal life in an attempt to uncover a salacious bit of news that might draw attention to the book, maybe even goose its sales, because King *readers* don't give a damn; they are not celebrity-hound sniffers.

Also, in contrast to *The Stephen King Story*, I've decided not to "date" it by adding detailed appendices. I hope to use another publication for that purpose—my quarterly zine, *Phantasmagoria*, in which I'm able to update readers and provide the kind of timely information on King that my books on him cannot provide.

Obviously, to have written as many books as I have on King, the presumption—at least to new readers—is that the book that follows is a hagiography, but it is not. I've enjoyed almost all of King's fiction, but there are still some books I haven't gotten around to reading; and in terms of the quality of writing, the books vary: good-faith efforts like *Gerald's Game* cannot be compared to, say, *The Green Mile*, but they came from the same writer. Hey, *nobody* bats a thousand; it's enough to play in the league, and end the season with an average of three hundred.

Finally, a note of thanks.

Preface

As the writer of this book, I shoulder full responsibility for its perceived successes or failures.

During what proved to be one of the most trying years of my life, there were a few bright spots, and invariably those beacons of light were my friends and family who, as always, were there when I needed them most.

In no particular order these good angels include:

• My long-suffering wife, Mary, who has joined me up, and down, the ladder of success. (Mary, you've got the Right Stuff.)

• Donna and Rex Martin. Donna's my editor at Andrews McMeel Publishing and, more important, a cherished friend. We've done a number of books together and in each instance she's brought a lifetime of editorial acumen to each project and has never failed to bring the best out of each book and out of me, as well. And her husband, Rex, whom I see far too infrequently, has always made me feel welcome whenever I visit Kansas City.

• My many friends at Andrews McMeel Publishing, too numerous to mention, but I do want to single out Tom Thornton, who, in 1988, took a chance and bought *The Stephen King Companion*, not knowing what to expect. (I wish I could say to him, "Many happy returns!" which would otherwise be appropriate, but not in the book trade. But you get my drift: Tom's one of the few gentlemen left in what *used* to be a gentleman's business. I am proud to have him bring out my books.) Thanks, too, to Matt Lombardi—another gentleman whose behind-the-scenes work on my books has improved them immeasurably.

• Stephen Spignesi, who wrote the foreword, Stuart Tinker, Charlie Fried, and David Lowell—my main men.

• And, finally, Colleen Doran—artist, writer, publisher—to whom this book is dedicated. Ten years ago, when we both toiled in the Mines of Donning, we commiserated over munchies at Ginger's on Fridays, while waiting for traffic in the Hampton Roads bridge tunnel to clear, so we could head to the Peninsula. There's been a lot of water under the bridge since then, but one thing has remained: a friendship of rare quality.

George Beahm
February 8, 1998
Williamsburg, Virginia

Stephen King
AMERICA'S BEST-LOVED
BOOGEYMAN

❧ 1 ❧

STEPHEN EDWIN KING was born on September 21, 1947, at the Maine General Hospital in Portland, Maine. The only natural-born child of Donald Edwin King and Nellie Ruth Pillsbury King, Stephen King was a welcome but somewhat unexpected addition to the family. The Kings had adopted at birth David Victor King two years earlier, having been told Nellie King could not bear children.

On the surface it appeared that the Kings were the typical nuclear family of the fifties: the husband, who worked for Electrolux as a door-to-door salesman, supported the wife, who stayed at home to raise the children. Beneath the surface, however, was a dark side to Donald King that no one in the family suspected. This family man, a former captain in the Merchant Marine, told his wife that he was stepping out for a pack of cigarettes . . . and never returned.

It was as if the earth had opened up and swallowed him whole. Nobody in the family ever heard from Donald King again or, if they did, they kept silent.

After Donald King—formerly David Spansky—abandoned his family, Nellie Ruth King had to pick up the slack, and fast. According to Stephen King, she ". . . landed on her feet, scrambling. My brother and I didn't see a great deal of her over the next nine years."[1]

For several years, the King family moved around the country, staying with relatives on both sides of the family, in Maine, Massachusetts, Illinois, Wisconsin, Indiana, and Connecticut. In 1958, however, they moved back to Durham, Maine, which would be home to Nellie King, her two sons, and her parents, Guy Pillsbury and Nellie Fogg Pillsbury, both in their eighties and in failing health.

Living in a modest, two-story home in the part of Durham called Methodist Corners, because of the proximity of the West Durham Methodist Church, the Kings lived a blue-collar life, as did most of the people in Durham, a town that counted less than nine hundred souls in the sixties.

Durham was, as King's childhood friend Chris Chesley observed, "a working-class town, a hard-luck town. Right around here was farming, but the majority of towners went out-of-town to Lewiston, Auburn, or Brunswick."[2]

Like most of rural Maine, Durham was not much to look at. Standing on the porch of the King house, to the left was the one-room schoolhouse, where Stephen King had attended fifth and sixth grades; the West Durham Methodist Church, a focal point for the community, where the Kings attended Bible classes and church services; and, further down, the home of Alex and Joyce Hall, who had three teenage boys. To the front was an open field, with one house in sight: the home of King's aunt and uncle, Oren and Ethelyn Pillsbury Flaws. To the right, about a mile down the road, was Runaround Pond, a large lake, and to its right the home of the Chesleys.

In January 1959, Stephen King's older brother—then thirteen—decided to publish a newspaper, drawing on local news. The admittedly home-brewed effort would never get more than twenty paid subscribers; the first issue, in fact, had a print run of only two copies, since each had to be individually typed by its publisher, David King, who told Don Hanson of the Brunswick *Record* that, "Until I get a mimeograph machine, things are going to be rather rushed."

After David King got a mimeograph machine, he was able to go into maximum overdrive as a publisher, typing directly on stencils that would be wrapped around a drum for printing. The mimeograph machine was a poor cousin to offset printing but effective nonetheless: corrections could be made using correction fluid, a sticky liquid called corflu, and art could be hand-drawn directly on the stencil. Then, using fiber-toned paper to absorb the heavy black ink, the machine could run off as many copies as necessary, limited to the durability of the stencil itself—easily hundreds of copies, more than enough for King's purposes.

Copies of *Dave's Rag* cost five cents for a single issue, or if you really wanted to break the bank, a buck for a long-term subscription.

In the summer 1959 issue, a budding writer reported on the current television offerings:

> Well, the fall T.V. season is in full swing, and it has the newest and best shows since the beginning of T.V. There's T.V. for every fan. Like adventure or espionage? Try the "Trouble Shooters" or "Five Fingers." Westerns your preference? How about "The Deputy" or "Man from

Blackhawk." Westerns are more numerous this season. Science fiction? Try "Man into Space" or "Twilight Zone." Roughly *20* new fall shows. Happy Viewing. Steve King.

In *Dave's Rag*, classified ads promoted subscriptions to new "Steve King" books. One such ad, promoting a condensed anthology book, proclaimed: "New book by STEVE KING! Thirty-One of the Classics! Read KID-NAPPED, TOM SAWYER, and many others! If you order in three weeks, only thirty cents."

In another issue, an ad promoted an Edgar Rice Burroughs–like story by Steve King. "Exciting story of 21 prisoners on an island that should have been extinct 1,000,000 years ago. Order through this newspaper."

It was obvious to everyone that Stephen King at an early age had an overactive imagination, but what was even more obvious was that he stood out physically, as well. Prematurely tall for his age, Stephen King towered six feet, two inches. Chris Chesley, who grew up with Stephen King, remembers the first time he saw him at school. "He looked like a kid with those old-fashioned, black-rimmed glasses. He was kind of slow, and chunky but not fat."[3]

Like Chesley, Brian Hall, who lived down the street, recalls Stephen King in a similar light. "Steve was a big, klutzy kid. Walking down the road you knew he was going to fall down or walk into a sign, reading his book."[4]

When King didn't have his nose in a book, he enjoyed going to nearby Lewiston on Saturdays, where he and his friends spent hours at the Ritz watching the matinees. Enveloped in the dark at the theater, King was entranced by the black-and-white movies that flickered to life on the silver screen. According to Chesley, "King, in effect, learned *how* to write from what he saw on the screen at the Ritz—the place where parents sent their kids on Saturday."[5]

After one such movie, the 1961 release of *The Pit and the Pendulum*, King self-published a novelization on his brother's mimeograph machine, one of several early efforts to see print. As King explained, "I bought a stapler and some staples, and I printed, on Dave's machine, about two hundred and fifty copies of this book. I slugged in a price of a dime on them, and when I took them to school, I was just flabbergasted. In three days, I sold something like seventy of these things. And all of a sudden, I was in the black—it was like a license to steal. That was my first experience with bestsellerdom."[6]

Of King's self-published effort, Chris Chesley recalled, "This was *not* a takeoff on the story. King had seen the film and in effect novelized that movie. We ran off copies and sold them in school for a dime or a quarter, but the teachers made us stop doing that."[7]

The inventive King later wrote a twenty-page "hostage" story that was a trial cut for *Getting It On*, later published as *Rage* under King's pen name, Richard Bachman. "It was a story where he used real kids who had taken over the grammar school," Chesley recalled. "Of course, the people that were in the story read it; and because of things like that, King was lionized. He could take real people and set them into this setting where we were heroes and died fighting the National Guard. The kids he liked best 'died' last; so, naturally, we were all wondering when we were going to 'die.'"[8]

Geographically trapped, so to speak, in rural Maine, King compensated with his imagination, which took him far away from the mundane life of small-town U.S.A. As Chesley pointed out, "The country dirt roads, the stands of pine trees, the hayfields run to seed, the antique-copper Maine sun, all of it common and real enough, yet within King's room, as if an actual atmosphere, as if breathed out on the air directly from the imagination of the kid who owned the typewriter, extraordinary things were vivid and real enough—more real, for an afternoon, than all the prosaic territory outside."[9]

King escaped through his fiction, submitting to the science fiction pulps of his day, though he clearly did not write science fiction, which has as its fictional premise that current events can be extrapolated, with the "what if?" based on solid scientific principles. He loved reading science fiction but couldn't write it. The hard science fiction written by men like Murray Leinster, Robert A. Heinlein, A. E. Van Vogt, and their contemporaries revealed a thorough grounding in the sciences, which King lacked.

The young King had yet to find his niche.

The turning point came when he discovered a legacy from his father, stored in his aunt and uncle's attic at their house down the road. As King tells it, he came across a box of books that had belonged to his father. The box contained an assortment of cheap paperbacks, mostly horror novels, including fiction by New England's dour supernatural writer, Howard Phillips Lovecraft.

It was then, King said, that he discovered his Great Interest. The needle, King said, finally swung to true north.

That same needle had also swung north for other writers who were influenced by Lovecraft's seriousness in writing horror fiction; they, in turn, influenced King. They broke from tradition and rescued horror fiction from the moldy confines of its traditional European settings by writing in contemporary prose, instead of the baroque style that their revered Lovecraft favored—a literary style that seemed hopelessly antiquated.

These postwar writers like Ray Bradbury, Robert Bloch, Charles Beaumont, Jack Finney, and Richard Matheson wrote their tales of terror set in a distinctive American milieu. Dark fantasists all, these devotees of films—most of them active in the film and television community—adopted a cinematic style, which a young Stephen King emulated.

King had finally found his way home, literarily, and realized that horror could be found in his own backyard, in Maine, in New England, and on Main Street, U.S.A.

As Chesley explained, "What Steve learned from Lovecraft was the possibility of taking the New England atmosphere and using that as a springboard. Lovecraft showed him a milieu that was definitely New England horror. *Dracula* could be moved to Durham, basically."[10]

The pieces of the puzzle finally came together; but then, as now, horror fiction was considered a bastard form of writing, the province of hack writers who should stick to publishing in cheap paperbacks and leave the hardbacks to the literary writers.

"As a kid growing up in rural Maine," King wrote, "my interest in horror and the fantastic wasn't looked upon with any approval whatsoever—there went young Steve King, his nose either in a lurid issue of *Tales from the Vault* or an even more lurid paper of some sort or other. . . ."[11]

King's elders—conservative adults with no sympathy for the kind of fiction he obviously preferred—felt that the young boy was introspective to a fault. According to Chesley, "Everybody thought—considering how much he read and how much he wrote—that he spent way too much time in his room, in his imagination, and it was thought to be unhealthy and abnormal behavior. . . . Given his nature, the isolation was necessary to make him what he became."[12]

King's contemporaries, though, shared his enthusiasms and tastes for popular culture, for the science fiction and horror movies, for magazines like *Famous Monsters of Filmland*, for comic books, and the lurid pulp magazines. (On the West Coast, two other baby boomers—Steven Spielberg and George Lucas—gorged themselves on similar, pop culture fare.)

For King and his fellow baby boomers, growing up in the dark shadow of the mushroom clouds that hung over Hiroshima and Nagasaki, the fifties and sixties were a time to look to the skies. The war was over but it was no time to let down the guard, because Communist Russia was flexing its power.

As U.S. servicemen stood in the deserts of Nevada to witness atomic blasts —wearing only sunglasses—civil defense shelters and bomb drills became commonplace; in fact, the idea of having your own bomb shelter beneath your house didn't seem so far-fetched after all.

The atomic-generated fear of the fifties and sixties, transmogrified through the popular culture of comics, pulp fiction, and movies, put a Jekyll and Hyde face on technology: the same atomic-powered technology that some-day might fuel starships to seed the planets outside our solar system was the same source of energy that transmuted bugs into giant, marauding creatures, turned people into rampaging giants, and created human monsters. In short, for the baby boomers, fear found a face in atomic technology. Science was the boogeyman, serving the growing military-industrial complex.

More than anyone else, Chris Chesley—a talented writer in his own right—saw the budding literary talent that his best friend possessed. As Chesley explained:

> When I went to Stephen King's house to write stories with him, there was the sense that these things weren't just stories; when you walked inside the walls of his house, there was a sense of palpability, almost as if the characters in the stories had real weight. . . . Imagination didn't just make it real for him—it made it real for *me*. To go inside his house was like being pulled into a different world unlike old, unimaginative Durham with its cowsheds. And that's what drew me to go see him. He had that ability. If you went inside those walls and you were at all sus-ceptible, you would be drawn into that. And when you read stories with him, or read his writing, or participated and wrote stories with him, the stories took on weight. . . . It was a world unto itself, and I was privileged to enter it. Even as a kid, a teenager, King had the power to do that. It was an amazing thing.[13]

Looking to make his mark professionally, King began submitting to the magazines he enjoyed reading. Hammering away on a manual Underwood typewriter, Stephen King submitted stories to *Fantastic*, a science fiction pulp magazine, and the literary cream of the crop, *The Magazine of Fantasy and Science Fiction*, edited by Ed Ferman. Predictably, these early efforts were rejected in due course and, as David King recalled, his brother "got lots of rejection slips. If I remember correctly, there was a nail pounded in the wall up in the bedroom, and he'd spear all the rejection slips on it."[14]

Even at an early age, King could tell a story, but they weren't publishable because he didn't send them to the right markets. "These stories had the trappings of science fiction, but they were really horror stories."[15]

Reflecting back on those times, Chris Chesley observed:

> Stephen King is aware of what he needs to preserve himself—the time and space and distance that allows him to write. That's pretty much what he is, and that's pretty much the way it always was. . . . He was certainly not a recluse; he had friends like the rest of us, but when he was done, he would always return to the typewriter. Watching him at his writing, you knew that's where he belonged.[16]

❧ 2 ❧

Because Durham, Maine, was too small to have a high school, students attended nearby schools. Stephen King, in the fall of 1962, began attending Lisbon High School in Lisbon Falls, northeast of Durham. (Stephen's brother David attended Brunswick High, southeast of Durham.)

Because Durham couldn't justify spending money on a school bus for a handful of students, the town leased a converted hearse that served as transportation. One of its occupants, according to King, was a strange girl who was the model for the fictional character Carietta White in *Carrie*. According to Brian Hall, who lived down the street and made the round-trip journey from Durham to Lisbon daily, there was a mad rush to get the best seats. "You didn't want to ride all the way to Lisbon with Carrie on your lap."[1]

Chris Chesley, who attended a nearby prep school, still hung out with his childhood friend, but as Chesley pointed out, "I saw Steve periodically on the weekends. He never talked much about his high school years. It was understood that we got together to talk about movies, TV and books."[2]

Under the name of Triad Publishing Company, in 1963, Stephen King and Chris Chesley self-published *People, Places, and Things—Volume I*, using David King's mimeograph machine. Of the eighteen stories, King wrote eight, Chesley nine, and one was a collaboration. The print run was, according to Chesley, around a dozen copies.

In its foreword, the proud authors set the stage for the one-note stories that followed:

> *People, Places, and Things* is an Extraordinary book. It is a book for people who would enjoy being pleasantly thrilled for a few moments.
>
> For example: take Chris Chesley's bloodcurdling story, GONE. The last moments of a person left alone in an atomic-doomed world.
>
> Let Steve King's I'M FALLING transport you into a world of dreams.
>
> But if you have no imagination, stop right here. This book is not for you.

If you have an imagination, let it run free.
We warn you . . . the next time you lie in bed and hear an unreason-
able creak or thump, you can try to explain it away. . . . but try Steve
King's and Chris Chesley's explanation: *People, Places, and Things*.

King's stories included: "Hotel at the End of the Road," "I've Got to Get
Away!", "The Dimension Warp," "The Thing at the Bottom of the Well,"
"The Stranger," "I'm Falling," "The Cursed Expedition," and "The Other
Side of the Fog."

Similarly titled, Chesley's fantasy and science fiction titles included
"Genius, 3," "Top Forty, News, Weather, and Sports," "Bloody Child,"
"Reward," "A Most Unusual Thing," "Gone," "They've Come," "Scared," and
"Curiousity [sic] Kills the Cat."

The final story, "Never Look Behind You," was the collaboration between
King and Chesley.

Chesley remembers those early days fondly, when the words came easily,
despite having to use a typewriter that, over time, lost its type, forcing them
to fill in the manuscripts by hand.

> I had gotten into the habit of visiting Steve, who liked to make up scary
> stories. I'd come over and contribute what I could, when I could. We'd
> have a good time, especially on hot August days, collaborating on sto-
> ries about thunderstorms over big dark houses. We'd write on an old
> typewriter. One of its metal letters was broken. When you finished a
> page, you had to fill in the missing letters with a pencil.[3]

Chesley didn't write much on his own afterward, since this was more of
an amusement. Unlike his friend Steve, Chris never felt the fire in his belly,
the burning desire to write, to publish professionally.

Like all born writers, King started out toward the deep waters as soon as
he could. The fiction grew in word count, just as King's story productivity
increased in number. "What I remember," Chesley said, "is a progression.
When we started hanging out together, he was writing short stories. Then
they got longer and turned into novellas, and then into novels. It was a very
gradual process."[4]

A year later, in June 1964, Triad and Gaslight Books—King's amateur
press—published a two-part, 3,000-word "book," *The Star Invaders*, a de-
rivative work that owes much to the science fiction pulp magazines of that
time, replete with eye-popping covers of bug-eyed monsters (BEMs), scant-
ily clad girls (FEMs) in danger from the BEMs, and atomic weapons.

In *The Shorter Works of Stephen King*, by Collings and Engebretson, Michael R. Collings summarizes *The Star Invaders*:

> In Part I, Jerry Hiken, one of the last defenders of the Earth, has been captured by the Star Invaders and tortured to force him to reveal the location of Jed Pierce, the brilliant mind behind the Counter Weapon. When Hiken resists, they use psychological torture; he breaks, telling everything he knows, then kills himself [by smashing his head against the floor]. Part II shifts to Pierce's hideout, where work on the Weapon is nearly finished. The Invaders attack. Pierce destroys ship after ship, ignoring the increasing danger as machinery overheats. When the last ship is destroyed, Pierce races to the atomic pile and single-handedly averts a meltdown. The Weapon works; Earth now has a defense against the Invaders.[5]

The Star Invaders was the last of King's self-published juvenalia. At a time when most writers would be grappling with the difficulties of telling a story, King's innate sense of storytelling—cinematic, not literary—was obviously present. The length of a short story, *The Star Invaders* laid the groundwork for more ambitious works that would soon follow.

In 1965, King broke into print in *Comics Review*, published by Marv Wolfman. The title, inspired by movies like *I Was a Teenage Werewolf* and *I Was a Teenage Frankenstein*, said it all: "I Was a Teenage Grave Robber."

Approximately 6,000 words in length, this narrative, told in the first person, has a straightforward plot, according to Michael Collings: "An orphaned teenager accepts a job as a grave robber for a scientist who, with all the flair of the 1950s 'mad scientist' stereotype, experiments with radioactivity and in the process creates monsters from the maggots inhabiting the corpses. The young man must rescue his girlfriend and destroy the monsters."[6]

The visual imagery in the story is arresting, clearly a cinematic style that goes unerringly for the gross-out:

> A huge, white maggot twisted on the garage floor, holding Weinbaum with long suckers, raising him towards its dripping, pink mouth from which horrid mewling sounds came. Veins, red and pulsing, showed under its slimy flesh and millions of squirming tiny maggots in the blood vessels, in the skin, even forming a huge eye that stared out me. A huge maggot, made up of hundreds of millions of maggots, the feasters on the dead flesh that Weinbaum had used so freely.[7]

In 1963 King wrote *The Aftermath*, a short novel of 50,000 words, conceived a year after the Cuban Missile Crisis, a time when Americans collectively held their breath, wondering if the nuclear-tipped missiles in Cuba with first-strike capability would be targeted and used against U.S. cities.

President Kennedy and Soviet Premier Khrushchev engaged in a deadly battle of wills, but it was Khrushchev who blinked. Although the missiles were removed from Cuba, the political climate remained frigid. With the advent of long-range nuclear missiles for which no defense was possible—except a preemptive strike—the science fiction movies of the fifties, notably *Earth vs. the Flying Saucers*, didn't seem so far-fetched after all. "Look to your skies . . . a warning will come from your skies . . . look to your skies," Americans were told, and it seemed like a prudent thing to do.

If the Russians launched first, there would be nothing left in this country. There would be only stragglers left in the aftermath of the destruction—the theme of King's apocalyptic short novel.

Ironically, King's first journalistic efforts appeared in print as a result of a self-published parody, the *Village Vomit*, lampooning the Lisbon Falls High School newspaper, for which he was a staffer and, as a junior, its editor. Earning him the respect of his fellow students, the *Village Vomit* also initially earned him a three-day suspension.

Fortunately for the indiscreet young writer, the administration decided to let the punishment fit the crime. Instead of suspension, they assigned King to cover sports for a local paper, the *Lisbon Enterprise*, where he earned a half-cent a word.

Years later, King said that John Gould, the paper's editor, taught him a valuable lesson. Reading King's effusive efforts, Gould took out a red pen and edited heavily, cutting adjectives and flowery language to get to the heart of the story. Writing, King realized, was rewriting. Nobody gets it right the first time. It would be an important lesson to learn.

On the whole, King's four years in high school were pretty typical. Academically, he did well enough to make the honor roll in his first two years, but only average in the hard sciences, chemistry, and physics. In addition to working on the school newspaper and playing in a rock 'n' roll garage band, King was on the football team, in the position of left tackle, where he didn't exactly cover himself in glory. But he was large and had to play, or the other students would have thought there was something wrong with him.

In terms of what he read, everything divided neatly into what his teachers wanted him to read—classics like *Moby Dick* and *Hamlet*—and works by writers he wanted to read: John D. MacDonald, Ed McBain, Shirley Jackson, Wilkie Collins, Ken Kesey, Tom Wolfe essays, Robert E. Howard, Andre' Norton, Jack London, Agatha Christie, Margaret Mitchell's *Gone with the Wind*, and, of course, countless comic books.

Other influences included Richard Matheson, Thomas Hardy, William Golding, John Fowles, John Steinbeck, and television shows, notably *Outer Limits* and *The Twilight Zone*.

Looking back on his high school days, King recalls that "my high school career was totally undistinguished. I was not at the top of my class, nor at the bottom. I had friends, but none of them were the big jocks or the student council guys or anything like that."[8]

King, who clearly identified with the outsider, who didn't move with the "in" crowd, saw high school for what it was: a rigid class system in which there were only two groups: the winners—and the losers. It was a caste system in which being cool meant everything: on the one hand, there were the jocks and cheerleaders and student council members; and, on the other, everyone else—the geeks to be gawked at.

"I've always assumed that Steve didn't have a wonderful high school experience, that it wasn't that great a time for him in his life," Chesley observed.[9]

He was right. Years later, King echoed Chesley's observation, saying that his great fear then was "not being able to interact, to get along and establish lines of communication. It's the fear I had, the fear of not being able to make friends, the fear of being afraid and not being able to tell anyone you're afraid. . . . There's a constant fear that *I am alone*."[10]

It would be a theme that King would later explore at length in *Carrie*.

In the spring of 1966, King graduated from high school and, lacking the finances to attend Drew University in New Jersey, elected to follow in his brother's footsteps and attend the University of Maine, which had given him a scholarship.

That summer, he began work on a novel tentatively titled *Getting It On*, amplifying the story he wrote earlier about kids who take over a classroom and try unsuccessfully to fight off the National Guard. This novel, which took its title from a rock 'n' roll song by T. Rex, "Bang a Gong (Get It On)," was an intense psychological study, tapping into King's fears in high school of being an outsider, a time when he characterized himself as being filled with rage, worried whether or not he'd go crazy.

❧ 3 ❧

Located north of bangor, Orono is a small town flanked by the Penobscot River, which runs north-south. Its population of 10,000 is mostly college students and faculty.

A freshman, Stephen King felt decidedly out of place, disoriented by his new surroundings. In a column for the school newspaper, King recalled:

> There I was, all alone in Room 203 of Gannett Hall, clean-shaven, neatly dressed, and as green as apples in August. Outside on the grass between Gannett and Androscroggin Hall there were more people playing football than there were in my home town. My few belongings looked pitifully un-collegiate. The room looked mass-produced. I was quite sure my roommate would turn out to be some kind of a freako, or even worse, hopelessly more With It than I. I propped my girl's picture on my desk where I could look at it in the dismal days ahead, and wondered where the bathroom was.[1]

College, typically an academic refuge, a respite from the pressures of the real world, was anything but that for Stephen King and his contemporaries, who were swept up in the events that made the sixties a time of dissent and turmoil, when civil rights, women's liberation, and the Vietnam War dominated the news.

The decade, which had opened on a note of optimism as President Kennedy urged Americans "to commit themselves to public service and seek new frontiers,"[2] would see man set foot on the moon. But back home the country would be torn apart by internal strife, punctuated with the assassinations of President Kennedy, his brother Bobby, and the black civil rights leader Martin Luther King.

It was a turbulent time, aptly characterized as "a decade of dissent. The civil rights and anti-war movements drew millions of people into the streets, where public protests raged. Bloody riots erupted, and cities and flags burned. . . . Long hair, mod dress, drugs, sexual freedom and anti-establishment ideas were hard to find ten years ago; now they are every-

13

where, as affluent kids embrace a counterculture fueled by rock music and a sincere yearning for brotherhood and peace."[3]

In his freshman year, King took general courses in geology, history, physical education, sociology, public speaking, and freshman composition.

Sanford Phippen, a graduate of UMO, recalls what Jim Bishop, King's freshman composition teacher, said about the budding writer. "Steve was a nice kid, a good student, but never had a lot of social confidence. Even then, though, he saw himself as a famous writer and thought he could make money at it. Steve was writing continuously, industriously and diligently. He was amiable, resilient and created his own world."[4]

During that first year, King completed his first full-length novel, *The Long Walk*. "I thought of it while hitchhiking home from college one night," King said.[5] As King recalled, "I submitted *Walk* to the Bennett Cerf/Random House first-novel competition . . . and it was promptly rejected with a form note . . . no comment of any kind. Hurt and depressed, sure that the book must really be terrible, I stuck it into the fabled TRUNK, which all novelists, both publishing and aspiring, carry around."[6]

Inspired by John Kennedy's fifty-mile walkathons, the novel can be seen as a grim commentary of the times. It is the story of teenage boys who must walk south on U.S. Route 1 from its northernmost point, Fort Kent, Maine, until only one walker survives. (The stragglers get three warnings; after that, they're simply shot, putting them out of their misery.)

Although it was a publishable novel—in fact, it was subsequently published in 1979 as a paperback original by NAL—King, as a writer, lacked the confidence to resubmit it. Had he not received a form rejection note, the novel might have made the rounds, but King was convinced it was unpublishable and, for the time being, put it aside.

Despite the crushing blow dealt him by Random House, King persisted in submitting short fiction and, in the summer of his sophomore year, finally broke into print professionally. "I was walking down a dirt road to see a friend, and for no reason at all I began to wonder what it would be like to stand in a room whose floor was a mirror. The image was so intriguing that writing the story became a necessity," King wrote.[7]

After five years of submitting short fiction, King had made his first fiction sale—thirty-five dollars. "I've cashed many bigger ones since then," King recalls, "but none gave me more satisfaction; someone had finally paid me some real money for something I had found in my head!"[8]

In a reader's poll, "The Glass Floor" took fifth place. Since it hadn't taken a top position, King could take comfort in the fact that it at least placed. In other words, the story was not so forgettable that the readers ignored it completely.

Perhaps emboldened by his first professional sale, King decided to get a second opinion on *The Long Walk* by showing it to his American literature teacher, Burton Hatlen, who years later recalled the excitement of finding a new writer among his students. "I brought it home and laid it on the dining room table," said Hatlen. "My ex-wife picked it up and started reading it and couldn't stop, which was also my experience. The narrative grabbed you and carried you forward. That was what was most striking about *The Long Walk*. King had a fully developed sense of narrative and pace. It was there already. It was quite amazing to see that."[9]

Hatlen was sufficiently impressed with this student novel to show it around the English department, where Edward Holmes, a creative writing teacher, enthusiastically endorsed Hatlen's assessment, saying that they had a writer on their hands.

"Professor Hatlen said I should give this to you to read. It's a novel. I wrote it,"[10] said King, handing a pile of manuscript to Carroll F. Terrell, a professor in the English department.

Terrell recalled that the book "posed certain technical problems which would require more practice for him to solve. The design of the book made the action repetitive and got him into a kind of 'another Indian bites the dust' trap." Terrell suggested to King that "the solution to that might be a more extensive use of flashback to flesh out the characters."[11]

King's response, according to Terrell, "was precise and (as I eventually came to realize) correct. He said, in effect, that the sameness and routineness were deliberate and part of the point. On the road to life few people become distinguished from the mass; they just stagger along until they conk out."[12]

Terrell assumed that *The Long Walk* was a first novel, unaware that King had been writing, and submitting, since his early teens. "I should have known that it could have been no such thing: No one could have written such a balanced and designed book without a lot of practice; not just aimless practice, but conscious and designed practice."[13]

Terrell also saw an early incomplete draft of King's next project, *Sword in the Darkness*. King sought out Terrell's advice, hoping to make a book sale:

After he'd finished about half of it, he asked me if it would be a good idea to send it to a publisher to get an advance. At the time, I knew nothing of his serious financial difficulties. I told him it would do no harm, but it wouldn't do any good. I thought the book was potentially marketable, but not something in 1969 that a publisher would given an advance on. So I told him they'd read it, tell him it showed great promise, and invite him to send the completed version, but they wouldn't give an unknown either an advance or a contract. A few weeks later, he handed me a letter from a publisher and said something like "At least you hit the nail on the head."[14]

Sword in the Darkness, completed on April 30, 1970, was a 150,000-word novel (485 manuscript pages) that made the rounds in New York, thanks to a professor who knew a literary agent, who believed in it enough to represent it to the book trade. Patricia Schartle Myrer of McIntosh and Otis sent it to Doubleday and eleven other houses, but the book didn't sell.

A reading of the manuscript, on deposit at the Special Collections at the Raymond H. Fogler Library at the University of Maine at Orono, reveals why the book is unpublishable: it is relentlessly downbeat, clearly the work of a young writer influenced by the naturalists, whose fictional worldview posited that life was Darwinian in nature; survival of the fittest mattered, and those who couldn't adapt or survive . . . died.

In this novel set in the small town of Harding, Arnie Kalowski is a bright young man planning to attend MIT in Cambridge, Massachusetts. Unfortunately, Kalowski suffers the loss of his mother, who had a brain tumor that proved fatal; his sister Miriam becomes pregnant and, distraught, commits suicide after she declares her love for her boss, Bill Danning, who rejects her utterly; and the effect of both deaths puts his father in a permanent state of mental disconnect.

Meanwhile, the town officials of Harding learn that Marcus Slade, a black activist lawyer from San Francisco, is coming to town. His arrival, they fear, may touch off a riot . . . and it does. A local gang starts the riot and the city burns.

What's remarkable about this novel is its narrative drive and the care with which King delineates the secondary characters in sufficient detail to make them come alive. That the riot doesn't in fact take place until page 400 in a 485-page book probably never struck King as a major flaw.

King, however, seemed much more interested in character development; and in that department, his cast of characters, with their human foibles, come alive: Henry Coolidge, the principal of Harding High School, who is sexually obsessed with his niece, Kit Longtin, a student at his school; Kit Longtin—a sexy young thing who sees her uncle's obsession with her as a ticket out of this dead-end town—who has blackmail on her mind; Meg DeClancy, who tries to seduce one of her teachers but fails, then cries rape to discredit him; Bill Danning, who knocks up Arnie Kalowski's sister and coldheartedly tells her that he doesn't love her, precipitating her suicide; and to stir the soup even more, Arnie, who fails at initiating a normal relationship with a good girl, Janet Cross, because—like Henry Coolidge—he can't resist the vamp from hell, Kit Longtin.

If a novel is only a failure if the writer fails to learn from his mistakes, then *Sword in the Darkness* is not in fact a failure: King learned that unrelenting misery is a tough sell in fiction, because people don't need to be reminded about how damnably difficult life can be. They go to fiction because they want to be entertained and diverted, to identify and live vicariously through a character in a book.

In *Sword in the Darkness*, however, there's too much darkness, few sympathetic characters, and too much human misery to make it an entertaining read. Downer fiction, King realized, doesn't play in Peoria, nor get bought in Publisher's Row in New York City, either.

King considered the book "a badly busted flush" and lamented that he couldn't "even like it when I'm drunk."[15]

By his sophomore year, King's classes were top-heavy in courses that would form a good mix for any writer. He took Burton Hatlen's American literature class; English, American, and twentieth-century literature; second-year and advanced composition classes; a creative writing class, which he felt was a constipating experience; a psychology course, useful for insights into human behavior; a sociology course on rural life; a course in the production of plays; and, finally, a teaching course, a prerequisite to getting certification to teach at the high school level.

Contrary to popular thinking, a writer can't learn how to write by taking courses in writing. One can learn the mechanics of writing, grammar, and fictional techniques, but the actual writing requires hours of sitting down in front of a typewriter, pulling words out of your head and onto paper, and being able to do so in an entertaining manner, sufficient to engage the reader's attention and get him to pay money for it.

In that sense, King's creative writing courses didn't teach him how to write; they "are very important," King said, "but I don't think they're necessary. It's a supportive experience. The best thing about it was that the art of writing was taken seriously, and that's an awfully good thing."[16]

King was a frequent contributor to *Ubris*, the school's literary magazine, with stories sufficiently professional that he sold them to paying markets in the years after graduation. In his junior year, he published "Strawberry Spring," "Here There Be Tygers," and, most notably, "Cain Rose Up."

The theme of the individual cracking up, going crazy, was one that King had explored earlier in *Getting It On*, but the fictional premise for "Cain Rose Up" was not based on King's imagination but on real-world events: Charles Whitman—a former Marine with a heavy caseload at school, who worked part-time after school—mentally snapped and had to get it on. He took a high-powered rifle for target practice from the top of a twenty-seven-floor tower at the University of Texas in Austin. He killed a dozen people and wounded thirty-three others. At the time, "University officials were at a loss to explain Whitman's actions. They said he had never been treated at the student health center for psychiatric disorder and had no record of being disciplined."[17] (What the officials didn't know: Whitman's journal entries clearly indicated that he knew he was acting irrationally and that he was suffering from a brain tumor.)

As a junior, King took courses in Shakespeare and twentieth-century British literature; an introductory course to radio and television; a debate class; an education class, Growth Learning Process; and a seminar on contemporary poetry, taught by Burton Hatlen and Jim Bishop. The class was limited to a dozen students who had to apply individually. King made the cut, though several others—including Tabitha Spruce—did not.

In *Moth*, Jim Bishop explained the appeal of the course:

> From that seminar . . . came a half dozen or so energetic and highly individual young poets who have been rapping in the hallways, in coffee shops, in front of Stevens Hall, or wherever any two of them chance to meet, ever since, and that original group has grown this year to a dozen, sometimes as many as twenty, who meet every other Friday in an informal workshop to read their poetry, alternatively to read and reassemble one another, and hopefully to emerge with a better understanding of themselves, their world, and their work.[18]

Though *Sword in the Darkness* never sold, King returned his attention to *Getting It On*, which he completed. He also made his second professional sale of thirty-five dollars, a short story to Lowdnes's a magazine, "The Reaper's Image," the story of an antique mirror in which the Grim Reaper appeared, a skeptic named John Spangler inspects the mirror, which claims him as its latest victim. (Years later, the device of the mirror would be used to greater effect in *Rose Madder*.)

On February 20, 1969, King's unique brand of commentary began appearing regularly in *The Maine Campus*, edited by David Bright, who recalled that "Steve came into the campus office and said he wanted to write a column. We were there to let students write, so he just did whatever he wanted to do. I said, 'Steve, you're more than welcome to write a column. My rules are that it's got to be here Tuesday at noon, and it has to fit the space.' Then King would show up and type it."[19]

As a journalist, King never suffered from writer's block. According to Bright, "The guy is very prolific; he likes to write and is excellent at it. He'd come in and bang those pieces out. They'd be letter-perfect and he'd lay them on the desk."[20]

A staffer from the paper observed that "King was always late. We would be pulling our hair at deadline. With five minutes or so to go, Steve would come in and sit down at the typewriter and produce two flawless pages of copy. He carries stories in his head the way most people carry change in their pockets."[21]

The first installment of "King's Garbage Truck" ran in the February 20, 1969, issue of *The Maine Campus*. Approximately 700 words, the first installment reviewed *Hush, Hush, Sweet Charlotte* and a program put on by students at a Vermont college.

Subsequent columns were free-ranging, from the serious (controversial campus activities, the Vietnam War, and birth control) to popular culture (book, movie, and record reviews) and the pleasures of everyday campus life (baseball and girl-watching).

The forty-seven installments of "King's Garbage Truck," so named because, said King, you never knew what you'd find when you read the column, ran until May 21, 1970, followed by eight installments of a comic western, "Slade," a trial cut on *The Dark Tower*.

Even as an undergraduate, King stood out, according to Burton Hatlen. "King was so different from most students. He had such a clearly defined identify and a sense of purpose. I think that's quite unusual."[22]

At that time the college was reassessing its curriculum and solicited input from the faculty and students alike, looking for new approaches. King, an outspoken advocate of popular culture, took the stand, as Burton Hatlen recalled:

I remember a meeting in which the students and faculty got together to talk about the curriculum of the English department. Several people have a memory of Steve standing up at this meeting and denouncing the [English] department because he had never been able to read a Shirley Jackson novel in any of the courses he had taken.

He criticized the curriculum and insisted on the value and impor-tance of popular culture and mass culture, and people listened to him. It was an important moment. King wanted to conduct a special semi-nar on popular American fiction, which produced a crisis. Here was an undergraduate proposing to teach a course.[23]

King, who had read widely and deeply in the literature of popular culture, subsequently became the first undergraduate in the history of the Univer-sity of Maine to teach a course. Although Popular Culture and Literature was technically taught by Graham Adams, King was in fact the teacher.

In his senior year, King concentrated on courses in English and, as prepa-ration for teaching high school, Education: The Teaching Process, Teaching Reading in Secondary School, Poetry of the Romantic Movement, The Earlier English Novel, and Directed Writing under Edward Holmes in which the students worked independently but met once a week for workshopping.

Diane McPherson, one of the twelve who took the Contemporary Poetry course with King, also took Directed Writing, which was ". . . great fun, often hilarious. I was the ideal audience for Steve's wild inventive fantasies. My thing then was to cut all the extraneous adverbs and adjectives. Steve was pretty pop. He was writing exciting stories, but with no control."[24]

In the last semester, King took a modern literature course, Educational Sociology, Man and His Environment, and continued to take Directed Writ-ing under Holmes. Also, as a prerequisite to obtaining certification to teach at the secondary level, King student-taught at Hampden Academy in a town south of Bangor.

Like many college students in the sixties who rebelled against the estab-lishment and did their thing, Stephen King was surprised when told that long hair wasn't within the guidelines established by the administration at Hampden Academy, and reportedly, King was told to get a haircut.

It seems likely that the incident prompted King to write a "Garbage Truck" column (February 12, 1970) on his right to wear his hair long. "Can you imagine a country supposedly based on freedom of expression telling peo-ple that they can't grow hair on their head or their face? Since when have we descended to the point where we care more about what people look like than what they think like?"[25]

Welcome to the real world.

Appearances can be deceiving, though; and when King took a job in the library, he was pointed out to Tabitha Spruce, whose surface impression of the hulking, hirsute man who badly needed a haircut prompted her to say sarcastically, "I think I'm in love."[26]

It was love, however, when Spruce realized that here was someone who was very serious about writing—just as she was—and didn't give a crap about how he looked, about status symbols, about being with the "in" crowd and being popular. All he cared about, recalled Spruce, was "getting everything he could out of school and writing his head off."[27]

Looking back, Stephen King explained that it was impossible to be unaffected by the turbulent times, unless you were oblivious to what was happening around you.

> When I was in school, Vietnam was going up in flames, and Watts was going up in flames, and Bobby Kennedy and Martin Luther King had been shot, and these little dollies were bopping into their eight o'clock classes with nine pounds of makeup on and their hair processed to perfection, and the high heels and everything, because they wanted husbands, and they wanted jobs, and they wanted all the things their mothers wanted, and they wanted to get into a big sorority. Big deal.[28]

To Stephen King, the big deal was taking advantage of the four years to get serious about writing, because it was his one shot at escaping the horrors of perpetually teaching high school English, which was the only other job for which he was trained. Of the two, writing seemed a far preferable but distant goal.

In June 1970, Stephen King graduated from the University of Maine, with a Bachelor of Science degree in English and certification to teach at the high school level.

He had entered college as a wide-eyed kid from a small Maine town and emerged world-weary but wiser. In the last installment of "King's Garbage Truck," King acknowledged that, along with his classmates, it was time to enter the real world and announced the "BLESSED (?) EVENT" of graduation. At twenty-two years old, standing six feet three inches, weighing 208 pounds, King cynically observed that future prospects were "hazy, although either nuclear annihilation or environmental strangulation seemed to be definite possibilities."[29] King concluded that, insofar as he was concerned, "This boy has shown evidences of some talent, although at this point it is impossible to tell if he is just a flash in the pan or if he has real possibilities. . . . he does not feel very bright-eyed by this time: in fact, he feels about two thousand years old."[30]

⊌ 4 ⊌

Upon graduation King moved into a riverside cabin in Orono. After seeing a spaghetti western, he idly wondered what it would be like to cross that genre with heroic fiction. Unlike "Slade," the humorous western story that was serialized in the campus newspaper, this story was no laughing matter. It would be an epic story of a gunslinger in search of the Dark Tower, inspired by "Childe Roland to the Dark Tower Came," the Robert Browning poem:

> A knight errant crosses a nightmare landscape in search of the Dark Tower . . . he eventually reaches the Tower and blows his horn defiantly at its foot. The poem ends with the title phrase, and there is no indication of what happened next. Because the story is told by the knight himself, the poem's form raises insoluble problems of interpretation, and the poem is both profoundly satisfying as a dream narrative and profoundly disturbing, as an impenetrable allegory—of life, or art, or of both. Browning consistently refused to explain the poem, saying simply that it had come upon him as a dream.[1]

Using bright green paper discovered in the library, King used a manual Underwood typewriter and began what would be his most ambitious work to date. "The man in black fled across the desert and the gunslinger followed."[2]

King, who had shared the beginning of the first story with Chris Chesley during a trip home to Durham earlier, trusted him to give it a fair reading. "He held up these sheets—about ten of them—titled *The Dark Tower*. I read them and said, 'Steve, this is the most amazing thing you've ever written. What are you going to do with it?'"[3]

Whatever King's plans were, *The Dark Tower* went on hold for the foreseeable future, since job-hunting became King's immediate priority. Unfortunately, teaching jobs were scarce, so King took whatever work he could find. In his case, it was pumping gas in Brewer, a small town south of Bangor. A gallon of gas cost less than a quarter; King earned $1.25 an hour.

After that stint, King moved up the pay scale, earning $1.60 an hour, $60 a week, at the New Franklin Laundry in Bangor. The experience would not go to waste; he used it as background for a short story, "The Manger."

King, who studied the fiction markets carefully, realized that his best bet was to submit to the "B-grade" men's magazines, the ones that might give a young writer a break—skin magazines that featured young women, with sexually explicit advertisements in the back part of the magazines offering marital aids, 8mm porn movies, and inflatable rubber dolls.

Ironically, King never saw a copy of his first published "slick" story, "The Float," which was purportedly published in *Adam*. Because the magazine paid on publication and King got a check for $250, he presumed it was published, though he never saw a copy himself.

Regardless of whether or not it was published, King did get paid, and that encouraged him to submit to other men's magazines, notably *Cavalier*, edited by Nye Willden, who demanded above all that stories be well written. As King recalled, "I have a particular warmth for *Cavalier*, because they published my own first marketable horror stories. Both [Publisher] Doug Allen and Nye Willden are warm and helpful, and if your story is good, they'll publish it. They report in four to six weeks and pay from $200 to $300 depending on length and previous numbers of stories published."[4]

King made his fictional debut in *Cavalier* in its October 1970 issue. "Graveyard Shift," which drew heavily from King's experiences after school and during the summers of his high school years at a textile mill in Lisbon Falls, was originally written in the offices of *The Maine Campus*. "I had this idea for a story: Wouldn't it be funny if these people cleaned out the basement of the mill—which is a job I had at one time—and found all these big rats? Wouldn't that be gross?"[5]

It was not only gross, it was grossly profitable for King, who would go on to sell numerous stories to Willden, who knew good writing when he saw it.

Writers draw on experience, observation, and imagination to write, and for "Graveyard Shift," King drew on all three:

> The real impetus to write this particular story was the mill I worked in. It was a non-union shop, and when they had vacation week, the people who had "tenure" got a paid vacation; the rest of us also got the week off—without pay, unless you wanted to work the clean-up crew, which was going to go down in the basement. . . . I worked in the bagging area. They'd blow fabric up into these huge bins and we would bag it. Between the times you were waiting for your bill to fill up, you'd throw cans at the rats, because the rats were everywhere. They were big

guys, too; some of them would sit right up and beg for it like dogs. So when I was asked to join the clean-up crew I said, "No, I can't do that. I'm going to beg off. You guys have a good time."[6]

It's questionable whether or not the workers had a good time, but one thing was certain: the rats in the cellar were, as one member of the cleanup crew recalled, "as big as puppies."[7]

Real life provided King with everything he needed to write "Graveyard Shift," with the injection of the gross-out that would later become a King trademark. In this story, the rats mutated and the sadistic foreman got his just desserts.

On December 29, 1970, when King was living at 112 North Main Street in Orono, he and Tabitha Jane Spruce were issued a marriage certificate. On January 2, 1971, they got married in Old Town, with clergyman John M. Anderson performing a Catholic ceremony, because Spruce was raised as a Roman Catholic; however, King was raised a Methodist, so the reception was held at a Methodist church.

Two months later, King sold *Cavalier* a second story, "I Am the Doorway." Although it had the trappings of science fiction, it was clearly a horror story. A spaceman returns from Venus and brings home a little surprise—eyes that grow on his hands, wanting to take control of his body. Horrified, he burns his hands, but the eyes grow back again . . . on his chest.

In May 1971, Tabitha King graduated from the University of Maine, with a B.A. degree in history. Having worked her way through college, she discovered that the degree and a quarter would get you the proverbial cup of coffee at a Dunkin' Donuts in Bangor, which is where she worked.

The blue-collar jobs didn't pay much, and although those meager incomes were supplemented with an occasional short story sale to *Cavalier*, King knew that his ticket to ride would be novels. Not only did they pay more but if you were lucky, a book would earn back its advance—a loan from the publisher against expected earnings—and produce royalties. Also, there was always the possibility of a subsidiary sale to a book club or a paperback reprint house, which would bring in even more money.

Money grew very tight after Naomi King was born, so Stephen King finished *Getting It On* and submitted it to Doubleday, since the firm published hundreds of books annually, among them Loren Singer's *The Parallax View*, which was similar enough to *Getting It On* that he felt it might be possible to make his first book sale. King sent a query letter to Doubleday to the attention of the editor of *The Parallax View*, not knowing that its flamboyant editor had left Doubleday, leaving that book, requesting that the book be turned over to the capable hands of another Doubleday editor, William G. Thompson.

Thompson, in turn, wrote back and invited King to submit the finished manuscript.

If the book sold, King knew, it would mean he could quit the laundry and do what he had always wanted to do, write full-time for a living.

The manuscript arrived, but Thompson couldn't convince the editorial board that it should be a Doubleday novel. Thompson regarded the novel as "a masterful study in character and suspense, but it was quiet, deliberately claustrophobic and it proved a tough sell within the house. I'd asked Stephen —for by now we were on a first-name basis—for changes which he willingly and promptly made, but even so I couldn't glean sufficient support and reluctantly returned it."[8]

King, in turn, was gravely disappointed. "Doubleday declined, a painful blow to me, because I had been allowed to entertain some hope for an extraordinarily long time, and had rewritten the book a third time, trying to bring it into line with what Doubleday's publishing board would accept."[9]

For a persistent writer like King, hope springs eternal, but there's a point at which reality sets in; and, in his case, the reality was that he'd have to put his dreams on hold and get a full-time job, because it didn't look like Stephen King the writer was going anywhere fast.

In the fall of 1971, King took a teaching position at Hampden Academy, where he had student-taught in college. The job paid $6,400 a year and King was glad to get it, because the novels weren't selling—yet.

For any writer, taking a full-time job is, if not an admission of failure, then one of temporary defeat. Predictably, King worried that his dreams as a writer would remain just that—nebulous dreams; and that he'd have to teach full-time for a living instead of writing, which he felt was the ultimate nightmare.

The Kings moved to Hermon, a small town on Route 2, west of Bangor. Their rented double-wide trailer sat on a hilltop in the middle of nowhere, which is exactly where King felt his life as a writer was going.

King's days were spent teaching; his nights were spent grading papers and preparing for classes; and the time devoted to writing grew increasingly scarce, though he always managed to find time late in the evenings to sit in his makeshift office, the furnace room of the trailer, to bang away on Tabitha King's Olivetti typewriter, a manual that would, in time, bear testimonial to Stephen King's dedication: his fingerprints would be imbedded in the keys.

That winter, Stephen King—out of desperation, perhaps, or out of blind hope—hammered out a novel over a long weekend during a school vacation. It was an investment in time that, unfortunately, would not pay off in the short term. The novel, *The Running Man*, was an imaginative fusion of the game-show mentality and a classic short story, "The Most Dangerous Game."

King promptly submitted it to Thompson, but it, too, was declined. King, who had faith in this short but intense story of a man under siege, trying to provide for his family under desperate circumstances. He then submitted it to Ace Books, since they published a science fiction line in mass market paperbacks—the perfect format for this kind of book, King decided. Unfortunately, its publisher, Donald A. Wolheim, rejected it with a curt note. "We are not interested in science fiction which deals with negative utopias. They do not sell."[10]

Wolheim, a well-regarded editor/publisher, knew his market and his readers well. He knew they read fiction to get away from the depressing realities of life; they wanted to read and be entertained. *The Running Man*, however, was no fictional diversion but, in fact, a reaffirmation about how tough life is—something King knew firsthand, after he pondered this latest turn-down.

King put *The Running Man* in his writer's trunk, alongside *Blaze* and *Getting It On*, and went back to work, depressed with the notion that he could sell an occasional short story but not a novel—the only way he could make a living writing.

On June 4, 1970, the Kings had a second child, Joseph. Money, which was already tight, became tighter; and although King would go on to sell four more short stories to *Cavalier*, getting rates of up to $300 each, the distinctive, well-written stories remained relatively unknown, just like their writer. Who, after all, would expect to find good fiction between the covers of a magazine with lurid headlines and salacious girls posing suggestively on the cover? *Cavalier* wasn't exactly *The New Yorker*.

The financial troubles mounted. The teaching salary was insufficient to cover the monthly expenses. King, an overworked and stressed-out teacher by vocation and writer by avocation, found himself "drinking too much,"[11] because the financial nightmare never seemed to end. Even the phone had to be removed to save money and, as usual, their seven-year-old Buick was always breaking down, running up repair bills instead of running down roads.

"I began to have long talks with myself at night about whether or not I was chasing a fool's dream," King recalled.[12]

Like the Beatles song, King felt very much like the fool on the hill, sitting perfectly still. Life had ground to a halt and King's dreams of writing full-time seemed to be a remote possibility.

In 1967 Ira Levin's horrific evil-seed novel, *Rosemary's Baby*, was successfully adapted for the screen, bringing horror to a mainstream audience that, four years later, was reinforced with back-to-back horror novels tapping into its new-found mass appeal: William Peter Blatty's *The Exorcist* and Thomas Tyron's *The Other*.

Against the backdrop of these three books, Stephen King began writing an engaging short story about a teenage girl named Carietta White, an ugly duckling who could trigger kinetic powers when stressed out. Drawing heavily on his remembrances of his high school days and the recollections of a girl who lived down the street from his Durham home, Stephen King wrote the first few pages of the story, crumpled them up, and threw them in the trash. Fortunately, Tabitha King fished them out of the trash can, read them, and encouraged her frustrated husband/writer to get on with the story.

"I persisted ... because I was dry and had no better ideas," King said.[13]

King's persistence paid off, but not in the way he had hoped. His expectation was that he would have a $300 short story to sell to *Cavalier*, but instead he had a 25,000-word novella, which was too long to be published in a magazine but too short to be published as a paperback novel. King, in short, had invested his precious free time in writing a story that had no market, which translated to "no money."

"My considered opinion was that I had written the world's all-time loser," King said.[14]

✌ 5 ✍

BECAUSE *Carrie* was too short to be submitted as a novel, King beefed up the wordage with bogus documentation, transforming the novella to a short novel.

In January 1973, King submitted *Carrie* to Doubleday.

William Thompson read the novel and wrote back to King, suggesting changes to its ending. King readily complied and, later, observed that "Thompson's ideas worked so well that it was almost dreamlike. It was as if he had seen the corner of a treasure chest protruding from the sand, and unerringly driven stakes at the probable boundaries of the buried mass."[1]

Thompson agreed. "Basically, the editorial process means understanding what the author wants to do and helping him get there. With *Carrie*, I don't think at any time before or after, have I as editor been so in tune with the author's conception of a book."[2]

With what Thompson considered to be a publishable manuscript in hand, he enthusiastically worked in-house to sell the book to "the profit-center types—sales, publicity, subsidiary rights."[3]

Working against the book: it was a first novel from an unknown who had to date published only a handful of stories, mostly in *Cavalier*. Working for the book: it was a terrific story that, with its first sentence as a narrative hook, engaged the reader's attention, and didn't let go until the story's end. It worked for Thompson, but would the story appeal to the rest of the Doubleday staffers outside of the editorial department?

Reasonably certain that a sale was imminent, Thompson invited King to New York for a publisher's lunch. King paid his own way, borrowing money from his in-laws to make a long trip on a Greyhound bus. He arrived early in the morning at a main terminal in Manhattan.

King, who wore new shoes that had to be broken in, couldn't afford to take a taxi, so he walked the dozens of blocks to the Doubleday office.

At lunch, King—desperate to make a good impression—drank gin and tonics on an empty stomach and was "almost immediately struck drunk"[4] and ate a pasta dish, its remnants soon lodged in his beard.

Thompson told King that the odds were in his favor, but hedged his bets. Having had to reject two novels previously, Thompson didn't want to give the unpublished novelist false hope. Fortunately for King, Thompson's instincts were correct. *Carrie* made the rounds in house and, in his words, "it was magic time."[5] In what King called the glamour world of book publishing, decisions were being made on *Carrie* that would irrevocably change his life.

King, meanwhile, went back to work as a teacher by day, writer by night, and began a new novel, *Blaze*, which he finished on February 15, 1973. The story of a kidnapping, *Blaze* was a clear departure from *Carrie*. A short novel of 50,000 words, *Blaze* was suspense fiction, but *Carrie* was clearly—for lack of a better term—horror fiction.

Back in New York, Doubleday finally gave the green light to *Carrie*, a moment Thompson recalls. "When the rights director's eyes lit up and when the advertising manager called it a 'cooker,' I knew we were home free."[6]

The original advance was only $1,500, but Thompson got it bumped up to $2,500, the equivalent of ten short story sales to *Cavalier*. The difference, however, was that the short stories would have been published and forgotten, and would not help build King's career. But *Carrie*, as a first novel, held the tantalizing promise of showcasing a new talent, one who could conceivably be developed into a brand name.

In March 1973, Thompson sent Stephen King a telegram. He would have preferred calling with the good news, but the Kings had no telephone.

Chris Chesley, who was attending UMO and renting a room in the double-wide trailer, recalled what happened after returning from classes the day the telegram arrived.

> After I hitchhiked home, I came down the little dirt road his house was on. I had just gotten in the yard when Tabby ran out of the front door, waving a telegram. She said, "Look, look at this!" I took it, Tabby jumped and shouted, I jumped and shouted, and when Steve got home later that day, I got out of the way. They just hugged each other and cried. It was one of the best days that I have ever had.[7]

When the standard Doubleday book publishing contract arrived, King and Chesley sat in the living room, drank beers, and went over the contract, clause by clause.

Years later, in a special collector's edition of *Carrie*, Tabitha King wrote, ". . . it was the end of a cycle for us, though we didn't know it. . . . We got evicted from the trailer in Hermon and moved back to Bangor."

The Kings moved into a modest second-story apartment on Sanford Street. It was a step up in terms of lodging, but not much better than the trailer in Hermon. At least now, the Kings could afford a phone.

King, who had wrestled with the demons of ill-fortune, now wrestled with the demons of good fortune. The days of what he rightly termed "shit work" were behind him: janitor, bagger, dyer, and sewer in a textile mill, gas station attendant, and laundry worker.[8]

On May 12, 1973, King got the phone call from Thompson that changed his life forever. Doubleday had sold paperback reprint rights to New American Library, for $400,000. King, as per the book contract, would get half of that.

"To say that Tabby and I were flabbergasted by this news would be to understate the case; there may be no word in English capable of stating our reactions exactly."[9] To mark that moment, Stephen King went across the street to a drugstore and bought Tabitha a hair dryer for $16.95.

David Bright, a reporter for the hometown newspaper, published the first ever interview with King, in which the budding writer wrestled with the demons of temptation—stay and teach or write and leave? As Bright explained:

> Steve King can't quite make up his mind whether or not he should retire. For King, the book marks his first hit after three strikeouts in trying to break into the novel business. That the book is about Maine high school life is no coincidence, for King wrote his first book while in high school himself. His first rejection, along with a letter that perhaps he should try another field of endeavor, came that same year. King says teaching often takes up time he'd rather spend at writing. . . . Five of his students at Hampden Academy have asked his advice on novels they are writing and he is encouraging them as best he can, which is one of the reasons he hasn't decided to quit teaching despite his new-found fortune.[10]

In the end, King made the most logical choice. "It was a great feeling of liberation, because at last I was free to quit teaching and fulfill what I believe is my only function in life: to write books. Good, bad, or indifferent books, that's for others to decide; it's enough to *write*."[11]

In June 1973, after the school year ended, the Kings packed up and moved to North Windham, a small town by Sebago Lake, near Portland.

With the publication of *Carrie* less than a year away—in April 1974—King turned his attention to *Second Coming*, a supernatural novel about a vampire who preys on a small Maine town.

Thompson, having read *Blaze* and an early draft of *Second Coming*, recommended that King publish *Second Coming*, which they both felt was the better of the two novels.

The year of promise, however, ended on a note of family tragedy. Stephen King's mother, Nellie Ruth King, who had been diagnosed with cancer the previous year, finally succumbed on December 18, 1973.

King, devastated by the loss, began a new novel, *Roadwork*, which would serve not only as catharsis for the reader but for its writer as well. "I think it was an effort to make some sense of my mother's painful death . . . a lingering cancer had taken her off inch by painful inch. Following this death I was left both grieving and shaken by the apparent senselessness of it all. . . . *Roadwork* . . . tries so hard to be good and to find some answers to the conundrum of human pain."[12]

Nellie Ruth King, who had always found the money for postage so her son could send off submissions to magazines, who gave her sons pin money she couldn't afford to give them while they were in college, did live long enough to see an advance galley of *Carrie* but not long enough to see the book get published.

With *Roadwork* finished in January, King turned his attention to the prepublication push on *Carrie*, which had begun to heat up. Advance reading copies went out to key media, accompanied by a letter from its editor, William Thompson.

> Doubleday is pleased to present you with this special edition of *Carrie*, by Stephen King. We feel it may be *the* novel of the year—a headlong narrative with the drive and relentless power of *The Exorcist*, with the high voltage shock of *Rosemary's Baby*. More than that, it is part of a rare breed in today's fiction market—a good story. Don't start it unless the evening in front of you is free of appointments; this one is a cooker.
>
> *Carrie* is the story of a girl who has been the odd one all her life, the misfit, the born loser. Torn between her fanatic mother who sees sin everywhere—in the nudity of a girl's shower room, in any friendship Carrie might develop with girls her own age, and especially in dating— and her own pathetic wish to become part of the world that shuns and

attracts her, Carrie becomes the butt of every cruel joke, the object of any malicious prank. But Carrie is different, more than a victim of forces she cannot understand, she possesses a strange and frightening power which she can hardly control. And when one final prank is played, the unleashing of Carrie's power proves as spellbinding as it is devastating.

We hope that *Carrie* will excite you as much as it has us. A tremendously readable ESP novel, it is also a quietly brilliant character sketch of a young and unusual girl trying to find her way out of a very personal hell. We think *Carrie* and Stephen King have a bright future, and we welcome this chance to share both of them with you.[13]

Carrie's first printing was 30,000 copies. Priced at $5.95, the 199-page book sported a cover illustration that had nothing to do with the book itself: a painting of a doe-eyed brunette with long, flowing hair, dressed in an exotically patterned black garment—a far cry from the pathetic misfit that King wrote about in his novel.

Though the novel reviewed well in the traditional prepublication journals that catered to the book and library trades, the book, said King, ". . . didn't get within hailing distance of anyone's bestseller list, it wasn't announced with trumpet flourishes from the first three pages of any critical magazine, and as far as *Playboy, The New Yorker, The Saturday Review, Time* and *Newsweek* were concerned, it didn't exist at all. Ditto book clubs."[14]

Carrie the book carried the day, but Doubleday's subsidiary rights department had gotten interest from Hollywood, and in time that would take King to the top of the bestseller lists.

❧ 6 ❧

In April 1974 Doubleday bought King's second novel, *Second Coming*, which had gone through three drafts before being accepted. Retitled after the fictional town that served as its setting, *'Salem's Lot*—an abbreviation for Jerusalem's Lot—would reinvent the vampire novel, transporting a Dracula-like vampire from his inaccessible aerie in the Carpathian Mountains of Transylvania to small-town America.

As with *Carrie*, the lucrative paperback rights to *'Salem's Lot* were sold to NAL, for $500,000, with King getting half—a boilerplate clause that King perceived as exceedingly generous to the publisher for what was in effect a sales commission, at a time when literary agents got 10 percent. Why, King thought, should the publisher keep half the money just for making a subsidiary sale?

No matter . . . for now. With the publication of *'Salem's Lot*, following on the heels of *Carrie*, it was enough for Doubleday to position King, to pigeonhole him to booksellers as a horror novelist. As King explained:

> *'Salem's Lot* had been read at NAL with a great deal of enthusiasm, much of it undoubtedly because they recognized a brand name potential beginning to shape up. Horror was big in those days . . . and I showed no signs with my second book of exchanging my fright wig and Lon Chaney makeup for a pipe and tweed jacket and writing something Deep and Meaningful.[1]

Having set two books and several stories in Maine, Stephen King decided it was time for a change of scenery, in his real and fictional life. Randomly pointing to a map of the United States, King's finger landed on Colorado, so the Kings packed up and moved to Boulder, where they rented a house at 330 South Forty-second Street.

King began writing *The House on Value Street*, inspired by the real-world kidnapping and brainwashing of Patty Hearst, daughter of the California newspaper publisher Randolph Hearst. As Douglas Winter noted in *Stephen King: The Art of Darkness*, "The book was never written; King attacked it for six weeks, but nothing seemed to work."[2]

King abandoned the book and picked up a novel idea inspired by Ray Bradbury's short story "The Veldt," in which a child's playroom of the future becomes something far more sinister. *Darkshine* would explore the idea of dreams that turned into reality; a little boy acted as a psychic receptor and amplifier. "I wanted to take a little kid with his family and put them someplace, cut off, where spooky things would happen."[3]

It was a promising idea, but the setting of the novel, an amusement park, proved unworkable, as King soon realized. "The thing is, you can't really cut a family off in an amusement park; they'll go next door and say, 'We've got some problems here.'"[4]

Unfortunately, King had some other problems, as well. He had attempted, and subsequently abandoned, two novels. As with most writers, King realized when it was time to call it quits and let his ideas percolate.

Unlike *The House on Value Street*, which seemed to go nowhere fictionally, the germ of the idea—the little boy with the psychokinetic powers—stuck in King's mind, and the novel that was *Darkshine* would, after a fortuitous weekend trip, develop into a book called *The Shine*.

It's hard to imagine a spookier place than the Colorado mountains in the dead of winter. Snow can fall as early as October and, as the Kings found out when they decided to spend a Halloween weekend away from the kids back in Boulder, the more posh resort hotels closed early for the winter because the roads would soon be impassable.

On the recommendation of the locals, the Kings drove to the Stanley Hotel in nearby Estes Park. A grand hotel with a long history, the Stanley was in the process of shutting down for the season when the Kings arrived.

The Kings assumed they could check in with their American Express card, but all the blank receipts had been shipped back to the home office; fortunately, one was found, so they were able to check in.

The Kings checked into room 217 and, as they walked down long corridors with coiled firehoses mounted on the wall, King's imagination, fueled by the spooky location, began conjuring up a new story. "By then, whatever it is that makes you want to make things up . . . was turned on. I was scared, but I loved it."[5]

That night the Kings dined in the cavernous dining room, attended by a waiter who sepulchrally intoned, "What would you like? We have one choice. You may have Colorado beef—or you may have nothing."[6]

They ate the beef, to the accompaniment of taped music piped through loudspeakers. The other chairs had been upended on the tables, and the band had left days earlier.

After dinner, the Kings returned to their room. Tabitha went to bed immediately, but King's imagination kept him awake, so he took a long walk and, at the hotel bar, was served drinks by Grady, its bartender.

When King left, he got lost in the maze of corridors, then found his way to room 217, where he went to the bathroom, pulled back the pink curtain drawn across the bathtub, and noticed the clawfoot porcelain tub. "What if somebody died here? At that moment, I knew that I had a book."[7]

The book was titled *The Shine* and, because it was impossible to concentrate and write in the small house they were renting, King rented a room in downtown Boulder.

Darkshine never passed muster, but King salvaged its best aspects—the little boy with an unusual power, the idea of a geographically isolated place where horrific things could happen—and incorporated them into the new novel. In *The Shine*—a reference to Danny Torrance's ability to exercise his paranormal powers—King also exorcised his personal ghosts, which had haunted him for some years. Fears of general inadequacy, fears of failure, and fears of inadequate parenting were at the core of the main character, Jack Torrance, a reformed alcoholic and former schoolteacher who was expelled for attacking a student but given a new lease on life: the opportunity to be the caretaker of the Overlook Hotel for a winter season. If he failed at this last chance—a job obtained through a family connection—he was, he knew, a dead man.

As King wrote *The Shine*, it transported him back to Maine, to the snow-capped hill in Hermon on which his trailer perched, where he thought his worst fears would be realized. "I was able to invest a lot of my unhappy aggressive impulses in Jack Torrance, and it was safe."[8]

Bracketed by a prologue and epilogue, *The Shine* was an inventive, rich novel that brought together many of King's strengths in a classic reinvention of an all-too-familiar theme in horror literature, the haunted house. Instead of a traditional haunted house, however, the setting was even more forbidding: a cavernous hotel with a shady past, set apart, and above everything else geographically, just as the Marsten house in *'Salem's Lot* looked down on its town.

In January 1975, on a visit to New York to see William Thompson, King went over the copy-editing for *'Salem's Lot* and also took the opportunity to tell Thompson the plot of *The Shine* at Jaspers, a hamburger joint.

Thompson was not enthusiastic, pointing out that it bore an uncanny resemblance to a 1973 novel by Robert Marasco, *Burnt Offerings*, which King was familiar with and, in fact, admired. "First the telekinetic girl, then the vampires, now the haunted hotel and the telepathic kid. You're gonna get typed," Thompson said.[9]

Thompson's concern was, up to a point, entirely justified. He felt that King would be typed as a horror writer, which King perceived as a compliment but Thompson knew was a significant long-term detriment in terms of public perception. King cited a long list of writers who worked in the spook field whom he admired: "Lovecraft, Clark Ashton Smith, Frank Belknap Long, Fritz Leiber, Robert Bloch, Richard Matheson, and Shirley Jackson. . . ."[10] Guilt by association didn't bother him, and he didn't care what labels people put on him.

When King returned to Colorado, he finished *The Shine* and, a month later, picked up *The House on Value Street*, which he felt was salvageable, but it went nowhere after six weeks of continual effort. King finally abandoned it, reluctantly, but found himself fascinated by a news story, an "accidental CBW [chemical-biological warfare] spill. . . . All the nasty bugs got out of their canister and killed a bunch of sheep. But, the news article stated, if the wind had been blowing the other way, the good people of Salt Lake City might have gotten a very nasty surprise."[11]

It brought to mind "Night Surf," a story he had published in 1969 in *Ubris*, the college literary magazine at UMO, later reprinted in an expanded version in *Cavalier*. The story focuses on a handful of teenagers in Maine awaiting their inevitable deaths at the hands of a superflu bug nicknamed "Captain Trips," which had already killed off the rest of the world's population. Like much of King's fiction, it explored the consequences of technology unchecked by morality. The world as they knew it was ending . . . and its cause? "Just the flu."[12]

The idea of the accidental CBW spill occupied King's mind and the germ of a new novel came to mind, brought into focus by George Stewart's novel

Earth Abides, about the end of the world, and a preacher broadcasting from a nearby town who spoke of a generational plague.

The danger would not come from the skies, from spacemen in flying saucers carrying weapons of mass destruction, but from within, recalling Pogo's oft-quoted observation that "We have met the enemy and he is us." Our technology, King realized, had outstripped our morality. And the ultimate joke was that we built weapons of mass destruction, hoping and praying we'd never use them. But they were there, immaculately maintained and precisely accounted for, until the system started breaking down . . . and, to his mind, it eventually would.

The Stand, which developed the idea of "Night Surf" to its logical conclusion, would be King's morality play, a classic story of the eternal struggle between good and evil. In this case, the forces of good were represented by Mother Abigail and her followers, drawn to her from across the country to do battle with Randall Flagg and his minions—the Dark Man would make his satanic stand in Las Vegas, Nevada.

The large canvas, however, required more room than King had initially realized. The book became "my own little Vietnam, because I kept telling myself that in another hundred pages or so I would begin to see the light at the end of the tunnel."[13]

That summer, the Kings moved back to Maine and, that fall, bought their first home, in Bridgton. Located on the west side of Long Lake, RFD 2, Kansas Road was the perfect writer's retreat. (Portland, the nearest metropolitan city, was only forty miles distant.)

In Bridgton, King worked on the first draft of *The Stand* while awaiting the hardback publication of *'Salem's Lot*. Even with only one book published—the hardback edition followed by the paperback edition that was released in April—King began to see the encroachment of the fans, who would track him down to Bridgton to ask locals where he could be found.

Appropriately, *'Salem's Lot*—a vampire novel set in small-town Maine—was published near Halloween. A $7.95 hardback, this novel was over twice the size of *Carrie*, which had a $5.95 cover price.

An astonishingly rich and inventive novel, *'Salem's Lot* later made the cut for *Horror: 100 Best Books*, with Al Sarrantonio extolling its many virtues:

> While *Rosemary's Baby* and *The Exorcist* mined supernatural niches in the bestseller list, I would argue that *'Salem's Lot*, because of its genuineness, its verve, its originality, its willingness to reflect, expand and

celebrate its sources, and, most importantly, its establishment of Stephen King, after the sincere but *un*seminal *Carrie*, not as an interloper but as a pioneer in a field ripe for reinvention, was *germinal* and *originative* of the entire boom in horror fiction we find ourselves in the middle of— with no culmination in sight.[14]

Reduced to a popular culture parody of itself, the vampire—most notably in films, but also in paperback novels—was something of a joke, especially in the horror genre, festooned with quickie paperbacks featuring vampires and lurid covers, usually with a pretty young woman cowering in a nightgown in her bedroom as the vampire approached.

King, however, went back to the original source, the seminal vampire novel, *Dracula* by Bram Stoker. Even a century after its publication, the book still wielded its hypnotic power over King, who decided to play it straight and breathed new life into a pop culture cliché.

King's original notion was that the idea of a vampire in contemporary America simply wouldn't ring true, since modern crimefighters, equipped with new technologies, could seek out and find Dracula or his counterpart in short order. But, years earlier, over the dining room table, Chris Chesley and Tabitha King both pointed out that there were small towns in Maine in which you could get lost forever, where nobody would ever find out.

King realized that was true, so he transported Dracula from the mountains of Europe to a small Maine town. As Leonard Wolf explained:

> *'Salem's Lot*—the name is a contraction of Jerusalem's Lot—is a vampire fiction set firmly in America. In addition to being a master plot maker, one of the things King does best is rendering the feel of American small-town life. In this novel one of those small towns, 'Salem's Lot, is invaded by a vampire named Barlow who, like Dracula, has left Europe in search of juicier prey in America. Like his Transylvanian predecessor, Barlow must have a mortal open doors for him. That doorman is Straker, an elegant, bald man whose name, I'd guess, is derived from Stoker himself. . . . Barlow and Straker open an antique shop in the village. Not much later, the horrors begin, as, one by one, beginning with the Glick family, villagers are vampirized.[15]

The reading public likes big, fat books to read during the summer; and Thompson, who was no exception, told King he had "lost one entirely sunny summer weekend with Ben Mears, Susan Norton and the company in the town of Jerusalem's Lot, Maine."[16]

For King, however, the real horrors of success began to surface. Now perceived as an overnight success—after two hardback books, a movie deal for *Carrie*, and six-figure paperback book deals—the author in the small Maine town was haunted by his Constant Readers, who weren't satisfied with just reading his books.

Just as the ordinary people in *'Salem's Lot* became vampires and went out to search for new victims, King found himself besieged by the media and fans alike, as Mel Allen explained in an article for *Writer's Digest*:

> One of the newest pressures is the demand from reporters, schools, clubs, service organizations and the like for interviews and appearances. These have risen as fast as his meteoric climb to the top of the bestseller lists.
>
> He's starting to say no for the first time. But he feels torn. "On the one hand I want to accommodate people; on the other, I need time for myself. Yet every time I say no, I hear them thinking, 'That stuck-up bigshot writer. . . .'"[17]

It didn't help that King owned a $150,000 home with a new Cadillac in the driveway—the outward signs of success that King's readers could not overlook. *This*, they thought, *is how a successful writer lives!*

Like vampires and succubi descending on Bridgton, the fans proved disruptive, expecting King to stop being a writer to help them become writers, or be there for them in other ways. Mel Allen chronicled those times in his article:

> . . . [H]e's had his phone number changed, and the local operator tells countless people every day, "No, I'm sorry, we are not permitted to disclose that number," because strangers call from all parts of the country to ask for money, interviews, help in finding a publisher for the 800-page novel they've written about werewolves, or advice on how to do away with the demonic neighbor who has caused their vegetables to succumb to root rot.[18]

For the rest of the year, King's attempts to start new books failed. King, who rarely is blocked as a writer, likely found himself distracted by the persistence of the fans who wanted his books and a piece of his time as well. *Welcome to Clearwater*, *The Corner*, an early draft of *The Dead Zone*, and a start at *Firestarter*—all were fictional busts.

Meanwhile, the reading public snapped up the paperback of *'Salem's Lot* just as they snatched up the paperback edition of *Carrie* earlier. King's reinvention of the vampire novel quickly sold a million copies.

In November, when *Carrie* the film was released, its surprise success turned many of King's viewers into paperback readers, who then went to the bookstores and boosted his sales. The fallout: 1.25 million more copies of *'Salem's Lot* were sold.

The ricochet effect—a hardback and a paperback reprint, followed by a movie—worked to great effect with King's books, since he was not only capable of producing a book a year, but also capable of writing in a cinematic style that translated easily to the screen.

King was headed for best-seller country, but would *The Shining* be the vehicle?

It was clear to King that his success as a writer demanded professional representation to the book trade. A writer who represents himself has a fool for a client, as King said, and it was certainly true in his case. As a newly published writer, King didn't have the experience factor in contracts that Doubleday—or any other publisher—would have; consequently, Doubleday's clauses proved advantageous to the firm, more than the writer, and lucrative film and subsidiary rights were signed away.

At a New York literary party in 1976, Stephen and Tabitha King met a transplanted literary agent from Minneapolis who, at that time, was already representing several horror writers. Kirby McCauley, only thirty-four, was at the right place at the right time, but ironically had little knowledge of the writer who would redefine the horror genre permanently:

> I had heard of Steve, but frankly, when I went to the party I had only read one thing by Steve. Before the party, I went out and got a copy of *'Salem's Lot* and was blown away by it. I loved it. So I went to the party and said to Steve, "I love that book, but to be honest, I haven't read anything else by you." So we started to talk about writers in general and the field of horror and science fiction. As it turned out, Steve's interests and my interests were very much alike. He was more interested in talking about relatively unknown writers like Frank Belknap Long and Clifford Simak and people whom I knew or represented, than he was in staying in the corner and talking with James Baldwin.[19]

Even though King badly needed representation, he took his time in making up his mind. In the interim, to test the waters, he gave McCauley several short stories to place, to gauge his effectiveness as an agent. King, who was unable on his own to break into the mainstream "slick" magazines, felt this was McCauley's chance to prove himself. After that, he'd consider taking him on to sell more ambitious properties.

The more immediate concern was the imminent publication of *The Shining*. Though King's two previously published novels were critical successes, neither made any of the national best-seller lists, though the paperback reprints did very well.

What King didn't know was that the third time would be the charm. *The Shining* would be the novel that would make it clear—if anyone had any doubts—that there was a new king of horror . . . and his name was Stephen.

7

For many writers, when Hollywood comes knocking, the stardust in the eyes is soon replaced by sand: the film community is a world unto itself, built on a verbal tissue of double-speak. Blinded by the glamour of Hollywood, writers soon realize that in the pecking order they are the Carries of the film industry: a book is optioned and a screenplay is written, but it never gets produced; the movie gets produced, but its budget is minuscule, so it doesn't get any distribution; the movie gets distribution, but early reviews and word-of-mouth kill the movie, as the box office receipts drop with each passing weekend, until the movie mercifully is taken out of distribution.

In the book trade, the writer is king; but in show business, in Hollywood, the scriptwriter is at the bottom of the pecking order, and his work will almost certainly be rewritten, from the producer down to the girlfriend of the assistant to the makeup artist—creative meddling developed to an art form.

Carrie the book was a low-budget film ($1.8 million) directed by a filmmaker known for his horror films (Brian De Palma), and cast with unknown film talent—Sissy Spacek, Amy Irving, William Katt, Nancy Allen, and John Travolta.

It was clearly the kind of movie that seemed to have no future beyond a quick first-run in some theaters, followed by obscurity. Fortunately, the story that worked so well as a novel—the tormented high school girl who wanted desperately to fit in—worked wonderfully well as a movie.

Released in November 1976 by United Artists, directed by Brian De Palma, produced by Paul Monash, with a screenplay by Lawrence D. Cohen, *Carrie* was ninety-seven minutes of pure entertainment. In her role as Carrie, the put-upon, down-and-out teenage girl, actress Sissy Spacek turned in a performance that earned her an Academy Award nomination.

In the role of Carrie's mother, Piper Laurie—the only name-brand talent on the set—gave an impressive performance as an evangelical Christian, earning her an Academy Award nomination, as well.

The movie, to everyone's surprise, grossed $30 million domestically. It would be the first of many movies that would later be made of King's fiction, but one of the very few good ones.

If there was any doubt after *Carrie* and *'Salem's Lot* that Stephen King was a horror writer, *The Shining* put those doubts permanently to rest. But just in case its readers weren't sure, the publisher made sure they knew: On the dust jacket for *The Shining*, King was championed as "the undisputed master of the modern horror story."

The Shining, unlike *Carrie* and *'Salem's Lot*, was cut to keep the cover price under $10. The published book, which retailed for $8.95, was 447 pages; had it included the prologue and epilogue, though, as King had originally intended, the book would have been well over 500 pages.

The original title, *The Shine*, was changed to *The Shining*, because of its pejorative meaning. The change, however, had an unintended side effect: following the lead of the undisputed master of the modern horror story, competitive paperbacks came out with similar-sounding titles. "I won't name any by name. But I see a lot of books that must have been inspired by some of the stuff I'm doing. For one thing, those 'horror' novels that have gerund endings are just everywhere: *The Piercing*, *The Searing*—the *this*-ing and the *that*-ing."[1]

As disappointed readers of these books found out, they couldn't judge a horror novel by its cover, the title or the cover art. A quick reading of the text, however, usually revealed what the cover concealed: the book was often a quickie cheap paperback, designed to tap into the market enlarged by King, a one-man shock wave in the publishing industry, who took horror literature out of the dark and into the light of mainstream, popular fiction.

Within horror circles, the novel quickly gained a well-deserved reputation as a book that stood on its own merits, one that showed King to be no writing fluke. *Carrie* may have been a case of lightning striking once, but after *'Salem's Lot* and now *The Shining*, King looked to be a brand-name author in the making. In its first year, *The Shining* sold 50,000 copies, making it King's first hardback best-seller. In paperback, it went on to sell 2.3 million copies. Clearly, King was developing both a hardback and paperback audience and, to boot, he seemed to be building up a movie audience, as well.

A longtime favorite among King readers, *The Shining* was consciously structured as a five-act play. To King, the structure "imposed an artificial but very useful discipline on the book; each chapter . . . was carefully staged. . . . I can't emphasize the wonderfulness of this sense of order enough. The job of the writer is to impose order on chaos, to create the necklace we call 'story' from the various beads of ideas, images, character, tone, mood."[2]

When King finished the novel, it seemed to him that the book required an epilogue, "After the Play," which then unbalanced the book, requiring a prologue, "Before the Play," detailing the unsavory history of the Overlook Hotel.

More than just another supernatural tale well told, *The Shining* is a claustrophobic study in the disintegration of the modern American family. Jack Torrance, an ex-alcoholic, is slowly sinking into madness, as his wife Wendy and son Danny watch in horror, unable to stop his descent. Haunted by his past and haunted by the hotel for which he must serve as caretaker, Jack Torrance is a doomed and damned man who seems almost certain to take his family with him.

To the world at large, it appeared as if King was a happy Doubleday author, but that was only a surface impression, and an incorrect one, at that. King was far from happy—so far, in fact, that the contracts were like albatrosses around his neck, which made him realize it was time for a sea change: a literary agent was no longer a luxury but a necessity.

King decided to make a stand against Doubleday and its firmly entrenched policies that rankled him, especially the onerous, nonnegotiable policy of the fifty-fifty split on paperback reprint sales.

According to *Newsweek*, there were several points of contention. First, after King had "started raking in millions for Doubleday, his publisher still continued to dole out paltry advances."[3] *Carrie* had sold to NAL for $400,000, *'Salem's Lot* for $500,000, and *The Shining* and *The Stand* each brought in over a half million in subsidiary rights income.

With *Night Shift*, a collection of short stories, and *The Stand* awaiting publication, Doubleday had a lot more at stake than it realized. It might not be fair to say that Doubleday lacked the imagination to realize the potential sales of King; but in retrospect, it is fair to say that losing King had to be a decision the company profoundly regretted—a smaller percentage of the rolling gross is better than 100 percent of no gross. Authors who, early on, sell in the millions of copies are likely to continue writing for decades afterward, selling many millions more. The question, then, remained: Which publisher would milk King's cash cows?

Doubleday paid $77,500 for King's first five books, which in retrospect makes the publisher look downright cheap, considering that it had no risks involved financially, since the books were immediately sold for six figures to NAL, recouping the "investment" many times over.

By this time, however, publishing a new King book was a no-lose proposition; King had a growing track record that appeared as if it could only go up.

Despite King's obvious financial value to Doubleday—after all, what is the intrinsic value of any publishing house without its stable of best-selling writers?—Thompson observed that King had to be reintroduced to the executives at Doubleday each time he visited the office.

There was another sticking point: King wanted to publish a limited edition of *The Stand*, but Doubleday, citing contractual conflicts with book club licensing deals, flatly refused.

Regardless of the other points of contention, the big one was Doubleday's firm policy of a 50/50 split on paperback reprint money that, said King, "finally led to our parting of the ways. . . ."[4]

Kirby McCauley, armed with King's solid track record, negotiated a three-book deal with NAL, bringing King his first king-sized advance: $2.5 million. Instead of Viking buying the book and selling the reprint rights to NAL, the reverse was true—NAL owned the hardcover and paperback rights, and licensed the rights to Viking, a creative deal that resolved King's long-standing unhappiness with the normal order of book publishing: sell to the hardback house, which in turn sells to the paperback house but pockets—to King's mind—a disproportionate share of the proceeds.

The newly inked contract was a giant leap up for King and for McCauley, as well. It was one thing to get $2,500 for *Carrie* when King was an unknown, but it made no sense for King to get paltry advances after having proven himself as a bankable, brand-name writer, even at this early stage in his career.

McCauley, who saw the future of horror and saw that it was his client Stephen King, said, "It put me in a whole different league. Not just income, but now that of a major agent."[5]

King, who has always been an acute observer of the book publishing industry, realized that "the paperback industry is now the giant of the publishing world."[6] In terms of marketing, sales, promotion, and book packaging, the paperback houses were aggressive and commercial, whereas the hardback houses seemed mired, by comparison, in the past, resting on their laurels and expecting the paperback houses to subsidize them through subsidiary rights sales.

The three books included *The Dead Zone*, *Firestarter*, and *Cujo*.

Predictably, the three-book deal made the news in *Publishers Weekly*, unlike *Rage*, a paperback original published by NAL under its Signet imprint, for $1.50.

In what was one of publishing's best-kept secrets, known only to a handful of people at NAL on a strict need-to-know basis, Richard Bachman was no newcomer to the scene. Bachman was in fact Stephen King, writing under a pen name. (Even Robert Diforio, the president of NAL, wasn't in on the secret.)

A claustrophobic study of adolescent rage originally titled *Getting It On* but retitled *Rage*, this mainstream novel is the story of Charlie Decker, a student at Placerville High School, who flips out, kills a teacher, takes over a class, and then invites the students to "get it on" with him, examining their lives as he had done.

King, who as a teenager had filled a scrapbook with clippings about serial killer Charlie Starkweather, felt a sense of enormous frustration, of adolescent angst and rage, himself, so it was not altogether terra incognita to King.

> Like most people, I suspect, I have trouble remembering my teenage years . . . but one thing I do remember is that the fury and terror and jagged humor . . . found in that story had only one real purpose, and that was the purpose of all my early fiction: to save my life and sanity. What made me feel so crazy so much of the time back then? I don't know, Constant Reader, and that's the truth. My head felt like it was always on the verge of exploding, but I have forgotten why.[7]

Because the book was a paperback original, it received few reviews, though it did get one in the July 25, 1977, issue of the industry's trade journal, *Publishers Weekly*:

> Even a lesson in Latin grammar would have been more involving than what goes on in the Maine classroom in which psychopath Charlie Decker holds fellow students hostage. Charlie is in a rage, but it's never clear why, other than that he's got a grudge against both his father and the high school authorities who put him on probation for assaulting a teacher. Now Charlie has killed two teachers, set a fire in the school and taken over his classroom at gunpoint. When the other kids begin to act like clones of Charlie, playing mean-spirited games on one another,

they too turn out to be merely rebels without a cause, but apparently the author considers their violence sufficient to engage our interest.

What would *PW*'s reviewer have written if he or she had known the book was an early work by Stephen King?

The book shipped out, filled the paperback racks, and after a brief shelf life approximating milk, the remaining copies were pulled off the shelves, their covers stripped for credit, and the books pulped. End of story.

In the fall of 1977, the Kings sold their home in Bridgton and headed to England for what they planned to be a one-year stay. They knew exactly what they wanted to rent and put a classified ad in the *Fleet News*: "Wanted, a draughty Victorian house in the country with dark attic and creaking floorboards, preferably haunted."[8]

The ad worked and the Kings moved into their haunted house at Mourlands, 87 Aldershot Road, Fleet Hants. According to the *Fleet News*, King wanted to move to England because he wanted to write a book "with an English setting. When the novel is finished . . . it will be set back in a fictitious place, although it will be based on Fleet."[9]

The paper reported that the two older kids—Naomi and Joseph—had enrolled at a local school, St. Nicholas. As for the youngest, son Owen, born seven months earlier, he was "already getting his teeth into Dad's books—literally."[10]

Hopeful of acquiring another haunted house novel on the order of *The Shining*, NAL released a press release to inform the book trade that King had temporarily moved to England. "With its history of eerie writers and its penchant for mystery, England should help Stephen King produce a novel even more bloodcurdling than his previous ones—a novel that will only go to prove his title of 'Master of Modern Horror Novel.'"[11]

For whatever reasons, King was never able to write a book with an English setting. Instead, he began work on a book set in his fictional town of Castle Rock, Maine. The creative impetus came from two sources. First, a clipping from a Portland, Maine, newspaper, in which "This little kid was savaged by a Saint Bernard and killed," recalled King.[12] Second, King's experiences from a year earlier when his motorcycle died and, on one ailing cylinder, barely made it to a local shop.

> I drove into the house driveway, and the bike died. I put it on the kickstand and got up. Then I hear this noise that sounds like a motorboat, and coming out on the other side of the road was the biggest Saint

Bernard that I ever saw in my life. He started to walk across the road. His head was down, his tail was down, he wasn't wagging his tail; and he knew what he wanted—he wanted *me*. . . . The guy who ran the place came out of the rusty, corrugated garage and walked across the road. "Don't worry," he said. "That's just Joe. He *always* does that."[13]

The dog, recalled King, coiled on its haunches and started growling, but its owner took a wrench and struck the dog's rump, then looked at King and said, "Joe must not like you." The sound, King said, "sounded like a woman beating a rug with a carpet beater."[14]

The English novel never materialized, but the trip wasn't a total waste; King found a kindred spirit in Peter Straub, a transplanted American writer living in Crouch End, a suburb of London.

When Stephen and Tabitha King visited the Straub home, the Straubs were, at first, a bit taken aback. "They burst in full of energy, on a torrent of talk. It is safe to say that they were completely un-English, which at first was disconcerting—we'd been there ten years, and were used to a less muscular social style—but then finally refreshing."[15]

King, who was previously known to Straub through insightful blurbs that he had written for *Julia* and *If You Can See Me Now*, not only impressed Straub socially but professionally. Straub admired King's fiction for its unrestrained qualities, its exuberance, and its plain but flexible writing style. Citing *The Shining*, Straub wrote: "It made a virtue of colloquialism and transparency. The style could slide into jokes and coarseness, could lift into lyricism, but what was really striking about it was that it moved like the mind itself. It was an unprecedentedly direct style, at least to me, and like a lightning rod to the inner lives of his characters."[16]

King's stories, self-characterized as ". . . plain fiction for plain folks, the literary equivalent of a Big Mac and a large fries from McDonald's,"[17] was accessible in a way usually associated with popular fiction, but unlike a lot of popular fiction, King's work—despite its supernatural trappings—showed the hand of a careful writer who had more in common with Shirley Jackson than the hack novelists in the field who wrote unambitious, potboiling insubstantial novels that catered to the lowest possible common denominator in readership.

Straitjacketed by the genre, those writers who took their work seriously were overlooked and ignored, well known to fantasy and science fiction fans but virtual unknowns outside of that small world. As King explained:

The field has never been highly regarded; for a long time the only friends that Poe and Lovecraft had were the French. . . . The Americans were busy building railroads, and Poe and Lovecraft died broke. Tolkien's Middle-Earth fantasy went kicking around for twenty years before it became an aboveground success, and Kurt Vonnegut, whose books so often deal with the death-rehearsal idea, has faced a steady wind of criticism, much of it mounting to hysterical pitch.[18]

It was time, King and Straub agreed, that their brand of fiction transcend the genre from which it was derived. Supernatural fiction, they knew, would have to go mainstream.

Like King's, Straub's supernatural stories, regardless of writing quality, were not taken seriously outside of the fan field. Both writers were aware of this eternal damnation of horror literature, and both resented it.

At a Thanksgiving dinner at the Kings' home in Fleet Hants a short time later, King and Straub, collecting firewood outside, talked about the mainstream dismissal of their work. Both writers were in agreement that they wanted their work to be taken seriously, on its own merits, and that they wanted to be published in a serious manner, instead of being treated like second-class citizens at the publishing house, writing fiction that was considered a subset of fantasy.

It was time to change the literary scenery, they knew, and these two gunslingers reckoned they were the ones to do it.

❧ 8 ❧

There's no place like home and, for the Kings that meant Maine. After three months in England, they headed home, purchasing a contemporary-style house at Center Lovell, located in the Lakes region in southern Maine.

In February 1978, Doubleday published *Night Shift*, King's fourth book for that house. With an illuminating introduction by novelist John D. MacDonald, *Night Shift* contained twenty short stories, all but four of which had been previously published in *Cavalier*, *Gallery*, *Penthouse*, *Maine*, and *Cosmopolitan*.

"The books are visual," King explained. "I see them almost as movies in my head. When I sign a copy of *Night Shift*, if I'm not pressed for time, what I usually sign is, 'I hope you've enjoyed these one-reel movies,' which is essentially what they are."[1]

A short story collection typically does not sell anywhere near as well as a novel by the same author, so publishing houses usually do it as a favor to an author. Even still, *Night Shift* sold a respectable 24,000 copies, about half of *The Shining*, and would go on to much greater sales in a paperback edition.

The "one-reel movies," as King called them, were pretty good shorts. So good, in fact, that with the exception of an epistolary story, "Jerusalem's Lot," all had been optioned for visual adaptations. Unfortunately, even though *Cavalier*, at King's request, had reverted all rights, Doubleday probably handled the sales of the stories, which in time would come back to haunt King. The stories that had earned him a modest $300 each in the early years of his career now sold for lucrative sums to producers eager to cash in on the man who they hoped would be king of the horror cinema.

In September Doubleday published *The Stand*, King's apocalyptic tale of post-plague America, modeled after Tolkien's "Ring" trilogy, *The Lord of the Rings*. At 823 pages, it was King's biggest book to date.

A $12.95 hardback, *The Stand* received excellent reviews, including a glowing one from the book industry's trade journal, *Publishers Weekly*, which exclaimed that King

> outdoes himself in this spine-chilling moral fantasy where gritty realism forms the basis for the boldly imaginative raid upon the bizarre.
> . . . King's message is simple, but his characters are compellingly real, his complex, nightmare scenario is so skillfully done one almost believes it.[2]

Like readers of *The Lord of the Rings* who lost themselves in Middle Earth and didn't want the story to end, many of King's readers got caught up in the sweep of *The Stand*, and wished there was more. What they didn't know was that the story, as written, *was* longer than the published version. Doubleday insisted that 100,000 words be cut, so King had no choice and decided to perform the surgery himself, vowing that he'd restore the wordage someday.

With *The Stand* published, the last book he owed them, King took up residence at his new home, NAL; his editor at Doubleday, William Thompson, also left, finding a home at Everest House, where he would serve as its senior editor.

There had been another compelling reason to leave Doubleday: King's hands were tied financially in an arrangement that, when instituted at the beginning of his career, initially made sense but in time proved detrimental, according to *The Writer's Home Companion*:

> A number of publishing houses, such as McGraw-Hill and World Publishing, initiated a royalty payout plan for a few of their successful authors. The arrangements varied, but all were done to help the author defer taxes on earned royalty.
>
> Doubleday was among these publishers, and they had two plans: one a boilerplate clause available to every author, and another slightly different plan offered to only a few of their most successful authors. Both arrangements allowed Doubleday to pay a fixed yearly amount, which was selected by the author, no matter what the royalty earnings were, with the balance to be invested by the publisher.
>
> The young Stephen King was offered this plan and opted for an annual payment of $50,000, seemingly a princely sum, but his kitty soon swelled to over $3 million. Realizing that, at $50,000 a year, his Doubleday income would outlast him . . . King, no longer a Doubleday au-

thor, asked to have the agreements ended and a lump sum payment made. Doubleday refused, saying that if it ended the agreement without a "due consideration," the IRS would conclude that all such agreements could be easily terminated.

Because no agreement could be reached, the money would stay at Doubleday under its control, until the "due consideration" was rendered by King.

When King first taught a college course, he was a promising undergraduate student, and a talented but unpublished novelist.

How times had changed! Back then, King had to take a stand to get his voice heard and, in time, get his way. Now, with classroom experience at Hampden Academy behind him and his track record as a successful novelist, the university invited him back to teach, beginning September 1978. According to Burton Hatlen:

> When Ted Holmes was forced to retire in 1975 . . . we had the question of what to do with a creative writing position. The English department decided that instead of bringing in a permanent creative writing teacher, we would invite writers for relatively short periods. . . . We invited Stephen King on the understanding that it was for one year.[3]

The appointment would mean that King would have to live within commuting distance. The Kings decided to temporarily move to Orrington, a small town southwest of Bangor. Route 15, the main road through town, a major route to Bangor, was heavily trafficked by large diesel trucks carrying lumber and goods to and from the seaport. Predictably, with the houses lining the highway, a winding ribbon with hills that concealed the oncoming vehicles, the road claimed an annual toll of animals, especially cats and dogs, most of whom belonged to neighborhood children.

For King, the teaching stint was a welcome break. "I'm looking forward to teaching on a college level because we can focus more on creativity than grammar."[4] It would also mean that he'd have, for the first time, a real office. "This is great," King enthused. "I've never had a real office before. Now I can say to my wife, 'Dear, I'm going to the office.'"[5]

Like most college instructors, King probably spent little time in the office, since the classroom and prep work at home demanded so much; still, it was a fortuitous change of pace and scenery.

One night in November 1978, wrote King, ". . . I was sitting at the kitchen table with a beer, trying to dope out a syllabus for [Themes in Supernatural

Literature] . . . and musing aloud to my wife that I was shortly going to be spending a lot of time in front of a lot of people talking about a subject in which I had previously only felt my way instinctively, like a blind man."[6]

Coincidentally, that night William Thompson called. "Why don't you do a book about the entire horror phenomenon as you see it? Books, movies, radio, TV, the whole thing. We'll do it together, if you want."[7]

King didn't agree immediately, but eventually decided to do it. It would be a long, hard look at the genre he loved, a book to be edited by an editor he trusted. It, King said, would be ". . . my Final Statement on the clockwork of the horror tale."[8]

Later that month, on Thanksgiving Day, horror stuck home: Smucky, Naomi King's cat, was claimed as the latest casualty on Route 15, which was within a stone's throw of their rented house. "Naomi was really upset. I just wanted to tell her, 'Gee, I haven't seen the cat for a while.' But my wife said that we should tell her, because she's got to find out about death sometime."[9]

Smucky was buried in a local pet graveyard that the neighborhood kids had called "Pets Sematary." Located nearby, behind a house on a hill, the children's pet graveyard never lacked for burials, because Route 15 claimed its grisly tribute on a regular basis.

Not long thereafter, when King was crossing the road, the germ of a story idea came to him. "On one side of the road, I wondered what would happen if that cat could come back to life. By the time I got to the other side, I wondered what would happen if a human came back to life."[10]

It was an idea that had been explored to its logical conclusion in the W. W. Jacobs short story "The Monkey's Paw," with which King was familiar. In that story, a man finds a monkey's paw and makes three wishes, which he's granted . . . but not in the way he had expected: the first wish brought him the fortune he wanted, but it was blood money—his son was the price he paid for the first wish; with the second, the man wished his dead son back; and with the third, when he realized what he had done, when the son appeared at their house, knocking on the door, the man uses his final wish to send his son back to the grave. "It's what the mind sees that makes these stories such quintessential tales of terror. It is the unpleasant speculation called to mind when the knocking on the door begins . . . and the grief-stricken old woman rushes to answer it. Nothing is there but the wind when she finally throws the door open . . . but what, the mind wonders, *might* have been there if her husband had been a little slower on the draw with that third wish?"[11]

What, indeed? A dead boy brought back to life . . . a real Stephen King nightmare; in fact, any parent's worst nightmare.

The idea for *Pet Sematary* took hold and the result would be a dark novel, with a worldview echoed by Halloran, who in *The Shining* tells Danny Torrance:

> You listen to me. I'm going to talk to you about it this once and never again this same way. There's some things no six-year-old boy in the world should have to be told, but the way things should be and the way things are hardly ever get together. The world's a hard place, Danny. It don't care. It don't hate you and me, but it don't love us, either. Terrible things happen in the world, and they're things no one can explain. Good people die in bad, painful ways and leave the folks that love them all alone. . . . You grieve for your daddy. . . . That's what a good son has to do. But see that you get on. That's your job in this hard world, to keep your love alive and see that you get on, no matter what. Pull your act together and just go on."[12]

Naomi King, however, would have none of that. "The next day . . . we heard her out in the garage. She was in there, jumping up and down, popping these plastic packing sheets and saying, 'Let God have His own cat. I want my cat. I want my cat.'"[13]

The incident with Smucky and Naomi's reaction, the thoughts that would form *Danse Macabre*, the nonfiction look at the horror field, and the course work that lay ahead, plus the notion of the pet cemetery and the Jacobs story . . . all coalesced, putting King in a metaphysical frame of mind, pondering the nature of life and its natural end:

> Death is it. The one thing we all have to face. Two hundred years from now there won't be any of us walking around and taking nourishment. That's it. Sooner or later, God points at you and says, "It's time to hang up your jock, the game is over, it's time to take a shower. It's the end." But the point is, this is something that every creature on the face of the Earth goes through, but so far as we know, we're the only creatures that have an extended sense of futurity. We are the only ones who can look ahead and say, "Yes, that's right, it's going to happen. And how am I going to deal with the idea of my own conclusion?"
>
> Well, if you stop and think about it, and you stop to realize how clearly we grasp the concept, the answer should be, "We can't cope with it. It'll drive us crazy." For me, the fact that it doesn't is one of the really marvelous things in human existence, and probably also one of the

true signs of God's grace on the face of this earth. The ability to go on, day after day, to build meaningful lives, to prepare children in the face of all that, is akin to the act where they talk about a man pulling himself up by his bootstraps. At the same time, we have to prepare for it in some way; we have to experience all the possibilities. And so, for a lot of us, one of the ways we do it is to take a worst-case analysis. You say to yourself, *Okay, let's go see a horror movie and see how bad it can be, and then if I die in bed it won't be so awful.* You try to experience that in as many different ways that you can.

For a long time, death has been one of the great unmentionables in our society, along with sex and how much money we make. It's generally something you try to keep from the kids.[14]

In May 1979, King had completed the first draft of *Pet Sematary*. Its disturbing content greatly disturbed him, however, and he put it away. In his previous books, he had danced around the subject, talked about it, but never grappled with it. With *Pet Sematary*, he finally came to grips with it, imagining what it would be like to suffer the loss of a child—a thought that was real, not make-believe, horror. It cut too close to the bone and, like the boy in the Jacobs story, King felt it was best to let this one remain unseen.

About that time, King's year in residence at UMO had ended. "We tried to talk him into extending it, but he didn't want to,"[15] said Hatlen.

The University of Maine's most famous alumnus headed back to Center Lovell, to get back to the typewriter, where there were always more tales waiting to be told.

9

In the summer of 1979 Richard Bachman published his second novel, *The Long Walk*. Like its predecessor, *Rage*, this novel was a paperback original, cover-priced $1.95.

Virtually ignored by the world at large—it was, after all, the work of a little-known paperback writer—*The Long Walk* and its author were well known at UMO's English department, where the book had circulated during King's college days.

Burton Hatlen, in fact, thought very highly of the book. "I still think *The Long Walk* is a first-rate book. I think it was the best thing he wrote as an undergraduate, and the best thing he wrote until *'Salem's Lot*. I think it's a better book than *Carrie*."[1]

King, however, did not share his former teacher's enthusiasm. "Both *The Long Walk* and *Rage* are full of windy psychological preachments (both textual and subtextual), but there's a lot of story in those novels—ultimately the reader will be better equipped than the writer to decide if the story is enough to surmount all the failures of perception and motivation."[2]

In sharp contrast to *The Long Walk*, King's new novel from Viking, published in August, with a first printing of 80,000 copies, showed King the wisdom in switching publishers. Unlike the usual cheapie Doubleday book, *The Dead Zone* was beautifully packaged, with a striking dust jacket cover design conceived by One + One Studio.

King was pleased with the new look. "I like the jacket pretty well. I think that, in a large measure, it's been responsible for some of the book's success because it's a very high contrast type, something I think Viking might have lifted from the paperback houses."[3]

There was, in King's eyes, a world of difference between the "look" of King's Doubleday books and his first Viking book. "I like books that are nicely made," King said, "and with the exception of *'Salem's Lot* and *Night Shift*, none of the Doubleday books were especially well made. They have a ragged, machine-produced look to them, as though they were built to fall apart. *The Stand* is worse that way; it looks like a brick. It's this little, tiny squatty thing that looks much bigger than it is. *The Dead Zone* is really nicely put together. It's got a nice cloth binding, and it's just a nice product."[4]

As to the extent to which the design affected the sales of King's books, who knows for certain? One thing, though, was certain: *The Stand* had sold a respectable 50,000 copies, but *The Dead Zone* sold an impressive 175,000 copies.

Unlike *The Long Walk*, which King rightly faults for its perception and motivation problems, *The Dead Zone* is, plotwise, driven by motivation. It is the story of John Smith, who, having suffered a fall on a frozen lake as a child, later suffers an auto accident that puts him in a coma for four years. After emerging, Smith has prescient abilities; he can "see" events before they unfold, but he cannot close his eyes to the horrific consequences if Greg Stillson, the leading candidate for presidential office, is elected — nuclear holocaust.

Like Carietta White in *Carrie*, like Ben Mears in *'Salem's Lot*, like Charlie Decker in *Rage*, and like Jack Torrance in *The Shining*, John Smith is an outsider who must make choices to change the circumstances and affect the future in a positive manner, or suffer the consequences.

A favorite King novel cited by Anne Rivers Siddons, who wrote *The House Next Door*, a novel King greatly admired, Siddons put her finger on why *The Dead Zone* is, in terms of writing, a step forward for King. "It is such a *human* horror. *The Dead Zone* is one of King's few books that does not depend on a literal monster for its impact, except as we ourselves are capable of monstrosity. The monsters here — the press, the politicians, the religious zealots (Greg Stillson in particular) — they are us. We see as clearly as in a mirror what King wants us to see: We poor humans have all the horror we need within us."[5]

If there was any doubt in anyone's mind, *The Dead Zone* put them to rest: King, best known for his traditional trappings of fictional horror, could spin a horrific yarn by cutting closer to the bone. He could write about the *real* monsters — us.

For readers who prefer horror fiction, there's only one convention to attend, the World Fantasy Convention. Unlike the World Science Fiction Convention, which had become big business and a colossal fan undertaking, with many thousands of attendees, the World Fantasy Convention was smaller, much more intimate, and the perfect place to get it on with fellow fans, ogle at the otherworldly art hanging in the art show, and see the pros chat amiably, pontificate, or argue vigorously at panels.

In 1979 the fifth WFC was held in Providence, Rhode Island, the city made famous by H. P. Lovecraft, the seminal American horror writer, who, in his lifetime, saw the bulk of his work published in pulp magazines. Lovecraft was the opener of the way for everyone else in the field—you could not be unaware of the lantern-jawed, dour man who invented the Cthulhu Mythos stories and inspired a host of writers who, in turn, would be influences on a young Stephen King.

At this convention, Frank Belknap Long, one of the original members of the Lovecraft Circle, was be feted as a co-guest of honor; the other guest was Stephen King, who had received World Fantasy Award nominations for *The Stand* and *Night Shift*.

Fritz Leiber, a former Shakespearean actor turned writer who lived in California, made the trip simply because "It was in Providence, H. P. Lovecraft's city, and I felt I just had to go."[6]

Leiber, who had not read King's work previously, observed that King "behaved modestly and said several sensible things on panels and in the course of his winningly brief guest of honor speech."[7]

Awash with guilt at his financial success, King was in a particularly suggestible state when approached by Christopher Zavisa, the publisher of a small press, Land of Enchantment. Zavisa wanted King to do a project with him: a calendar with a fictional vignette for each month, to be illustrated by the premiere horror artist in the field, Berni Wrightson.

"I was, after all, rubbing elbows with writers I had idolized as a kid, writers who had taught me much of what I knew about my craft—guys like Robert Bloch . . . Fritz Leiber . . . Frank Belknap Long. . . . They had labored long and honorably in the pulp jungles; I came bopping along twenty years after the demise of *Weird Tales* . . . and simply reaped the bountiful harvest they had sown in that jungle."[8]

King agreed and subsequently made several abortive attempts to write the vignettes, but nothing clicked, so he did not force it. Something was wrong, he knew, but he couldn't put his finger on it. Maybe it was the format—the imposition of the calendar idea—or maybe it was the need to rework one of the most overworked clichés in the horror genre, the werewolf. For whatever reasons, King couldn't pull it together. "Every now and then," King wrote, "I would look guiltily at the thin sheaf of papers gathering dust beside the typewriter, but look was all I did. It was a cold meal. Nobody likes to eat a cold meal unless he has to."[9]

For the remainder of the year, the manuscript lay gathering dust. The calendar idea simply couldn't be made to work, despite King's best good-faith efforts.

As the year drew to a close, King saw *'Salem's Lot* air on national television. Originally optioned by Warner Brothers in 1975, this richly complex novel had eluded previous attempts to distill, as numerous screenwriters had attested. The problem, they agreed, was lack of running time. Finally, a decision was made to produce it as a television miniseries, hoping that it would give the book enough breathing space to tell its story.

For financial reasons, the miniseries was shot in a Northern California town that resembled New England, instead of shooting on location in Maine, which would have been ideal. (In the years to come, however, filmmakers would realize that it simply made good sense to shoot King's films *in* Maine, instead of trying to cut costs by shooting elsewhere.)

The 225-page script resulted in a four-hour miniseries that aired on November 17 and 24. Unfortunately, the shift from theater to television meant that, in terms of what was deemed acceptable visually, the movie had to be adulterated. Standards and Practices guidelines, adhered to by all the major networks, effectively neutered the horror story, ripe with erotic overtones of ritual neck-biting and violence, integral to the plot. King, however, took it in stride. "Considering the medium, they did a real good job. TV is death to horror. When it went to TV, a lot of people moaned and I was one of the moaners."[10]

❧ 10 ❧

In June 1980 the long-awaited, eagerly anticipated Kubrick film *The Shining* hit the theaters nationwide, to mixed reviews. Kubrick, a controversial director who likes to put his cinematic mark on any work he adapts, had attempted to create the ultimate horror story. Although his intentions were good, the resultant film—curiously miscast with Jack Nicholson as Jack Torrance and Shelly Duvall as Wendy Torrance—had its moments, but as a whole, the film never explored the nuances of the book, rich in its exploration of the disintegration of the Torrance family, as the haunted Overlook Hotel took its inevitable toll.

For King fans who loved *Carrie* as a book and a film, *The Shining* would be the first in a long string of disappointing adaptations that failed to faithfully translate King's fiction to the screen. As King opined: "Many people who love my books have turned away from the movies, particularly since *The Shining*—they don't find me in the movies—whatever *me* is. Writers don't have style so much as they have soul; it's between the lines of the prose that they write, it's that interior tension, the stuff that you don't say or the way that you say the things that you *do* say."[1]

Chris Chesley saw *The Shining* with Stephen King. "I could tell from sitting there beside him and watching him that although he didn't say so in so many words, he liked what the director had done, but the supernatural side of it had been excised—it wasn't his vision at all. That's what he said when we left the theater. It wasn't *his* book—it was *Kubrick's* movie."[2]

Carrie worked as a movie because it was mostly about character; the supernatural aspect, while important, did not overshadow the straightforward story, which King economically told in his short novel. *The Shining*, as a fictional construct, was considerably more complicated; unfortunately, the requirement existed to shoehorn it into 143 minutes.

A visually stunning film with an appropriately eerie score, *The Shining* proved to King that there were no guarantees as to the fidelity with which his books would be translated to the screen. Despite Kubrick's best effort, the road to hell proved to be paved with good intentions, and had cost a fortune. "*The Shining* cost roughly $19 million to produce as a film; it cost roughly $24 to produce as a novel—the cost of paper, typewriter ribbons, and postage."[3]

King could afford to be philosophical about it:

> When you sell something to the movies—and I love the movies, and it's immensely flattering to have somebody want to turn a book into a movie—there are two ways to go about it: one is to get involved, all or part of the way, and stand up and take the blame or criticism for everyone else; and the other is to say, "I'm going to sell it. I'm going to take the money."
>
> You know what John Updike used to say about it—it's the best of all possible worlds when they pay you a lot of money and *don't* make the movie.
>
> But when you don't get involved, you are in a no-lose situation, when you can say, "If it's good, that's based on my work." And if it's bad, you can say, "I didn't have anything to do with that."[4]

In this instance, King in fact had nothing to do with *The Shining*. It was Kubrick's vision, from the first to last frame. King had in fact written his own screenplay, but Kubrick reportedly refused to read it. "It was pegged a lot more to the history of the hotel because I was really interested in the idea that an evil place calls evil men—which is a line from '*Salem's Lot*. The screenplay that I wrote begins with total blackness on the screen and the sounds of people talking. It turns out that there are Mafia hit men, and there are shotgun flashes and screams. Then this voice says, 'Get his balls.' There's another scream, then you see the hotel."[5]

King summarized *The Shining* by saying that it was "a beautiful film. It's like this great big gorgeous car with no engine in it—that's all."[6]

In the summer of 1980, the Kings bought the William Arnold House, an Italianate villa originally built in 1856 for $6,000. Located in the Historic District, on the most fashionable street in Bangor, the house cost only $135,000, but the Kings would need to spend considerably more to renovate it to suit their needs, not only as a private residence but also as home offices for not only Stephen King but Tabitha King, who had been working on *Small World*, her first novel, scheduled for publication in 1981 by NAL.

The creative impetus to move to Bangor was Stephen King's desire to write a long novel set in a major Maine town, which narrowed the choice down to Portland, Bangor, and Augusta.

It was Bangor that would serve as the real-world model for the town of Derry, Maine, on the same fictional map as Castle Rock, Maine. "I had a very long book in mind," King wrote, "a book which I hoped would deal with the way myths and dreams and stories—stories, most of all—become a part of the everyday life of a small American city. . . . Oh, my Lord my Lord, the stories you hear about this town—the streets fairly clang with them. The problem isn't finding them or ferreting them out; the problem is that old boozer's problem of knowing when to stop."[7]

Characterized by King as a "hard-drinking, working man's town,"[8] Bangor felt right to King.

From a practical viewpoint, Bangor simply made good sense. Unlike Augusta, Bangor had a major airport—an important consideration, since King's career demanded frequent trips around the country, often on short notice. Bangor's library, essential for researching books, was one of the finest in New England. Bangor was a half hour away from Orono, where King would have access to the University of Maine and his supportive network at the English department. And, in addition to a major hospital and a number of independent bookstores, Bangor had recently built a multiplex theater, essential to someone who loves movies as much as King does.

Also, from a personal viewpoint, Bangor had a lot to offer: a good public school system, in which to enroll the three children, and proximity to Old Town, where Tabitha King grew up.

King assessed Bangor, saying that "I think a place is yours when you know where the roads go. They talk my language here; I talk theirs. I think like them; they know me. It feels right to be here."[9]

The locals agreed. An out-of-town journalist from *Entertainment Weekly* came to interview King. She got in a cab and asked if the cabbie knew Stephen King. The cabbie replied that of course he knew him, and that he was "one of us."[10]

Bangor was also far enough north to dissuade all but the most hardy to make a trek to see King. (Years earlier, when he lived near Portland, he was too accessible; fans could always find him, or give it their best shot.)

That summer, as the Kings went through their house in Center Lovell in preparation for the move, Stephen King ran across mountains of original manuscripts that presented a storage problem. Fortunately, an answer had presented itself years earlier, in 1975, when Eric Flower, the Head of Special Collections of the Fogler Library at UMO, reminded King of his intent to deposit *Carrie*.

That summer, King carried six boxloads of manuscripts to UMO. Flower, citing King's importance as a Maine writer to "future researchers of Maine literature,"[11] was happy to acquire the papers, though King felt that there was not much "Maine-ness" in his fiction.[12]

Flower, like the members of the English department at UMO, knew better. King was not only a popular novelist but his work was firmly entrenched in a growing Maine myth uniquely King's, a thesis Burton Hatlen had put forth in a long essay, "Beyond the Kittery Bridge: Stephen King's Maine."

An important regional writer, King's work was worth preserving, according to Flower, so anyone with a legitimate need to read King's unpublished and early drafts could now do so.

In addition to *Carrie*, King deposited drafts, proofs, and galleys for *Second Coming* (and its successive drafts as *'Salem's Lot*), *The Shining*, *The Stand*, and *The Dead Zone*. The real motherlode, however, consisted of three unpublished manuscripts, *The Aftermath*, *Blaze*, and *Sword in the Darkness*, which King intended to keep unpublished.

The Special Collections would make the material available, but no photocopying would be allowed; researchers would have to read the material on the premises and could make notes, but that was the extent of it.

Just as the Kings made the move from Center Lovell to Bangor, "The Mist," which was written in the summer of 1976, saw print as the lead story in Kirby McCauley's anthology *Dark Forces*.

Originally intended as a short story, it grew in its telling to 40,000 words. McCauley was surprised but pleased. He had expected "an ordinary-length story and ended up with a short novel by the most popular author of supernatural horror stories in the world."[13]

McCauley's drum-beating aside, the truth remained: "The Mist" was quintessential King, combining all of King's fictional trademarks, which had made him, in a few short years, a brand-name writer: the first-person voice, told in a conversational tone; the vivid imagery, from the opening sequences of a storm over the nearby lake, to the haunting imagery of monsters in the mist; the sympathetic characters, including a little boy and his concerned father; a small-town Maine setting; fears about the nature of technology and the sinister machinations of the federal government; and, most of all, monsters straight out of the classic fifties films.

If *Night Shift* was a collection of one-reelers, then *The Mist* was a short feature film that would scare the beejesus out of the reader.

Set in Bridgton, Maine, where the Kings had lived for two years, the fictional story is told in the first person by David Drayton, who witnesses a freak summer storm at the lake near his house. The next morning, as the cleanup crews repair the downed power lines, Drayton, his son, and a neighbor head into town to the grocery store for supplies, only to find themselves in a nightmarish situation: a strange mist rolls in, bringing with it unimaginable monsters—a tentacled beast that attacks the loading dock in the back of the store, a pterodactyl-like creature that breaks through a window and flaps monstrously through the store, large buglike creatures, spiders, giant lobstrosities, and, as Drayton and company make their escape from the store and get on the interstate, a creature so vast that all they can see are its monstrous legs, twin pillars that rise up into the mist.

An homage to the monster films of the fifties, "The Mist" was the perfect opener of the way for *Dark Forces*.

King recalls the genesis of the story, which came to him during a routine shopping trip to Bridgton:

> I got the idea doing one of these dull chores where your wife says to you, "Will you go to the market?" and hands you a list. I went to the market and got all this stuff, and I'm rolling up and down the aisle. And if you're a writer, you suddenly realize that in the daytime, between nine and five, the world belongs to the women, but that's another story. People are looking at you and saying, *What's wrong with you, turkey? You on welfare?*
>
> I was totally bored and I was walking down an aisle that was lined with canned goods, and I thought, *Wouldn't it be funny if a pterodactyl just came flapping up this aisle and started knocking over Ragu and Hunt's and all this other stuff?*
>
> The image delighted me and I started writing this story around this one little irritant. I don't know if you'd call this story a pearl, but it's there, anyway, and it began with that. The story is nice, and it's nice to be paid for the story, but it's just as good to have had that freedom from boredom.[14]

More than a pearl, the story was a gem, and readers of *Dark Forces* were bowled over with the imagination King invested in "The Mist." Recalling the horror movies of the fifties, King said, "You're supposed to visualize that entire story in a sort of grainy black-and-white."[15]

As King worked on *It*, his incendiary novel *Firestarter* went to press with 100,000 copies and would go on to sell 285,000 copies in its first year.

A riff on *Carrie*, *Firestarter* further explored a favorite fictional premise that King used in "The Mist"—the government, which tells us only what it feels we need to know, is the boogeyman. (Later, in the paperback reprint, King added an afterword in which he stated, "The U.S. government, or agencies thereof, has indeed administered potentially dangerous drugs to unwitting subjects on more than one occasion."[16])

Firestarter is the story of a pyrokinetic girl, Charlie McGee, pursued by an unnamed agency of the government called simply The Shop, because they want to harness her power for military use. The offspring of two penurious college students who themselves had been administered a bad lot of experimental drugs, Charlie's parents are hunted down and killed, leaving her an orphan with an awesome power.

A story told in straightforward fashion, the novel is, as critic Michael R. Collings wrote, "a midrange novel, certainly an interesting read, but representative neither of his strongest nor of his weakest works."[17]

In October, at the World Fantasy Convention, King received an award for "special contributions to the field." The award, a small bust of H. P. Lovecraft, meant a lot to King, but he knew it was a consolation prize of sorts; he would have preferred to win one for one of his short stories or novels, and not for the cachet he had brought to the horror community at large.

❧ 11 ❧

As the new year began, King, who had flailed away at the Zavisa project, simply couldn't find his way into the werewolf story, so when the publisher called and asked for a progress report, "Guilt rushed over me anew," King wrote. "Lying through my teeth, I told Chris it was coming real well."[1]

A month later, the Kings went to Puerto Rico for a family vacation. For Stephen King, it was a busman's holiday; he took the work in progress, thinking he'd knock out the vignettes, but soon came to a dead stop. "The vignette form was killing me," King admitted.[2]

The story began moving, however, when King decided to tinker with it, trying it as a short story, at which point it quickly wrote itself. King called Zavisa with the mixed news: the bad news was that the calendar idea was unworkable; the good news was that the story could be published as a book.

Zavisa responded enthusiastically to King's suggestion, who "wondered if it wasn't what he had sort of wanted all along, but had been, maybe, a little too shy to pitch."[3]

Zavisa knew that a book simply made more sense. The market, for one thing, was bigger for a book than a calendar; and, of course, the book could be published in several editions and priced accordingly.

In April 1981 Everest House published the hardback of *Danse Macabre*. The book was the brainchild of King's former editor at Doubleday, William G. Thompson, who was now an editor at Everest House. King's only nonfiction book to date, its first printing was 60,000 copies, plus 250 signed and numbered copies. A survey of the horror field since the fifties, *Danse Macabre* was King holding forth on his favorite subject. ". . . I cannot divorce myself from a field in which I am mortally involved," he wrote in *Danse Macabre*.[4]

Dedicated to six writers in the field—Robert Bloch, Jorge Luis Borges, Ray Bradbury, Frank Belknap Long, Donald Wandrei, and Manly Wade Wellman—*Danse Macabre*, written in King's conversational tone of voice, is an excellent, informal overview of the field, covering movies, television, radio, and books.

For King, it served two purposes: first, it gave him ammunition for those who would inevitably ask, "Why do you *write* this stuff?" As if to ask: What's *wrong* with you because you write horror? And, second, it gave King the opportunity to crystalize his thoughts on the genre—it had been good preparation for the college course that he was then teaching at UMO.

As for King: ". . . I thought that here was an opportunity to talk about a genre I love, an opportunity few plain writers of popular fiction are ever offered."[5]

A stark contrast to the usual jargon-ladened, academic books on the subject, *Danse Macabre* was a breezy read, and a critical and financial success for Everest House.

Publishers Weekly sang its praises:

> Knowledgeable and engaging, King is a perfect tour guide. King's narrative style is refreshingly informal. . . . Yet such informality can and does lead to an annoying amount of digression. Nevertheless, King's account is perceptive and remarkably inclusive. A solid history both for those who are King's fans and for those who aren't.[6]

In May 1981 George Romero began shooting *Creepshow* in Philadelphia. An anthology movie—stories tied together with a framing device—budgeted at $8 million, it was a big step up for Romero, who cut his teeth on the horror classic *Night of the Living Dead*, with its modest budget of $127,000—an investment that returned millions.

Unlike *Carrie*, *The Shining*, and *'Salem's Lot*, *Creepshow* saw King's active participation, not only as the screenwriter but as an actor in a role that his critics would say was typecasting—King in the role of Jordy Verrill, a hayseed farmer in bib overalls who foolishly retrieves a meteor to sell to the local university, with disastrous personal consequences.

Working in Philadelphia, King spent his evenings writing in longhand a bizarre novel, *Cannibals*, which was "all about these people who are trapped in an apartment building. Worse thing I could think of. And I thought, wouldn't it be funny if they ended up eating each other? It's very, very bizarre because it's all on one note," King said.[7]

Cannibals sounded similar to J. G. Ballard's *High-Rise*, in which "the inhabitants of a massive multistory apartment block gradually revert to savagery as the amenities of civilisation, which form a restrictive veneer around their lives, break down."[8] King decided not to publish the novel and put it in his writer's trunk. (The theme of cannibalism, explored in "Survivor Type," would, years later, be food for thought for ". . . a tale about a planet where people for some reason turn into cannibals when it rained . . . and I still like that one, so hands off, y'hear?")[9]

Creepshow, unlike King's other movies, also had a unique visual tie-in—Berni Wrightson, the macabre artist who made a name for himself in the comics field. Wrightson, who drew (in part) his inspiration from William Gaines's E.C. line of horror comics, was the perfect choice to re-create the long-deceased comic line that King and Romero as teenagers found gruesome but appetizing fare.

Unlike *Cycle of the Werewolf* and *Danse Macabre*, King's new novel from Viking, *Cujo*, published in October 1981, would be the major King offering of the year. Rolling off the assembly line with a first printing of 350,000 copies, the $13.95 novel was set in King's mythical small town of Castle Rock, Maine.

Atypical for King, *Cujo* was no supernatural novel. The evil element is the family dog, a 200-pound St. Bernard that, after pursuing a rabbit into a cave, gets bit by bats and becomes rabid. Cujo then lays siege to Donna Trenton and her son Tad, trapped in their Pinto at the edge of town at Joe Camber's garage.

Cujo is a relentless, claustrophobic novel, a reading experience in which the reader feels not so much an observer but a participant. Not a novel of external horror but internal horror, *Cujo* brings the horror home with its exploration of a favorite King theme: a family in crisis on multiple fronts: Vic Trent, worried that his small ad agency will lose its one big account; Donna Trent, worried about a sleazy affair she has with a local tennis pro who strips her furniture and then her; and their son Tad, who like Danny Torrance in *The Shining* is the unwilling victim of forces he cannot control—not supernatural in origin but, in fact, originating from what was once a lovable, harmless St. Bernard that wanted nothing more than to be a GOODDOG but became a BADDOG.

Publishers Weekly praised the novel. "With a master's sure feel for the power of the plausible to terrify as much or more than the uncanny, King builds a riveting novel out of the lives of some very ordinary and believable people in a small Maine town, and an unfortunate 200 lb. St. Bernard."[10]

In contrast to *Cujo*, *Roadwork* was published with little fanfare. A $2.25 paperback original under NAL's Signet imprint, the third Richard Bachman novel was not considered by King, in retrospect, to be one of the better Bachman books, as he later wrote in an omnibus collection:

> The most recent of the Bachman books offered here . . . was written between *'Salem's Lot* and *The Shining*, and was an effort to write a "straight" novel. . . . I think it was also an effort to make some sense of my mother's painful death the year before—a lingering cancer had taken her inch by painful inch. Following this death I was left both grieving and shaken by the apparent senselessness of it all. I suspect *Roadwork* is probably the worst of the lot simply because it tries so hard to be good and to find some answers to the conundrum of human pain.[11]

The year ended with King covered in glory, as they say. In addition to a World Fantasy Award nomination for "The Mist," King's short story "The Way Station" was nominated for a Nebula Award, voted upon by the members of SFWA (Science Fiction Writers of America). He also received a special British Fantasy Award for contributions in the field, similar to the award he had previously won at the American convention, the World Fantasy Award.

The year closed with recognition for King outside the fan field. King's alma mater honored him with a Career Alumni Award.

❦12❦

Beginning with the first draft of his only collaboration, *The Talisman*, and ending with a self-published novel in progress, *The Plant*, 1982 was a year of fictional exploration and experimentation. In between, however, King published *The Running Man* (the last Bachman novel published as an original paperback), *Creepshow* (his only graphic album), *Different Seasons* (a quartet of exceptionally memorable stories), and the first book in a long series, *Dark Tower I: The Gunslinger*.

"I never can understand how two men can write a book together; to me that's like three people getting together to have a baby," Evelyn Waughn wrote.[1]

In the case of *Talisman*, the "third" person was the distinctive voice that formed when King and Straub merged their prose styles, creating a literary voice that was clearly neither King nor Straub.

For both writers, the book would be a challenge to write, because neither had previously done a book-length collaboration, complicated by geographic considerations: King lived in Bangor, but Straub lived in Connecticut.

The solution was to write the book in parts, with each writer sending the text by computer modem to the other—a literary round robin that, in effect, bounced back and forth until completed. King banged on his Wang word processor, whereas Straub used an IBM Displaywriter. The remainder of the year would be spent in creating a first draft, which later would be ruthlessly edited over a Thanksgiving weekend to a publishable length.

May 1982 saw the publication of *The Running Man*, the fourth Richard Bachman novel published by Signet as a paperback original, retailing for $2.50. Like the other three Bachman novels, this one was published with little fanfare, written when King was teaching high school. "Writing it was a fantastic, white-hot experience; the book was written in one month, the bulk of it in the one week of winter vacation."[2]

Set in 2025, the chapter headings emphasize the passage of time, a clock ticking down, from "Minus 100 and counting," as the protagonist, Ben

Richards, plays a deadly game of hide-and-seek, in a jaded society that watches game-show contestants battle, gladiator-like, to their deaths.

In the end, "Ben Richards, the scrawny, pre-tubercular protagonist . . . crashes his hijacked plane into the Games Authority skyscraper, killing himself but taking hundreds (maybe thousands) of Free Vee executives with him; this is the Richard Bachman version of a happy ending,"[3] wrote King.

Perceived as a cheap paperback of genre fiction—the dreaded "sci fi" label scaring off all but the hardy band of Bachman fans and the science fiction community at large—*The Running Man* got the usual treatment: dumped into wire spinner racks and, in time, pulled out, and its covers stripped and returned for credit.

In contrast to the "stealth" publication of *The Running Man*, *Creepshow* was an appetizer for its main feast, the Halloween release of the film. A $6.95 trade paperback in full color, the graphic album featured cover art by Jack Kamen, one of the original E.C. artists, and interior art by Berni Wrightson.

The cover art depicts a boy in bed, at night, reading a comic book ("First issue collectors edition, 10¢, CREEPSHOW, Jolting Tales of Terror"); his wall is decorated with posters (*Dawn of the Dead, The Shining, Carrie*); and a skeletal figure lurks outside the window, backlit by a full moon, with a bare tree in the background.

Creepshow showcased moral fiction: bad things happened to bad people—they got their just desserts, as they did in the E.C. comics. (Unfortunately, E.C. comics died prematurely when a *real* boogeyman, Dr. Frederic Wertham, testified before Congress, claiming a link between juvenile delinquency and crime/horror comics.)

The stories included "Father's Day," "The Lonesome Death of Jordy Verrill," "The Crate," "Something to Tide You Over," and "They're Creeping Up on You."

In the best E.C. tradition, the skeletal figure on the cover introduces each story: "Heh-Heh!! Greetings, kiddies, and welcome to the first issue of CREEPSHOW, the magazine that dares to answer the question "WHO GOES THERE?"

The following month, King followed with his major book of the year—not a novel, as his fans had expected, but a collection of four novellas, titled *Different Seasons*.

His editor at Viking, Alan Williams, had thought in terms of another horror novel. "Loved *Cujo* . . . have you thought about what you're going to do next?"[4] When King responded that he wasn't going to follow up *Cujo* with another novel but in fact with a collection of four novellas, Williams was understandably crestfallen.

Williams would have no reason to worry, since *Different Seasons* went on to sell 140,000 copies in hardback—nothing like *Cujo* but certainly very respectable numbers. (Afterward, when King told him that he was following up *Different Seasons* with a novel about "a haunted car,"[5] Williams responded with predictable enthusiasm.)

In the afterword to *Different Seasons*, King wrote about this misperception. "But is horror *all* I write? If you've read the foregoing stories, you *know* it's not . . . but elements of horror can be found in all of the tales. . . . Sooner or later, my mind always seems to turn back in that direction, God knows why."[6]

Reviewers, conditioned to seeing haunted houses and haunted hotels and haunted dogs from King, responded with high praise for this quartet of dark fiction. *Publishers Weekly* called it "some of his best work,"[7] and *Book World*, echoing *PW*, stated, "The important thing to acknowledge in King's immense popularity, and in the Niagara of words he produces, is the simple fact that he can write. He can write without cheapening or trivializing himself or his audience."[8]

Outside of the book trade, reviews were also enthusiastic, from small-time newspapers to major consumer magazines like *Cosmopolitan*, which put its finger on the pulse of the book. "No demons chortle from the closet, no vampires droll beneath the moon. Instead King's ragged claws reach from ambush into the wholesome light of daily life—what could be more frightening than that?"[9]

What, indeed?

The book begins with "Rita Hayworth and Shawshank Redemption," an awkward title for an extraordinarily good story. A prison story set in the late forties when Rita Hayworth was a movie pinup queen in her heyday, the story is narrated by a prison inmate nicknamed "Red," who has a reputation for being able to secure select items outside of the prison and arrange to have them smuggled in, befriends Andy Dufresne, who wants a poster of Hayworth to decorate his drab prison wall. The poster, which draws attention to itself, conceals the hole he'd dug that provided his eventual escape.

An evocative story with sharply defined characters and a penetrating study in character motivation, the novella sets the tone for the remainder of the stories to follow. Leave your preconceived notions at the door, King seems to suggest, because when you enter my hotel of stories with its many rooms, there's a story behind each closed door, and you don't know what you'll find.

In the second story, "Apt Pupil," the element of surprise is paramount: a prototypical thirteen-year-old Californian, Todd Bowden, who discovers by accident his "GREAT INTEREST"[10] which turned out to be a morbid fascination with the Nazi death camps.

To his initial horror but subsequent delight, Bowden discovers that Kurt Dussander, a former camp commandant, lives in the neighborhood, and decides to confront the old man with the evidence he unearthed. The result: a perverse symbiotic relationship between Bowden, an apt pupil, and his new teacher, Dussander, who recalls the glory days of being in power, of wearing his uniform, which gave his life dignity and meaning at a time when the Germans had none.

The escalation of violence initiated by this unholy partnership reaches a fever pitch as Bowden, armed with a .30-.30 rifle, takes up a field position near a freeway, waiting until the authorities relieve him of duty permanently.

More than any other story in the collection, "Apt Pupil" hits a raw nerve. This wasn't entertainment or diversion from the realities of life—it drilled to the monstrous core of Bowden, who told Dussander, "I want to hear about it. . . . Everything. All the gooshy stuff."[11]

At Viking, the editors were concerned that the story was *too* real, hitting too close to home, according to King:

> I got a really strong reaction to the "Apt Pupil" story. . . . My publisher called and protested. I said, "Well, do you think it's anti-Semitic?" Because it's about a Nazi war criminal, and he begins to spout all the old bullshit, once the kid in the story gets him going. But that wasn't the problem. It was too real. If the same story had been in outer space, it would have been okay, because then you'd have that comforting layer of "This is just make-believe, so we can dismiss it." . . . So they were very disturbed by the piece, and I thought to myself, "Gee, I've done it again. I've written something that has really gotten under someone's skin." And I do like that. I like the feeling that I reached right between someone's legs . . . like that. There has always been that primitive impulse as part of my writing."[12]

A radical departure from "Apt Pupil," the story that followed, "The Body," is a quiet, elegiac piece. More than any other work of fiction King had published to date, "The Body" is very autobiographical, drawing heavily on his childhood experiences as a young teenager living in rural Maine.

On the surface, the story's plot suggests little of its complexity. A rite-of-passage story, "The Body" tells the tale of its narrator, Gordon LaChance, who in the company of three friends heads out on foot for an extended trip to view the dead body of a boy killed by a passing train.

Imbedded in "The Body" are two short stories that, in fact, were published by King during his college days ("Stud City" in *Ubris* and "The Revenge of Lard Ass Logan" in *Maine Review*).

"The Body" spans the narrator's life:

> I'm a writer now, like I said. A lot of critics think what I write is shit. A lot of the time I think they are right . . . but it still freaks me out to put those words, "Freelance Writer," down in the *Occupation* blank of the forms you have to fill out at credit desks and in doctors' offices. My story sounds so much like a fairytale that it's fucking absurd.[13]

Not to put too fine a point on it: "The Body" is King at his finest, exhibiting all of his strengths as a writer: his ability to evoke the Maine landscape in a way that we feel at home there; his ability to carefully delineate individual characters, each with his quirks and foibles; his ability to tell a story in a conversational manner, with a dead-on ability for writing dialogue that is in fact much closer to how young teenage boys talk, as opposed to how adults *think* they talk; and, most of all, his ability to bring all of these disparate elements together in a cohesive whole, resulting in a poignant story that tugs at the heartstrings and evokes a nostalgia for our own lost youths and, inevitably, our own falls from innocence, as we moved on to adulthood through experience.

The final story, "The Breathing Method," is closest to what King's readers have come to expect: a story of quiet horror, told—as are all the stories in this collection—in a distinctive voice. The shortest of the four in the book, "The Breathing Method" is narrated by an elderly gentleman, an attorney, who is a member of a storytelling club that meets at an anonymous brownstone at 249B East Thirty-fifth Street in New York City. Called simply The Club, it has as its host a curious man named Stevens, who appears to be ". . . older than he looks. Much, *much* older."[14]

The members of The Club, who take turns telling stories, listen that night to a doctor who tells a bizarre story: Sandra Stansfield dies in labor but not before delivering a macabre surprise.

After the telling of the tale, the story's narrator asks Stevens if there are more rooms upstairs in the building. Stevens replies: "Oh, yes, sir . . . A great many. A man could become lost. In fact, men *have* become lost. Sometimes it seems to me that they go on for miles. Rooms and corridors . . . Entrances and exits."[15]

When asked by the narrator if there will be more tales, Stevens enigmatically replies, "Here, sir, there are *always* more tales."[16]

On that note, the book closes, its fourth and final story told, the curtain falls, and King comes out to address the audience in a chatty Afterword, in which he talks *about* the stories, but is careful not to reveal any of his stage tricks. Then, in characteristic fashion, King quickly exits, stage left. "Okay. Gotta split. Until we see each other again, keep your head together, read some good books, be useful, be happy. Love and good wishes, Stephen King."[17]

Shifting from *Different Seasons* to *The Dark Tower: The Gunslinger* was a radical change in subject matter. An epic in progress, *The Dark Tower*, the first in what King projected as a seven-book series, had been serialized previously in *The Magazine of Fantasy and Science Fiction*, considered to be the most literary journal in the field.

The chapters included "The Gunslinger" (October 1978), "The Way Station" (April 1980), "The Oracle and the Mountains" (February 1981), "The Slow Mutants" (July 1981), and "The Gunslinger and the Dark Man" (November 1981).

For his part, King had no plans to publish *The Dark Tower* in book form, since it was a radical departure from what he considered his norm—tales of horror or suspense. "I didn't think anybody would want to read it. It wasn't like the other books. The first volume didn't have any firm grounding in our world, in reality; it was more like a Tolkien fantasy of some other world. The other reason was that it wasn't done; it wasn't complete."[18]

Despite King's misgivings, Donald M. Grant knew better—he knew that this was *exactly* the kind of book fantasy fans loved to read. A specialty publisher in Rhode Island who issued small runs of illustrated books, beautifully designed and manufactured, Grant—a quiet but convincing man—knew it was the right project for him.

At a public get-together at the college where he worked as its Publication Director, Grant broached the subject and prevailed in the end. Plans were made to issue a small run in hardback to be illustrated by Michael Whelan, an artist mutually agreed upon by Grant and King.

As Grant explained, "We both thought that Michael was at the top of the game," adding that King "certainly liked Michael's work, so we were in accord there."[19]

Whelan, who had previously illustrated the limited edition of *Firestarter*, was an ideal choice: a classic illustrator who was a fan of King's fiction.

Whelan turned in a spectacular set of illustrations, including a full-color piece that was used for endpapers, five full-page color illustrations, and black-and-white decorations throughout.

The cover, a striking painting of the Gunslinger with Zoltan the talking crow on his shoulder silhouetted against a misty image of the Dark Tower in the background, would be the definitive "look" of the Gunslinger, in a way that Frank Frazetta had defined the "look" of Conan for the Robert E. Howard novels published by Lancer in paperback.

The back cover illustration showed the Gunslinger sitting on a beach as the sun set, with the Dark Tower appearing as a misty tower in the clouds.

Whelan, best known for his fantasy, horror, and science fiction art, found the novel to be an artistic challenge to illustrate. The story was like no other book he had illustrated before. It was, he said, ". . . one of the most unremittingly bleak (though engaging) Stephen King novels I've ever read. . . . If the book hadn't been so interesting, it would have been hard to maintain my enthusiasm through the completion of the work."[20]

The Grant edition would be limited to only 10,000 copies, the largest first printing of any Grant title, and a numbered and signed edition of 500 copies, slipcased in matching cloth.

In early ads, Grant pulled out all the stops:

> Written over a period of twelve years, *The Dark Tower: The Gunslinger* is the first cycle of stories in a remarkable epic, the strangest and most frightening work that Stephen King has ever written. It is the book of Roland, the last gunslinger, and his quest for the Dark Tower in a world in which time has no bearing.
>
> Against the weird background of a devastated and dying planet— with curious ties to our own world—the last gunslinger pursues the man in black. It is a time when man's thirst for knowledge has been lost, and the haunted, chilling land harbors strange beings: the Slow Mutants, less-than-human troglodytes dwelling in the darkness; a Speaking Demon, laired beneath a forgotten way station; and a nameless vampiric presence, held captive in an ancient circle of altar stones.
>
> Herein lies a tale of science-fantasy that is unlike anything bestselling author Stephen King has ever written; indeed, it is unlike anything anyone else has ever written. . . .[21]

For King, it was a way to give back to the fan community that he loved, the world of fan conventions where you could haunt the dealer's room and see collectibles and look at back issues of *Weird Tales,* and stare agog at the dark treasures in the art show, or hit the bar and see old friends and renew old ties.

"To issue such a book, of course, is one of the few ways I have of saying that I am not entirely for sale—that I'm still in this business for the joy of it, and that I have not been entirely subsumed by the commercial juggernaut I have cheerfully fueled and set in motion."[22]

What the "bestsellersaurus rex"—as King termed himself—didn't realize was that insofar as his fiction was concerned, his readers wanted the right to make a decision as to what they wanted to read; they didn't want King to make that decision for them.

The entire print run of *The Dark Tower: The Gunslinger*—$20 hardbacks and $60 limited editions—was snapped up immediately, and the book quietly went out of print.

On the secondary market, fueled by book dealers who bought and resold books, the prices began to rise dramatically. "The book was published at twenty dollars, and I was a little bit horrified by what happened. The price jumped and it became a collector's item, and that hadn't been my intention at all, to see these books climb from $20 to $50 to $70, to whatever," King observed.[23]

Nobody—not even the dealers—could have guessed that, years later, the $20 book would eventually sell for $600!

Stuart David Schiff, editor of *Whispers,* which had published a special King issue (#17/18), praised King's generosity to the field:

> I am certain that there is not a single person reading this who needs an introduction to Stephen King. His meteoric rise to the top of the book-publishing field is one of the incredible stories of the past decade. Despite his new and lofty position, Steve has kept his roots. His support of small presses and authors who have not been as successful as himself is ample evidence of this. Without Steve wanting *Whispers* to share in his success, this issue simply would not have been possible.

Like any other King collectible published in the fan market, *Whispers* sold out all its copies, including the signed edition, and once again, the market realities of supply and demand drove the price up.

The price King paid for his success—the loss of his anonymity—became apparent to him when he attended the World Fantasy Con that year:

> I'm still a fan at heart and one of the things which is real rough is not being able to go to a convention and go into the huckster's room and

look around, maybe pick up some copies of *Weird Tales* or other pulps, without having people come for autographs, or talk about something they've written. They're hitting on you all the time.[24]

Locus magazine, the newsletter of the SF field, reporting on the convention, said that "Stephen King spent a lot of time in his suite, because he was mobbed wherever he went."[25]

The result—King's growing disenchantment with conventions. "I love conventions, but may have to give them up if this continues."[26]

The World Fantasy Convention wasn't a complete bust, however, since King won an award for a short story, "Do the Dead Sing?"

A classic King story in which a ninety-five-year-old woman living on Goat Island, Maine, walks across the frozen waterway—called The Reach by locals—and reconnects with her past but dies in the attempt.

At another convention—the World Science Fiction Convention—*Danse Macabre*, King's nonfiction look at the horror field, took a Hugo; and, at an overseas convention, *Cujo* won a British Fantasy Award—the small irony was that *Cujo* was the novel King wrote instead of the haunted house novel he had planned to write while visiting England.

Much more than just a prominent figure in the field, King was well on his way to becoming *the* brand-name writer in the field and a household name, as well. In fact, he was so obviously America's best-loved boogeyman that when the ad agency Ogilvy & Mather wanted to run a spooky ad, who else were they going to call?

King, flattered to be asked, hammed it up in the best acting role of his life, convincingly playing himself. In the thirty-second ad, King—appropriately attired in an after-dinner jacket, haunts a mansion on a dark and stormy night. He looks at the viewer and, rhetorically, asks:

> *Do you know me?* It's frightening how many novels of suspense I've written; but still, when I'm not recognized, it just kills me. So instead of saying "I wrote *Carrie*," I carry the American Express card—without it, isn't life a little scary? The American Express card—*don't leave home without it.*[27]

The ad aside, it was killing King to *be* recognized, but how could he not? At six feet four inches, King stands out in a crowd, with a trail of fans following him at public gatherings—bad enough under normal circumstances, but on Halloween, in his hometown of Bangor, the frenzy reaches a fever pitch: the town turns out to gape at the house and its famous inhabitant, who has come to define the holiday. (The Kings now routinely leave town, placing a small ad in the local paper to announce their temporary absence.)

"I hate Halloween," King opined. "I've turned into America's giant pumpkin and I can't relate to that."[28]

"My idea of a perfect horror film," King said, "would be one where you'd have to have nurses and doctors on duty with crash wagons because people would have heart attacks. People would crawl out with large wet spots on their trousers. It would be that kind of experience. They'd say, 'What the hell are you doing with me?' The answer: 'What *you* wanted. We're scaring you.'"[29]

The only thing scary about *Creepshow* was its low box office receipts. The plan was to have a horrifying film that would scare the crap out of the viewer, but the combination of horror and camp didn't work. Though perfect for the E.C. comic line, the same vision, translated to the screen, failed to terrify or horrify, and King had to resort to the gross-out, the lowest level to which horror can achieve, according to King's fear barometer.

Book publishing traditionally plans its year in terms of a spring and fall season, but for King, this had been a year of different seasons—a pseudonymous novel, a comic book, a novella collection, a limited-edition small-press book that had previously been serialized in a specialty magazine, ending with a self-published book, *The Plant*, sent to 200 handpicked people on the Kings' Christmas card list. Explaining his rationale, King said:

> It's sort of an epistolary novel-in-progress.
> A couple of years ago I got thinking about Christmas cards and how mass-produced they were. You buy them from the Girl Scouts and it says, "Best Wishes," and inside in red print it says "The Andersons."
> It didn't seem like a sincere, personal thing. So I thought, "Well, I'll do this little book every year and print it, and send it out to friends."[30]

The Plant would be the first bonafide publication of *Philtrum Press*, King's small press that, with the help of Michael Alpert, whom King knew from his college days, would go on to publish small runs of elegantly designed books to be sold only by direct mail.

These limited editions of King's works were known only to those in the fantasy community, which led Underwood-Miller books to cater to this growing audience of King collectors, who wanted not only to read books *by* King but *about* him, as well.

Fear Itself: The Horror Fiction of Stephen King made its debut in hardback and a signed limited edition as well. King contributed a long essay, "On Becoming a Brand Name," and signed the limited edition.

A collection of essays about King, *Fear Itself* was eagerly snapped up by his fans eager to learn more about their favorite author, creating a monster industry in books *about* King.

The thought must have been in the air, because Starmont House, a small press in Washington State, published *Stephen King* by Douglas E. Winter, who in his introduction prophetically wrote, "It is the first book-length study of King's fiction, but it certainly will not be the last."

King, for better or worse, was no longer just a writer, able to write in relative anonymity. Predictably, the Bangor house became, to his horror, a tourist attraction. You couldn't miss it. Even on the historic street with turn-of-the-century houses, each unique in design, King's house stood out.

When King had originally bought the house, he assumed that people would leave him alone, but he was dead wrong. The house was a magnet, drawing fans and curious onlookers as well.

King finally had to post a discreet sign near the ringer on the front door, saying that both he and his wife were writers and couldn't be disturbed; but that didn't deter the hardy, who showed up with books in hand, ringing the doorbell, wanting to see Bangor's boogeyman personally.

Reluctantly, King came to the conclusion that if the readers wouldn't leave him alone at the house, he'd have to force the issue by erecting a fence around the entire property.

The fence, however, had to meet three requirements: first, it had to be suitably gothic; second, decorative and functional, high enough to keep the curious from scaling it; and third, within the guidelines dictated by the architectural committee that approved of modifications to the houses on Broad Street, part of the town's Historic District. An old friend of the Kings, Terry Steel, took on the challenge, recalling:

> I brought a lot of magazines showing examples of ironwork to my first conference with the Kings, along with a lot of photographs I'd taken of fence and gate work around Beacon Hill in Boston. The Kings also had books with drawings of ironwork, and we discussed possible designs. It was important for the fence and gates to work with the ar-

chitecture of the house, to be graceful and attractive, and yet reflect the personalities of the occupants, as well. King wanted bats worked into the design; his wife wanted spiders and webs.[31]

Looking back at the job, Terry Steel observed, "The commission took a year and a half to finish—270 lineal feet of hand-forged fence, weighing 11,000 pounds, punctuated by two gates composed of spiders, webs, goat heads, and winged bats. The editor of the local paper called the project a major contribution to the architecture of the city of Bangor. A neighbor comes over to tell me the fence is 'just what the house needed,' and turns to eye her own front yard. One thing's for sure: Anyone touring Bangor trying to pick out the house where Stephen King lives will have little trouble finding it."[32]

✌13✌

En route to a speaking engagement, King stopped off at the summer house in the dead of winter, January 1983. A story idea King had been toying with finally crystallized. "It was the perfect time and place," King recalled, "to start such a story: I was alone in the house, there was a screaming northeaster blowing snow across the frozen lake outside, and I was sitting in front of the woodstove with a yellow legal pad in my hand and a cold beer on the table."[1]

King wrote thirteen pages in longhand. The story's working title was *The Napkins* and, unlike his previous novels, this one wasn't written for the money —King could afford to take the time and write whatever he wished, without the financial pressure of having to write to make money. Its creative impetus, as King explained, was his attempt to reach out to his teenage daughter Naomi, who wasn't among his Constant Readers. "Although I had written thirteen novels by the time my daughter had attained an equal number of years, she hadn't read any of them. She's made it clear that she loves *me*, but has very little interest in my vampires, ghoulies, and slushy crawling things."[2]

It was a good beginning and he'd finish it later, but he had to get to the speaking engagement.

In April, *Christine* rolled off the Viking assembly line. Unlike his other novels, King took a token advance—one dollar—explaining that

> I wanted not to be taking a lot of cash which I didn't need, and it ties up money other writers could get for advances. We took a lot of money on *The Dead Zone*, *Firestarter*, and *Cujo*, and [the publishers] are ahead of me right now. They paid out the advance in yearly installments—lots of money. Before they had finished paying the advance in five or six staggered payments, the books had earned into the black, but they're not required to pay royalties until they've finished paying the advance.
>
> On *Christine*, the first time they sell a book, they're in the black, I'm in the black. There are no staggered payments—it's hard to stagger a dollar! [3]

Christine, set in a middle-class suburb of Pennsylvania in 1978, taps into one of King's recurring themes: the outsider looking in at a life he wants but can't have. Arnie Cunningham—recalling the name of Ritchie Cunningham, a role played by Ron Howard in the television sitcom *Happy Days* set in the late fifties—falls in love with the new girl in school, Leigh Cabot, but his real love is a 1958 Plymouth, a two-toned red car that he buys and restores to life . . . a *haunted* car.

Just as the book had gone to press, *Christine* the movie had begun principal shooting in California. Richard Kobritz, the producer of *'Salem's Lot*, had gotten an early copy of the manuscript and optioned it for $500,000. Devouring the book in a three-day read, Kobritz felt a strong affinity for the novel of teenage angst:

> The one just seemed very, very special to me. It was teenagers, it was rock 'n' roll, it was taking America's love affair with the automobile and turning that into a horror story. King has a great ability to render familiar objects scary, and when he can do that with a car, that's special. And it was a fun book, as opposed to *The Shining*, which is the serious side of King.[4]

The book, a dark *American Graffiti*, was according to King "a monster story. But it's also a story about cars and girls and guys and how cars become girls in America. It's an American phenomenon in that sense. *Christine* is a freeway horror story. It couldn't exist without a teenage culture that views the car as an integral part of that step from adolescence to adulthood. The car is the way that journey is made."[5]

It was one thing to make a monster of a person, as in "Apt Pupil," but quite another to make a car believable as a monstrous entity, which is why *Publishers Weekly* praised the book with some reservations, saying that it "contains some of the best writing King has ever done; his teenager characters are superbly drawn and their dilemma is truly gripping. However, Christine, we soon realize, is just a car, a finally inanimate machine that does not quite live up to the expectations King's human characterizations have engendered."[6]

Kobritz, working on the film, would soon come to grips with that problem, but on a larger scale. How do you make a car appear haunted? Can you make it believable? It would be a visual challenge for the film's director, John Carpenter, to convince a sophisticated movie audience that the car was evil . . . and alive.

Ironically, *Christine*—heavily promoted and advertised—turned out not to be the King book of the year. *Pet Sematary*, which King refused to promote, would be the leader of the pack, with an announced first printing of 500,000 copies.

The novel, *Newsweek* noted, had an interesting history: King's old contract with Doubleday forbade the lump sum payment of accumulated royalties doled out on an annual basis. Concerned about IRS complications, Doubleday demanded "due consideration" in the form of two books, but subsequently took one book—*Pet Sematary*.[7]

For *Pet Sematary*, King granted only one interview—to Douglas E. Winter, for *Stephen King: The Art of Darkness*—and then closed that gate permanently.

Regardless of King's lack of promotion, *Pet Sematary*, which had gone to press with 335,000 copies would go on to sell 657,000 copies.

King, who felt the book was dark and nasty, found that unlike *Christine*, which got mixed reviews, *Pet Sematary* struck critical paydirt. The *Portsmouth Herald* called the novel "a work of such skill and quality that it transcends the horror genre to become an unforgettable piece of literature about death and bereavement," adding that "At 36, [King] is not only far from running out of steam but becoming a better novelist."[8]

Even more laudatory, *Publishers Weekly* said, "King's newest novel is a wonderful family portrait that is also the most frightening novel he has ever written. . . . [T]he last 50 pages are so terrifying, one might try to make it through them without a breath—but what is most astonishing here is how much besides horror is here. . . . Witty, wise, observant, King has never been a more humane artist than he is here."[9]

Pet Sematary is the story of Louis Creed, a physician who must question his faith in science to believe in the reanimating powers of a pet graveyard—spelled by neighborhood children as "pet sematary"—in which the dead can come back to life.

Because of his faith in science, Creed is naturally a skeptic of the Micmac Burial Ground's supposed magic, but soon becomes a believer when he sees the family cat come back to life, and then decides to bring back his son—run over by a truck—from beyond the grave.

In a note preceding the novel, King wrote that "Death is a mystery, and burial is a secret" but what kinds of secrets are unearthed when death is no longer a mystery? What is the nature of life . . . and death?

Like Dr. Frankenstein who plays God, Louis Creed, following in his footsteps, realizes that there are some things man was not meant to know.

Pet Sematary also brought one of King's earlier books back from the dead—a book King had never intended reprinting. *The Dark Tower* was dutifully listed as a 1982 novel by King, which set off a feeding frenzy among King's fans, who had faithfully haunted the bookstores but somehow had missed out on it.

Consequently, fans turned to booksellers who themselves knew little or nothing about the book, since the entire 10,000-copy print run sold by mail order to the science fiction and fantasy community.

The letters continued pouring in from everywhere to his publishers. The company sent them on to King, who still held his ground, refusing to allow a trade edition from NAL.

The $20 hardback suddenly rocketed even higher than before on the collector's market, creating a moral dilemma for King. "I wanted to do something about it, and Don [Grant] wanted to do something about it. He was upset. We talked on the phone one night and I said, 'What if you published another 500 or 5,000?' There was a long sigh. And I said, 'That would be like pissing on a forest fire, wouldn't it?' He said, 'Yeah.' "[10]

Hell hath no fury like a King fan denied the opportunity to buy a new King novel, so King authorized a second printing, for what was termed the piss-on-the-fire edition—10,000 copies, set for publication next year, but that, said King, would be it: *No more copies.*

More than anything else, this situation made King realize that he was no longer just a writer but a popular writer on a very large scale:

> I started out as a writer and nothing more. I became a popular writer and have discovered that, in the scale-model landscape of the book business, at least, I have grown into a Bestsellasaurus Rex—a big, stumbling book-beast that is loved when it shits money and hated when it tramples houses. I look back on that sentence and feel an urge to change it because it sounds so self-pitying; I cannot change it because it also conveys my real sense of perplexity and surprise at this absurd turn of events. I started out as a storyteller; along the way I became an economic force, as well.[11]

The book beast had definitely defecated dollars with the publication of *Pet Sematary*, but had unwittingly trampled on the fans with the general nonavailability of *The Dark Tower*, which would be a thorn in his side for years to come, since the series was far from over, and with each new book, the general fans would likely become more pissed.

It was a far cry from those days when he was perched on a hill in a rented trailer in Hermon, Maine, which he described to *Playboy* with candor as being, if not the asshole of the universe, then within farting distance of it.

Not surprisingly, after reading that, the officials in Hermon decided to cancel an upcoming Stephen King Day as well as plans to erect a King museum on the original trailer site, as if Stephen King would care. After reading the self-righteous letter in his hometown newspaper, King responded with his own barrage, saying that Hermon was never one of his "favorite places."[12]

King wasn't averse to being feted, but he was damned if it would be under these conditions, from a place that held nothing but thoughts of misery.

Just as King saw two books published that year, he saw three movies adapted from his books: *Cujo* in June, *The Dead Zone* in October, and *Christine* in December. Because of the proximity of the release dates—three movies in six months—reviewers carped at what they derisively called the "Stephen King Movie of the Month" club, knowing full well that it was more a matter of coincidence than choice on King's part.

Cujo, an effective book, made an effective movie, as well. Budgeted at $5 million, directed by Lewis Teague, and released from Warner Brothers, *Cujo* featured noteworthy performances by its cast, especially Dee Wallace as Donna Trenton, trapped in the family Pinto with her sick son as Cujo relentlessly attacks.

In a radical departure from the book, in which Trenton's son dies, Lewis Teague felt strongly that the too-dark film couldn't be a total downer, so in the movie version, Tad lives.

The Dead Zone, directed by David Cronenberg, and released by Paramount Pictures, opened with respectable box office numbers, boosted by excellent reviews. An easier novel to adapt than a traditional horror film, *The Dead Zone* relied heavily on believability of the main character, Johnny Smith, more than aptly portrayed by Christopher Walken, a versatile actor who in retrospect was the perfect choice for the role.

Christine, directed by John Carpenter, and released by Columbia Pictures, boasted no name actors, which had two benefits: it put the spotlight where it belonged—on the haunted car itself—and it allowed room in the budget for more special effects, a critical component to the look and feel of the movie.

Christine the movie, despite its promising opening, eventually ran out of gas; teens, the target audience for the movie, preferred their gore straight up and in-your-face.

Christine was no match for Freddy Kruger.

Chris Chesley, who had moved to Truth or Consequences, New Mexico, had never gone on to write professionally like King, but they kept in touch. Chesley usually didn't have to buy King's books, since he got them free, directly from King.

Lois Chesley, who went into the local library to check out *Different Seasons*, told the librarian that the reason she had to borrow it was that "King didn't send us one." The librarian, Ellanie Sampson, responded, "How'd you get on his mailing list?" Lois Chesley replied that they were good friends with the Kings. "The next time you talk to him, ask if he'd come out and give us a talk," Sampson replied.[13]

The Chesleys talked to King, who agreed to come out for a talk.

On November 19, 1983, the big day arrived. Festivities began when Mayor Elmer Darr presented the key to the city to King, officially proclaiming it "Stephen King Day." After the presentation, King signed books for two hours at the convention center, then rode in a caravan to the Damsite Restaurant for a barbecue luncheon in his honor, sponsored by the Chamiza Cowbelles, a local civic group.

After lunch, King gave a public talk to a crowd of eight hundred people at the Middle School, then attended a reception in his honor later that evening at the Geronimo Springs Museum, where he signed so many autographs that his writing hand blistered.

The year ended with matters close at home occupying King's attention. Because King's main secretary, Stephanie Leonard, would soon go on maternity leave, he interviewed and subsequently hired Shirley Sonderegger, a manager at a local bank that Leonard frequented. And, on an unrelated note, King had an opportunity to buy a radio station, which he didn't expect to be a sound investment; WZON, operated by the Zone Corporation, would rock and roll at 530 on the AM band. "I didn't do it to make money; if I had, I'd have to count the venture as a failure. I did it because the cutting edge of rock and roll has grown dangerously blunt in these latter days."[14]

As with the previous Christmas season, the Kings sent out their version of a Christmas greeting—a second installment of *The Plant*, which went out to 226 fortunate recipients, most (if not all) appropriately inscribed. Designed by Michael Alpert, *The Plant* was a Philtrum Press publication. This time, unlike *The Dark Tower*, *The Plant*, another work-in-progress, was kept under wraps from the general public and, wisely, not listed in the front matter of King's other novels.

By now the firestorm of protest from fans regarding the general non-availability of *The Dark Tower* had fanned across the country. What the fans didn't know was that, like *The Dark Tower*, another King book had just been published without their knowledge: the Land of Enchantment edition of *Cycle of the Werewolf*, an oversized book with beautiful pen-and-ink and color illustrations by Berni Wrightson, sold by mail order to fans in the fantasy community.

The 7,500-copy trade edition as well as the 250-copy signed edition were quickly snapped up; the book went out of print, leaving King with a second book for which no trade edition existed.

In the publishing world, where King had sold 25 million copies of his books to date, it seemed futile to publish anything of his in such a minuscule run. The only advantage in publishing a small-press book, King knew, was that it guaranteed a sell-out eliminating the risk in what is otherwise a very risky business. The disadvantage, King soon realized, was that his Constant Readers constantly complained, loud and clear to everyone in earshot, if he published a book they couldn't buy.

Who, King probably asked himself, does the book belong to? To the writer . . . or the readers? He would come to realize that the fans wanted what they wanted, and expected King to deliver, like a milkman making his rounds.

What would the fans have said if they had known there were not only three books (*The Dark Tower*, *The Plant*, and *Cycle of the Werewolf*) unavailable but four books under the Bachman pen name?

❧14❧

Two years before, Douglas E. Winter—a lawyer by vocation and a writer by avocation—had published *Stephen King* at Starmont House. A small-press book, it had the effect of a small rock thrown in a lake, with correspondingly small ripples. Deciding that the subject warranted expansion, Winter sold King's publisher, NAL, on the idea of publishing what he called "a critical appreciation; it is an intermingling of biography, literary analysis, and unabashed enthusiasm, spiced with commentary by Stephen King transcribed from our more than twelve hours of recorded conversations. . . ."[1]

Unlike *Stephen King*, the new book would be the equivalent of throwing a large rock in a lake, with correspondingly large ripples. Set for publication in October of 1984, Winter's book would tell King fans everything they wanted to know about the Boogeyman from Bangor . . . except the King-Bachman connection.

On January 14, 1984, while visiting King at his home in Bangor, Maine, Winter got early warning on the fifth Bachman book:

> Stephen King and I huddled before a wood-stove fire, watching in silence as a terrifying blizzard descended upon Bangor, Maine. After a time, he handed me a manuscript entitled *Gypsy Pie*. His eyes were suddenly alight with sardonic humor.
>
> "Dicky Bachman is back from the grave," he said. "I thought that the brain tumor had gotten him . . . but he's back."[2]

King had no plans to write another Bachman book, but according to Winter, what was originally planned as a short story became a novel; and instead of publishing it under his own name, King elected to publish it as a Bachman book instead—a decision King would come to regret.

In May, *Thinner* made its debut in the form of advance reading copies at the American Booksellers Convention. Published as trade paperbacks, to precede the November release of the hardback, the advance reading copies were literally stacked on pallets, given out freely to any bookseller willing to take a look at an author whom NAL was promoting in a big way.

Bachman's breakout book—the one NAL hoped would bring him to the attention of a hardback audience—was introduced with a characteristically understated letter that was laid in each copy of the book. "Richard Bachman is an incredibly talented writer, and *Thinner* is a riveting novel that gives a new meaning to the word 'horror.' Read it and enjoy."[3]

At a convention where the brand name is king, it's easy to see how *Thinner* got lost in the shuffle; there were, after all, thousands of other similarly promoted books, prominently displayed to catch the eye of the bookseller, and pallets of other free books.

What bookseller had time to pay attention to *Thinner* when *The Talisman* was shipping that fall?

The Talisman, the much heralded King-Straub collaboration, was the centerpiece for Viking at the ABA. The book, a 646-page hardback with a first printing of 600,000 copies to be laid down nationwide in a single day, was backed with a $500,000 ad budget to insure it wasn't going to get lost in the shuffle.

Richard Bachman, however, *was* lost in the shuffle. Just another paperback novelist trying to break into hardback, the booksellers thought. And they couldn't be bothered because Bachman, unlike King, wasn't a brand name . . . yet.

If the previous summer had been perceived by the movie critics as being crowded with King movies, they experienced *déjà vu* in the summer of 1984. Unfortunately, it would be slim pickings, starting with *Children of the Corn*, a film with a torturous production history, finally shot in less than a month on a meager $3 million budget. Heavily promoting "*Stephen King's Children of the Corn*," hoping King's brand name would offset what was obviously a flawed movie, its producers twisted, mutilated, bent, and warped the short story to make a ninety-three-minute movie infested with corn smut.

In "Lists That Matter," King singled out ten films that he felt were among the worst movies of all time, including *Children of the Corn*, about which he said:

> Here is another horror movie, and to me the most horrible thing about it is that it was based on one of my stories. Not very closely—just closely enough so the producers could call it *Stephen King's Children of the Corn*, which it really wasn't. . . . I understand this gobbler made

money, but so far I haven't seen any of it, and I'm not sure I want to. It might have corn-borers in it.[4]

Linda Hamilton, in the role of Vicky Baxter, probably wished at some point during production that the movie could have been terminated, but if so, she never got her wish: this modestly budgeted film made a profit by virtue of having low overhead, generating additional TV, video, and overseas rentals that laid the groundwork for the inevitable dreaded sequel, *Children of the Corn 2*. (The only saving grace was that it didn't have King's name attached to it.)

Of the summer King movies that failed to ignite the interest of the movie-going public, *Firestarter* was the more tragic case, because unlike *Stephen King's Children of the Corn*, *Firestarter* was a big-budget film ($15 million) with name-brand talent (George C. Scott, Martin Sheen, Art Carney, and, oh yes, Drew Barrymore). Furthermore, its director, Mark Lester, came into the project with considerable enthusiasm but ended it with the feeling that he got unjustly singed by the critical comments of Stephen King, who said it was "the worst of the bunch" of his film adaptations.[5]

For his part, Mark Lester kept his silence for years, but finally exploded, speaking out against what he considered to be bad manners on King's part:

> When you make a film, you try your best. You hope it succeeds with the public, and I think *Firestarter* did. It's enough in show business that we have critics that write about our pictures, sometimes rightly, sometimes wrongly. But to have a person so intimately involved, who actually approved the script and loved the movie, and collaborated every step of the way in the making of the film, come out and attack the movie, to me is sickening. . . . I've wanted to say this for years because he's attacked me so many times in print.[6]

King fought fire with fire. Knowing *Firestarter* would detract, not add, to the luster of his name in Hollywood, King said:

> I see that Mark Lester has finally revealed my dark secret: I'm a two-faced son of a bitch, a liar, and an all-around *eevil* guy. Actually, I'm none of those things, and neither is Mark; he's just another director who ended up with his scalp dangling from a pole outside the lodge of Chief Dino De Laurentiis. . . . Mark's assertion that I saw the movie and loved it is erroneous. I saw *part* of an early rough cut. When I saw the final cut . . . I was extremely depressed. . . . There were $3 million worth of

special effects and another $3 million of Academy Award-winning talent up there on the screen, and none of it was working. Watching that happen was an incredible, unreal, and painful experience.[7]

When $15 million is invested in a film project like *Firestarter*, expectations run high—sometimes unrealistically so. The movie's special effects, involving extensive shots of live fire, made for a difficult shoot: dealing with any of the natural elements—especially fire—is a dicey proposition, at best.

Unfortunately, the principal reason the movie failed to win over its viewing audience was its reliance on the child actress who would have to play Charlie McGee. Thoroughly engaging and believable in *ET*, Drew Barrymore couldn't carry the movie on her shoulders.

Harlan Ellison called it right on this one: ". . . this motion picture is (forgive me) a burnt-out case. We're talking scorched earth. Smokey the Bear would need a sedative. Jesus wept. You get the idea."[8]

Though it was a tepid season for King's movies, it would be quite a different season for King's books, with *The Talisman* leading the way. After six months of anticipation, *The Talisman*, with its distinctive red, black, and yellow cover design, finally shipped.

On October 8, 1984, nine warehouses throughout the country, coordinating the shipment of the book, laid down an estimated half million copies on a single day.

This time, no low-priced book club edition was available, forcing King fans to buy it from booksellers.

Understandably, reviews of the book were mixed, as reviewers scratched their heads, wondering where King left off and Straub began. Depending on whom you believed, the book was either greater than the sum of its parts or, as *People* magazine asserted, a literary experiment gone awry: "In horror fiction, two heads are better than one only if they're on the same body."

Esquire, known for its literary fiction, took a whiff of the book and summarily dismissed it:

> King, whose own style is American yahoo—big, brassy, and bodacious—has always expressed admiration for Straub's cooler, less emotional diction, and Straub in turn has praised the grand, "operatic" quality of King's work. Their collaboration is both cool and operatic—and very, very scary. It's a horrific work of art. But is it really art? Probably not. We are talking about mass-market books and popular music here. People consume horror in order to be scared, not *arted*.[9]

The reviewer, however, missed the point: King and Straub had written an American quest novel, a book that was clearly a fantasy construct. An ambitious and richly complex novel that could easily have been two or three times its published length of 650 pages, *The Talisman* was for King a one-time literary experiment. "As Casey Stengel used to say, you've got to put an asterisk by it," King said.[10]

In the wake of *The Talisman*, which would go on to sell 880,000 copies within two months after publication and perch on top of the best-seller lists for twenty-eight weeks, the pseudonymous Bachman novel *Thinner* went to press with a printing of only 26,000 copies.

Just as *The Talisman* was a book judged by its cover, *Thinner* was not; in fact, the author's photograph of Bachman seemed to suggest nothing out of the ordinary—nope, nothing wrong here—but careful readers in the fantasy and science fiction community had suspected something was awry. *Thinner* had the unmistakable texture of a Stephen King novel, despite all the sand thrown in the public's eyes. (At one point, a character in the book, Dr. Houston, admonishes Billy Halleck: "You were starting to sound a little like a Stephen King novel for a while there. . . .")[11]

A careful reader, noting all the allusions in the text to King's work and life, could have connected the dots and seen that it was indeed King—as some had already suspected and said in print, in and outside of the small circle of fans in the science fiction community—but the world at large remained oblivious, casting a dispassionate, if not cold, eye on the $12.95 hardback from a paperback novelist who wrote "sci-fi" stories but changed his tune to write a horror novel, probably to cash in on the horror craze.

That same month NAL also released in trade hardback *Stephen King: The Art of Darkness*, by Douglas E. Winter. A handsome book of 252 pages, complete with a sixteen-page photo insert printed on glossy stock, *Stephen King: The Art of Darkness* told you everything you'd possibly want to know about King . . . except the Bachman connection.

Winter was in on the secret, as were a handful of others with a "need to know" basis, but he couldn't spill the beans. His book, written in a taut but accessible prose style that bridged the gap between the scholarly tone found in articles for *Fear Itself* and the uncritical fanboy burblings of self-appointed critics in fan circles that beamed with delight at each new King offering, lent an air of respectability to a new area ripe for scholarly strip-mining: books *about* King.

Stephen King: The Art of Darkness had sold 20,000 copies, and would be reprinted in trade paperback, to be followed by a mass market paperback edition, as well.

The Stephen King Gold Rush was on, and regardless of whether there was fool's gold or real gold to be found, other writers, inspired by the success and visibility of Winter's book, began penning their own tomes. Stephen King's story was compelling enough to spawn, in the years to come, more books *about* him than *by* him—biographies, trivia quiz books, encyclopedias, concordances, bibliographies, collections of interviews and profile pieces, and companion-style books.

King quickly distanced himself from all those books. The only cold comfort was that the books treated him and his work with respect—nobody went looking for the skeletons in his closet, if any existed.

The year ended with the publication of *The Eyes of the Dragon*, self-published in a sumptuous edition from King's own Philtrum Press, with a print run of 1,250 copies: 1,000 signed and numbered in black ink, to be sold, so that the remaining 250 copies, signed and numbered in red ink, could be given away to people on the Kings' Christmas list.

Imagine what it must have been like for the recipients, expecting the third installment of *The Plant* but receiving in its place an oversized hardback, with a matching slipcase. (Those not fortunate enough to be on the Kings' Christmas list had to put their names in a lottery, for the opportunity to buy it at $120.)

The Philtrum Press edition, designed by Michael Alpert, with pen-and-ink illustrations by Kenny Ray Linkous (using the pen name Kenneth R. Linkhauser), was 8.5 x 13 inches in size, with handset type on an acid-free paper that had the texture of hand-made linen (recalling the original title, *The Napkins*, which figured in as a major plot device). With its hand-sewn signatures and sturdy cloth binding, the book was an art object in its own right. Written for the young at heart of all ages, this edition was designed to be handed down from generation to generation. "With good care," Alpert said, *"The Eyes of the Dragon* will stay in fine condition for centuries.[12]

King, who had grown increasingly disenchanted with the idea of allowing the publication of so-called limited editions that, in fact, were simply autographed editions of his trade books, made a fine distinction between those kinds of books and a book like *The Eyes of the Dragon*: the former were available in such large quantities that the loss of copies would not significantly diminish the world supply; but with only 1,250 copies of a book that did not exist in *any* other edition . . . that's another story:

A real limited edition, far from being an expensive autograph stapled to a novel, is a treasure. And like all treasures do, it transforms the responsible owner into a caretaker, and being a caretaker of something as fragile and easily destroyed as ideas and images is not a bad thing but a good one . . . and so is the re-evaluation of what books are and what they do that necessarily follows.[13]

❧ 15 ❧

STEPHEN KING has never been comfortable with the idea of a fan club devoted to him or his work. Like most writers, King would prefer to have *readers*, not *fans*. The distinction is an important one: Readers are interested in books, but fans are interested in celebrity. The former will likely leave you alone, but the latter will drive you to misery.

A Mainer by birth, by inclination, and by choice, King values his privacy, in a state where privacy is a byword. New Englanders are by nature standoffish at first, warming up slowly to newcomers, but afterward can be counted on for steadfast loyalty.

As a popular writer and celebrity figure in pop culture, King hated the notoriety that brought him the unwelcome attention from people intent on peering through his windows and digging through his trash, so to speak.

For these reasons, and more, King had never officially endorsed any fan publication about him, nor has he lent his official support to any books about him, with the notable exception of Winter's *Stephen King: The Art of Darkness*.

Still, it became obvious that demand for timely, accurate information about King required an official or unofficial publication for his readers. It was enough for his publishers to keep his books in print and issue new ones; someone else would have to take up the slack and serve as a source of definitive information on King's comings and goings.

That person was Stephanie Leonard, his sister-in-law, his main secretary. Figuring that it'd be a good way to answer the bulk of the mail inquiries—the 500 letters a week, of which most required a personal reply—Leonard began *Castle Rock*, an informal newsletter on King that would "serve as a vehicle for communication between the fans. So *Castle Rock* was born with Stephen's blessing, and on the condition that he would have nothing to do with it."[1]

The first issue, printed letter-size, with its type set in an appropriately gothic but unreadable typeface—Old English—went to press with 500 copies. "Our goal," said Leonard in her editorial, "is to keep you up-to-date on the work of this prolific writer."[2]

There was a lot of ground to cover, from books in multiple editions to film adaptations, from magazine publications to personal appearances. In short, Leonard could easily fill an informal, eight-page newsletter, and do so on a monthly basis.

Taking its name from the mythical town on a map that can only be found in King's imagination, *Castle Rock*, in its premiere issue, teased its readers with the promise that there would be "a secret revealed at long last. . . . "[3]

The secret revelation: Richard Bachman was going to emerge from the shadows, pull aside his fake mask, and reveal his true identity as Stephen King—read it here first, folks, Leonard hinted.

Since the inception of the pen name, it became more difficult with each passing year to conceal Bachman's secret. Although it was relatively easy to keep denying it when the paperbacks were out, even though they had obvious references to people, places, and things in King's life, *Thinner* was too visible, unlike the four previous books, which were released in stealth mode: the readers' radar never registered their presence.

Like Dussander in "Apt Pupil," when confronted by the evidence unearthed by Todd Bowden that revealed his true identity, King could almost be heard echoing the words of Dussander himself: "How did you find out?"

In early January, Steve Brown, a part-time bookstore clerk in Washington, D.C., suspected that King was writing behind the Bachman pen name. Brown went to the Library of Congress to do a copyright search, to look at the registration forms. Of the four books, three bore the name of Kirby Mc-Cauley, King's agent, and Bachman as a registered pen name. But on the copyright form for *Rage*, someone at NAL had screwed up and put King's name as its author.

Armed with incontrovertible evidence, Brown wrote to King, who called him back to discuss what to do about it.

In truth, there was nothing King *could* do about it. Had his name not been on the copyright form, King could and would have denied authorship, since it would have remained a matter of speculation. But denial was no longer an option and Richard Bachman died of "cancer of the pseudonym."[4]

Brown was not the only one who had his suspicions, however. In the science fiction community, it was an open secret, but until now there had been no confirmation. One bookseller, in fact, had connected all the dots a half year earlier, but decided not to do a copyright search, because, as he put it, if King wanted to keep it his secret, let him at least have *that*, since he had so little privacy otherwise.

In late January, when the television show *Entertainment Tonight* ran a story speculating as to the King/Bachman connection, the thread had begun to unravel on a national scale. It would be only a matter of time until Bachman would be laid bare.

On February 9, 1985, King's hometown newspaper, the *Bangor Daily News*, planned on breaking the story, with or without his consent. Joan H. Smith, a staff reporter whose beat included King, ran her story, "Pseudonym Kept Five King Novels a Mystery."

King, under attack from all over the country, now had to fight off the locals, and gave up the good fight. "You know when you're carrying home some groceries in the rain and the whole bag just kind of falls apart? Well, that's how it's been with Bachman lately."[5]

When it rains . . . it pours, and the trickle turned into a torrent. Early reaction from the fans was mixed. On one hand, most were glad to find out that five new King novels had been published; on the other hand, only two books, including *The Running Man* and *Thinner*, were in print. Opined one reader who thought that King was deliberately denying them the books, "That is so mean. Cruel, too."[6]

In the rush to get her story printed, Joan Smith's story was peppered with errors that aggravated the situation.

In a letter to the editor (March 5, 1985), King wrote to set the record straight:

1. He did not try to time the release of the information to benefit two Bachman books optioned for the movies; both had sold on their own *before* the revelation came to light;

2. He had in fact confirmed the pen name to Steve Brown a month earlier; Brown, for his part, had planned on running his story in the *Washington Post* in late January, but Smith had beaten him to the punch;

3. He felt there was no point in further denial and opted to confirm Smith's story, since the news story would have run, anyway; and

4. He felt compelled to respond to fan criticism about his use of the pen name, pointing out that they had confused "enjoyment with ownership," or in other words, just because they enjoyed his work didn't mean they *owned* it. It wasn't meanspiritedness on his part, he wrote.

In a world in which King had damn little privacy, what little was left—his pen name—was now being taken away from him, and he was righteously indignant:

> I was pissed. It's like you can't have anything. You're not allowed to because you are a celebrity. What does it matter? Why should anyone care? It's like they can't wait to find stuff out, particularly if it's something you don't want people to know. That's the best. That's the juice. It makes me think about that Don Henley song, "Dirty Laundry." Hell, give it to them.[7]

After Brown's story saw print in the *Washington Post*, in its April 9, 1985, edition, the sales of *Thinner* leaped up. As Bachman, King ruefully noted, "the sales of *Thinner* were 28,000. But as *Stephen King*, the sales were 280,000. That, King noted, might tell you something. . . ."[8]

It said a number of things, loud and clear. First, King could forget about any privacy surrounding his life. The encroachers and the poachers would be in his backyard, looking for what King termed "the juice." And the dirtier, the more salacious, the better. Even though a pen name hardly qualified as "juice," it was juicy enough to warrant research in the Library of Congress. Second, King's fans reacted with a wide range of emotions, from surprise to shock, from indignation to delight.

Another thing: his fans wanted all he could write, even if it broke the holiest of marketing rules: *Thou shalt publish but one major novel a year by a bestselling writer.*

In the wake of the revelation, it was open season on King and the subject of pen names. Might he have used another pen name? Were there any other novels out there that the fans didn't know about?

Stephanie Leonard, who never got a chance to break the story, tried to quell the readers' concerns by stating definitely in the April 1985 issue of *Castle Rock* that the subject was a dead issue: "As to whether or not he has any other pseudonyms, except for using the name John Swithen . . . he has never used any other pseudonyms. Really . . . Trust me. . . ."[9]

After years of denial from King, fans were hard-pressed to take the word of anyone, even if it was the truth; and in science fiction circles, rumors flew that a Laser Book edited by anthologist Roger Elwood was a King novel in disguise; set in Maine, *Invasion* was the story of a family attacked by aliens.

Who else could have written it? In truth, it was Dean Koontz, but some fans didn't want to believe *that*, either.

More galling, King was cited as the author of a pseudonymous Beeline book, *Love Lessons*, supposedly written when he was in college. Now, the book had been reprinted in a limited edition hardback, according to the review that ran in *Fantasy Review*.

On the face of it, the story seemed very plausible. King could have cranked it out. As was well known in the fan community, King had, in fact, attempted to write a porno novel when he was in college, because he was financially strapped and figured he could knock one out in a weekend, but abandoned it when it was clear that he couldn't bring himself to finish it. Also, Beeline Books published all of their aptly named "stroke" fiction under assumed names, so the pen name was a given. *Love Lessons*—especially as a bootleg item—would be a hot King collectible.

The limited edition hardback never existed, however, except in the imagination of Charles Platt, who wrote the fictitious review as a marketing device to test the "pull" of the magazine, to gauge readership response.

It did indeed draw attention, but not in the way its publisher, Robert Collins, had hoped: Collins got a legal nastygram from King's lawyers, who made it clear that their client was not happy with this latest development.

From the publisher's point of view, *Thinner* proved that, contravening conventional wisdom, King's readers would happily buy each new book by him, regardless of release dates; the more, in fact, the merrier, so bring 'em on!

Armed with that information, a Stephen King firestorm—the publication of four books in fourteen months—would soon set the book world ablaze: *It* would be published in October 1986, followed by *The Eyes of the Dragon*, *Misery*, and *The Tommyknockers*.

As if to presage the firestorm, 1985 would see four books published: two editions of *Cycle of the Werewolf* (one of them, a movie tie-in edition with King's screenplay included, in *Silver Bullet*), *Skeleton Crew* (a Putnam book, a collection of short fiction), and an omnibus collection, *The Bachman Books*.

In April 1985, *Cycle of the Werewolf* appeared as a trade paperback reprint of 128 pages. Reprinting the Wrightson art, this edition featured reset type and an introduction explaining the history of the calendar-turned-book project.

Two months later, Putnam published a large collection of short King fiction, *Skeleton Crew*. Collecting stories from diverse sources—from a college publication, regional magazines, fantasy magazines and anthologies, and mainstream magazines—*Skeleton Crew*'s stories spanned seventeen years.

Opening with "The Mist" and closing with "The Reach," *Skeleton Crew* ended with a "Notes" section in which King gave the genesis of each story, for those who wanted to know the story behind the story.

Selling 600,000 copies that year, *Skeleton Crew*'s sales figures were hellishly impressive for a short fiction collection. Numbers like that were normally reserved for bestselling writers publishing novels. It was proof positive that King fans had an insatiable appetite for his fiction in any form, as if *Thinner* had left any doubt.

An impressive collection of short fiction, *Skeleton Crew* was a bargain in the Putnam trade hardback at $18.95, but in terms of value to collectors, the $75 Scream Press edition was unquestionably the best buy: A numbered edition of one thousand copies, imaginatively illustrated by J. K. Potter, signed by author and illustrator, printed on expensive matte paper, magnificently bound in black cloth, with an illustrated slipcase, the book was clearly underpriced at $75. In fact, $125 to $150 should have been its price, but publisher Jeff Conner underestimated costs from the onset. The result: He took advance orders at $75, but it was not sufficient to cover the increasing production costs. In the end, his undercapitalized small press absorbed the blow, but as he told another small press publisher, the titanic book—a flagship for his company—nearly sank his firm.[10]

Meanwhile, cognizant of the high visibility of King in the marketplace, Starmont House in Mercer, Washington, geared up its ambitious publishing program to meet the demand for books about King. Since they no longer had *Stephen King* as a title—the book went out of print after *Stephen King: The Art of Darkness* was published—Ted Dikty was anxious to sign on a prolific but discerning critic to tackle the multiple books. Fortunately, he found such a critic in Dr. Michael R. Collings, a college professor who taught English at Pepperdine University in California. An academic with impeccable credentials, Collings loved the literature of the fantastic, took it seriously, and was himself a versatile and prolific writer: poetry, essays, nonfiction, and short fiction—all of high literary quality.

Starmont House signed Collings to write *The Many Facets of Stephen King*, *Stephen King as Richard Bachman* (an appropriately timely subject), and in collaboration with a student of his, David Engebretson, *The Shorter Works of Stephen King*. (Another book was also in the works: *Discovering Stephen King*, edited by Darrell Schweitzer.)

"The Stephen King Phenomenon," as Collings termed it, was not mere hyperbole but fact: King was a one-man publishing industry, with a not too shabby track record in the film industry, as well.

In April 1985, MGM/United Artists released *Cat's Eye*, an anthology movie like *Creepshow*. Produced by Frank Capra, Jr., shot entirely in Wilmington, North Carolina, from a script written by Stephen King, this $6 million film starred the apple of De Laurentiis's eye, Drew Barrymore.

Like *Creepshow*, *Cat's Eye* used a framing device to loosely link its unrelated stories together: from the *Night Shift* collection, "The Ledge" and "Quitters, Inc.," and "The General," written especially for this film.

Unfortunately, *Cat's Eye* didn't have nine lives—it had one. Neither a critical nor a financial success, *Cat's Eye* was clearly just another uninspired King film, causing King fans to shake their heads and wonder if the next adaptation could be any worse. (In October, *Silver Bullet*, based on a King screenplay, would be released. Sadly, it would fare little better than *Cat's Eye*, disappointing King's fans and providing ammunition to King's film critics who by now could cite a long list of mediocre King films, some of which bore King's name as the screenwriter.)

Perhaps needing a change of pace—certainly needing a break from the pressures of writing—King changed hats and, with some initial misgivings, took Dino de Laurentiis up on his offer to direct a movie. The vehicle of choice would be *Maximum Overdrive*, a movie from King's screenplay, based on his short story collected in *Night Shift*.

A vocal critic of the less faithful screen adaptations of his books to movies—notably *Firestarter*—King began principal photography in Wilmington, North Carolina, in July, one month after Rob Reiner had begun principal photography in Eugene, Oregon, on his King movie, *Stand by Me*, based on "The Body," from *Different Seasons*.

In a trailer for *Maximum Overdrive*, King said, "A lot of people have made movies out of my stories . . . but I thought it was time I took a crack at doing Stephen King. . . . After all, if you want it done right, you have to do it yourself."[11]

From the beginning, King had set himself up for a nearly impossible task. For starters, King had no real-world experience behind or in front of the camera. Acting and directing require years to learn and a lifetime to master; and although King gave it his best shot, he would miss the target by a country mile.

For King, writing was not work—it was a form of play. *Directing*, King realized, was *work*. It meant getting up six days a week, riding to work on his

Harley motorcycle, stopping briefly at McDonald's for a quick breakfast, then shooting all day in the unbearable heat and humidity of coastal North Carolina, and hoping the weather cooperated, since he shot on location at a dummy truck stop off the interstate, sufficiently convincing that truckers pulled in, looking to get their eighteen-wheel diesels topped off.

After work, King would review the dailies, then stop off at a local Zip-Mart for beer, pick up dinner at a local fast-food restaurant, and get back to his rented house early in the evening. Then, after drinking the beer and wolfing down a high-caloric dinner, he'd switch gears to work on revisions to *It*.

All work and no play makes Jack a dull boy. . . .

Writing, to King, was a part-time job, but making movies—being the director and calling the shots—was a full-time commitment. Although it was a radical change from his normal writing routine, directing stretched him, forcing him to look at life and his work in a new light. He probably had a new-found appreciation for the work of the producers and directors that he had dissed in the past. It was a *lot* harder to pull off than he realized; there was an art to filmmaking, just as there was an art to storytelling.

When asked afterward if he enjoyed his new job as a director, he replied, "I didn't. I didn't care for it at all. I had to work. I wasn't used to working. I hadn't worked in twelve years."[12]

The $70,000 he was paid to direct the movie was chump change compared to the $5 million he would have made if he had spent the time writing a new novel. The economics of it simply didn't make any sense, as King soon realized: ". . . as far as I'm concerned, it was disaster pay. This whole [moviemaking] business is so . . . unreal."[13]

If the work didn't get him down, local politics sure did. During the time he filmed *Maximum Overdrive*, North Carolina had passed a restrictive anti-pornography statute that, literally overnight, cleaned the shelves of *Playboy*, *Penthouse*, and all other men's magazines and adult videos, as well. It was, King said, as if the Porn Fairy waved a wand and made everything the least bit objectionable disappear. And if the Porn Fairy wasn't diligent enough, the local police took up the slack: At a Waldenbooks, King saw a cop searching through cheesecake calendars, hoping to find "topless" material. "In North Carolina, bare breasts and cocaine are both crimes. I think that's the real obscenity," King said. The right to choose what we read was at stake here: "It's our responsibility. Pass a law like this, and the question of what's obscene passes out of your hands once and for all; you've given up your freedom to judge for yourself, which is one of the things America is supposed to stand for—or so we teach our children in school. Get rid of the hard-core and what goes next?"[14]

In early October, King wrapped up *Maximum Overdrive*, just as another De Laurentiis production hit the theaters, also from a King screenplay. *Silver Bullet*, retitled *Cycle of the Werewolf*, was budgeted at $7 million but failed to earn back its initial investment. As difficult as it was to handle the special effects on *Firestarter*, it was even more difficult for an audience to believe the actors dressed up as werewolves. In fact, it seemed almost a satire on the genre, and moviegoers howled with laughter, not fright. Afterward, they shook their heads, lamenting the fact that another King movie had bit the big one.

In October, NAL issued an omnibus collection, *The Bachman Books*, bowing to the demand of the readers who wanted all four of the early books under one set of covers. Simultaneously released in trade hardback and trade paperback, the edition featured reproductions of each book cover, preceded by a King essay, "Why I Was Bachman," in which he said wanted to ". . . turn the heat down a little bit."[15]

The year ended on an ironic note: The third installment of *The Plant* was published and dutifully mailed in time for Christmas, but a remake of *The Little Shop of Horrors* convinced King that it was pointless to complete the novel-in-progress. Both his story and the movie were headed in the same direction, so he killed *The Plant*; nor were there any plans to reprint in any mass edition the previously published material.

More's the shame, according to Harlan Ellison, who stated that *The Plant* was a singular work for King. "And once in a while," Ellison wrote, "as in the *Night Shift* and *Different Seasons* collections, he sings way above his range. And those of us who have been privileged to read . . . *The Plant*, King's work-in-progress privately printed as annual holiday greeting cards, perceive a talent of uncommon dimensions."[16]

❧ 16 ❧

"THERE IS MORE THAN ONE WAY to burn a book. And the world is full of people running about with lit matches," wrote Ray Bradbury in an introduction to *Farenheit 451*.[1]

Horrified by the censorship he saw in North Carolina, King saw the new year begin with the flames of censorship being fanned in his own backyard. The firestarters were at it again.

The Maine Christian Civic League had, a year earlier, conducted a poll and—surprise, surprise!—concluded that the public "favored restrictions on pornography."[2]

The league, after getting the required number of signatures, forced the issue; and at the 112th Maine Legislature, a bill was introduced to "make it a crime to make, sell, give for value, or otherwise promote obscene material in Maine."[3]

It sounded good on the surface—after all, who wants to stand up and be counted *for* pornography?—but the sticky problem remained: What's pornographic and by whose standards? Who's to judge? And where is the line drawn?

"Do It for the Children" became the slogan around which Reverend Jack Wyman of the Christian Civic League rallied his troops, including the Guardians for Education for Maine, the Pro-Life Education Association, the Maine chapter of the Eagle Forum, and the Women's Christian Temperance Union.

The anticensorship group countered with their own slogan: "Don't Make Freedom a Dirty Word," and that group consisted of the Maine Civil Liberties Union, the Maine chapter of the National Organization for Women (NOW), The Maine Teacher's Association, the Maine Library Association, the Maine Women's Lobby, the Maine Citizens Against Government Censorship, and magazine and book distributors in Maine.

The war began in earnest, as the Christian League mobilized its Christian soldiers: information packets were distributed to 1,500 churches throughout the state; petition signers were contacted and urged to contribute money to the self-financed campaign by joining the membership of the Christian Civic League; and two ads "stressing the link between pornography and child sexual abuse" aired on television, at a cost of $100,000, with Wyman fanning the flames, debating the issue on radio and television stations.

In an op-ed piece in the *Bangor Daily News*, Wyman expressed his viewpoint:

> Hard-core and violent pornography debases and destroys lives, families and marriages. It is a cultural, social and moral blight. It lowers the entire tone of civility upon which a free public depends. It exploits and threatens innocent women and children. The statewide law we have advanced will not totally eliminate pornography in Maine nor will it end rape and child abuse, both of which have been linked to pornography. This law, however, will help control the extreme manifestations of this cultural disaster. Those charged with enforcing and interpreting the anti-obscenity law will, we believe, do so fairly, reasonably and with intelligent discernment.[4]

"Want to hear something *really* scary?"[5]

That was the question King posed in television ads, designed to counter Wyman's inflammatory rhetoric.

As the war of words continued unabated, King wrote a newspaper piece, "Say 'No' to the Enforcers." "I think the idea of making it a crime to sell obscene material is a bad one, because it takes the responsibility of saying 'no' out of the hands of the citizens and puts it into those of the police and the courts. I think it's a bad idea because it's undemocratic, high-handed and frighteningly diffuse. I urge you to vote on June 10, and I urge you to vote 'NO.' "[6]

Stephen King's oldest son, Joseph, also spoke his mind in the hometown newspaper, in an op-ed piece. "There are a few holes in the idea of an obscenity law. Unfortunately, these holes are big enough to drive Mack trucks through."[7]

Fighting fire with fire, the anticensorship forces bought more television advertising, showing a leather-jacketed man setting fire to books by John Steinbeck, Alice Walker, and Jean Auel. The voiceover intoned, "If the censorship referendum passes, your freedom could go up in smoke. Vote 'No' on the censorship referendum."[8]

Though effective, the ad didn't strike the right tone with King, who admitted, "I hate that ad. I mean, the guy in it looks like a Nazi. . . . But you know, once you start down that road [to censorship], it might not be that far off. . . ."⁹

As the most prominent figure spearheading the anticensorship movement, King found himself on the radio in a public debate with his opponent, Reverend Jack Wyman. Christopher Spruce, in *Castle Rock*, reported on the event:

> Stephen King, who has had his books banned from some school libraries, said he didn't know what the law might result in. "Jack," he told Wyman during the radio debate, "you can sit there and say you know what [the law] will do, but you don't. No one does. And that's why I'm against it. I'm against what I don't know about."¹⁰

Better the known evils of pornography than the unknown evils of censorship, though Reverend Wyman would hardly agree. Fortunately the citizens of Maine, who have historically preferred to make up their own minds and not let others make them up for them, agreed with King—the referendum was voted down by a resounding margin: 72 percent voted against it, making it clear that Mainers chose intellectual freedom and the right to choose.

Crestfallen, the Christian Civic League admitted its defeat, but not without trying to put a positive spin on their efforts:

> We fought the good fight. Our cause was noble. We can be proud of our accomplishments. While our opponents waged a shameful campaign, we can only acknowledge their cleverness and appreciate their success. I wish we could have won. . . . I of course wish we could have won for our children. . . . God surely had His purposes, even in dealing us this defeat. We will come back stronger, with His help, I assure you.¹¹

On another front, King found himself manning the ramparts again, this time on behalf of his own movie, *Maximum Overdrive*, which had just been screened by the reviewing board of the Motion Picture Association of America, which gave it the dreaded *X* rating.

Scheduled to open in thousands of theaters nationwide in August, *Maximum Overdrive* would prematurely die on the vine if released with the *X* rating, which meant that newspapers would refuse to carry advertising for the film—the kiss of death.

The film was then edited, its objectionable scenes excised—including a boy run over by a steamroller—to secure the *R* rating, at which point it lumbered out into theaters nationwide, hoping to roll over the competition.

King, who had either lost all objectivity about the movie or felt dutybound—as screenwriter, actor, and director in this production based on a short story he wrote—to put on his best face, optimistically stated, "For the record, I don't think the picture is going to review badly."[12]

For the record, the movie not only reviewed badly but some reviewers—even one for his hometown newspaper—seemed to take special delight in savaging the film, especially *this* one, on the premise that a king-sized target was too tempting.

Robert H. Newall, in the *Bangor Daily News*, was not atypical in his dislike for the film, but he seemed to take it as a personal affront. "As I left, I felt the urgent need of a hot bath. . . . I wanted to scrape off the grime of a scurrilous, mindless film. . . . It lacks . . . taste, grace, civilization and, above all, humanity."[13]

A marvelously inventive short story, reprinted in *Night Shift*, "Trucks," the basis for *Maximum Overdrive*, was a gem, perfect for television adaptation. Padded out to a movie, however, its point became belabored—how we have become slaves to technology, serving it instead of it serving us—and repetitive.

The Boston Globe said that "Stephen King's latest movie . . . is a factory reject. . . . King makes his debut as director of his own material, and his treatment of horror is boneheadedly banal."[14]

It was for King a learning experience, albeit an expensive one. The $10 million movie returned, in its initial short run, less than $4 million, proving that even King couldn't necessarily take his fiction from the page to silver screen—it was a *lot* harder than it looked. King's low-octane *Maximum Overdrive* had run out of gas and, by summer's end, sputtered to a dead stop.

A sanguine King, looking back at the experience, said, "I don't have any plans to direct, but sooner or later I would like to do it again . . . in Maine. The nice thing about directing is that you control everything; and the terrible thing about directing—the real drawback—is that you control everything."[15]

The most recent in a string of less than successful King adaptations, *Maximum Overdrive* evoked memories of *Cat's Eye, Children of the Corn, Silver Bullet,* and *Firestarter*—all movies that failed to ignite the interest of the public.

The cachet of the Stephen King name, which routinely worked its magic in bookstores, had worn off with moviegoers, now accustomed to summer's flood of unremarkable King movies.

In Hollywood, nothing exceeds like excess, but the seemingly endless trail of uninspired King movies poisoned the well—it was too much, too soon, and offering too little.

In an interview, Rob Cohen elaborated on that thesis:

> Hollywood is always looking for some way to *market* films, more than they're looking for a good story. They're looking for marketable hooks. If you can create a marketable hook for a movie, you've got a much better chance of getting it sold, even if the script is inferior. You can say, "I have a *Stephen King* picture!" So [producers] flocked, in the early part of the Stephen King-Hollywood romance; they flocked because they thought, "My God! We have a trademark!"
>
> That didn't work. The trademark alone is not enough to make a successful picture.[16]

In September, another King movie hit theaters nationwide, but not in the same fashion as *Maximum Overdrive*, hyped to the max and trading extensively on the King trademark to convince viewers to pack the theaters.

Adapted from a novella in *Different Seasons* ("The Body"), *Stand by Me*, which took its title from the Ben E. King (no relation) classic that served as a musical leitmotif throughout the quiet film, was directed by Rob Reiner for Columbia Pictures.

A stark contrast to King's other film adaptations, *Stand by Me* was not horror; and, fearing that association would scare off potential moviegoers who would otherwise give the film a chance, the decision to downplay King's association would, it hoped, allow the film to be seen on its own merits.

The strategy worked. In contrast to the 1,000 to 1,500 theaters that normally opened a King film, *Stand by Me* opened in sixteen key cities nationwide, where it quickly benefited from the kind of promotional push that every filmmaker hopes for but seldom gets—word of mouth.

The story, stripped to its essence, was, as *USA Today* put it, "A boy and his buddies set out on a hike to find a dead body."[17]

Now, having read that as a capsule review, would *you* rush out to see it? Probably not. But, as the favorable word of mouth grew, it was clear that this film was the summer sleeper—the surprise hit of the year. Forget the heavily hyped *Maximum Overdrive*, King fans were telling their friends, but don't forget to see *Stand by Me*.

Truth be told, *Maximum Overdrive*, like *Christine*, faced an uphill battle:

How do you make machinery appear malevolent? Both films relied too much on the ability of the moviegoer to actually believe the impossible, but *Stand by Me* had no such handicap.

Set in the summer of 1960, *Stand by Me* was that rarest of treasures: a fictional story that had been faithfully translated to film, without losing the writer's original voice in the translation. Not since *Carrie* had there been a King film that captured the essence of King's fiction.

Stand by Me, in short, was a film that King fans could stand by, and so could a mainstream audience, hungry for something more than the mindless action-filled movies that typified the summer, the least of which was *Maximum Overdrive*.

Rob Reiner, who had not read King previously, was bowled over by the story on which the film was based:

> When you read King's books, and because so many people have seen his films, people assume that Stephen King is just a schlocky kind of horror writer. But if you read his books, you'll discover he is a brilliant writer. His characters are very well drawn, his dialogue excellent, his references great.
>
> I think one of the reasons he is popular is because he has the horror aspect, the supernatural aspect to his work—people like those kinds of things. But if you take all of that out and just look at the way he draws his characters, he's really good. That's what attracted me more than the horror aspect, because I'm not a big horror fan.
>
> That's what attracted me to "The Body." To me, it wasn't really a horror piece—it was a character piece about four boys who go through a rite of passage.[18]

Predictably, the close juxtaposition and ironic divergence in quality between *Maximum Overdrive* and *Stand by Me* invited comparisons, none too complimentary for the former, though enough laudatory adjectives could not be found for the latter. Typical of the praise, from the *Newark Star-Ledger*:

> Considering what a disaster Stephen King's *Maximum Overdrive* is, directed by the best-selling horror novelist himself, it's a pleasure to report that *Stand by Me*, based on the novella "The Body," is an almost unqualified success. . . . [O]ne of the extremely rare films ever to convey a sense of what it is truly like to be a 12-year-old boy in rural America. Ignore the stupefying title and go see *Stand by Me*, which at its best has overtones of Mark Twain and Faulkner.[19]

David Brooks, in *Insight*, enthused: "Who could have predicted that a movie, let alone a good movie, could be made from a story about four 12-year-olds hiking to find a dead boy?" He concluded that the movie was a "stunning accomplishment" and a "powerful, affecting and completely original movie."[20]

The sixteen theaters that opened the film were followed by seven hundred more, fueled by positive reviews, continued positive word of mouth, and a film score that, with its rock and roll score, seemed to hit all the right notes.

Stand by Me, a picture-perfect film, showcased King as a writer with uncommon sensibilities, able to evoke a bygone time and re-create the world of preteen boys, achieving a verisimilitude that for any writer is the essence of story.

It helped, of course, that the casting was perfect: Wil Wheaton in the role of Gordie LaChance, the narrator of the story; River Phoenix as Chris Chambers, Gordie's best friend; Corey Feldman as Teddy DuChamp; and Jerry O'Connell as Vern Tessio. (King's brother, David, observed that when they were growing up, King resembled O'Connell in this movie—King was the ungainly outsider.)

The most autobiographical story King had written, the story-turned-film grossed $46 million in its first four months, making it a financial as well as critical success.

In the company of King, Rob Reiner had screened the film, carefully watching for a reaction, to see how closely the film hit home, concerned because from the beginning it had been an uphill battle to secure the rights to do the film—King, by all accounts, was reluctant to sell it, a clear departure from his normal policies. According to Reiner:

> After meeting him, after he saw the film, I understood why he had been so reluctant. After the screening he appeared very, very moved and really couldn't even talk to us. He said, "I have to go away." And he went away for about 15 minutes. Then, he came back and we sat around and talked about it and he told us how much of the story had been his life—and how upsetting it was to him. . . . He said it was upsetting to sit there and see all these kids he grew up with on screen, brought back to life when—well, you can't ever get them back.[21]

In October, Viking released the first of four books in the King firestorm—*It*, four years in the making, was a wonderfully monstrous book, in size and content, as well.

That month, *Time* magazine put King on its cover, profiling King as "The Master of Pop Dread." It would be typical of what the media would do—

paint King as the boogeyman from Bangor, a pop culture writer steeped in Americana, instead of the kind of writer who could write standout stories like "The Body" that clearly showed his ability to write nonhorrific material.

It, however, would merely affirm *Time*'s assessment that King was a horror writer. The biggest King book to date, with 1,138 pages, *It* was bound to invite criticism because of its length, as King pointed out in a letter to Dr. Michael Collings, who received a photocopy of the manuscript, which Collings carefully read and then wrote to King to express his enthusiasm in an essay on the book.

King responded:

> Thank you for your kind letter and the accompanying essay. I'm pleased that you liked the book so well. Actually, I like it pretty well myself, but when I saw that ludicrous stack of manuscript pages [a foot high], I immediately fell into a defensive crouch. I think the days when any novel as long as this gets much of a critical reading are gone. I suspect part of my defensiveness comes from the expectation of poor reviews, partly from my own feeling that that book really is too long.[22]

Considering the complexity of the novel—spanning nearly three decades with seven main characters as children, then adults, coming to grips with an ancient evil, Pennywise, who haunted them in the past and, in present day, still haunts them unless the group bands together to take a stand against him—*It* is a complex novel but also a convenient target for critics who felt King wrote not so much by the word but by the pound.

At over a half million words, *It* is not an easy read, but it's easy for any King reader to see where the book fits in the King canon: If *Danse Macabre* was his final summation on the nature of horror, then *It* was his final summation on children and traditional monsters, as King carefully, lovingly recreated the fictional Derry, Maine, from his childhood memories of growing up in Stratford, Connecticut, and geographically set the story in Bangor, Maine.

In the book's dedication, King said that *It* was ". . . gratefully dedicated to my children. . . . My children taught me how to be free. . . . Kids, fiction is the truth inside the lie, and the truth of this fiction is simple enough: *the magic exists*."[23]

Because of its length and complexity, reviewers either loved *It* or hated *It*. There was no middle ground.

David Gates of *Newsweek* praised the novel—the first part, which focused on the children in Derry, Maine, in 1957—and downplayed the rest of the book. "The exciting and absorbing parts of *It* are not the mechanical show-downs and shockeroos—but the simple scenes in which King evokes child-hood in the 1950s. If—fat chance—he ever takes a vow of poverty and tries for true literary sainthood, this intensely imagined world would be a good place to begin his pilgrimage."[24]

Other reviewers—even the redoubtable *Publishers Weekly*—savaged *It*: "Get *It*. Buy *It*. Everybody's reading *It*. The catchy sales pitches are innu-merable. But how about forget *It*? . . . Overpopulated and under-charac-terized, bloated by lazy thought-out philosophizing and theologizing, *It* is all too slowly drowned by King's unrestrained pen. . . . [T]here is simply too much of *It*."[25]

Walter Wagner of the *New York Times Book Review* lamented, "Where did Stephen King, the most experienced crown prince of darkness, go wrong with *It*? Almost everywhere. Casting aside discipline, which is as important to a writer as imagination and style, he has piled just about everything he could think of into this book and too much of each thing as well."[26]

Some reviewers alluded to King's need for a Maxwell Perkins to edit his monstrous-sized manuscripts, but King's readers ate *It* up. King, who had no misgivings about the kind of reception he'd get just based on the book's length, explained:

> I knew *It* would be long since I was trying to focus and understand all the things I had written before. You see, my preoccupation with monsters and horror has puzzled me, too. So, I put in every monster I could think of and I took every childhood incident I had ever written of before and tried to integrate the two. And *It* grew and grew and grew. . . .[27]

Despite the critical drubbing King received for *It*, his readers didn't care. They wanted as much King as they could lay their hands on; and this open-ing shot, the first of four books in a one-year period, was a king-sized feast.

In a curious parallel, that year saw the publication of four books *about* King, as well. Starmont House issued two more books by Michael Collings—a much-needed bibliography of primary and secondary work by and about King, *The Annotated Guide to Stephen King*, and a text-only guide to *The Films of Stephen King*.

Underwood-Miller, happy with the success of *Fear Itself*, followed up with a second, stronger collection of articles about King, *Kingdom of Fear*; and even NAL got into the act with a co-published book, *Stephen King at the*

Movies, by Jessie Horsting, which featured full-color and black-and-white stills from the movies, from *Carrie* to *Stand by Me*, and television and independent film productions, as well.

Adding to the profusion of books about King, Underwood-Miller's collection of King interviews, *Bare Bones*, had been erroneously listed as a book *by* Stephen King in *Forthcoming Books*, which confused bookstores, librarians, and readers alike. In any event, King probably never imagined that one day so many books would be written about him, much less compilations like *Bare Bones*.

❧17❧

WHEN KING COMPLETED *The Eyes of the Dragon*, he gave it to its intended audience of one, his daughter Naomi, who "took hold of the finished manuscript with a marked lack of enthusiasm. That look gradually changed to one of rapt interest as the story kidnapped her. It was good to have her come to me later and give me a hug and tell me the only thing wrong with it was that she didn't want it to end. That, my friends, is a writer's favorite song," King wrote.[1]

Very much a tale for children and adults, *The Eyes of the Dragon* was a bonafide children's classic, appealing to the child in every reader, evoking a sense of wonder that is the hallmark of timeless fiction.

Set in the fictional kingdom of Delain, *The Eyes of the Dragon* clearly had an audience beyond the 1,250 who had read King's privately published edition; and with the publication of Viking's trade edition, which sold 525,000 copies in its first year, King's fantastic imagination was showcased. Here there be dragons, kings, princes, and, of course, an evil sorcerer plotting his machiavellian schemes.

King Roland's heir to the throne will be one of his two sons: Prince Thomas, a pawn for the evil magician Flagg, who intends to rule the kingdom through Thomas, or Prince Peter, the good prince. Setting his evil plot in motion, Flagg looks as if he will have his way and the kingdom will be under his sway, unless Prince Peter escapes from the tower in which he was imprisoned.

Readers who expected King to talk down to them in his so-called children's novel were pleasantly surprised by the richness and inventiveness of the story, combining stereotypical characters in a fresh and engaging way.

Margi Washburn, who wrote a letter of comment to *Castle Rock*, opined that after reading the flap copy on the book, she decided not to buy it. "Why? Because Mr. King had written for a thirteen-year-old, and not for me. I am thirty-four."[2]

Washburn, however, changed her mind after a librarian enthusiastically recommended it. Picking it up, Washburn said, "It took me three days to finish this treasure. . . . I laughed and cried and prayed it would not end."[3]

As King explained to the book's readers, "I respected my daughter enough then—and now—to try and give her my best . . . and that includes a refusal to 'talk down.' Or put another way, I did her the courtesy of writing for myself as well as for her."[4]

In contrast to the delightful illustrations by Kenny Ray Linkous, published in the Philtrum Press edition, Viking chose to have the book illustrated by David Palladini, whose work lacked the evocative quality of Linkous's art; Palladini's work, to be honest, simply failed to enchant—a real disappointment, considering that artists like Michael Whelan, Tim Kirk, or Colleen Doran could have breathed life into the illustrations.

But like all stories, *The Eyes of the Dragon* had to end, and on an upbeat note, King ends the tale with the promise of more to come:

> All I can tell you is that Ben and Naomi were eventually married, that Peter ruled long and well, and that Thomas and Dennis had many and strange adventures, and that they did see Flagg again, and confronted him.
>
> But now the hour is late, and all of that is another tale, for another day.

Three months later, in May, another book centered around a tower was published, but not by Viking. Donald M. Grant published the long-awaited second installment of Roland's epic quest. *The Dark Tower II: The Drawing of the Three*, in its minuscule (by comparison to a Viking run on a King book) 30,000-copy run, plus 850 copies signed and numbered by King and its young illustrator, Phil Hale, whose hard-edged, rawhide interpretation of Roland and his world was a clear departure from Whelan's romantic vision.

Like the first book, *The Dark Tower: The Gunslinger*, this edition sold out—albeit not as quickly—and, once again, there was another King book published that many of his fans could not read, for the simple reason that they had no idea who Grant was or how to order it.

With the publication of this second installment, pressure mounted for King to publish them through a trade house, bringing them to a larger audience, since his mainstream fans clamored for an affordable edition.

With that in mind, King's agent, Kirby McCauley, had begun talks with NAL to release what was undoubtedly King's most ambitious story to his millions of other fans, the ones who had no idea that small presses were issuing sumptuous first editions of King's books, including numbered and signed copies.

That same month, *Creepshow 2* was released, directed by Michael Gornick and produced by Laurel Productions, distributed by New World Pictures. Like its predecessor, *Creepshow 2* was an anthology movie, with three stories that tried to terrorize, or at least horrify, but failed to please the mainstream audience. (It returned less than half of the box office receipts of its predecessor.)

"Old Chief Wood'nhead," the opening installment, written by King, is a predictable revenge story: The Spruces, viciously murdered by two teenagers, are avenged by their store's wooden Indian who comes to bury the hatchet—in their heads.

The second installment, "The Raft," adapted the short story collected in *Skeleton Crew*. The story, originally titled "The Float," was purportedly published in *Adam* magazine, but as King tells it: "*Adam* paid on *publication*, dammit, and since I got the money, the story must have come out. But no copy was ever sent to me, and I never saw one on the stands, although I checked regularly. . . ."[5]

A typical one-noter, "The Raft" is the story of four college students who encounter a malevolent blob of black goo in a remote lake that relentlessly attacks the raft on which the students take refuge, until all are killed. End of story.

The final installment, the best of the bunch, is an in-your-face black comedy. An adulterous Annie Lansing, anxious to beat her husband home, drives her Mercedes like a bat out of hell and runs over a hitchhiker, who comes back to haunt her, who won't stay dead, no matter how many times she runs him over—first, by accident, then by intent. When she finally gets home, the hitchhiker makes his final appearance.

Sometimes, as King knows, they come back. . . .

Best-selling writers like Stephen King are no strangers to life's misery. Once the transition is made from unknown to known writer, from a moderately successful to a hugely successful career, the writer's landscape changes; the dream becomes a nightmare, fueled by the expectations of the publisher, booksellers, and ultimately the readers.

In "The Fault in My Lines," an introduction to *Slippage*, Harlan Ellison explains the nature of fan obsession: "Not all, but some, of one's readers become obsessive and act as if a writer is denying them their mainline fix if they don't get a new book when they want it. No matter that one has more than sixty *other* books they can enjoy . . . they want the *next* one. And they demand it!"[6]

King, who heard the plaintive hue and cry of the fans denied *The Dark Tower*, knew exactly what Ellison was writing about: King, like Ellison, lives uneasily with the fans' expectations, with their assertion: *Well, we made you who you are, so why are you to deny us, your loyal fans?*

As King's main secretary, editor/publisher of the King newsletter turned newspaper *Castle Rock* and sister-in-law, Stephanie Leonard experienced firsthand, on and off the job, the intrusiveness of the fans.

One time, she said, the Kings were at a restaurant in North Carolina, enjoying the rarest of luxuries: a quiet meal in a public place. Someone in the King party expressed surprise that nobody had approached the table for autographs, and wasn't *that* a real change? Those good old boys in North Carolina obviously had good manners. And they did—they had waited *outside* the restaurant, where King was surprised to see a long line of admirers wanting autographs.

Stephanie's husband, Jim, knew all too well the intrusiveness of the fans. As a employee working at the King home in the Historic District, Jim witnessed on a daily basis the crush of crowds—peaking in the summer and, predictably, on Halloween—that pressed upon the fence that surrounded the house. Jim Leonard had seen thousands of fans come and go, taking pictures of the house and, usually, a picture of themselves in front of the distinctive bat-and-spider gate.

No wonder the dedication to *Misery* read: "This is for Stephanie and Jim Leonard, who know why. Boy, *do* they."

Misery, one of King's finest books, tapped deep into his writer's psyche to explore a writer's worst fear: the inversion of the writer-reader relationship, in which the writer, through his book, doesn't hold the reader in sway, but the reader literally holds the writer hostage—the ultimate misery for any creative person.

"The public is frequently possessive and unforgiving, without seeming to understand that what they are attempting to exercise is a kind of emotional slavery," observed Tabitha King. "Money and fame attract the self-seeking, who are willing to do anything . . . even if it hurts or kills you. . . ."[7]

Misery is the story of Paul Sheldon, a frustrated writer whose serious work is overlooked in favor of his commercial work, a series of bodice rippers featuring the heroine Misery Chastain.

Sheldon, forcing the issue, decides to end his misery by killing off Misery Chastain, and in doing so invokes the misery-turned-wrath of his "number-one fan," Annie Wilkes, who forces him to write *Misery's Return*, which earns her its dedication.

King originally envisioned the novel as a simple escape story—Sheldon's efforts to free himself from the confines of the house and out into the real world.

While the novel certainly explored that aspect, there was more to it—a psychological underpinning that comprised the scaffolding he came to see as the *real* story:

> I thought it would be about escape, pure and simple. About halfway or three-quarters through, I found out I was actually talking about something as opposed to just telling a story. I thought to myself, you're talking about *The Thousand and One Nights*, and you're talking about what you do. The more I wrote, the more I was forced to examine what I was doing in the act of creating make-believe; why I was doing it and why I was successful at it; whether or not I was hurting other people by doing it and whether or not I was hurting myself.[8]

After *Misery* shipped its first printing of 900,000 copies, the fan mail, predictably, included letters from fans who took the book *Misery* personally. In an article for *Castle Rock*, Tabitha King wrote, "I have read several pained, angry, and offended letters from fans who mistakenly believe that Steve was recording his true feelings about his readers in *Misery*."[9]

It underscored what King, and every other writer, knew: that the art of storytelling is an exercise in make-believe, grounded in reality, but hardly a transliteration of a writer's feelings, thoughts, and emotions.

Even at that, Tabitha King had to admit that *Misery's* "exploration of the worst aspects of the celebrity-fan connection is obvious and real."[10]

What, precisely, was the nature of the relationship between writer and reader? Stephen King, who has always maintained that he writes for an audience of one (himself), is very aware of his readers' presence: "I feel a certain pressure about my writing, and I have an idea of who reads my books; I am concerned with my readership. But it's kind of a combination love letter/poison-pen relationship, a sweet-and-sour thing. I feel I ought to write something because people want to read something. But I think, 'Don't give them what they want—give them what you want.'"[11]

Curiously, the flap copy of *Misery* reads: "Stephen King is arguably the most popular novelist in the history of American fiction. He owes his fans a love letter. *Misery* is it."

The book is certainly no "love letter," but King does give his readers what they want: an intense work of fiction that, for a few hours, takes you away from the real world and puts you into the fictional world of Paul Sheldon. But, unlike most popular fiction, *Misery* doesn't comfort or placate the reader, catering to his preconceived notions and mundane sensibilities — the novel is a straight-from-the-heart imagining of every writer's worst nightmare: the number-one fan who holds him captive.

"People really like what I do," said King, though he admitted that "some of them are quite crackers. I don't think I have met Annie Wilkes yet, but I've met all sorts of people who call themselves my 'number-one fan' and, boy, some of [them] don't have six cans in a six-pack."[12]

The Kings had been lucky, but soon their luck would run out. Like lightning to a rod, the crazies would seek him out.

In contrast to *Misery*, with its mammoth first printing, the latest Philtrum Press offering — King's own homegrown books — broke with tradition and, instead of publishing King's fiction, published Don Robertson's *The Ideal, Genuine Man*.

The dust jacket flap copy made it clear that this was a standout book by a standout writer who deserved more attention. ". . . *The Ideal, Genuine Man* marks the finest work yet from the man who may be America's least-known and most articulate novelists.

"Set in Houston — a Houston which in Robertson's hands becomes a shimmering nightmare landscape — it is the story of Herman Marshall, a retired truckdriver whose wife is dying of cancer and who is himself trying to come to grips with the fact of his own old age in a society where the elderly are discarded like empty beer-cans."[13]

In the "forenote" to the novel, Stephen King — the book's publisher — wrote: "Don Robertson was and is one of the three writers who influenced me as a young man who was trying to 'become' a novelist (the other two being Richard Matheson and John D. MacDonald)."

Philtrum, King explained, is ". . . a very humble storefront in a world dominated by a few great glassy shopping malls."[14] It's more a labor of love — books like *The Plant* were all given away, and even *The Eyes of the Dragon* was not designed to make a profit but to break even, to allow the gift distribution of 250 red-numbered copies.

Why, then, publish this book at Philtrum? Because, as King pointed out, he had no choice: "Publishing this book is no thank-you note, but a simple necessity. To not publish when I have the means to do so would be an irresponsible act."[15]

In time, the book sold out its limited edition and the first trade edition, as well, but the second printing was remaindered by a trade publisher that took on its distribution.

In November, the fourth of the Bachman novels, *The Running Man*, was released by Taft Entertainment. Boasting the bankable Arnold Schwarzenegger as the hapless Ben Richard, *The Running Man* was a $27 million film. But despite its special effects and big budget, it failed to capture the audience's imagination.

Schwarzenegger—an overpowering, unstoppable figure in *The Terminator*, *Terminator 2*, *Commando*, and *Predator 1*—played the role of the hunted, not the hunter. As a result, the audiences didn't go for it; they wanted to see Arnold grumble, in his characteristic accent, "I'll be *back!*" What they didn't want to see: their hero running like Wile E. Coyote, trying to evade the deadly game-show assassins who tried to hunt him down and kill him, while the public cheered.

Also in November, just in time for Christmas, Putnam rolled out *The Tommyknockers*, a science fiction–horror novel that went to press with 1.2 million copies—a far cry from the tiny print run of *The Ideal, Genuine Man*.

The plot: "The townspeople of Haven are 'becoming'—being welded into one organic, homicidal, and fearsomely brilliant entity in fatal thrall to the Tommyknockers."[16]

An ancient, evil race whose spaceship has been buried with only the nose tip extruding from the surface, the Tommyknockers' effect is long-lasting and deadly. The townfolk are able to build devices to solve their nagging simple problems without realizing that those same devices, if left unchecked, could have disastrous consequences.

The novel, in essence, is a morality play. Said King to Winter, "*The Tommyknockers* is a gadget novel. . . . Our technology has outraced our morality. And I don't think it's possible to stick the devil back in the box."[17]

At 558 pages, *The Tommyknockers* is everything *Misery* is not. A tight, controlled novel, *Misery* has the impact of a well-placed knockout punch, whereas *The Tommyknockers* took it on the chin.

Part of the problem was that King could refuse to make editorial changes unless he wanted to, since his publishers weren't likely to force the issue and, in the process, lose a book that would earn millions of dollars. Better to let King have his way—a danger that King himself recognized:

> At this point, nobody can make me change anything. . . . [W]here does a 10,000-pound gorilla sit? The answer is, any place he wants. That's why it becomes more and more important that I listen carefully to what people say, and if what they say seems to make sense, I have to make those changes even when I don't want to, because it's too easy to hang yourself. You get all this freedom—it can lead to self-indulgence. I've been down that road, probably most notably with *The Tommyknockers*. But with a book like *Misery*, where I did listen, the results were good.[18]

The same reviewers who praised *Misery* were the ones who knocked *The Tommyknockers*, including *Publishers Weekly*:

> *The Tommyknockers* is consumed by the rambling prose of its author. Taking a whole town as his canvas, King uses too-broad strokes, adding cartoonlike characters and unlikely catastrophes like so many logs on a fire; ultimately, he loses all semblance of style, carefully structured plot or resonant meaning, the hallmarks of his best writing. It is clear from this latest work that King himself has "become" a writing machine. . . .[19]

❧18❧

From January to May 1988, Stephen King suffered from writer's block for the second time in his life. (The first occurred in college, when he felt constipated as a result of the writing classes he took.) A form of creative impotence, writer's block is when you want to get it on but can't. The result: misery and rage.

Publishers Weekly's assertion aside—that King had become a writing machine—the simple truth is that King's storytelling machinery froze. It happens to the best of them, for all sorts of reasons, but usually because stress outside the writing overwhelms the writer, to the point of literary impotence.

Frank Herbert, author of *Dune*, said that "The successful writer listens to himself. You get a writer's block by being aware that you're putting it out there."[1]

King, very aware that he was putting it out there, with short stories, nonfiction, books, and movies in the mill, likely became too self-conscious of being a Best-Selling Writer with an Audience of Millions, instead of the writer who originally wrote to please himself—the only barometer by which he could accurately gauge his work.

Unable to write novels, King played with a short story idea, to start the storytelling machinery going. It worked. The writing block finally ended after he finished "Rainy Season," an odd story that appeared in a semipro magazine, *Midnight Graffiti*.

This story about summer people is simply told: John and Elise Graham, out-of-towners visiting Willow, Maine, during its rainy season, a rare meteorological event that occurs only on June 17, at night, once every seven years. But it doesn't rain the proverbial cats and dogs—it rains, instead, malevolent toads that demand their bloody sacrifice: a man and a woman, and this year it's the Grahams. The next morning, the toads evaporate with the rain, and the locals thank their lucky stars that, once again, the out-of-towners have unwittingly sacrificed themselves, preserving the status quo.

An imaginative riff on Shirley Jackson's short fiction, recalling "The Lottery" and "The Summer People," King's "Rainy Season" used a premise previously explored in "The Children of the Corn" and in "You Know They Have a Hell of a Band"—lost tourists who find themselves in a nightmarish situation.

The story, though not wholly original, ended King's dry spell and, ". . . all at once, everything opened up and flooded out. I've been writing horror since then," King explained.[2]

Unfortunately, the drought meant that, for the fall, there would be no King book from Viking, which had for years dutifully issued a novel just in time for the Christmas trade.

Faced with that grim prospect, a decision was made to publish a book that would use King's name to maximum effect; and that book would be a coffee-table book, retailing at $24.95, with photographs of gargoyles by f-stop Fitzgerald. King's contribution? An essay commissioned especially for the book—10,000 words.

Which came first: the chicken or the egg? Was it the photos that required the name-brand introduction, or the intro that required the photos?

As most publishers know, collections of photos, no matter how beautifully printed, have a small audience: photographers. What publishers want but rarely find are best-selling authors, who even with less ambitious fiction books or nonfiction can move a lot of copies: *Danse Macabre* was book-length nonfiction; and *Cycle of the Werewolf* was only a short story, enhanced with illustrations to produce a 128-page book.

Nightmares in the Sky, however, was neither fish nor fowl. Admittedly, its 100 duotone photos and 24 full-color photos were visually arresting, and King's chatty intro was a good read, but it was hardly the picture-perfect King project.

In King's words, his contribution to the book was ". . . an essay on gargoyles as a kind of preface to the book of extraordinary photographs. . . ."[3] On the cover, however, the distinction is not made clear. King fans who picked up the book, thinking it would have a lot of text by King, were surprised to discover that the text was up front, and the bulk of the book was photography, about which they could care less. *Who is f-stop Fitzgerald? Is that supposed to be a joke name, or something? And what's this thing with gargoyles? I mean, enough already!*

Regardless of these considerations, or perhaps thinking that King's name would pull his fans in like a tractor beam, Viking issued 250,000 copies, crossed their fingers, and prayed. *"Nightmares in the Sky* is a visually stunning book, one which would make an ideal gift for anyone interested in horror, Gothic architecture, photography, and the darker side of daydreaming," the flap copy breathlessly stated.[4] But despite the multiple markets and King's introduction, the book never reached sales expectations.

The nightmare, as it turned out, wasn't in the sky; it was in bookstores, as the stacks of *Nightmare in the Sky* failed to move—a real publisher's nightmare. An estimated 100,000 copies were returned, according to the *Washington Post*'s David Streitfeld,[5] and in the months that followed, the book was marked down to a few bucks, each copy bearing a remainder bar on the side of its pages.

King's fans sent a message, loud and clear, to King's publishers, after *Nightmare in the Sky* bombed: They weren't willing to pay $25 for an essay by King in book form, no matter how attractively packaged.

Plume, NAL's trade paperback reprint line, had no such problems with the reprint of *The Dark Tower: The Gunslinger*, which was published in September, preceded in July by an unabridged audiotape reading of the novel by King himself, hyped by NAL's Robert Diforio, who gushed that King was "as mesmerizing in audio as he is in print. [King] has an incredibly seductive quality that just draws you in. He's clearly not a professional actor or reader, but it doesn't matter, because what you get is Stephen King himself. I think his fans will be thrilled."[6]

King's self-evaluation of himself as an audiobook reader was more on the mark. "I thought that even though I don't have a professional voice, I know what the story means to me, which is a great deal. It seems built to be heard around a fire. A lot of fantasy is that way," he said.[7]

Reasonably priced at $10.95, the Plume edition was a facsimile reprint of the Grant edition, which gave it a striking appearance. Finally, King's millions of readers could follow Roland's long quest to reach the Dark Tower, without having to pay scalper's prices or look for the hard-to-find individual installments that appeared in *The Magazine of Fantasy and Science Fiction*.

Though there were no new books by King—*The Dark Tower* being a reprint—there were four new books *about* King that fall.

Underwood-Miller published *Bare Bones*, a collection of interviews, and *Reign of Fear*, a second collection of essays. Additionally, two scholarly books were published, including *Landscape of Fear: Stephen King's American Gothic*, by Tony Magistrale, and *Stephen King: The First Decade*, by Joseph Reino, whose thesis was "Primarily thematic and favorable, this book strives for critical objectivity, highlighting in-depth examinations of psychology, symbolism, imaginative wordplay, and mythic and current cultural analogies."[8]

In King's personal life, the fall marked a change of seasons on several fronts.

The official Stephen King publication, *Castle Rock*, would change hands—from Stephanie to Christopher Spruce, whose skills in layout, editing, and printing had vastly improved its look and feel; what had begun as a modest newsletter was now a monthly newspaper, tabloid size, pasted up in the offices of WZON, King's radio station, which Chris Spruce managed.

Castle Rock, it seemed, had found a comfortable niche and wanted to remain, like its namesake town, small in size. "With a publication like this, there's a point of diminishing returns. It's all mail circulation and time-consuming to put it out. I'm fairly comfortable with the circulation where it is now [in the low thousands]. It's manageable and I'd like to keep it that way."[9]

Not only did *Castle Rock* undergo a change, but WZON underwent changes, too. "All the change means is that Z-62 will offer its programming commercial-free. That means more music and no commercial interruptions. Commercial AM rock 'n' roll is nearly dead. Resurrecting the Z as a non-commercial rocker may be one way of keeping the format alive on AM."[10]

The biggest change, however, was that King, for whatever reasons, decided to change literary agents. After months of speculation in the science fiction fan community, Stephanie Leonard, in the September 1988 issue of *Castle Rock*, cleared the air and set the record straight. "A recent article in *Fantasy Newsletter* mentioned a shake-up at the Kirby McCauley agency. It is true that Stephen King is no longer represented by Kirby McCauley, as the article implied. At this time he has not signed with any other representatives."

Speculation ran rampant in fandom, but the simple truth was that King didn't *need* a literary agent per se—McCauley or anyone else. As King had said before, in an article on writing, you *need* an agent only at the point at which he needs *you*.

When King was at Doubleday, he clearly needed a literary agent, someone who could be objective and view the contracts with a cold eye, and improve the god-awful boilerplate contracts, written by the publisher's lawyers to suit the house. For his work, McCauley got 10 percent, perhaps even 15 percent of the gross, which was good money when you're dealing with millions on each book sale.

King needed a professional manager, not simply an agent. He needed someone who could integrate all of his financial matters under one umbrella, including agenting; and that person would be Arthur B. Greene.

In December, Greene represented King on the next book deal, which would be, for King and NAL, a very big deal indeed.

❧ 19 ❧

Robert Diforio, the president of NAL, got the Christmas gift he had hoped for—a contract with King for four new books. "This is simply wonderful to report," Diforio said. "We enjoy being King's publisher and we're happy that we'll be continuing that relationship."[1]

The relationship, *Castle Rock* reported in its front-page story in its February 1989 issue, would guarantee a book a year: *The Dark Half* in 1989, *Four Past Midnight* in 1990, *Needful Things* in 1991, and *Dolores Claiborne* in 1992.

Diforio had more cause for celebration, because in March 1989, NAL's Plume imprint published a facsimile edition of *The Dark Tower II: The Drawing of the Three*. A bargain at $12.95, the novel would bring more readers into the fold, into the dark world of Roland and his nemesis, the Man in Black.

In King's Afterword, in which he projected the series to be comprised of "six or seven books," he told the reader:

> My surprise at the acceptance of the first volume of this work, which is not at all like the stories for which I am best known, is exceeded only by my gratitude to those who have read it and liked it. This work seems to be my own Tower, you know; these people haunt me, Roland most of all.[2]

The story, King said, had haunted him for seventeen years . . . but even he had no idea when the next book, *Wizard and Glass*, would be written. Fans would just have to wait for this serialized work in progress, even if it meant years.

With each passing year, prices on King limiteds have continued to rise, but in the spring of 1989, prices took a sharp leap upward. With King no longer the province of the small presses in the fantasy field, the prestigious Whitney Museum of American Art contacted King for a story, suitable for illustration by Barbara Kruger, a graphic artist, a King reader who had suggested the idea.

May Castleberry, the project coordinator at the Whitney, contacted King but, hearing nothing for weeks, expected King was too busy with other commitments to participate. In time, though, she received a forty-page story of approximately 9,000 words.

The story, "My Pretty Pony," was actually extracted from an aborted novel titled *My Pretty Pony*, a Richard Bachman book that had gone bad. A self-contained story, "My Pretty Pony" explored the nature of time, as explained to Clive Banning by his grandfather.

Kruger worked on the design without the benefit of talking with King. "Not only did I not want to go up to Maine, I didn't even ask to get from King any instructions on how to handle the text," she said.[3] Kruger, who had very firm ideas on how to illustrate the book, decided to focus on the temporal nature of time as a visual motif. From the inlaid liquid crystal display clock on the cover to the illustrations themselves, the book achieved—in her mind—the desired visual effect:

> Because it's so much a story about life and death and time, I really wanted to visualize the literalness of time passing, so I used a real digital clock embedded in a piece of stainless steel as the cover. It was important for me to design the book using my experience in graphic design. I had to visualize the text not only in pages but also in terms of how the book is organized: the size of the materials, the typeface, the spacing and leading, the colors, and the papers we used.[4]

The result: 280 copies of a book, of which only 150 were for sale to the general public. The prepublication price was $1,800; the postpublication price, $2,500. The books were signed but not numbered.

Measuring 13.5 x 21 inches, the book was clearly not only for the most ardent, and rich, King collector but for art collectors who followed Kruger's career, as well.

Plans were made for a facsimile reprint, to be published by Knopf: a 68-page hardback book, with matching slipcase, in a run of 15,000 copies, that would sell for $50.

For King collectors who were used to more reasonably priced limited editions, *My Pretty Pony* was a surprise, not only in price but in design and illustration. Kruger may have her advocates in New York, but elsewhere in the United States, at least among King fans, their tastes ran more toward Michael Whelan, Phil Hale, and others who drew representational art.

King, always sensitive about the "look" and pricing of the limited editions made from his work, later expressed his misgivings about the production:

"My Pretty Pony" was originally published in an overpriced (and overdesigned, in my humble opinion) edition produced by the Whitney Museum. It was later issued in a slightly more accessible (but still overpriced and overdesigned, in my humble opinion) edition by Alfred A. Knopf.[5]

King, however, had no misgivings about the limited edition of *Dolan's Cadillac*, published by the prestigious Lord John Press, well known in the fan community but also in mainstream circles because of its publishing affiliation with contemporary authors.

Founded in 1977 by Herb Yellin, the small press was a one-person operation, with minuscule print runs, rarely more than a few hundred. Using hand-set type, Yellin's broadsides and books included literary luminaries like John Barth, Donald Barthelme, Ray Bradbury, Raymond Carver, and Ken Kesey, and former President Gerald Ford, as well.

Like all the small presses in the field, Lord John Press was anxious to publish a King project, but its publisher, Herb Yellin, was in no hurry. It was "seven or eight years after I had met him in San Francisco, and he had promised that I was third on his list of small presses to do a book. I am patient and *Dolan's Cadillac* fits in more with the type of books we publish. It is a story of revenge, a theme that I understand and appreciate, so the 'fit' was good."[6]

The "fit" resulted in 1,000 numbered copies, signed by King, with a price of $100; and 250 deluxe copies, quarter-bound with marbled paper, at $250.

The book was a small gem. Only 64 pages, *Dolan's Cadillac* originally appeared as a serialized story in the first four issues of *Castle Rock*, but was revised for its first book appearance from Yellin's press. Said King: "Because I love his books, which are small, beautifully made, and often extremely eccentric, I went out into what I think of as the Hallway of Doom and hunted through my boxes to see if there was anything salvageable."[7]

There was something salvageable—the short story that had been published in 1989, King's take on a familiar Poe story, "The Cask of Amontillado," in which a man is entombed alive. King's version, however, was deliciously ironic: the mob boss is, along with his bodyguard goons, buried alive in a reinforced Cadillac that he traveled in precisely *because* of its tank-like protection.

Charity begins at home. For Stephen King, that meant using his influence to force an issue that had rankled him: Despite all the movies made from his work, none had been filmed in Maine. A clean industry, the film community would come, set up, pump a small fortune into the local economies, and then clean up, leaving nothing behind except local businessmen, happy with the influx of cash.

In any state, the influx of film dollars was a good thing, but especially so in Maine, which has a per capita income of only $17,306.[8]

King flexed his muscles to insure that, for the first time, if someone wanted *Pet Sematary* it would have to be shot in Maine:

> Because *Pet Sematary* of all my novels was the one I thought would be the most difficult to film, I just simply made it an unbreakable part of the deal that whoever was going to do it, would have to do it in Maine. And Laurel came along, and Bill Dunn came along and said, "Yeah, OK, we'll make it in Maine."
>
> And, again, why not? You've got production facilities, lab facilities, and an acting pool to draw on here in New England. And if you need to go to Boston and New York, they're 600 miles down the road, and they're closer than, say, San Francisco is to Los Angeles.
>
> We've got stuff up here that nobody's seen. Maine's supposed to be Vacationland. And, ideally, what should happen is that people should look at the movies and say, "We'd like to go there." And they should come and say, "Gee, this is as great as we saw it." In other words, a movie like *Pet Sematary* . . . should serve as a commercial for the state, as much as all the movies made in California, Los Angeles, and New York have served as commercials for those places.[9]

In truth, *Pet Sematary* would, at best, be an advertisement for the film industry looking to shoot in Maine, more than it would be an advertisement for the tourists who come to Maine and stay predominantly near U.S. Route 1 and flock lemming-like to coastal towns like Freeport, which harbors 1.5 million visitors a year at its outlet stores, or picturesque Bar Harbor, where the yuppies congregate.

Pet Sematary—notable for its horrific, dark imagery of talking corpses with bloody brains, not to mention the dead cat, child, and wife coming back to life, and a foreboding Indian burial ground—would not likely bring in additional summer people on the strength of its landscape. That's *not* the way life should be.

King, who knew that *Pet Sematary* would be a start, continued to beat his drum. He knew the Maine Film Commission could use it as a drawing card for the film, not tourist, industry. King explained:

If you're going to tell about Maine, why not come here? People like Bill Dunn have helped to blaze the way for that, to create a precedent for it, so I think it'll happen more. I think that one thing you can count on is that I will try as hard as I can to get film production up into this particular area. I can do it to some degree with my own work—it's not going to become my life's crusade—but nonetheless, the more film that comes up here, the stronger the Film Commission gets.[10]

King was successful in his lobbying efforts—speaking softly and carrying a king-sized economic stick for clout—and *Pet Sematary* pumped considerable amounts of cash, mostly to small businesses that provided goods and services, into the local economies, grateful to see its influx. (The movie itself grossed $26 million.)

King's philanthropy extended beyond Maine's borders, as well: At the Milton Academy in Massachusetts, its newly constructed arts and music center had gotten a big boost when the Kings donated $6 million.

Milton Academy, the private school that the King children attended, named its newly built theater after Ruth King. "As children," King said at the dedication ceremony, "we need to have our dreams encouraged and nurtured. My mother did that for me."[11]

Closer to home, the Kings made a major donation to a local library—$1.5 million, approximately half of what would be needed to build a 6,000-square-foot addition to the public library at Old Town, where Tabitha King grew up.

Since 1980 the King's Bangor home served double duty, as a principal residence and an office, where a staff of secretaries arrived on weekdays to help manage King's burgeoning career.

It was time, however, for a change. King's home would, finally, become his castle—albeit always under siege, year-round, from the tourists—and he'd bar the gates forever, making it a refuge for family and friends.

That winter, King moved his office staff out of the house and into a nondescript, one-story office building near the Bangor airport on the outskirts of town.

The office was staffed by two secretaries overseen by Shirley Sonderegger, though King usually didn't make an appearance until the early afternoon, because he did his real work, his writing, at his home office.

Unlike the house, encircled by the wrought-iron fence, with signs posted on the property to indicate there was no trespassing, the office was open to anyone. But its phone number and location would remain a closely guarded secret; the fans who came from out of town could always find the King house easily enough, but the office was sufficiently off the beaten track.

In November 1989, Viking published *The Dark Half*, in time for the Christmas trade. The 431-page novel, retailing for $21.95, had an impressive first printing of 1.2 million copies, like *Tommyknockers*.

In contrast to *Tommyknockers*, *The Dark Half* garnered positive reviews. Originally intended as a King-Bachman collaboration, *The Dark Half* would be, like *Misery*, an exploration of the dark side of the writing profession. This time, however, it would not be a fan that holds the writer hostage, but the writer's alter ego—his dark half—that came to life to haunt him:

> Thad Beaumont is a writer, and for a dozen years he secretly published novels under the name of "George Stark" because he was no longer able to write under his own name. He even invented a slightly sinister author biography to satisfy the many fans of Stark's violent bestsellers. But Thad is a healthier and happier man now, the father of infant twins, and starting to write as himself again. He no longer needs George Stark, and in fact has a good reason to lay Stark to rest. So, with nationwide publicity, a bit of guilt, and a good deal of relief, the pseudonym is retired.[12]

Like *Misery*, *The Dark Half* was a brilliant transmutation of life enhanced by a writer's imagination: *The Dark Half*'s notion of George Stark, a pen name who refused to die, had its basis in the disclosure that King was writing as Bachman—a secret that would have been revealed by King in the second issue of *Castle Rock*, but King's cover was blown prematurely by a Washington, D.C., bookstore clerk.

"He took on his own reality, that's all, and when his cover was blown, he died. I made light of this in the few interviews I felt required to give on the subject, saying that Richard Bachman had died of cancer of the pseudonym, but it wasn't actually shock that killed him: the realization that sometimes people just won't let you alone," wrote King.[13]

The Dark Half, King said, is "a book my wife has always hated, perhaps because, for Thad Beaumont, the dream of being a writer overwhelms the reality of being a man; for Thad, delusive thinking overtakes rationality completely, with horrible consequences."[14]

In *The Dark Half*, a part-time bookstore clerk and law student, Frederick Clawson, uncovers Beaumont's pen name. Clawson, who had gone to extreme lengths to secure incontrovertible proof—placing invasive phone calls to people in the publishing industry, taking a trip to the post office in Brewer, where he staked out the box which Beaumont rented—gets more than he bargains for: Not only does Beaumont refuse to provide him with an "assistance package" but he deliberately discloses the pen name, insuring Clawson doesn't get anything out of the secret.

But the creepazoid Clawson does get his just desserts: George Stark, tracking a bloody path to Beaumont, viciously kills Clawson.

In a discussion after Clawson's murder, Thad Beaumont's wife Liz observed, "'When a genuine Creepazoid gets his teeth in you, he doesn't let go until he's bitten out a big chunk.'"[15]

Publishers Weekly praised "the new King thriller . . . so wondrously frightening that mesmerized readers won't be able to fault the master for reusing a premise that puts both *Misery* and *The Dark Half* among the best of his voluminous work."[16]

For King, *The Dark Half* could be perceived as a fictional form of closure on the matter of the Bachman revelation, putting it to rest.

Art imitates life, and life imitates art: Presaging *Needful Things*, in which Castle Rock is destroyed, *Castle Rock*, the King newspaper, folded after fifty-five issues.

Castle Rock's last issue was cover-dated December 1989, and its 1,500 subscribers, who shelled out $20 for an annual subscription (twelve issues), would have to find their King news elsewhere. The homegrown publication, which started out with 300 subscribers, rising to a high of 5,000 subscribers during the period that NAL extensively promoted it in the back pages of King's paperbacks, fell victim to real-world considerations. Its editor, Chris Spruce, felt it was time to head back to school, to get his master's degree at the University of Maine. Besides, there was the matter of King's lack of involvement in recent years. As Spruce pointed out:

> I'm not sure he has been entirely comfortable with the idea of a newsletter devoted to "Stephen King." After all, he is yet a tried-and-true Yankee possessed of that sometimes endearing quality of self-effacement who just might be a little embarrassed by all the fuss. At the same time, he understands his faithful fans need both a source of information about him and an outlet for their comments about their favorite writer.[17]

One of *Castle Rock*'s subscribers—the late Ray Rexer—penned a poem for the occasion:

It's been around for five full years
with stories and reviews,
and screaming editorials
and horrifying news.
For five full years it crammed me full
of Stephen King-ish stuff,
then Mr. Spruce, The Editor,
proclaimed "Enough's enough!"

Enough *was* enough, and with Spruce's departure, King fans were left bereft, with nothing to give them a monthly king-sized fix of news about their favorite writer. Like the Bachman pen name, *Castle Rock* was put to rest.

Cover for *Carrie* (1974), Stephen King's first novel.

Chris Chesley, King's childhood friend, with whom he collaborated
on several self-published projects, at the Harmony Grove Cemetery.

Harmony Grove Cemetery in Durham, Maine, the inspiration for
the fictionalized cemetery of the same name in *'Salem's Lot.*

A local haunt in Durham, Maine, where Chesley's and King's imaginations ran wild.

Runaround Pond in Durham, Maine, which was an inspiration for King's classic coming-of-age story "The Body."

The Shiloh Chapel in Durham, Maine, which is mentioned in *'Salem's Lot* and, guesses Maine writer David Lowell, was probably part of the inspiration for the Marsten House.

Trestle and track in Lisbon Falls, Maine, the small town where
King attended high school.

Chris Spruce, editor/publisher of *Castle Rock*, displays the current issue.

Famous cover story on King in *Time* magazine (October 6, 1986), with an allusion to *It*.

Paul Bunyan—a symbol of Maine's past—looks out across downtown Bangor, Maine.

Stephen King addresses a capacity crowd in Bangor, Maine, at a fund-raiser for the Bangor Public Library.

NOTICE

Electronic Surveillance and Alarm Equipment is in use. Please do not enter the grounds.

Thank you

In the wake of the break-in at the King residence, a sign makes it unmistakably clear that new security measures have been instituted.

Perched on the wrought-iron fence that surrounds the King residence, a three-headed creature stands guard.

Maine writer David Lowell in front of the famous bat-guarded
gate at the King residence.

An Aladdin's Cave of Kingly Treasures: Betts Bookstore's
King collectibles for sale.

Surrounded by fellow Skemers in Betts Bookstore, club founder Michelle Rein shows off her copy of *The Dark Tower IV: Wizard and Glass.*

A week before official publication date, the Grant edition of *Wizard and Glass* makes its first bookstore appearance at Betts Bookstore, displayed by proprietor Stuart Tinker.

King's home is his castle: to shelter the house from prying eyes,
a new row of shrubbery goes up.

❧ 20 ❧

W HEN *The Stand* was originally published in 1978, King was selling millions of copies of his books, but even that didn't give him the editorial clout to force Doubleday to publish the book as he had envisioned—*The Shining* and *The Stand* suffered textually.

In its first incarnation, *The Stand* had been cut to keep the retail price down. To King and his readers, it didn't make any sense; it was one thing to cut a novel that badly needed pruning, but quite another to prune it just to save money on the production costs. According to the *New York Times*:

> King's editor at that time, William G. Thompson, who is now with another publisher, says he edited the manuscript strictly for editorial reasons. "There was no pressure on me to cut it because it was too big," Thompson told the *New York Times*.
>
> However, Thompson left Doubleday before *The Stand* went into production, and according to King, Doubleday's publisher Samuel S. Vaughan, told him that the book would have to be cut even more, to keep the retail price down.
>
> Vaughan, now a senior vp and editor at Random House, says, "Steve has always made me the heavy in the story. It's the book that was heavy. By trying to keep the price down so that it was not prohibitive, we were trying to build the career and sales of a young author."[1]

Considering what a cheap job of manufacturing Doubleday did with the original edition, it's especially hard to justify cost-cutting as the rationale. A clear case of the publisher not knowing his market—thinking that a few dollars would deter a King fan from reading the book—Doubleday forced the issue and cuts were reluctantly made by King, who had the last word— he restored the book to its original length and had it published by the very house that originally published the book years ago.

In the introduction to the new edition—the biggest King book to date— King wrote that "approximately four hundred pages of manuscript [100,000 words] were deleted from the final draft. The reason was not an editorial one; if that had been the case, I would be content to let the book live its life and die its eventual death as it was originally published."[2]

Certainly the success of the Bachman books was a major part in Doubleday's rethinking of this issue. Also, the clamoring fans made it clear that they wanted, even at this late date, the author's vision for the book, not the publisher's.

Doubleday reissued all their other King titles—upgrading the typography, paper stock, binding, and jacket designs to finally produce good-looking books instead of cheap book club editions—in the hope that a new look for all the books would translate to enhanced sales in the bookstores.

In his introduction to the new edition, King made it clear that this was an *expansion* of the original book, reassuring his fans, who wondered if he would take this unique opportunity to rewrite it, to add new plot twists and new characters.

The new *Stand* added 150,000 words, updated the time frame from the eighties to the nineties, and bookended the story with a new beginning and ending. The book also included a dozen pen-and-ink illustrations by Berni Wrightson, whose work enhanced *Cycle of the Werewolf* and, to a lesser extent, *Creepshow*.

A brilliant pen-and-ink artist specializing in the macabre, whose work for *Frankenstein* astonished and delighted his fans, Wrightson produced illustrations for *The Stand* that complemented the text nicely.

The flap copy for *The Stand* read, in part, "For the hundreds of thousands of fans who read *The Stand* in its original version and wanted more, this new edition is Stephen King's gift." It conveniently overlooked the fact that the *reason* the first version had been truncated was that Doubleday forced the issue.

But all of that is history and, the second time around, Doubleday published a classy edition that did justice to the book King called "this dark chest of wonders."[3]

The trade edition was impressive enough, but Doubleday went even further, publishing the signed, limited edition that King had originally conceived in 1978.

The most beautiful edition of any King book ever done, the book was limited to 1,250 numbered copies ($325) and 52 lettered copies (not for sale). Using the motif of the book (a "long tale of dark Christianity")[4] as the starting point for the design, Peter Schneider's vision of the book was positively inspired, matched only by Doubleday's willingness to go the extra mile.

The book itself was bound in black leather, like a Bible, with metallic gold and red foil stamping; the type had been reset and the book had been printed on heavier stock than was used on the trade edition; two-color printing was used, with red ink for ornamental designs and black ink for the main text.

Encasing the book, a varnished wooden box, painted in flat black; the case was lined with red silk, like a coffin. A brass plate, with the title, was affixed to the top of the two-piece box, and to assist in getting this sumptuous book out without upending the box, a red silk ribbon was sewn in, so the book could be slowly raised out of the box.

The book was distributed by allotment through the in-house sales reps, who each got only a few copies. And the dealers who normally carried the King limiteds in the fantasy field found themselves cut out, for the most part, unless they had Doubleday accounts. Regardless, this was clearly a case in which demand would *far* exceed supply—a demand so frenzied that Doubleday turned down prepublications offers of up to $1,250 for guaranteed copies.

Clearly a showcase book, a prestige book, the limited edition of *The Stand: The Complete & Uncut Edition* soon became one of the hottest King collectibles ever, since this was *the* edition of *the* book that King fans preferred above all others, as King noted:

> So here is *The Stand*, Constant Reader, as its author originally intended for it to roll out of the showroom. All its chrome is now intact, for better or for worse. And the final reason for presenting this version is the simplest. Although it has never been my favorite novel, it is the one people who like my books seem to like the most.[5]

Like it? Hell, they *loved* it! No matter what else King had written, this was *the* book his fans rallied around. So, they asked, what about the rumored film adaptation?

Fans had mixed feelings: Fearing that an unfaithful adaptation would mar their memories of their best-loved book, some of them argued that no film adaptation should be done. The book, they asserted, should be left alone. Others, however, felt differently, asserting that given enough time and money, a faithful adaptation *could* be done, that not every King book-turned-movie had to be a disaster.

King wrote:

> I am inevitably asked if it is ever going to be a movie. The answer, by the way, is probably yes. Will it be a good one? I don't know. . . . But in the end, I think it's perhaps best for Stu, Larry, Glen, Frannie, Ralph,

Tom Cullen, Lloyd, and that dark fellow to belong to the reader, who will visualize them through the lens of imagination in a vivid and constantly changing way no camera can duplicate. . . . The glory of a good tale is that it is limitless and fluid; a good tale belongs to each reader in its own particular way.[6]

Benefiting from the brouhaha surrounding the reissue of *The Stand*, Viking's *Four Past Midnight* went to press with 1.2 million copies. A big book—763 pages—*Four Past Midnight* was, like *Different Seasons*, not a novel but a collection of novellas, which made comparisons between the two books inevitable.

"When this book is published," King wrote, in the introduction to *Four Past Midnight*, ". . . I will have been sixteen years in the business of make-believe." Along the way, King wrote, "I had become, by some process I still do not fully understand, America's literary boogeyman. . . ."[7]

In retrospect it's easy to see how King would come to be labeled the leading spooksman, as it were, for the field: No other writer had achieved the popular success King had enjoyed, nor the visibility. Certainly the movies contributed to that, as did his cameo appearances in some of them, but the frequent television appearances on network talk shows, the profiles and interviews in the print media, and the American Express ad—all contributed to making him a household name. King, the writer, had also become King the celebrity, to people who had never read his books or seen his movies but knew of him by name.

Four Past Midnight is not *Different Seasons*, as King acknowledges in his introductory note. *Different Seasons*, he noted, was a collection of four undeniably powerful stories, each with its own virtues, with all but one story devoid of the supernatural element that had become King's trademark. "I knew it was good; I also knew that I'd probably never publish another book exactly like it in my life," King wrote.[8]

Four Past Midnight stands apart from its predecessor, alike only in its number of stories. Each story is prefaced by King's usual, chatty introduction, and all are horror stories; but beyond that, the stories are strikingly dissimilar. "The Langoliers," "Secret Window, Secret Garden," "The Library Policeman," and "The Sun Dog" have no relationship to the others, each exploring in its own way "Time, for instance, and the corrosive effects it can have on the human heart. The past, and the shadows it throws upon the present—shadows where unpleasant things sometimes grow and even more unpleasant things hide . . . and grow fat."[9]

"The Langoliers" is, if anything, a nod to the past, the kind of story that would have made a fine episode of *Twilight Zone*. In this story, a red-eye flight from L.A. to Boston is anything but routine: All but a dozen passengers can be accounted for—the rest have mysteriously vanished—and when the plane lands in Bangor, Maine, it becomes clear that the landscape of the world as they know it is changing . . . the Langoliers, racing across the land, headed toward them, are in the process of literally erasing the world.

"Secret Window, Secret Garden" is a riff on *Dark Half*, completing a trilogy, as it were, of stories about the art of story making. According to King, between the writing of *Misery* and *The Dark Half*, "I started to think that there might be a way to tell both stories at the same time by approaching some of the plot elements of *The Dark Half* from a totally different angle."[10]

This dichotomous approach, which King would use to even greater effect years later, was perfect for this story, which tells of a writer, Mort Rainey, who is accused by John Shooter of plagiarism.

"The Library Policeman" had its genesis in an offhand remark King's youngest son, Owen, made over the breakfast table about his fears of returning a book because it was overdue and he feared the Library Police; it foreshadowed a longer work to come, *Gerald's Game*. Ostensibly the story of Sam Peebles, who forgets to return an overdue book, the story soon takes on a sinister tone that explores childhood horrors long since forgotten, buried deep in his memory, in his abused past.

Fascinated by the Polaroid cameras that spit out instant prints and develop before your eyes, King ". . . became fascinated with this camera. . . . The more I thought about them, the stranger they seemed. They are, after all, not just images but moments of time . . . and there is something so *peculiar* about them."[11]

Developing that story idea, a haunted Polaroid camera spits out photos of ordinary scenes that, in the background, inexplicably shows a dog approaching in leaps and bounds, but to what end?

Besides its nod to the past—Pop Merrill's nephew is Ace Merrill from "The Body"—"The Sun Dog" is a nod toward the future. It is an appropriate story with which to close this collection, an appetizer that reacquaints readers with Castle Rock, where a storm is now brewing—a storm with cataclysmic results for the town, bedeviled by Satan.

For King, the book is a bridge that straddles the past and links it to the future, eschewing the safety net of writing about familiar things in favor of trying new things, new methods of storytelling.

Painfully aware of the passage of time, King, who turned forty-two as the decade changed to the nineties, realized that, as a writer, it was time for him to move on creatively:

> I'll never leave Maine behind, but Castle Rock became more and more real to me. It got to the point where I could draw maps of the place. On the one hand, it was a welcoming place to write about. But there is a downside to that. You become complacent; you begin to accept boundaries; the familiarity of the place discourages risks. So I am burning my bridges and destroying the town. It's all gone—kaput. It's sad but it had to be done.[12]

It's Halloween night in Bangor and the teenagers too old for trick or treat line up at the multiplex theater in town, dressed in costumes ranging from the traditional to the unconventional. They aren't in line waiting to buy a ticket to *Graveyard Shift*, because that night, all the tickets are free. It is the world premiere of *Graveyard Shift* that draws the local media in full force, since Stephen King will be present for the press conference—one of his few public appearances on Halloween in Bangor—along with John Esposito, who wrote the screenplay, and William J. Dunn, who co-produced the film.

Shot entirely in Maine, the film pumped $3 million into Maine's coffers, in Bangor, Lewiston, and Lisbon Center.

Seated at a table, the three men at the table were a study in contrasts: John Esposito, the screenwriter, looked nervous; William Dunn looked relaxed; and Stephen King, who had done this countless times, looked world-weary but accommodating, smiling on cue as cameras flashed and the television cameras trained their lenses on him, neatly ignoring the other two.

Based on a one-note story that was reprinted in *Night Shift*, *Graveyard Shift* is the story of a drifter, John Hall, who gets a job at the Bachman Mills in Gates Falls, Maine. As in the short story, the conflict is between Hall and the overbearing foreman of the mill, Warwick, who descend into the pit of the mill, the basement, where they find mutated rats.

Putting his best foot forward and his best face on, King told the media:

> *Graveyard Shift* was written by this 22-year-old kid who sold two pieces of fiction beforehand, both to specialty magazines. That kid was still in school when the story was written and rewritten. It's a very early piece of work. It is in fact the second earliest piece of fiction I've ever included in any of my published works.
>
> This movie was put together years later by seasoned people who have worked in this field a long time, in any number of capacities.

In a way, John Esposito and I are the perfect team, in terms of him adapting my material, because we were both starting out, cutting our teeth. And you have advantages that balance off the disadvantages of being new—boundless enthusiasm, which John has, and the ability to go for it all, which is automatic when you're starting off.

Whether or not *Graveyard Shift* does the job in terms of art, I don't much care. It works in terms of sitting back and putting your feet up and watching the movie and having a good time.

We'll let Martin Scorsese and those guys take care of themselves; they didn't make this movie—*this* movie was made by cannibals.[13]

To be fair to all the parties involved in *Graveyard Shift*, the original story simply didn't merit a motion picture treatment. At best, it would have been perfect for *Creepshow* or *Creepshow 2*, but the only justification for a movie is a story that requires two hours for its telling, which this movie clearly did not need.

Predictably, reviewers jumped on this one, calling it everything short of *Graveyard Shit*. The *Washington Post* said, "The acting and directing are substandard. Even the hackneyed plot is barely turned over. . . . Even the jaws of life couldn't extricate this film from the quick burial it deserves."[14]

The *Washington Post* expected far too much. This was a "check your brains at the door" movie, with no pretensions of greatness. Since it couldn't terrify or horrify, it went for the gross-out—the dictum King followed when writing horror fiction—and, if nothing else, the movie's focus on rats in every permutation certainly achieved *that* objective!

Graveyard Shift was soon put out of its misery, but King fans would find a real treat in *Misery*, the next Rob Reiner–directed King project to make it into the theaters. Featuring standout performances by James Caan (as Paul Sheldon) and Kathy Bates (as Annie Wilkes), *Misery* brought nothing but happiness to everyone involved in the project—especially Bates, who received both a Golden Globe Award and an Academy Award for her performance as the deranged fan who held Sheldon hostage.

As with "The Body," *Misery* appealed to Reiner because it stood on its own merits, not relying on King's name or supernatural trappings to sell the movie:

The thing that drew me to the book was not that it was a suspense thriller genre—that's not what I was interested in doing next. What I was drawn to was the theme: the artist's dilemma in attaining a certain success, and the fear of breaking away from that in an attempt to grow and change, and the fear that you'll lose your audience.[15]

As King said, for any creative person, the story at the heart of *Misery* is a very real fear: having to repeat yourself, by popular demand, and never being able to fulfill your creative vision, which by its very nature demands breaking the mold and venturing far afield.

Kathy Bates, like Reiner, is not a horror fan per se, but she had dealt with the horror of having a last name that recalled *Psycho*, an association from which she never could escape, as the witless indulged themselves at her expense:

> It's an old, tired joke. I leave my name at a restaurant or the dentist, and someone says, "Oh, like in Norman Bates—a relative of yours? I've admired King's work over the years, but I'm not a horror devotee. I read metaphysics and Jung and occasionally Clive Barker. I'm an eclectic reader. . . . After this film, it'll start again. More Norman Bates references, and *People* magazine will refer to me as Kathy "Misery" Bates. Everybody wants to type you. There's a human urge to pigeonhole. It's just rampant in Hollywood.[16]

The pigeonholing occurred not only in Hollywood but in the larger world as well, which by now had been so desensitized to King's name in connection with film adaptations that it prejudiced potential viewers.

As with *Stand by Me*, King's association was wisely downplayed, to give the movie a chance to stand on its own merits. The movie poster, in fact, has the names of Caan and Bates atop the title, set in a large typewriter-like typeface, with the slugline beneath it: "Paul Sheldon writes for a living. Now, he's writing to stay alive." Beneath that, a single house, lit from within, in shadows from the Colorado mountains, as a snowstorm descends at night; and, in *tiny* type at the bottom, the credits . . . including King's name, in tiny type—a contrast to how his book publishers print his name, bigger than the title, on all his books.

Lightning can accidentally strike twice, but in this case, it was a well-placed thunderbolt. Reiner's instincts had proven to be unerringly accurate, once again.

USA Today sang its praises in an understated review. Mindful of the critical drubbing King had gotten over the years by film critics, which scared off viewers, the newspaper reassured them: "Though *Pet Sematary* and *Grave-yard Shift* have inspired countless moviegoer moratoriums on Stephen King adaptations, even non-fans might consider giving *Misery* a shot."[17]

There's no question that a King story presents formidable obstacles for any-one seeking to adapt the work from print to film, while trying to preserve the texture of the prose—an admittedly difficult task, unless the book is action-packed. Now, throw in the need for expensive special effects to con-vince the audience to suspend disbelief, and what is relatively easy to do in print becomes an expensive proposition on the screen.

King's shorter works—principally novellas and short novels—have, by and large, made the transition most successfully, but movies have a time con-straint that further complicates King adaptations: a film must run between 90 to 120 minutes, so trying to shoehorn a novel like *It* or *The Stand* into a standard film is virtually impossible, without paring the story to the bone, which makes it pointless to produce the film in the first place.

The answer, some thought, was to adapt King to television. Mindful of the advantages a miniseries offers—enough time to tell the story, stretched out over multiple nights—the medium had two disadvantages: the need to work within the restrictions of television censorship standards, and the dis-ruptive effect of commercials airing every fifteen minutes.

With the widespread popularity of video, however, even those two con-cerns could be overcome: additional footage could be added in the video version, providing a reason to rent it; and commercials could either be placed up front as coming attractions or after the main feature.

With that in mind, *It* aired on ABC-TV over two nights in November 1990, spaced a day apart. Haunted by the memories of *'Salem's Lot* when it was adapted in 1979, King fans hoped for the best but expected the worst. After all, this was no mean feat: the novel, one of King's most complex, ran 1,138 pages. Covering two time frames and seven main characters, it was no easy task to adapt *It*.

Fortunately, the $12 million production, directed by Tommy Lee Wallace, pulled the proverbial rabbit out of the hat.

Understandably, reviewers felt—as they did when the book was pub-lished—that the story of the children, set in the past, was more evocative than the story of the children as adults, set in the present:

> The film seems best when it centers on the children. Indeed, the cast of
> young actors is superior to their adult counterparts mainly because the

script is more interesting, and palpable, when it deals with the horrors of childhood. . . . [King] should write more often about children because he's got a touch for reaching this level of innocence.[18]

Fittingly, with the eighties behind him, and the nineties ahead, it was a time for reflection, for King and everyone else as well. The biographical note on the dust jacket for *Four Past Midnight* underscored King's considerable achievement: "His first novel, *Carrie*, was published in 1974, and the 1980s saw him become America's bestselling writer of fiction. He's glad to be held over into the new decade."

Looking back, *The Magazine of Fantasy and Science Fiction* honored King with one of its rare cover stories, which previously had been done only a handful of times: Ray Bradbury, Isaac Asimov, and Harlan Ellison had also been so honored for their body of work and contributions to the field.

In his editorial, then editor-publisher, Edward Ferman, said simply, "Stephen King is unique." The issue then served up its tasty dishes, including "The Moving Finger," written especially for this issue; "The Bear," an excerpt from the front part of the third Dark Tower novel, to be published the following year in Grant's edition; a critical overview of King's career by writer/critic A. J. Budrys, and a bibliography of primary and secondary works, by and about him, compiled by one of his secretaries, Marsha DeFilippo.

Appropriately, the issue was published in both a trade and a limited, signed edition, with different cover stock, though the same interior pulp paper stock was used.

In the larger world, outside of fandom, King got kudos, too, for his visibility in the eighties: *Entertainment Weekly*, *People Weekly*, ABC-TV, and *Publishers Weekly*. By any barometer one would care to name, King was more than just a writer—he was a one-man entertainment industry, summed up by *People Weekly*:

> Nothing is as unstoppable as one of King's furies, except perhaps King's word processor. In this decade alone he has spewed out 15 novels that have sold close to 15 million copies. And what of the unliftable? At 1,138 pages, *It* weighed in at 3.5 pounds.
>
> King's popularity reflects his uncanny ability to exploit the anxieties that swirl around the modern American family. His audience—and his victims—are baby boomers, a generation that has had to reconcile the buoyant fantasies of the sixties with the dismaying realities of the nineties. In King's novels, ordinary people suffer appallingly contemporary fates.[19]

❧ 21 ❧

Standing in front of a crowd of 2,700 fans who had gathered in Syracuse, New York, at the Landmark Theater to hear their favorite writer talk, Stephen King told them that he was a "lightning rod" for his fans. In fact, he said, "I had one drop by to visit my wife last week."[1]

Predictably, he drew a big laugh, but as the audience soon learned, it was no laughing matter. "My little episode of terror," as King termed it, shook the Kings out of their complacency, that living in a town like Bangor, so far away from the rest of the country, would be a haven from out-of-town harassers. "Usually those people write, but they don't show up," King told his hometown newspaper.[2]

Erik Keene, a former fast-food restaurant worker who told his boss he was leaving to go to Maine, made the trip from Texas to haunt King's private residence and his office, as well. Keene had "told police . . . he had planned to do something to gain publicity" but nobody could have imagined what resulted.[3]

"He had become enough of a concern that I told a couple of people who work with me to call the police if he came back around," King told his hometown paper.[4]

On April 18, 1991, Keene dropped by King's office, to the surprise of the staff, previously alerted to his presence in town. "Marshal DeFilippo, who works in the office, said Keene wanted King to buy him a pair of contact lenses, house him for a couple of months and keep him supplied with cigarettes and beer."[5]

Keene left the office empty-handed, but sometimes they come back. . . .

Two days later, Keene made good on his word. He trespassed on the property at King's house on West Broadway—easy enough to do, since nothing barred his way.

It was 6 A.M. and the house was empty, except for Tabitha King. Nursing an ailment, she was home alone, while her sons and husband were off at a ballgame in Philadelphia.

She heard glass breaking, assumed it was the cat, but when she entered the kitchen, she saw Keene. "I didn't have time to be scared," Tabitha recalled. "I was just shocked. My body was already making the decision for me. I was already headed toward the door before he told me he had a bomb."[6]

Dressed only in her nightgown, she fled to safety at a neighbor's house. The police were called and, arriving in full force, sealed off the street. They sent in a canine unit to ferret the intruder out. They finally found him, in the attic, with what he called a "handheld detonator unit" made out of "cardboard and some electronic parts from a calculator."[7]

Keene later told the police, "I wanted to get into that attic. I did exactly what I planned to do by going up to that room. I looked at it as compensation for all the effort I went to."[8]

Asked by the police what he would have done if the police hadn't found him, he replied, "I don't know what I would have done, but it's an amusing thing to contemplate, isn't it?"[9]

Nobody—least of all Stephen and Tabitha King—was laughing.

As it turned out, Keene, according to the *Bangor Daily News*, was "on parole from Dallas County for theft." The *News* also reported that "the Texas man said he has been diagnosed as a schizophrenic and said he has spent years taking drugs prescribed by doctors who have treated him. Keene said he wants to write a book with King. He said he is tired of being poor and said he has been discriminated against because he suffered from a mental handicap."[10]

Keene later pleaded innocent to the burglary charge and innocent by reason of insanity to a terrorizing charge. (One wonders about the judicial system: Wouldn't it make more sense if the charge could read *guilty* by reason of insanity?)

Understandably shaken by the turn of events, Stephen King told the hometown newspaper that "after all, we've lived here for twelve years and this is the first time somebody has tried to plant a bomb in the attic."[11]

Realizing that life would never again be the same, King told the hometown newspaper: "I don't want to live like Michael Jackson or like Elvis did at Graceland. That's gross. It was bad enough when we had to put up a fence. It was worse when we had to put up a gate. I hate to think I have to keep that gate locked."[12]

King would not only have to keep the gate locked but the fence was extended, providing 100 percent protection around the property; the exposed driveway was barred with locking gates; and in time, closed-circuit television cameras would be mounted in key surveillance positions around the property and at the office. (The prominently posted signs forbidding trespassing had protected them for years, but no longer.)

After sentencing, Keene was released to Texas authorities:

> The man who broke into author Stephen King's house left town . . . escorted by Texas authorities.
>
> Eric Keene, 26, of San Antonio was extradited back to his home state for violating his parole there.
>
> Keene had been in Penobscot County Jail since his arrest after the April 20 break-in. . . . After his case took an unusual path through the judicial process, he ultimately pleaded guilty to the burglary, and the terrorizing charge was dismissed. He was sentenced late last month to the time he had already spent in jail, but remained there pending the arrival of police from Texas.
>
> During a two-year probationary period, Keene also is to stay away from the Kings and stay out of Penobscot County.
>
> Had Texas decided not to extradite him on the parole violation, his lawyer, Martha J. Harris, would have given him a bus ticket to Texas purchased with money donated by his friends and relatives. . . . Keene has contended that a main character [Annie Wilkes] in Stephen King's book *Misery* was modeled after convicted Texas Baby killer Genene Jones, whom Keene has said is his aunt.[13]

According to the *Bangor Daily News*, that wasn't the end of it. "Keene said he has many troubles. He added he has a lot of things planned if he ever gets out of jail. He said if he gets out he will give King a present 'from the macabre.' "[14]

The Kings were gravely concerned. Tabitha King, in an interview published four years previously, had expressed her concerns about the deranged fan mentality:

> I think it's unhealthy for people to live vicariously through others. John Belushi and Elvis Presley were truly victims of their fame—and hence their fans—because a weak character has no defense against sycophancy. Money and fame attract the self-seeking, who are willing to do anything they want, even if it hurts or kills you, because you can pay for it or because you are Somebody. Mark Chapman's assassination of John Lennon was the result of celebrity worship in a country where the mentally unbalanced have a de facto right to both lethal weapons and access to famous people. Chapman, by his own admission, was out to kill

someone famous; it did not matter to him whether it was John Lennon, or Paul Simon, or Steve [King]—all to whom he made personal approaches. Murder is the ultimate fan possession of the idol. It will happen again, given the American refusal to stop the epidemic of gun murder and the media-enforced insistence that a public person is public property.[15]

That same month, King found himself under attack again, on the legal front:

A woman is suing author Stephen King claiming the horror novelist plagiarized from her writings and based a character in *Misery* on her.

Anne Hiltner, of Princeton, is seeking damages, a share in book profits, and its removal from store shelves.

She claims King stole in 1986 or 1987 eight copyrighted manuscripts written either by her or her brother, James Hiltner.

Hiltner charges the author incorporated parts of her unpublished works into *Misery*.[16]

When the details came out, it was clear that this claim was not only meritless but put forth by someone who clearly believed she was victimized by King:

Anne Hiltner is suing King in New Jersey courts, alleging that the Bangor author broke into her home and a rented storage facility to steal her work. She also claims that King flew over her home in an airplane and eavesdropped with listening devices.

Hiltner, who has been sending letters to King for a decade, also alleged the Wilkes character in *Misery* is based on her life.

In an August 1990 letter to the *News*, Hiltner claimed she was a "victim of the assaultive books by Stephen King, and over 150 burglaries by King in 1990 alone."

Hiltner said in the rambling, unpublished letter that she had filed criminal complaints against King last July with the Bangor Police Department, and that King had called her last August. She also complained of receiving little help from Bangor police.[17]

According to Bangor detective Robert Welch, the meritless lawsuit was subsequently dismissed.

On June 2, 1991, at the New York Hilton, Stephen King sat down to have breakfast with 2,400 people.

One of the name-brand authors at a celebrity breakfast hosted by the

American Booksellers Association for independent booksellers, King—in the company of Dr. Ferrol Sams, Gloria Steinem, ABA president Joyce Mcskis, and NAL's Elaine Koster, all seated at the head table on the stage—eyed the convention attendees who had paid $35 each for crepes, bacon, coffee . . . and a good look at the King of Horror.

Writers at the ABA are commonplace; it is, after all, their moment to stand in the sunlight and bask in the warm recognition that comes with the territory of being a scribe for hire. But, to be honest, if you want to get people up early and pay good money to see and hear someone talk, it had better be a name-brand celebrity . . . and who better than Stephen King?

The assembled crowd talked politely among themselves before the people at the head table took their seats, but when King entered, a murmur swept through the room. All eyes were on him; this was clearly not just any writer but the biggest writer in the country, live and up front!

Had King talked first, the room might have emptied out slowly as each speaker took the stand, so King was wisely scheduled to speak last.

Dr. Sams spoke first. A Southern gentleman from Georgia, an entertaining speaker who gave an amusing talk ("If mama ain't happy, ain't *nobody* happy!"), he peppered it with jokes and homilies, having such a grand time that he went over his allotted time, cutting into Steinem's allotment.

Gloria Steinem followed, using the opportunity to promote her new book, *Revolution from Within: A Book of Self-Esteem*; like Sams, she, too, ran over the allotted time.

The cumulative effect: King was left with very little time to speak.

Finally, with only minutes left before the conclusion of the breakfast talks, King was introduced by Joyce Meskis, who recapped his career:

> It was the first work of a man who in catering to a public's worst nightmares would become a publisher's dream. It was the start of a record-breaking career that would redefine a genre and would push publishing into numbers that movie producers dream about. The book was *Carrie* and the author was Stephen King.
>
> Seventeen years and a phenomenal thirty books later, Stephen King has over 150 million copies of his books sold, and had a record five books on the various *New York Times* bestseller lists simultaneously last winter.
>
> His catalog of novels read like a "Who's Who" of the horror world: *It, Four Past Midnight, The Dark Half, The Stand*, and *Needful Things*.
>
> But how has King managed to grasp the minds and raise the blood pressure of the world's readers so consistently? How is he able to make

us care about killer clowns, malevolent cars, pet cemeteries and their remains? Why is he so incredibly popular?

It isn't just great writing, although he is a great writer; it is perhaps we tend to think of him as ours—America's Horror Writer Laureate. Where he leads, we gleefully follow. And whatever he writes, no matter how outrageous, we believe it.[18]

When Meskis called him "America's Horror Writer Laureate," King reacted, hitting the table with his fist, making the silverware clatter, to the laughter of the audience.

Meskis took her seat and King rose to the podium, as well as to the occasion, and spoke extemporaneously, as he had the audience figuratively eating out of his hands, hungry to hear the best-selling writer in America finally speak.

King reminisced about his mother, her love of reading, his role as a writer, and his appreciation for the booksellers who helped make him a success. He reminded the audience that

> Writers, novelists in particular, are actually supposed to be secret agents. We're supposed to be observers, but not observed. We're supposed to look around, record these things with our unblinking gimlet eyes, and take it back for the delectation of the rest—particularly a guy like me who lives with one foot in the twilight zone most of the time. And it used to be that way. I did not used to be a recognizable face.[19]

Cut short by the clock, King concluded, "You are the people who have allowed me to do for money what I would otherwise have done for free anyway," and sat down to loud, sustained applause.

After the talk, the writers held a press conference in a small room downstairs, in the bowels of the convention center, to answer questions from the media, waiting patiently for their arrival.

King, on automatic pilot, took questions from the media, answering the same questions he'd heard a million times before:

"How can a first-time author get published?"

King responded, "I'm not sure what you do about it. As to my own success, I was lucky enough to have a book that was adapted into a film that was a success. I've always wondered, if *Carrie* the film had been a failure, would I be where I am today? I'd like to think so, but who knows? I think it's something of a crapshoot, but I'll tell you one thing I do believe: talent almost always finds the light, even today. If you need proof of that, look at Amy Tan, who is a fantastic success story and deserves every bit of it. I just wish as many people knew Katherine Dunn, who wrote *Geek Love*, as know Amy Tan."

A caustic New York reporter from the *New York Times* asked, *What scares you?*

World-weary from answering that old chestnut a million times, King got a glimpse at her name tag and said, "the *New York Times*," which brought laughter from the crowd. The reporter realized she had been neatly skewered. King, no country bumpkin, was able to think on his feet.

Miffed because she didn't think her question was being taken seriously, she shot back, "Play it straight. Answer the question."

King, decided to rescue the reporter from her public embarrassment by answering at length, in as serious a tone as possible.

"The answer is the answer I gave," he began. "I think that the things that scare me are reading about what's happening to the environment, the destruction of the rain forest. I still wish that I didn't know about the statistics about the constant rate at which it's disappearing and what's happening to the atmosphere of the planet as a result."

Recalling an incident in which his flight was held up so an actor playing Ronald McDonald could also catch the flight, King, who sat next to the actor in first class, added: "And I think what's worse is this sort of existential comedy to make more grasslands to make more cows, so McDonald's can make more hamburgers, so Ronald McDonald can ride on the plane next to me. We're destroying the Earth for Ronald McDonald. Think about it. And they say *I* write horror."

The reference to horror sparked a question about *American Psycho*, a novel by Bret Easton Ellis which had been boycotted by the Los Angeles chapter of the National Organization for Women on the grounds that it was a how-to manual on the torture and murder of women. Since King was seated next to Gloria Steinem, the question was inevitable, but he fielded it easily, like a pop fly.

"*American Psycho*," he said, "is a disturbing book. It's disturbing because it's very difficult for me to separate my feelings of revulsion about what's going on in the book, and the violence that's directed across a broad spectrum, and not just toward women. It's directed toward the homeless, toward men and toward animals. It's hard for me to separate that from my pervasive feeling that something is really going on in that book, that Ellis is trying very hard to express an entire attitude of an entire alienated culture.

"The people in the book are extremely nasty, yet there is a ring of reality that can't be denied. At the same time, whatever he did, I don't feel he succeeded at it very well; and I think that in order to find out what Ellis was reaching for, you have to go back to some of the great naturalistic Grove Press books in the late fifties and sixties. I'm thinking of *City of Night* and *The Last Exit to Brooklyn*.

"So my feelings about the book are ambivalent, but ambivalent on the downside."

After more questions, fielded by King and Steinem, King made a surprise appearance in the main exhibition hall where his publisher, Penguin USA, had a corridor lined with booths.

As King made his way through the crowd, standing head and shoulders above the long trail of people that followed him—a trail that grew larger as he made his way through the hall—surprised attendees pointed to him and whispered, "Look! That's Stephen King!"

King arrived at one of the booths and, surrounded by a sea of people, signed copies of his books, promotional postcards for *Needful Things* ("Stephen King bids farewell to Castle Rock . . . Parting is such sweet horror."), and anything else pressed into his hands.

That evening, King attended a private party in his honor, at a nearby restaurant, the Café Society. According to the *Washington Post*, King took to the stage when John Cafferty and the Beaver Brown Band began to play. "King, a frustrated rocker, got up, grabbed a guitar and played (passably) and sang (too softly) 'Twist and Shout' and 'Whole Lotta Shaking Goin' On.'"

Sometimes, they come back. Dino de Laurentiis, who had closed his North Carolina studio in Wilmington that served up *Maximum Overdrive* and other forgettable movies, shifted from films to television adaptations, which were then released in theaters around the world.

Because *It* had done well in the ratings—a fact that did not escape the attention of De Laurentiis—he decided that since he still had rights to several King short stories, he'd adapt one for television. As a result, "Sometimes They Come Back," a story that had been published in *Cavalier* twelve years earlier, surfaced as a potential made-for-TV movie.

In the summer of 1991, "Sometimes They Come Back" aired on CBS.

The production company, named Come Back Productions, hired Tom McLoughlin to direct, based on a screenplay by Lawrence Konner and Mark Rosenthal.

McLoughlin, who rose to the occasion, was a baby boomer who felt that his generation, which included filmmakers like George Lucas and Steven

Spielberg, ". . . were all shaped by the same influences. So I can see where King is coming from. And I can appreciate King's genius for reinterpreting and drawing on those common influences."[21]

Like "Maximum Overdrive" when adapted to the screen, "Sometimes They Come Back" would have been perfect for a thirty-minute adaptation for a television anthology series, but the story didn't justify the additional length.

But as long as King's name had currency in the film and television industries, options on King's stories, like "Sometimes They Come Back," would be exercised.

The critical drubbings, though, were reserved for the sequels that had nothing in common with King's work, except the name connected to an earlier production—*Return to 'Salem's Lot* comes to mind, as do the endless *Children of the Corn* sequels, and *The Lawnmower Man II.* (When rights were sold to those original stories, option clauses allowed for sequels, as a condition of the original sale.)

King, however, now called the shots, so when CBS wanted a major King project, King proposed an original miniseries, which was for CBS a consolation prize of sorts. What CBS *really* wanted was King as the host of a horror anthology show, like *The Twilight Zone.* What they got was King's script and King, along with Richard P. Rubinstein, as a co-producer for *Stephen King's Golden Years.*

Jonathan Levin, CBS vice president of drama development, was happy but obviously not as happy as he would have been if he had been able to get King to go "booga booga" with his fright mask on—an image that King, in later years, would try to tone down, citing that horror wasn't *all* he wrote. As Levin told *USA Today,* " 'Golden Years' comes out of years of pursuit, but the end result was not what we originally intended."[22]

For King, the idea of doing an original miniseries had a certain appeal for him that his other television productions did not—*Stephen King's Golden Years* was an original presentation, from start to finish:

> In "Stephen King's Golden Years," Keith Szarbajaka . . . stars as Harlan Williams, a 70-year-old janitor who works at Falco Plains, a secret government lab located in upstate New York. Nearing retirement age, Harlan's fears about losing his job are soon eclipsed by a terrible explosion that occurs in the lab of Dr. Richard Todhunter (Bill Raymond), killing two assistants and exposing Harlan to an unknown combination of mysterious chemicals. Following the accident, General

Louis Crewes (Ed Lauter), who runs Falco Plains, has his head of security, Terrilynn Spann (Felicity Huffman), launch an investigation into the cause of the explosion. Spann soon begins to focus on Harlan and his recovery and is eventually joined by a government investigator Jude Andrews (R. D. Call), who may have his own reasons for keeping the accident a secret.

Though the doctors and Harlan himself detect no adverse effects from his proximity to the explosion, it is Harlan's loving wife Gina (Frances Sternhagen) who begins to notice subtle signs that all is not well with her husband. It is Gina's discovery that Harlan has somehow changed that begins an adventure for the couple, who discover that they have as much to fear from the lab authorities and the government as they do from any combination of chemicals.[23]

With considerable prepublicity, CBS launched the miniseries with a two-hour opener, to be followed by six more installments, one hour each.

Unfortunately, its slow pacing proved to be a major disappointment. As Matt Roush of *USA Today* observed, the miniseries was "too slow out of the gate" and, after getting underway, was "a bit shy of action in successive weeks."[24]

In reading a King novel, patience is a virtue. His readers have been conditioned to a slow pace. A King novel will unfold slowly, as you get to know the characters individually, and come to care about their lives. In TV land, however, the remote control rules, and if you can't keep and hold the viewer's attention, then the bored viewer will go channel surfing, in search of more engaging fare.

As the miniseries unfolded at its glacial pace, it was clear that this was not so much a miniseries as a major investment of time. Predictably, viewers yawned and tuned out permanently. As the series progressed, they tuned out in greater numbers and ratings continued to plummet.

The original hope was that the miniseries would justify expansion into a regular series, but that wasn't in the cards. The last installment that aired did end with the tagline, "To be continued," but not on TV, as it turned out; viewers who had stuck it out would have to rent the video.

For King, the best thing that came out of the summer was the Grant edition of *The Dark Tower III: The Waste Lands*. It had been four interminably long years since his fans were able to follow Roland on his quest for the Dark Tower.

A handsome hardback, with single-page and double-page illustrations by Ned Dameron in full color, and decorations in black and white, *The Waste Lands* was a literary tour de force, wrote *Locus* magazine's Edward Bryant:

> While clearly a symphony of traveling music, the novel is rather like an enormous chapter in some sort of cosmic radio serial. It's got so much color and bizarre imagery, so much action and speedily shifting backdrops, a new reader can probably get along relatively fine with only the cursory synopsis of the first two volumes the author provides. But be warned. . . . This third installment is full of converging plot lines, action scenes, stories within stories, and a bit of metaphysics. . . . One of the astonishments of these books is King's seemingly cavalier but still utterly coherent method of merging science fictional constructs with irrational fantasy. He shoves the superficially disparate concepts together with such force, the generated heat melds the elements. . . .
>
> King has suggested he doesn't think the "Gunslinger" novels are quite as attractive to the mainstream of his readers as are such fare as *Needful Things* or *Pet Sematary*. I suspect he's right. The simplest reason may be the quality of strangeness. So much of King's most popular storytelling is based on familiar, everyday jills and joes getting caught up in extraordinary circumstances. . . .
>
> It's not that this sideline of Stephen King is bad, not that it's difficult, non-entertaining, or unreadable in any way. It's just that it's strangely unfamiliar, dissimilar to anything else the author is doing. And if the imagination itself can be considered a bone that supports the musculature, flesh, and hide of a writer's private associative creative processes, then I suspect this work of King's cuts close to it.[25]

Put differently, complacency for a writer is a form of slow death. That, in fact, is one of the themes of *Misery*—the ultimate writer's horror of being *forced* to write, again and again, the same book, to please an audience that doesn't want to grow, to stretch with the writer.

For that reason, King felt it was necessary to move on, beyond the town limits of Castle Rock, Maine, a place that had become too familiar. Said King:

> It's easy to dig yourself a rut and furnish it. I've done that a little bit in Castle Rock. Going back to Castle Rock for me has been like going home and slipping into an old smoking jacket or an old pair of blue jeans and settling down. After a while, I started to feel excessively comfortable in Castle Rock.
>
> I don't think that's a good state for a novelist to be in, particularly if

you're in my situation and you've sold a lot of books. Let's face it: When you become extremely popular and you command extremely big bucks, bloat sets in no matter what you do. I'm just trying to postpone it as long as possible.[26]

Needful Things, subtitled *The Last Castle Rock Story*, struck different chords with the reviewers. *Publishers Weekly*, which is right more often than not, said that ". . . King bids a magnificent farewell to the fictional Maine town where much of his previous work has been set. Of grand proportion, the novel ranks with King's best, in both plot and characterization. . . . King, like Leland Gaunt, knows just what his customers want."[27]

Others felt the novel was a near miss, certainly not in the first rank of King's fiction. Joe Queenan gleefully fired away in the *New York Times Book Review* at a target so big you couldn't miss it: 690 pages in length, *Needful Things* took a broadside hit from Queenan:

Yes, the maestro of the macabre, the czar of the zany, the sultan of shock, the liege of loathsomeness, is back with another of his gruesome novels, this time bidding farewell to Castle Rock, Maine, the site of so much mayhem in his previous books. . . . If [the plot] sounds a tad adolescent, well, it is. *Needful Things* is not the sort of book that one can readily recommend to the dilettante, to the dabbler or to anyone with a reasonable-size brain. It is the type of book that can be enjoyed only by longtime aficionados of the genre, people who probably have a lot of black T-shirts in their chest of drawers and either have worn or have dreamed of wearing a baseball cap backward. Big, dumb, plodding and obvious, Mr. King's books are the literary equivalent of heavy metal.[28]

Queenan, who clearly wore blinders that made it impossible to read the book without dismissing it out of hand because he felt it was horror fare for the simpleminded, must have read only the dust jacket, or perhaps had speed-read the novel, because the book clearly stands on its own, without the crutch of having to appeal to horror fans alone. (Case in point: If it *did* appeal only to horror fans, how could Viking have sold over a million copies? It just doesn't parse.)

The best that any writer can hope for is that a book is read with an open mind; but as King knew, his reputation as a celebrity threw a long shadow over everything else, so reviewers—as he pointed out before—were more apt to review his book contracts than the books, blinded by the money paid for them, blinded by the large first printings, and blinded by the erroneous assumption that if it is popular and sells a lot of copies, it must not be good.

Writers are sometimes better off not reading their reviews, because the mean-spirited reviewers don't review best-selling books but the personality, as Professor Walter Kendrick had done in the *Washington Post*:

> Given the chance, [King] seems to say, we'd all blow our neighbors' brains out for the sake of our needful things. A mean message from America's most popular novelist. But King has spat in his readers' faces before, and they have lapped it up. I can only suppose that King's millions of fans agree with him on the amoral, vicious, brain-dead disgustingness of their fellow Americans. Now that's a scary thought.[29]

King, who rarely responds to any reviews, made an exception in this case. In a letter to the editor, King cited Kendrick's review as "a combination of academic arrogance, elitism and critical insularity," and said that "a critic's interest in statistics . . . usually says more about his shortcomings as a reader than his subject's shortcomings as a writer."[30] King put things in their proper perspective:

> At one point in his jeremiad—one cannot quite call it a review— Kendrick states that I have achieved my success as a popular writer over the bleeding bodies of reviewers who have pointed out my lack of moral vision and inability to deal with any concepts larger, say, than my own bank account. That is absolutely not true. I have never stepped over a bleeding reviewer in my life. I have stepped over a few who were bleating, however, as I now intend to do with Kendrick.[31]

Dr. Michael Collings, another academic, felt quite differently from Kendrick. Collings, who called them as he saw them, wrote:

> What would happen if a twentieth-century avatar of The Mysterious Stranger or The Man That Corrupted Hadleyburg decided to open a shop called "Needful Things" in the small New England town of Castle Rock and began selling dreams?
>
> In *Needful Things* the result is a chain of interlocking horrors that culminates in King's starkest, most powerful confrontation of the Dark powers and the White. . . . The result is a powerful tale of sin and redemption—sins past, long thought hidden and safe, as well as sins present; and redemption through trial and suffering and forgiveness. King uses horror, terror, fantasy, and magic to define fundamental human states, leading to an unequivocal conjuring of the White against the Black, a motif he has worked within a number of his novels.
>
> If *Needful Things* represents a capstone to a segment of King's career,

it is an appropriate one, taking leave of a familiar landscape by imbuing it with a forceful, complex, and ultimately uplifting parable of good and evil.[32]

Makes one wonder if Kendrick and Collings had read the same novel. . . .

Fall, trumpeted NAL, belongs to King! *Needful Things* was the first volley, but if you were in a bookstore that fall, you couldn't help noticing King's books everywhere: the mountains of *Needful Things*, the stand-up cardboard book dumps with headers that contained paperbacks of his books, and—wanting to tap into the collector's market—the first three books in the "Collectors Edition," a new series that would repackage all of King's fiction in uniform editions.

On the surface, the idea seemed like a good one. But below the surface, the idea—the brainchild of Michael Fragnito, an executive at Penguin USA—showed a misconception of the collector's market.

Backed with extensive promotion, *Carrie*, *'Salem's Lot*, and *The Shining* were published in first printings of 65,000 copies; the only difference between the existing texts and this series was the newly commissioned introductions—suggested by Plume's editor-in-chief, Elaine Koster.

The series, from the collector's point of view, was not steak, as NAL had hoped. Collectors had a big beef with the books, since these were not hardbacks and, more to the point, were not signed or numbered. In fact, the marketing behind this series seems to suggest that Penguin USA could create a collector's mentality among King's mainstream readers by merely offering a uniformly designed, new edition of King's fiction, albeit attractively packaged and reasonably priced.

Had the series been published in hardback, in a uniform edition, it might have tapped into the larger market—the same market that Book-of-the-Month Club tapped into with its "Stephen King Library," which was nothing more than King's canon reprinted in hardback, in red boards, in a uniform edition. (Those books, at least, *looked* good on the shelves.)

Though NAL did publish another three titles—*Cujo*, *The Dead Zone*, and *Firestarter*—the series never caught fire, and no further books in the series were published.

Fortunately, Plume did have a "no lose" King book on its hands for the Christmas trade. In December, a mere three months after Grant published his hardback edition of *The Dark Tower III: The Waste Lands*, a $15 Plume trade paperback reprint shipped over a million copies into stores nationwide, killing the sales of the $38 Grant edition.

Like *Needful Things*, *The Waste Lands* was omnipresent in bookstores nationwide. For King fans, it was a bonanza: not one but two new King novels!

Like any best-selling author, King is sought out by civic groups, bookstores, librarians, and other organizations that want to see him live and up front. Being able to pick and choose where he appears, King chooses carefully, knowing that his presence will be a big draw, attracting many thousands of readers who would pay money to see him.

On November 22, 1991, King made one of his rare public appearances, for a public benefit, Voices Louder Than Words. On a rainy night at the Sanders Theater at Harvard, the eight hundred attendees paid $10 (to hear the lectures) or $50 (to hear the lectures, get a copy of the trade edition of *Voices Louder Than Words*, and attend the reception), with the proceeds going to benefit the homeless.

After the other speakers had gotten up and delivered their talks, it was time for King to be introduced by another brand-name writer:

> My name is Robert Parker, and I'm sort of stuck. I'm supposed to introduce Stephen King. His publisher had promised to send me a biography, and they didn't. So how do I know what to say? Which one *is* he? [*Audience laughs.*]
>
> Well, being adroit, I'm going to wing it and maybe some of you out there are familiar with his work. You probably are. He is, after all, the most successful author in the entire world. Trying to explain his success, one reviewer said King is a force of nature, and I guess he *is* a force of nature. Reviewers know these things.
>
> But there are perhaps some less exotic reasons for his success, as well.
>
> For instance, he writes with a kind of fluent grace that makes every story flow like wine from a bottle. Everything he writes sounds as if it were easy to do, and maybe it is for Steve. But how come nobody *else* does it?
>
> Steve writes about the felt surface of life better than anyone else I know. He catches the odd grandeur of ordinariness the way Shakespeare could, for instance, and the way John Updike can; the way Melville could not, and the way Mailer can't. But more than that, in ways beyond my powers to explain them, his imagination seems to vibrate in precise consonance with our collective imagination, the way I wish *mine* would, for instance.

May I add finally that I've known Stephen King for, maybe, fifteen years, and aside from being a force of nature, he's a pretty good guy.

What's also nice is that he's just as good a guy now as he was when I met him fifteen years ago when he was merely successful. [*Audience laughs.*]

I have always liked Stephen King. I have always wished him well . . . but not *this* well. [*Loud audience laughter.*]

Ladies and gentlemen . . . *Stephen King!*[33]

"Thank you, Bob," King began. "I had a lot of mean things I was going to say about you, but you shot me out of the saddle. You've mellowed. But one thing I will repeat that was just too good to let go: fifteen years is a long time." King noting that Parker was heavyset, decided it was time to make a gentle joke. "I remember Bob when he still *had* a neck."

The audience roared with laughter—these two good old boys were just having fun with each other—and King, knowing he then had the audience in his hand, got serious:

I want to tell one quick story before I read, because that's what I do.

In late 1972 my wife and I were living in a trailer. We had two small children, both of whom are now in college; at that time, we weren't making out real well. I had a job, but we still had donated commodities like cheese in our cabinet and it was lousy-tasting, but my wife wasn't going to let that go. In fact, she may still have that block of cheese somewhere in the house, because hard times have a way of sticking with you.

I wrote a story called *Carrie* and sent it to a publisher in New York, Doubleday, which at that time was a publisher instead of a corporate entity. An editor said, "Why don't you come to New York? I think we want to publish this book." So I borrowed $75 from my grandmother-in-law after promising her I would give it back if I got an income tax return.

I caught a bus to New York, where I hadn't been since I was a little boy with my mother. I got off at the Port Authority terminal and walked out onto the street, oriented myself by my shadow when the sun came up, and walked east in brand-new shoes which raised blisters on both feet.

Finally, I got to Doubleday. I was supposed to be there for lunch, but it was only a quarter to eight in the morning. I was dressed in my best sweater—my *only* sweater—and the first thing that I saw was a man I took to be a corpse, near 227 Park Avenue, the Chemical Bank, a huge sandstone structure.

I watched people hurrying past the man, stepping over him, as though he weren't there. I saw a cop and, very aware that I was a country mouse, went over to him and said, "I think that man over there is dead."

The cop looked at the man, then looked at me, and then looked at the man again, and then laughed. I've never forgotten that laugh. He said, "Kid, if he was dead, we could *do* something about it." And that was it.

That guy was a homeless person and got a "place" to live that morning . . . somewhere in the back of my head. It's not a penthouse, just a little room. I never see his face; I just see this shape lying on the concrete, with an overcoat over him. And he's there. And I guess that's why I'm here tonight.[34]

Having said his piece about the homeless, King got on with the second part of his talk, a reading from a recently completed novel, which would signal a new fictional departure for him.

Castle Rock was gone, destroyed, blown up, but the Maine milieu remained, and the new novel would explore the interior landscape of a woman literally chained to a bed in a summer home in Maine at the end of the vacation season, with only her thoughts, her dead husband on the bedroom floor, a visiting dog, and Something Else lurking in the shadows. . . .

It seemed the perfect story for a cold, rainy night in New England . . . and King began:

I want to read to you from a book I've written called *Gerald's Game*. I generally don't try to read scary things, because when you get people in a big crowd, they generally don't get scared.

I like to get them alone.

But it's raining out, it's dark, and what the hell, just this one time, I'll try to scare the crap out of you.

This is actually chapter thirteen of this novel—sort of fitting—which means that I should have to stand here for a long time to fill you in on another one of my brilliant, complex plot devices; but in this case, it won't be necessary.

I wrote a book a little while ago called *Misery* that had *two* characters. That was quite successful, so I decided that since it had been, I would write a book with *one* character. On the drawing board next year is a book called *Living Room*—with *no* character! [*Audience laughs*.]

Actually, there's two characters in this story, Gerald and his wife Jessie, who have discovered bondage as they step into middle age.

On this one occasion, they decide to play this game with the handcuffs at their summer place, in the fall at the lake where there's nobody around to hear you if you scream. Nobody knows where they have gone, and nobody knows they're there.

Jessie's lying on this bed, wearing nothing but her underpants, with her hands handcuffed to the bedposts of the mahogany headboard. And she decides that she doesn't want to play this game at all. Her husband says, "That's very good. I almost believe you."

And what really infuriates Jessie is that she sees in his eyes that he *knows* she's not joking but pretends *he doesn't know*.

She kicks him . . . and I was glad.

Gerald—about forty-five, overweight, a heavy drinker, and a heavy smoker—has a heart attack and drops dead.

She's handcuffed to the bed and tries very hard to pull herself free.

The back door is unlatched, the wind is blowing, and a stray dog comes in and dines in on her husband. She sees this happen and, little by little, begins to realize that she may die, in a position that's akin to crucifixion.

She falls asleep and has a nightmare . . . and as Jessie awakes, she realizes she may no longer be alone in the house.

What I'm going to read you now is her awakening, after the sun has gone down. It's dark now and what really interests me here is not knowing what's real and what's not, what's there and what's not. For me, this is where I think a lot of fear lives.

"During their summers on the lake in the early sixties, before William was able to do much more than paddle in the shallows with a pair of bright orange water-wings attached to his back, Maddy and Jesse, always good friends despite the difference in their ages, often went down to a swim at the Neidermeyers.' "

With that, King held the audience rapt, like the Ancient Mariner in the famous Coleridge poem.

The chapter ends in a moment of horror for Jessie Burlingame, as she faints dead away. . . .

The appreciative audience clapped loudly and, afterward, the reception at the Harvard Faculty Club gave the seventy attendees a chance to eat finger foods, buy drinks at the cash bar, and meet the writers who, hours earlier, had taken the stage to speak in voices louder than mere words on a page.

❧ 22 ❧

WHEN KING PUBLISHED *Night Shift*, Doubleday acted as his agent for all the subsidiary rights, including film/television adaptations, and dutifully sold several to a British film producer, Milton Subotsky, who in turn sold several to Dino de Laurentiis. After Subotsky's death, his estate sold the rights to the sole King film property they owned, "The Lawnmower Man."

It is a bizarre, one-note short story in which Harold Parkette calls a lawn company, Pastoral Greenery and Outdoor Services, to come and cut his lawn. The lawnmower man is, well, not human — a fact that Parkette realizes when he sees the man chewing the grass cut by the "aged red power mower," which has a life of its own, mowing down a gopher, which the lawnmower man happily devours. Parkette, who had his doubts initially, is now damned sure convinced that he made the wrong call.

Parkette calls the police and is interrupted by the lawnmower man, whose possessed power mower claims its next victim — Parkette himself.

The rights to "The Lawnmower Man" were subsequently bought by Allied Vision and the resultant film was distributed by New Line Cinema.

The director of the film, Brett Leonard, told Allied Vision that "there wasn't a movie in the seven page short story about a guy being chased by a lawnmower. But they said, 'We're developing this. Do you have any ideas for expanding it?'"[1]

Leonard did indeed. "Leonard's idea was to combine King's story with *Cybergod*, an existing script cowritten with Gemil Everett, about a virtual reality experiment gone awry, a kind of cross between Daniel Keye's *Flowers for Algernon*, filmed as *Charly* with Cliff Robertson, and *Colossus: The Forbin Project*."[2]

The film, starring Pierce Brosnan, did have a scene in which a lawnmower comes to life, commanded by the cybergod, but it was clearly no more than a passing nod to King's story. Unlike *Return to 'Salem's Lot* or the forgettable *Children of the Corn* sequels, here was a clear case of misrepresentation, since it was billed as *Stephen King's The Lawnmower Man*. It was neither King's story nor King's movie and, in fact, King himself had no inkling that the film had even been made, until he saw, much to his surprise, its movie poster at a hometown theater three weeks before its release.

Predictably, reviewers who had taken the trouble to check out the original story realized that the only thing of any value in the film was King's name attached to it. Richard Harrington of the *Washington Post* said the film was "so loosely based on a Stephen King short story as to constitute fraud. . . ."³

King, like Harrington, felt the movie was selling the moviegoing public a bill of false goods:

> I hate it that New Line's got my name plastered all over the place. It's the biggest rip-off that you could imagine because there's nothing of me in there. It just makes me furious. . . . My name shouldn't be on it. New Line isn't interested in anything that's right or anything that's going to help the consumer. They're interested in exploiting me. My name is being strip-mined. . . . People can say this is stupid and I'm getting rich, but I don't feel that way. My name is my fortune and it's the only name I've got. I've got a minuscule percentage, but I'll never see a cent. Take my word on it.⁴

Defending himself against charges that the story was not the film, Bob Shaye—New Line Cinema Chairman and CEO—asserted that "We had nothing to do with changing the story. The story didn't come with the screenplay. We're the distributors. We bought the rights fair and square," adding that they felt they had bought the rights to King's name, as well. "That's what we paid for. That was part and parcel of why we bought this project. His name was the most important thing we were buying."⁵

King fought back, filing a lawsuit in New York, claiming that the movie "bore no meaningful resemblance" to his original story. The lawsuit demanded that "King wants all profits that can be attributed to the use of his name. . . . And he doesn't want his name used in the future in connection with either the movie or the planned comic book."⁶

King won the lawsuit, but the damage had already been done. Later, just as *'Salem's Lot, Children of the Corn*, and *Pet Sematary* spawned sequels that were possible because of clauses in the original contracts, *The Lawnmower Man* spawned a sequel, too.

Two months later, *Stephen King's Sleepwalkers*, distributed by Columbia, hit screens nationwide. Unlike *The Lawnmower Man*, this film had King's cooperation and consent; in fact, King had written the screenplay. In a promotional videotape, Columbia Pictures said:

> Stephen King has scared book lovers and movie audiences for years. Now, in his original screenplay, we're going to see what scares him. . . . You won't see this as a book by King. You won't see it as a graphic novel. It's a movie.[7]

The story was promising, but the execution was flawed; the film soon became just another forgettable horror movie. The plot: Charles Brady is not what he appears to be—an attractive young boy in high school, with a crush on the popcorn girl at the local cinema (the real-life inspiration for the story: King's son Joe had a crush on the popcorn girl at the Bangor cinema multiplex). On the prowl for young virginal girls, Brady wants them . . . for his mother, who achieves rejuvenation through their life forces. The Sleepwalkers—immortal catlike beings—have no choice but to feed periodically . . . or die.

King's assessment was that his movie was faithful to his screenplay. "*Sleepwalkers* came out real well. On a grading scale—if an A is 92 to 100 and a B is 84 to 91—I'd probably give it a B-plus."[8]

Well, what do you expect when a teacher grades his own work?

The critics disagreed. Richard Harrington (*Washington Post*) opined, "Another week, another Stephen King movie disaster."[9] And Susan Wloszczyna (*USA Today*) extended her claws and took a swipe at the film: "One can understand why horror honcho Stephen King was tired of screenwriting hacks turning his mega-selling stories into multiplex sludge. After all, as *Sleepwalkers* amply demonstrates, ol' Cujo Breath can come up with his own lousy script, thank you."[10]

Entertainment Weekly continued the catfight, calling it a "microwaved hash of slasher-movie thrills and werewolf-like metaphysics."[11]

Ironically, *The Lawnmower Man*, which could stand alone on its own, without King's name to sell it, was the box office standout of King's films that summer, and not *Stephen King's Sleepwalkers*, an unfortunate title, since some reviewers obviously felt that King, or someone else, had sleepwalked through the production of this motion picture.

Like *Thinner*, *Gerald's Game*—the first of three loosely connected novels, with the theme of physically or emotionally abused women—received a big promotional push at the American Booksellers Association convention in

Anaheim, California. Boxed advance copies were given out to selected book-sellers, with the expectation that it would start an early buzz and, hopefully, get the booksellers to hand-sell it to their favorite customers.

Stylistically, *Gerald's Game* seemed to say: *Okay, I'm done with the safe, the comfortable. Remember "Library Policeman"? Well, we're going to get inside the head of the main character to see what boogeymen lurk there!*

Backed by a $750,000 ad budget, *Gerald's Game* would have no middle-ofthe-road readers, because they would either love it . . . or hate it.

A Book-of-the-Month selection, *Gerald's Game* got the full cover treatment for its solicitation. Scott Warren Lynch made the dichotomy clear, so that none of King's readers would be in the dark about this one:

> Let me just warn you right off the bat: Stephen King pulls out all the stops in *Gerald's Game*. In King's latest horror show the master drives three distinct story lines, all screeching and swerving around, and then slams them together with the impact of a mack-daddy caddy hitting the median at 90. It's a heavenly (or hellish) brew of King's strongest evo-cations: insane, loopy fear, the special perspective of children, and nasty, nasty bad guys.[12]

For King readers, each new novel is cause for celebration, one with heav-enly expectations; King, after all, rarely hits a false note. With *Gerald's Game*, however, an old adage comes to mind: If you want to send a message, use Western Union. The book telegraphed King's thesis—that Jessie Burlingame's going to free herself from her past and not be a victim any longer—and readers were likely to feel as much a victim of the book as Jessie was in the story.

Held captive by her past, Jessie has to break free to become the woman she could be, symbolized by the handcuffs that chain her to the bed. But in order to set that scenario up, King decided that the only way it could work would be if Jessie and her husband decided all of a sudden to play a bondage game.

As those in the S&M community have pointed out—notably Susie Bright in her review of *Gerald's Game*—because of the safety risks inherent in bondage games, a safe word is used to say: *Stop!*

Bondage, according to its aficionados, is make-believe between consent-ing adults who act out a mutually agreed-upon fantasy, whether it's simu-lated master/slave relationships, physical bondage, or forced situations . . . all situations that involve protestations, which is why the safe word is the escape pod. Say it and the game stops—even Gerald's game. Fake protestations are part of the fantasy.

That Jessie would agree and then suddenly change her mind is not beyond imagination, but it does stretch credulity. If she truly had been as adamant about *not* participating, she would never have agreed in the first place; and if Gerald had persisted, that's not bondage but forcible rape.

That no safe word was used suggests that King was unaware of it as a safeguard, or thought the last-minute protestation by Jessie was motivationally justified and, plotwise, believable, but it rang a false note.

Besides which, think about how much more horrific it would have been if Jessie *had* used a safeword and Gerald *still* wanted to play his game. *That* would have been a real moment of horror, to see your spouse uncovered as a sadistic monster intent on using you as a living prop in a sex fantasy gone awry, regardless of whether or not you wanted to play.

Gerald, however, can't stick around to debate the issue, because he gets kneed in the groin and does a high-dive off the bed, landing on his head, and dies—again, necessary to the plot—and we are left with Jessie and her trapped-rat-in-a-maze thoughts of escape, as she hears voices from the past come to haunt her. Bookwise, what we have left is a story that's mostly moralizing, with a loose linkage to King's next novel, *Dolores Claiborne.*

For King fans who like his books without windy preachments, *Gerald's Game* was bound to disappoint. For King fans who found "Library Policeman" quietly effective, as it shifted from the light to the shadows, as its real story of child molestation was explored, this novel was a letdown. And for most everyone else, *Publishers Weekly* spoke for them:

> While this is one of the best-written stories King has ever published, it will offend many through sheer bad taste. . . . For the first third of the book he is at the top of his form, creating in Jessie one of his most intense character studies. . . . The gory stuff . . . is prime King, but this is subsumed in the book's general tastelessness. A lame wrap-up to what might have been a thrilling short story only further compromises the enjoyment readers might have found in this surprisingly exploitative work.[13]

Dr. Michael Collings, who has read all of King's fiction and most of his nonfiction, found little to like in *Gerald's Game*, echoing what *Publishers Weekly* had said. This novel, said Collings, was a radical change from what King had written in the past:

In the end, *Gerald's Game* seems more single-dimensional than one expects from King. Everything is neatly explained away, including Jessie's hallucinatory awareness that someone has been in the house with her (also initially described as monsters and the supernatural). There seems little growth, little change. In important ways, she is still as handcuffed to herself and her past as she was handcuffed to her bed for most of the story.[14]

Promoting *Gerald's Game* was certainly sufficient justification for King to attend the ABA, but he had another agenda: to raise money for anticensorship efforts and to help the homeless.

On May 25, 1992, before a large crowd in the main ballroom of the Disneyland Hotel in Anaheim, California, Garrison Keillor hosted "A Celebration for Free Expression: An Evening of Censored Classics," to benefit the American Booksellers Foundation for Free Expression.

Appearing at the celebration: a rock band, the Rock Bottom Remainders. This, however, was no ordinary band; this one was composed of some of the biggest names in the book business, with writers like Robert Fulghum (*All I Really Need to Know I Learned in Kindergarten*), Barbara Kingsolver (novelist), Amy Tan (novelist), Dave Barry (best-selling humorist), Matt Groening (creator of *The Simpsons*), and others . . . including Stephen King.

What few knew was that in high school, when King discovered rock and roll, it was for him, as it was for a generation of baby boomers, a pivotal moment. King, who grew up on Elvis and Buddy Holly and the other hard rockers who defined rock and roll in its infancy, had played in a high school band with the Mune-Spinners, and in fact had taken the stage at his senior prom to play the guitar and sing.

For King, the formation of the Rock Bottom Remainders was a godsend. He could indulge himself in one of his most cherished fantasies and hang out with his contemporaries and become just one of the guys. The king of the best-sellers could pretend to be the king of rock and roll for one night.

For the celebration, the Rock Bottom Remainders gave its first public performance, unplugged. The booksellers who attended were understandably surprised but delighted; they could eyeball some of the biggest names in the book business and hear them . . . sing?

The two songs, however, sounded okay—a promising sign, since the band could at least sing, no matter how it played. Those who had bought tickets to hear the band play in its plugged mode—with electric guitars and power amplifiers, already set up at the nearby Cowboy Boogie bar—looked forward to a night of hard rocking!

Although people had paid good money to hear the band play, the impression this band of writers gave was that *they* would have gladly paid for the privilege of getting together and jamming, practicing, and then performing in front of a live, appreciative audience—the ultimate baby boomer's fantasy.

Writers, for the most part, live solitary lives. As King had put it before, they sit in little rooms and write, trying to create something out of nothing. Here, in Anaheim, it was a different situation: they would be up front, personal, and *loud*. If nothing else, enthusiasm on the band's part would be sufficient to carry the day, but everyone knew they'd have a hell of a band.

King had no illusions about their musical abilities. They were a celebrity band that could afford to get together and have fun and have people want to hear them play, just for the novelty of it. And if by chance the music was good, that'd be a bonus but not a requirement. "I mean, when you get right down to it," he wrote, "we're just a bunch of bangers with only three days to rehearse (and during much of that we're apt to be distracted by press, autograph seekers, psychotic celebrity serial killers, etc.). If we charge too much up front, people are apt to expect a little too much. I'd rather have them come expecting to see a bunch of refugees from the Major Bowes Amateur Talent Hour and get an agreeable surprise when two or three numbers actually work . . .*get me?*"[15]

Judging from the crowd that gathered outside the Cowboy Boogie, including latecomers who begged for tickets at any price, *this* was *the* place to be that night. Anaheim, home of Mickey Mouse's Disneyland, would rock!

The money would be donated to charity, to benefit three local organizations: The Homeless Writers Coalition of Los Angeles, Literacy Volunteers of America, and The Right to Rock Network.

Supplementing ticket sales, a table had been set up inside with autographed collectibles, including photos and T-shirts signed by all the members, which were quickly snapped up.

Brazening it out, their motto said it all: "This band plays music as well as Metallica writes novels."[16]

The motto had been written by Dave Barry, who, as it turned out, was also pretty damned good on the guitar. The rest of the members, vocally or instrumentally, held their own, but to punch it up, to give it the extra musical juice, two ringers were brought on: Josh Kelly on drums and Jerry Peterson on the sax.

The band was flanked by two groups of vocalists: the Remainderettes on the left, and the Critics Corner on the right. The former included Tad Bartimus, Kathi Kamen Goldmark (the founding mother of the band), and Amy Tan; the latter included Roy Blount, Jr., Tomie de Paola, Greil Marcus, Dave Marsh, Joel Selvin, and Matt Groening.

Flanked between the vocalists, the band itself: Robert Fulghum, Barbara Kingsolver, legendary rocker Al Kooper, Ridley Pearson, Dave Barry, and Stephen King.

Play that funky music, white boys!

The band rocked and the crowd danced and everybody got down and dirty and felt they got more than their money's worth.

The musical selection was a blast from the past: "Money," "Gloria," "Louie, Louie," "Land of a Thousand Dances," and—believe it!—Stephen King, hit by a single light, with his guitar slung across his back, Bruce Springsteen fashion, as he crooned one of his favorite songs, "Sea of Love," as the rest of the band stood in the shadows.

"I think we blew the doors off that place," King said later.[17]

The band *definitely* blew the doors off that place, though the videotape that was produced from that evening failed to convey the excitement of the crowd, the wall-to-wall people dancing, and the admittedly unusual sight of Stephen King—the biggest, baddest, best-selling writer of the bunch—fulfilling what had to be a lifelong dream: being, for one night, a rock and roller belting out songs instead of words.

You had to have been there. In the words of Al Kooper: "They played like men."

After the concert, King shared his perceptions of his fellow band members: "Barbara Kingsolver, who's a poet and sensitive intellectual, is a really hot keyboardist who can boogie. Dave Barry is a hot lead guitarist, who would fit in with any '60s frat-house rock band. And Ridley Pearson has been playing bass for about a thousand years."[18]

When King got home, he told the *Bangor Daily News*, "I usually play chords on a word processor, which is a very private thing. . . . It was great. It was a lot of fun. If nothing else, at least I've improved my guitar skills."[19]

Though the band would later go on tour and also play at other bookselling venues, the first time was magic time. They came, they saw . . . and they *ruled*!

It was not surprising that King had lent his formidable presence to the ABA that year, with its emphasis on censorship and banned books. One of the most frequently banned contemporary authors, King had over the years seen so many of his books banned that he routinely refused to comment.

But after *The Dead Zone* and *The Tommyknockers* had been pulled from a school in Jacksonville, Florida, King wrote an op-ed piece for the *Bangor Daily News*, preceded by an editorial, "Read This Book":

> . . . Author Stephen King has some simple but sound advice for students upset because two of his books have been banned: Hit the public library, read the books, and find out what makes them so horrible that they must be yanked from the school library.
>
> Mr. King has plenty of experience with banned books. At various times around the country his novels *Carrie*, *'Salem's Lot*, *Firestarter*, *Cujo* and *The Shining* have been banned, and proposed bans have been laid on *The Stand*, *Christine*, and his short story "Children of the Corn" from the collection *Night Shift*. A junior high school in Jacksonville, Florida, now adds *The Dead Zone* and *The Tommyknockers* to the list of those banned.
>
> Banning books creates a dangerous precedent. The intellectual freedom generally assumed to exist in this country will continue only as long as citizens protect the right of authors to place their ideas before the public. That doesn't mean that a pornographic magazine belongs in an elementary school library, but it does mean that novels widely accepted by the public should not be banned.
>
> It's a testimony to the power of the written word that books that describe violent or sexual scenes or contain swear words are kept from teenagers, while television and the movies virtually are left alone. Television, even on the three major networks, guarantees a nightly primetime menu of murder, rape, disfigurements, shootings, stabbings, maulings and beatings. That's entertainment.
>
> Cable TV stations, to which almost all teens have access one way or another, regularly show movie versions of some of the very books by Mr. King that have been banned. No protests there.
>
> Books such as *The Adventures of Huckleberry Finn* and *The Catcher in the Rye* are willfully misinterpreted and banned every few years in some misguided hope that children will be shielded from the realities of the world. The world creeps in anyway, leaving the bans no purpose other than to restrain free speech.[20]

In his op-ed piece, King pointed out that book banning was "a kind of intellectual autocracy" and as for censorship itself: "It's a scary idea, especially in a society which has been built on the ideas of free choice and free thought. . . . No book, record, or film should be banned without a full airing of the issues."[21]

It would be a battle that would never end. King had seen the hydra of censorship rear its ugly head in North Carolina, then in his own home state by Reverend Wyman "for the sake of the children," and, again, elsewhere in the country. Cut one of the hydra's heads off and two would grow in its place. . . .

Charity, as Stephen King has often said, begins at home.

For King, that means giving back to the local community, using his name, presence, and good fortune to benefit everyone. (The Kings' philanthropy, in fact, was so widespread in Bangor that it took a magazine article to give the subject full coverage, in James Conaway's "The King of Bangor," which appeared in *Worth* magazine [December/January 1997].)

Sometimes, charity starts in your own backyard—in King's case, Hayford Park.

In 1989, King's son Owen played on the local Little League team, coached by Dave Mansfield. King assisted as part-time coach and full-time scorekeeper, and in the process chronicled the team's path from Bangor to the state championship. For father and son, it was a journey, one that seemed providential, as King observed: "My proximity to the Bangor West All-Star team . . . was either pure luck or pure fate, depending on where you stand in regard to the possible existence of a higher power. I tend toward the higher power thesis, but in either case, I was only there because my son was on the team."[22]

Like other parents, he didn't want to be simply an observer—traditional in his role as writer—but wanted to be a participant, as well. So when Dave Mansfield found in King a kindred spirit, someone who was one of them and clearly not a celebrity writer demanding preferential treatment, Mansfield was glad to accept King's offer to help.

The experience, chronicled in "Heads Down," appeared in *The New Yorker* magazine, which probably surprised its more staid readers who would not expect to see King in the pages of their very literary, highbrow magazine, filled with ads for yuppie toys.

When the readers got past their initial shock, however, they discovered that King could write with the best of them. As for King's part, he credited the magazine's editor, Chip McGrath, for having "coaxed the best nonfiction writing of my life out of me."[23]

With over a hundred pieces of nonfiction to his credit, King's down-to-earth personality, which translates with perfect, high fidelity in his fiction, also translates perfectly in his nonfiction—something frequently overlooked, since his spook novels commanded most of the attention.

The other thing that came out of King's experience: his realization that the playing fields for Little League ball in Bangor were inadequate. . . . Realizing that, King decided to dig deep in his pocket to come up with $1 million to make a field of dreams—inevitably nicknamed the Field of Screams, in the park behind his home on West Bangor Street.

Bob Haskell, a sportswriter for the hometown newspaper who has known King for two decades, said that for King baseball was much more than simply just another sport:

> It has been his oasis and his escape for more than 30 years—since marveling over Don Larsen's perfect game during the 1956 World Series that he watched on a tiny black-and-white television when he was nine and living with his mother in Stratford, Connecticut.[24]

King elaborated: "Baseball has saved my life. Every time I needed a lifeline, baseball was it. I grew up alone. My mother worked. I was a latch-key kid before anyone knew what a latch-key kid was. I would watch baseball when I got home from school. I listened to the games on the radio before that."[25]

Whether it was coaching a Little League team during college, or watching his beloved Red Sox lose game after game—hope springs eternal—or getting his hands dirty by maintaining the Little League field before his son's team trotted out to assume field positions, King and baseball are inextricable.

The ballfield itself, wrote Haskell, was designed for Little League, but nothing was little about the planning that went into it:

> "Steve told me last May that he wanted a state-of-the-art baseball field," said sandy-haired Gary Crowell, a carpenter and contractor from Stoneham, Me., who has worked on King's homes since 1978. "The field has been designed around a million-dollar budget," added Crowell, who was overseeing the construction. "We'll come in within five percent of that, one way or the other."[26]

Haskell wrote that the field had "two hundred tons of porous Georgia clay," "115,000 square feet of durable Kentucky bluegrass sod," "a grandstand for 1,500 fans," "a 15-foot-wide warning track of pine stone dust from Maine's renowned Mt. Desert Island," "a mile of four-inch drainage pipe beneath the soil," "a computer-driven, three-section sprinkler system," and "a lighting system meeting National Collegiate Athletic Association standards."[27]

King's big heart was matched only by his philanthropy—a fact that didn't escape the local paper in an editorial headlined "Kings' generosity":

> Coming out of a decade when the objective of having money was to hoard it and flaunt it, it is refreshing to see authors Stephen and Tabitha King dealing with wealth the old-fashioned way: They have earned it, and they have chosen to share it.
>
> Only the Kings know for certain the extent of their generosity to their community. There have been many quiet contributions, to very needy causes that they have not wanted made public. But their more conspicuous donations should improve the quality of life in two communities, in very different ways.
>
> The Old Town Public Library today is a $1.7 million testimonial to a community's commitment to learning, scholarship and the preservation of the written word. The $750,000 donated by Tabitha King constructed a wing that bears her name, but she helped the people of Old Town build something bigger, pride in an accomplishment that will serve generations.
>
> Stephen King added together two of the personal interests in his life: the welfare of children and a passion for baseball. Their sum is a $1 million ballfield that King will build at Hayford Park in Bangor, complete with seating for 1,500, concession stands and state-of-the-art lighting.
>
> According to King, the shortage of full-size baseball diamonds in the area severely limits the number of young players who can play and develop at the upper echelons of the Little League program.
>
> Because of his generosity, their dreams and aspirations will not die for lack of vision and opportunity.
>
> Philanthropy is rare. Rarer still are people who have much, and who could live above their community, but who instead have chosen to become part of it.[28]

The field opened in late June and Bangor's citizens, once again, saw that the King of Horror was a real prince to the local community.

For their outstanding civic contributions, the Kings received the Norbert Dowd Award for community service from the Greater Bangor Chamber of Commerce at its annual dinner.

Rising to the occasion, King said, "We're glad to be a part of Bangor.

We've never said, 'Maybe life would have been better if we had gone to the southern part of the state.' Whatever we've done for Bangor was the result of what Bangor has done for us."[29]

The Kings, clearly, were in a league of their own.

The Dark Half flew into theaters in summer and horrified its audiences — not, of course, in the way that *Maximum Overdrive* or *Graveyard Shift* did, but in the way that *Pet Sematary* and *Misery* did. In other words, it was a visual treat, faithfully adapted from the King novel in which Thad Beaumont literally confronts his dark half, his pen name that came to life, taking his two children hostage, and threatening to take his life, as well.

A riveting story made into a riveting film, the standout acting performance was the dual role played by Timothy Hutton, who took the parts of both Thad Beaumont and George Stark, in a performance that showed his virtuosity.

The film, with a screenplay by George A. Romero, was produced by Dark Half Productions and distributed by Orion Pictures. It was in fact ready to roll in early 1991, but financial troubles kept it from release until Orion's financial situation improved.

The Dark Half was followed by Castle Rock Entertainment's *Needful Things*, with a screenplay by W. D. Richter.

Running a little over two hours, *Needful Things*, like *The Dark Half*, translated effectively to the screen. It is story of Leland Gaunt, the devil himself, who comes to Castle Rock to open up a retail shop, Needful Things, where you can find anything you want for a price.

Leland Gaunt, played by Max von Sydow, works his magic and mischief over the spellbound inhabitants of Castle Rock, as a skeptical Sheriff Alan Pangborn (Ed Harris) sees Gaunt for who and what he is, and attempts to stop him.

Actions have consequences, *Needful Things* reminds us . . . a pivotal fact at the center of *The Tommyknockers*, which premiered on ABC on May 9, adapted by Larry Cohen, who previously had written scripts for both *Carrie* and *It*.

In *The Tommyknockers*, the inhabitants of Haven, Maine, build strange contraptions to rid themselves of their simplest problems, not knowing that these very machines, if left unchecked, would have catastrophic consequences.

Unlike *Carrie* and *It*, *The Tommyknockers* as a visual adaptation had its moments but was clearly not in the same league as *Misery*.

Just as *The Dark Half* and *Needful Things* proved to be a double-dip delight, King's fans who haunted the bookstores that year found two major King books. The first, *Nightmares & Dreamscapes*, the largest collection of King's short fiction to date—816 pages that included twenty-three pieces—was bookended by an introduction and notes, and followed by "The Beggar and the Diamond," a story told to King.

Opening with a rewritten version of "Dolan's Cadillac," the collection is a King reader's delight, bringing together a cornucopia of contributions with something for everyone.

In his Introduction, King points out, as he did in *Skeleton Crew*, that he wrote these stories because, over the years, no matter what else has changed, one thing has not:

> But it *isn't* about the money, no matter what the glossy tabloids may say, and it's not about selling out, as the more arrogant critics really seem to believe. The fundamental things still apply as time goes by, and for me the object hasn't changed—the job is still getting to *you*, Constant Reader. . . .[30]

If *Nightmares & Dreamscapes* didn't get to you—and it's hard to imagine that it wouldn't—then *Dolores Claiborne* surely did. A short novel of 305 pages, *Dolores Claiborne* is effectively told in the first person, from Claiborne's viewpoint—by now, an old, cranky woman whose no-account husband deserved what he got; likewise, she too gets what she deserves—the estate of Vera Donovan, her longtime employer, who gave her a lot of shit while she was living.

Dolores—plainspoken and unrepentant—gives a spellbinding account to the police, who at first are skeptical but come to be believers.

From the beginning, the reader knows that Dolores is somehow linked to her husband's death, which she readily admits to; she's also somehow linked to Vera Donovan's death as well, which sets up a difficult situation for King to resolve: How can you create a sympathetic character out of someone who appears to be a murderess?

King pulls it off in spades. He depicts a quintessential Mainer, a woman with a hardscrabble life and a no-account husband who drinks and abuses her. In the end, the reader is rooting for Dolores, who points out that sometimes an accident is a girl's best friend.

❧23❧

Ever since *The Stand* was published, fans began talking about whether or not it could be adapted visually without losing its special qualities—its scope, its carefully delineated characters, and most of its depiction of good and evil as embodied respectively by Mother Abigail and King's bad man, Randall Flagg.

Reduced to a one-liner: "It's about the end of the world," King said.[1]

But there's more—*much* more.

More than any other novel by King, *The Stand* is rich in scope and, with the exception of the multidimensional epic *The Dark Tower*, *The Stand* towers above his other novels.

An ambitious novel, *The Stand*'s length precluded a successful adaptation to the silver screen, but it was perfect for a miniseries, which aired on ABC in 1994.

Molly Ringwald, who played the critically pivotal role of Frannie Goldsmith in *The Stand*, spoke for everyone in the cast when she said of the viewers, "They weren't coming out to see Molly Ringwald, Gary Sinese, or Rob Lowe; they were coming out to see Stephen King."[2]

Because of King's brand-name recognition, it became *de rigueur* for his films to have his name in the title, up front, typically preceding it, so you knew it wasn't, for example, just *Sleepwalkers*, it was *Stephen King's Sleepwalkers*. Sometimes that helped sell a few tickets, and sometimes it didn't. It depended on the quality of the film that resulted. In this case, however, *Stephen King's The Stand* is appropriately titled, since King took a hands-on approach to the making of this epic film, which did justice to the book.

King wrote the screenplay and served as an executive producer; he even had a cameo in the role of Teddy Wiesak, who gives Nadine a ride in his truck.

Shot over a five-month period in ninety-five locations, drawing on the talents of 125 actors, *Stephen King's The Stand* was eight hours of prime time

Stephen King: Episode 1, "The Plague"; Episode 2, "The Dreams"; Episode 3, "The Betrayal"; and Episode 4, "The Stand."

A horror story on an epic scale, *Stephen King's The Stand* was also a very moral tale, telling the oldest story in the book: a classic good versus evil story, appropriately ending with the Hand of God making its appearance.

Directed by George A. Romero, this production boasted an all-star cast, with standout performances from all the principals, especially Ruby Dee as Mother Abigail, Molly Ringwald as Frannie Goldsmith, Gary Sinese as Stu Redman, Rob Lowe as the mute Nick Andros, Laura San Giacomo as Nadine Cross, and Jamey Sheridan as Randall Flagg, to name a few.

Dr. Michael Collings, writing about the revised edition of the book, could just as easily have been speaking about the spirit of this film adaptation:

> *The Stand* . . . is one of King's strongest novels. It is a consistent, readable, teachable response to life in a frighteningly technology-oriented world; it also reminds us that we may sometimes be forced to find a place for the spiritual and the supernatural within that world. The restored novel confirms King's position as a master storyteller; and at the same time, it provides even readers familiar with all of his works to date increasing insight into the growth and transformation over more than a decade of his abilities, his themes, and his narrative power.[3]

If *Stephen King's The Stand* was not enough good fortune in one year for King fans, *The Shawshank Redemption* fortuitously followed, from Castle Rock productions, which had established a name for itself with its previous King adaptations, *Stand by Me* and *Misery*.

Could this prison story, set in the thirties, be successfully adapted to the screen and retain the unique flavor of King's fiction?

Enter stage left, Frank Darabont, who years earlier, as an aspiring filmmaker, had asked King's permission to film "The Woman in the Room," a short story collected in *Night Shift*.

Of the story, King wrote:

> It had been written as a kind of cry from the heart after my mother's long, losing battle with cervical cancer had finally ended. Her pain—the *pointlessness* of her pain—shook me in a deep and fundamental way; it made me see the world in a new and cautious perspective. This was in addition to the natural grief almost anyone feels when a parent dies at the relatively young age of sixty-two.[4]

Whether Darabont knew how much the story meant to King is immaterial. What Darabont *knew* was that the story was poignant and begged to be filmed.

King's policy—then and now—is that any film student can shoot one of his short stories for the nominal cost of $1, and a finished copy of the film on videotape. The predictable result is the usual student fare, but occasionally there's a standout.

After King granted the rights, Darabont filmed it as a short feature, and, as per the standard student film agreement, sent a videocassette to King. ". . . I watched it in slack-jawed amazement. I also felt a little sting of tears. *The Woman in the Room* remains, twelve years later, on my short list of favorite film adaptations."[5]

Time is a circle and in due time things came full circle: Darabont wrote to King for an option on "Rita Hayworth and Shawshank Redemption," and King granted it, mostly because he was curious to see what kind of screenplay would result.

After the usual byzantine negotiations over a long period of years, Darabont and Castle Rock Entertainment began preproduction work in January 1993 on what would prove to be one of those rare King films that found an audience *outside* the horror market. In fact, it did so well with the critics—the same ones who relished putting King and his books and movies down—that it garnered seven Academy Award nominations: Best Picture, Best Actor (Morgan Freeman), Best Screenplay Based on Material Previously Produced or Published, Best Cinematography, Best Original Score, and Best Sound.

It didn't win any but, hey, as King said, ". . . the little gold statues aren't the point. . . ."[6] It did, however, win its fair share of awards *outside* of the Academy Awards, including: two Golden Globes (Morgan Freeman, Best Actor; Frank Darabont, Best Screenplay), a Director's Guild Award (for Frank Darabont), and two Screen Actors Guild Awards (Best Actor, for both Morgan Freeman and Tim Robbins).

In the wake of those awards, Frank Darabont must have felt like Tim Robbins, who, in the movie, and in the movie poster, is standing outside, at night, exuberant because he's now a free man and the rain falling down on him feels *so* good.

The film, while not a commercial success in the theaters, was certainly a critical success; but, when released in video a year later, it became a much-talked-about film and a commercial success in video sales and rentals.

It was not, by any stretch of the imagination, an easy shoot—it never is, as any dedicated filmmaker will tell you. (When Darabont had asked George Lucas why he hadn't directed in two decades, George "The Force" Lucas replied that it was, in so many words, too damned hard. ". . . [A]nd this coming from a man with the most tireless work-ethic I've ever seen," said Darabont.[7])

Five months of preproduction was followed by three months of production, as Frank tells it:

> Then the *real* work began. Three months of shooting in Mansfield, Ohio, working 15 to 18 hours a day, 6 days a week, with barely enough time to sit. . . . You wind up in a sort of zombie-like daze, functioning on autopilot, reduced to putting one foot in front of the other like the kids in *The Long Walk* by Stephen King, the finish-line some mythical Promised Land you try not to think about lest you go mad with homesickness and despair, knowing that if you drop in your tracks they'll shoot you and leave you behind for the buzzards to chow down on. Sleep becomes a dim memory. The mental and physical stamina required is awesome. The stress is beyond belief.[8]

Well, that explains *Maximum Overdrive* . . . but what about *The Shawshank Redemption*?

Gene Siskel of the *Chicago Tribune* said, "Frank Darabont, with this one work, declares himself a special talent."[9]

Glenn Kenny of *Entertainment Weekly*—a zine where King has gotten more than his fair share of lumps—begrudgingly admitted it was good, falling short of calling it a "masterpiece" by calling it a "provisional masterpiece," with a grade of *A*-, which was high praise.

For some authors, book tours can be exercises in futility and embarrassment, especially early in the writing career when the brand name isn't set in bigger type on the cover than the book's title. But when that's reversed, and your name's not only bigger than the title but set in embossed type or in metallic foil stamping, it's the equivalent of seeing your name up in lights on Broadway instead of in tiny eight-point type on the playbill.

When King decided to promote *Insomnia*, his 787-page novel for fall 1994 that was guaranteed to keep you up all night, he was able to pick and choose which bookstores he would support; and, because he could indulge himself, he decided to go not by jet but by motorcycle, his trusted Harley Davidson, decorated with its distinctive spiderweb trim.

Traveling across the country, with a van behind him, King rolled into town and gave signings only to the independent booksellers, the stores—according to King—that could use his presence to boost sales.

King started out in Vermont, at the Northshire Bookstore in Manchester Center; from here, he went to Ithaca, New York; Worthington, Ohio; Lexington, Kentucky; Nashville, Tennessee; St. Louis, Missouri; Manhattan, Kansas; Colorado Springs, Colorado; Sun Valley, Idaho; and Santa Cruz, California.

At the final stop, King was unpleasantly surprised to see Steven Lightfoot, who alleged that King killed John Lennon; Lightfoot had his message prominently displayed on his van, which was parked outside of the bookstore, Bookshop Santa Cruz: "Stephen King Shot John Lennon. Govt. Media Pushing Look-Alike; Chapman."

Lightfoot was subsequently arrested by the police on trespassing charges at the bookstore.

That night, at the Santa Cruz Civic Auditorium, King spoke to a capacity crowd. He prefaced his reading with an impromptu, chatty introduction, then read from *Insomnia*, and answered questions afterward.

King condemned the practices of the heavy discounters, the warehouse operators that skim the cream off the top and sell only a handful of best-selling titles, discounted up to 40 percent—a discount so deep that local booksellers, on occasion, go there to buy stock because it's more cost effective than buying them from a local book distributor.

"It's not right," King told the crowd, to loud, enthusiastic applause. "It's bad for diversity. It's bad for American thought when American fiction is represented only by Sidney Sheldon, Danielle Steele, Tom Clancy and Stephen King. That's not the way it's supposed to be, and it's a dangerous philosophy."[10]

Because it was nearing Halloween, King spoke briefly about his least favorite holiday, the one that had come to be associated with him, more than any other person on the planet. "I want to wish you all a Happy Halloween." Pause. "I fucking hate it. I've turned into America's version of the Great Pumpkin. It used to be Alfred Hitchcock, but he's dead. On Halloween night, six thousand kids show up at my house in their little Freddie Kreuger and Jason outfits."[11]

King had reluctantly become America's best-loved boogeyman, and Halloween was the night that recalled him to the world at large.

Insomnia, despite the publisher's best efforts, was not an easy sell. The size was off-putting and the story was atypical King—no surprise to King fans who knew he was going through a period of experimental fiction, eschewing the familiar trappings of horror, inside and beyond the city limits of Castle Rock.

Dr. Michael Collings, in his understated way, was correct in saying that:

> *Insomnia* is probably not to every reader's taste. A long novel that threatens an odd kind of stasis in its opening chapters, it has as its hero an old man of seventy, recently widowed and increasingly suffering from an unnerving kind of insomnia. It is not that he can't *get* to sleep but that he awakens a minute or so earlier every day until eventually he is living on two or three hours of sleep, constantly fatigued, almost hoping for death. This is a relatively long process, and King allows the novel to move slowly over the course of months, detailing the consequences of the affliction on Ralph Roberts's life and on his relationship with old friends and neighbors—some of whom simultaneously begin acting strangely, even threateningly.[12]

Some of his readers wondered what King was trying to achieve in his fiction. First *Gerald's Game*, now *Insomnia*, What next? Where are the haunted cars and haunted houses? What about the kids who could make things move by mind control or make them explode or even be able to see into the future a bit? What about something safe and familiar set in Castle Rock?

King was not interested in playing it safe, having made *that* clear after he took out Castle Rock, in a fashion that recalled *'Salem's Lot*, *The Shining*, and *The Stand*. *Just blow up the town!*

This seemingly maddening cycle of disparate novels had to come to an end . . . or would it? But King wasn't telling.

At the end of the talk, King word-teased the audience. "I can give you a sneak peek and tell you what *Rose Madder* is about. It's *about* . . . 450 pages long."

❧24❧

Wʜᴀᴛ'ѕ *Rose Madder* about? It's about . . . female empowerment, a theme King tentatively explored in *Carrie*, then reexamined in *Gerald's Game* and *Dolores Claiborne*. It's about Rosie Daniels, a battered wife whose husband, a policeman, is hell-bent on tracking her down; she's taken the bus to a city where she hopes he can't find her, but Norman Daniels is relentless; and what matters is that he wants to find his wife to speak to her up close, and get her to take her medicine. . . .

The publisher, hoping for good word of mouth, broke from its tradition of printing a few hundred advance galleys and reportedly printed 15,000 advance reading copies, bound in rose-colored covers.

W. David Atwood, senior writer for the Book-of-the-Month Club, explains that *Rose Madder* is, stylistically, new territory for King:

> King went from high-school English teacher to one of history's best-selling authors for one simple reason: He dared to confront the 20th century's unspoken fears. The dog in *Cujo*, the teenager loser in *Carrie*, the obsessive fan in *Misery*, the fatal disease in *The Stand*, the sexual experimentation of *Gerald's Game*, the crazed dad in *The Shining*, the sleeplessness of *Insomnia*—all aspects of modern life that scare us, of which we rarely speak openly.
>
> Now, in *Rose Madder*, King takes on one of our oldest taboos, one that is very much in today's headlines and, at long last, open for discussion: domestic violence. Rosie Daniels tries hard to be a good wife, but she keeps messing up in little ways—spilling iced tea or getting caught with a racy novel. And when she does, *he's* always there, every night, to punish her. People around town respect Police Detective Norman Daniels, the handsome, well-built high school sweetheart Rosie married 14 years ago. But they don't know what goes on each night in his own house: the carefully placed punches, the biting that leaves scars, the pencil-stabbing, or the shameful thing he did with his tennis racket.[1]

Mark Harris, writing in *Entertainment Weekly*, asked: "When did Stephen King's books stop being so scary?"[2] Citing *The Shining*, *Pet Sematary*, and *Carrie* as novels in which "the horror . . . springs from the ease with which evil can take hold of (or masquerade as) decent people,"[3] Harris felt that *Rose Madder* offered no "seductive ambiguity" (huh?), with an ending that he believed was simply "a cheat."

> She steps through an oil painting of a toga-clad woman warrior into another world, where she has some sort of empowering experience involving a feminist goddess, a maze, a magical stream, and something called the Temple of the Bull. Temple of the Bull, indeed. In the context of a novel that means to explore the psychology of a beaten woman, the random imposition of a supernatural gimmick—especially a wan, fairy-tale-ish conceit that's about as convincing as a CD-ROM game—constitutes a rather stunning cop-out.[4]

On the silver screen, it was a typical year for King, whose adaptations ranged from the eminently forgettable (*The Mangler*) to the middle-of-the-road effort (*The Langoliers*) and, finally, to the memorable—*Dolores Claiborne*.

Based on a short story originally published in *Cavalier* and collected in *Night Shift*, *The Mangler* was a one-noter, recalling *Maximum Overdrive* and other productions that didn't have enough story to justify being made into full-length feature films. If *Maximum Overdrive* was overkill, then *The Mangler* had to be the runner-up: based on King's real-world experiences in a laundry in Bangor, "The Mangler" is the story of a large, electric speed ironer and folder that comes to life and kills laundry workers, finally uprooting itself and going off in search of human prey.

The Langoliers, a much more ambitious effort, would have been perfect for a 30-minute television episode, but the strength of *Stephen King's The Stand* put this production, shot in Bangor, in the forefront of ABC's offerings for sweeps week in May 14 and 15, where it captured but did not hold the viewers' attention.

In "Just Plane Scared," Ken Tucker of *Entertainment Weekly* reviewed the production, gave it a *B*, and concluded that although it was "slow going in spots . . . it's also a lot more fun than most TV movies. . . . And even though the langoliers are pretty obviously computer-animated special effects, these little meatballs are still pretty scary. I'd rather watch them than a Susan Lucci TV movie any day."[5]

❧25❧

Burton Hatlen, who taught King at UMO, has always been an advocate for his star student. In fact, long before it became fashionable in some critical circles to acknowledge, much less praise, King, Hatlen beat the drum, standing up and saying in a loud voice: Take King seriously. Look past the fright mask he wears. He can write! We must pay attention to this man! Wrote Hatlen:

> Beginning with *Rage*, and *The Long Walk*, all of King's novels celebrate the possibility of community by looking at all the forces arrayed against it. It is his consistent concern with the way we live together that makes King—not, as Thomas Edwards suggests in a recent *New York Review of Books*, an "almost 'serious'" writer—but rather one of the most truly serious novelists writing today.[1]

Such an assertion, voiced too loudly, would likely bring catcalls from literary writers because, after all, King's just a horror writer, and his sales are proof of that—it's popular trash! But, please, pay attention to *my* books; they're *serious literature*.

In *Different Seasons*, one of the stories, "The Breathing Method," uses the framing device of a club whose members meet to tell tales. Over the mantle, engraved upon its keystone, the motto of the club speaks volumes: *"It is the tale, not he who tells it."*[2]

Serious writers find that difficult to swallow whole, because in order to truly believe in it, they must discard their egos, which prevent them from judging creative material without regard to its source. That is why, in the judging for the Screen Writer's Guild awards, the names of the screen/scriptwriters are removed—the work must stand alone.

What, then, can you go by? One barometer is to have an impartial judge call the shots; and in annual collections like *Best Short Stories* and *Prize Stories: The O. Henry Awards*, the work must speak for itself.

In *Prize Stories 1996: The O. Henry Awards*, edited by William Abrahams,

the calls were made; and considering who won first place, there was probably no joy in Mudville, where the Serious Writers resided.

The Atlantic Monthly said that *Prize Stories* was "widely regarded as the na-
tion's most prestigious awards for short fiction."[3] Abrahams prefaced the
1996 volume, saying he had judged its entries for three decades, but he was
now retiring. He made it clear that he felt there was no question as to the
literary quality of these stories:

> For the 1996 volume I have chosen twenty stories from among the ap-
> proximately one thousand that were eligible—stories by American au-
> thors published in magazines in the twelve-month period from summer
> 1994 to summer 1995. The winnowing and sifting procedure reduced
> the number of plausible candidates dramatically. Perhaps one hundred
> stories remained to be read and reconsidered. Then, another winnow-
> ing—and several worthy stories were reluctantly let go. Ultimately, I
> settled on the final twenty, making a collection about which I am pre-
> pared to say: This is one of the very best.[4]

The best of the best that year—the story that took the First Prize, was "The
Man in the Black Suit," written by . . . Stephen King.

Like the other stories in this collection, it quietly asserts itself, drawing attention not to the writer but to the work itself. A typical King story—a old
man reminisces about the past, when he was a little boy on a fishing expedition and goes too far into the woods, only to meet old scratch himself, the
devil.

"The Man in the Black Suit" pulls together many of the things that King
does so well as a writer: set in Maine, told in the first person, this poignant
gem evokes childhood memories, establishes a sense of familiarity with the
milieu, touches on a family relationship with a tragic element, and introduces a supernatural element so subtly that its presence goes unnoticed until
it's too late.

Set in the small Maine town of Motton, the story beat out (that year
alone) works by Joyce Carol Oates, Alice Adams, Jane Smiley, et al.

An interviewer said that, of late, the critics had been kinder to him, and
that the story was a "classic" King story. King responded:

> This is wonderful. But you're right, it is a classic Stephen King story. I
> was talking with somebody about "The Man in the Black Suit," saying,
> "I can't believe this, I won the O. Henry Award, I won the World Fan-
> tasy Award"—and I had never won a World Fantasy Award before for

a piece of prose by myself. I shared the award one year with Dennis Etchison and I got a "special" award, which means, "Thanks, Steve. Because everybody likes your books, a lot of us got contracts." But this seemed like every other story that I ever wrote in my life, and more boring than some. I think a lot of people who read the story don't recognize it as being typical of my work because they haven't read much of my work.[5]

Later that year, on October 11 and 12, 1996, a "Reading Stephen King Conference," held at UMO, brought together three hundred people who came to celebrate King's fiction. Organized by Brenda Power, an associate professor of literary education, the conference attracted fans, readers, and scholars from around the country, who gave addresses exploring every nook and cranny of the fictional universe of Stephen King.

Burton Hatlen, King's teacher, introduced King before his address, and explained what he felt was King's unique literary position:

> It has to do with this position he occupies between mass culture and high culture. How many people would write a novel like King does and include all these epigraphs from literature? He's a key mediating figure between mass culture and traditional culture. That split between high and mass culture can be debilitating. We can't just have high culture. But if all we have is a media culture, then we're impoverished. He has allowed us another possibility: to get these two perspectives together.[6]

Predictably, some of the papers read struck some of the participants as very highbrow. A graduate student in English at New York University, for instance, gave a talk on "Raising the Dead: Teaching Theory Through Non-Canonical Texts," explaining that King's "one of the best. Reading him is not discontinuous with traditional canonical horror works."[7]

At the buffet dinner, surrounded by a phalanx of friends, King went through the buffet line, picking up Hot Nadine Crossed Buns, Anne Wilkes's Chicken Fricassee, 'Salem's Lotsa Pasta, and Bull's-Eye Red Licorice.

The music in the background included theme music from *The Addams Family, Ghostbusters,* and that campy favorite, *Monster Mash.*

Wearing a Harley T-shirt, jeans, and cowboy boots, King made his own fashion statement of sorts.

One fan, who sat near the table where King and his colleagues gathered, remarked, "He's an amazing guy, really. I mean, I don't know him but you see him at the movies or at the baseball field. He's just one of the crowd."[8]

True enough . . . until King sits down to write and exercises what is likely to be one of the most imaginative storytelling minds in the book world, going to fictional places that exist only in his head and coming back with stories uniquely his own.

In terms of books, it would be Stephen King's golden year. Starting in March, the first installment of his serial thriller *The Green Mile* was published, titled "The Two Dead Girls."

A prison novel set in 1932, the novel was a literary experiment of sorts: King, who wrote that he was "a writer who exists more on nerve-endings than the process of intellectual thought and logic"[9] is not an outliner; he starts a story and, as it takes off, follows the characters as they go every which way.

The advantage of writing by intuition is that the story is as much a surprise for the writer as it is for the reader. The disadvantage is that, if you're not careful, you can paint yourself into a corner, as King did with *Cycle of the Werewolf* before changing from calendar to book format, or with *Christine*, with one narrator telling the first and last part of the story in the first person, and the second part being told in the third person because the narrator got hurt . . . and, besides, it would have been impossible to cover that middle part otherwise.

King, for his part, explained that it was a thrill for him to write without a safety net. "That is part of the excitement of the whole thing, though—at this point I'm driving through thick fog with the pedal all the way to the metal."[10]

That first installment would be followed by five more installments, so that in August, the final installment would be told, and the novel would be complete, requiring the reader to dutifully buy all six. "It's like a novelistic striptease," King told an interviewer. "It's old-fashioned. The opposite of instant gratification—like pushing a button online and getting something off your laser printer. Not this time."[11]

The idea appealed to King for two reasons: First, as a suspense novelist, he's always disliked the idea of readers skipping ahead to the end of the book, to take a peek and see how the book turned out. It was cheating, King felt, and he was frustrated because he had no control over the story once published. In this case, however, he still held the cards . . . and dealt them out poker-faced, one by one, to readers.

"I want to stay dangerous, and that means taking risks," he told *Entertainment Weekly*.[12]

The risk for King was that the story would take an unexpected turn and he'd be stuck, plotwise, with nowhere to go. But the payoff was that if he pulled it off, he'd have done something no other popular novelist in recent history had done—strung the readers along for six months, whetting their appetites, just as readers of the *Saturday Evening Post* (whose ranks included King as a teenager) had to wait for the next installment to see what happened.

It's a device that pulp magazines used years ago to maximum effect, so it seemed appropriate that the paperbacks, on cheap pulp paper, would be the vehicle instead of the usual hardback edition.

Like "Rita Hayworth and Shawshank Redemption," this was a prison story with a twist . . . and one of the best novels King has ever written. The story of John Coffey— a gentle black giant of a man with an extraordinary gift— delighted everyone, in and outside the horror field.

USA Today, one of King's harsher critics, enthused, "One of King's most immediately engaging page-turners . . . tantalizing mysteries . . . horrors . . . wonders."[13]

The *Boston Globe* gushed, "King surpasses our expectations, leaves us spellbound and hungry for the next twist of plot."[14]

And the cunning linguists at *Entertainment Weekly* who pride themselves on their clever headlines and catch phrases stated simply, "King's best in years . . . a prison novel that's as haunting and touching as it is just plain haunted."[15]

In the book trade, everyone sat up and took notice. Each installment blew out of the bookstores, selling over a million copies each, producing a record for King: six best-sellers in six months, paving the way for the two big fall titles, *Desperation* and *The Regulators*, which would add two more to the list—an astonishing *eight* best-sellers simultaneously, a record that had never been achieved in adult fiction in book publishing history.

Predictably, the imitators followed suit, starting with John Saul, who was anxious to follow after King had blazed the trail. Serial fiction, thanks to King, was making a comeback; and nobody was more surprised than King himself.

"Sure *The Green Mile* is doing well, they're having a ball, it's succeeding, it's making them all happy. But I guess you could say they had no option: if it fell flat, they're basically holding a dead, rotting corpse out there for six months and trying to tell everyone it's a bouquet of flowers."[16]

The fallout from *The Green Mile* set the stage for the "twinner" books, *Des-*

peration by Stephen King and *The Regulators* by Richard Bachman, to be published on the same day. "We didn't plan for *The Green Mile* to be an entryway to the fall novels, but that's what it has turned out to be," Elaine Koster of NAL said.[17]

It would be one hell of a fall for King.

Where does an 800-pound gorilla sit? Anywhere he wants to . . . which is the position King was in when he worked out the terms of publishing for two books that comprised both sides of the same coin: one side was stamped *Desperation*, by Stephen King; the reverse, *The Regulators*, by Richard Bachman.

NAL had its own mind on how to publish the books, but King forced the issue. First, King wanted the books published simultaneously, because of the thematic connection. "They didn't want to do it," King recalls.[18] Then they wanted to make sure everybody knew it was a Stephen King book, so they wanted to publish *The Regulators* with cover credit to make the connection clear, but King forbade that as well, because "you might as well then just say 'written by Stephen King.' "[19]

NAL acceded to King's wishes. The result: Stephen King's *Desperation* was published by Viking simultaneously with Richard Bachman's *The Regulators*, a Dutton title. Both in hardback, the books shared the same cover art by Mark Ryden, designed to be positioned side-by-side to show the King-Bachman connection.

NAL, for its part, would push 1.75 million copies of *Desperation* and 1.25 million copies of *The Regulators* simultaneously into bookstores, backed up with a $2 million ad/promo campaign, which included: a two-for-one pack, in which both books were shrink-wrapped together, with a "keep-you-up-all-night" book light, limited to 200,000 sets; a floor display unit with a revolving top, packaged with a dozen copies of the books, including some in the book light package; a special toll-free number (1-888-4Bachman) to get information on the Bachman book; abridged audios read by Kathy Bates (for *Desperation*) and Mary-Louise Parker (for *The Regulators*), although King preferred unabridged audios ("I couldn't bear to look at them," he said); thirty-second television ads (a million bucks' worth) to push the books as a pair; and linked web sites for those with Internet access.

The inspiration that drove *Desperation* occurred when, in 1991, on the way back from Oregon, where he picked up his daughter's car to bring it back to Maine, King drove through Ruth, Nevada, a small, desolate town. Wondering where all the people were, King thought to himself that the towns-folk were dead and then asked himself who had killed them, and the answer: "The sheriff killed them all."[20]

In the novel, David Carter must fight Tak, embodied in the form of the sheriff of the town, in a classic good versus evil confrontation, assisted by Johnny Marinville, who rode into town not on a horse but on his Harley. "I love Johnny," King said, " but I don't think he's a whole lot like me. Coincidentally, he rides the same motorcycle, but he's really a composite of every pontificating white male writer I ever grew up with, and I'm not going to name names. Besides, he's won a National Book Award and the way things are going I'm not making space on my shelf for one."[21]

The Regulators had its genesis in "The Shotgunners," an unpublished screenplay by King for Sam Peckinpah. "It was a strange story of vigilante ghosts from the last century appearing in a Western town to avenge a hanging. They came, not on horseback, but in three, long black Cadillacs with darkened windows. Peckinpah was in preproduction when, in 1984, he died of a heart attack."[22]

In the screenplay, the Caddys go down a normal, suburban street; the darkened windows on the cars go down; and shotguns emerge, opening fire on the unsuspecting victims.

According to Ann Lloyd, "King says it's one of his favorite pieces of work, and he cannot understand why nobody else has shown any interest in the project."[23]

Beyond the obvious—*Desperation* is the more optimistic book, but *The Regulators* is downright depressing, as you'd expect from a Bachman book—the two books fit hand-in-hand like a glove, so you can read either book first.

The limited edition of *Desperation*, from Donald M. Grant, was a numbered and signed edition of 2,050 tray-cased copies ($175), as well as a gift edition ($75, not numbered or signed), with dust jacket and slipcase.

Unlike *Desperation*, *The Regulators* presented a major problem as a signed edition: Its author, Richard Bachman, had died, so unless spirit writing could be used—appropriate but not reliable—another method had to be invoked.

The ingenious solution was to insert dummy checks, each signed by King *as* Richard Bachman. (The few that slipped through King's hands and were signed *by* him became even more collectible.)

Drawn on the First Bank of New England, the checks bore the return address of Richard Bachman: 432 Marsten Street, Starkeville, NH 03057. Each check was made out to fictional King characters or other personages, complete with memos that explained why the check was written. (Check #53, for instance, was made payable to: Quitters Inc., for $5,000.50 — the fee the firm charged for their services . . . and fifty cents for electricity.)

Designed by Joe Stefko of Charnel House, a small press known for its imaginative production values on its books, this striking edition was overseen by Peter Schneider of Penguin USA.

The Regulators had a limited edition of 500 copies ($325). "We decided that we would make the box for the book look like a toy box, like one of the MotoKops vans. It's a cloth-covered box with a color illustration by Allan M. Clark, of the van with the shotguns bristling out and the radar dish."[24]

In addition, fifty-two lettered copies were made, with an entirely different design: "We used a western theme. The box is basically a wooden tray-case, but the book inside is bound in full grain leather, with the name, the title of the book, and the author's name branded on the spine. Protruding from the cover are the heads of four Winchester .30-.30 bullets that stick up approximately a half inch; on the back cover, the ends of the fired cartridges protrude — the little pin marks show on the back of each cartridge, since Joe actually had them fired."[25]

As expected, sales of the trade and limited editions of both books exceeded all expectations. For King fans, 1996 was a year of plenty: *eight* books, carefully doled out, creating a year of reading riches.

King has never had a year quite like that again, nor is it likely that he ever will, because he has no plans to do another serialized novel. Regardless, Penguin USA called this one correctly, saying that it was "the year of Stephen King publishing."[26]

It was not, however, the year of Stephen King film adaptations, like the previous year. *Thinner* was thin gruel for King fans, tired of a diet of on-and-off adaptations. Barely grossing more than the anemic *Pet Sematary 2* ($14.5 million at the box office), *Thinner* was a minor footnote in an otherwise memorable year.

❧26❧

Κɪɴɢ, ᴡʜᴏ ꜱᴇᴇꜱ ꜰᴀᴍᴇ ᴀɴᴅ ᴄᴇʟᴇʙʀɪᴛʏ as states of misery, knows their downsides, as Douglas E. Winter observed: "Stephen King speaks rarely of the dark side of his success—the overeager fans, the genuine crazies, the never-private life, the omnipresent specter of exploitation. . . ."[1]

The upside is that, in terms of King's work, there's more control over its publication—witness *Desperation* and *The Regulators*—and, because of his track record, he can go back and get some things done right the second time: case in point, a film adaptation of *The Shining*, one of King's best novels.

"Why," asked *TV Guide*'s Mark Schwed, "spend $23 million on a six-hour miniseries for ABC when the 1980 Stanley Kubrick movie starring Jack Nicholson was so darn good that some movie buffs with a taste for the macabre consider it a classic? There are two answers: Because King *can*, and because the movie took liberties with his book about a hotel caretaker named Jack Torrance who goes mad while snowed in at a remote mountainside resort haunted by evil spirits. . . . He wanted to do it *his* way."[2]

Filmmaking, like life, is a capricious business.

Originally released in 1980, *The Shining* could justifiably be retitled *Stanley Kubrick's The Shining*, because it was clearly his film more than it was King's book. Of that adaptation, King said:

> Stanley Kubrick's version of *The Shining* is a lot tougher for me to evaluate, because I'm still profoundly ambivalent about the whole thing. I'd admired Kubrick for a long time and had great expectations for the project, but I was deeply disappointed in the end result. Parts of the film are chilling, charged with a relentlessly claustrophobic terror, but others fall flat. . . . Not that religion has to be involved in horror, but a visceral skeptic such as Kubrick just couldn't grasp the sheer inhuman evil of the Overlook Hotel. So he looked, instead, for evil in the characters and made the film into a domestic tragedy with only vaguely supernatural overtones. That was the basic flaw: because he couldn't believe, he couldn't make the film believable to others. . . . What's ba-

sically wrong with Kubrick's version of *The Shining* is that it's a film by a man who thinks too much and feels too little; and that's why, for all its virtuoso effects, it never gets you by the throat and hangs on the way real horror should.

I'd like to remake *The Shining* someday, maybe even direct it if anybody will give me enough rope to hang myself with.[3]

Since King had already done that with *Maximum Overdrive*, the decision was made to hire a bonafide director. But King did write the screenplay, serve as an executive producer, and made a cameo appearance as the tuxedo-clad leader of the Gage Creed Band.

With directing duties placed squarely in the hands of Mick Garris, the ABC miniseries was scheduled to air during sweeps week on April 27 and 28, and May 1, 1997. It would be titled "Stephen King's *The Shining*," and this time, ABC-TV and King meant it—this film would be his, from first to last frame.

When scoping out locations, Garris and some Warner Brothers executives went to Estes Park, where Garris took some shots with a camcorder, hoping to convince the suits that this was the place to shoot the film—not Canada, which was being seriously considered—since it would save money.

Garris sent his film to King. "Steve, what would you think if we were able to actually do it at the Stanley Hotel?"

King replied, "That would be a dream come true."[4]

King's dream came true.

The press conference for the film was held on January 9, 1997, at the Ritz-Carlton Huntington Hotel in Pasadena, California, where the cast and key crew fielded questions from the media: Mick Carliner (producer), Mick Garris (director), Stephen King (screenwriter, executive producer, actor), Steven Weber (in the key role of Jack Torrance), and Rebecca de Mornay (as his wife Wendy). Missing from the conference was Courtland Mead, the child actor who portrayed Danny Torrance.

Predictably, the media wanted to discuss this new version in light of the Kubrick version, but King had to curb his tongue— a precondition set by Kubrick prior to releasing the rights for a remake.

"Mr. King, there's been numerous reports that you weren't happy with the first interpretation. How accurate were they and how do you feel about it?"

King replied, "Well, I'll tell you, I came in last night, flew across the country. I hate to fly because there's no breakdown lane up there. If it stops, it's over; forget it. You don't have a chance—you're done. So I'm thinking to myself, I'm flying 3,000 miles to say, 'no comment.'"

The members of the media laughed, taken off-guard by King's honesty. This was the usual "sell the cast and push the movie" time, but at least it would be good for a few laughs—Stephen King and Steven Weber would see to that.

When asked how it felt to walk in Kubrick's footsteps, Garris replied, "Stanley Kubrick is a genius, one of the great filmmakers of our time; and the idea of doing it was daunting, but the actuality of doing it was that I was trying *not* to walk in his footsteps. Kubrick made Stanley Kubrick's *The Shining*. I felt my job was to make Stephen King's *The Shining*, so we went back to the book.

"There are a lot of very important elements in that book that we thought should have been treated in a cinematic manner, particularly the whole subject of abuse and alcoholism and responsibility, and the whole idea of familial and parental guilt. All of those things were, to my way of thinking, what the book was about, and what Steve's script was about, which was very faithful to the book."

King added, "What I did was to try to write the truest, most wrenching story. . . . *The Shining* is a story about a haunted hotel, but it's also a story about a haunted marriage. And the two things should work together. The reality of that abusive relationship should enhance and make the ghost story even more frightening than it is."

The end result, which had been preceded by teaser ads in the weeks leading up to the first night, was very much as King promised: *The Shining* was a story overtly about a haunted hotel but, in fact, really about a family disintegrating before their eyes, with Danny Torrance—endearingly portrayed by Courtland Mead—and his mother Wendy watching in horror.

A big point of concern—the casting of Jack Torrance—had been put to rest when Steven Weber (from the TV show *Wings*) delivered a convincing portrayal of an ordinary man, a former alcoholic, whose tenuous grasp on reality slips into madness, abetted by the ghosts that haunted him from without (ghosts from the Overlook's past) and from within (ghosts from his own past).

In "Hits & Misses," *TV Guide*'s Susan Steward explained:

> This version deepens and enriches both the novel and the 1980 Stanley Kubrick film without sacrificing a single shiver. Steven Weber is superb as the alcoholic writer. His demons are as dreadful as the killer topiar-

ies at the hotel where he, his wife and son endure a chilling winter. Structure echoes meaning: As the horror materializes, the family disintegrates. Their bloody endgame of croquet is both the climax of a great ghost story and the consummation of an intense relationship drama. My score (0-10): **10**.)

Supplementing the laudatory review, that issue also featured a cover illustration by Berni Wrightson who also illustrated a truncated version of "Before the Play" for this issue highlighting the remake.

Far from being a hands-off writer, King very much likes to do things *his* way, even when he doesn't need to. Case in point: the same month that saw the release of *Stephen King's The Shining* saw the publication of *Six Stories*, published only in a signed, limited edition of 1,100 copies (900 sold at $80, with 200 reserved for the press), collecting "Lunch at the Gotham Café" (a Bram Stoker award-winning story, published in *Dark Love*), "L.T.'s Theory of Pets," (a new story), "Luckey Quarter" (from *USA Weekend*), "Autopsy Room Four" (a new story), "Blind Willie" (from *Anateus*), and "The Man in the Black Suit" (from *The New Yorker*).

Beautifully designed by Michael Alpert, whose distinctive sense of design underscores his philosophy of form following function, the book featured beautifully set type, generous leading, and plenty of white space in the margins—refreshing at a time when young graphic designers today favor design over function, resulting in illegible type and eye-popping MTV design.

Sold on a first-come, first-serve basis, *Six Stories* sold out before publication through postings on the Internet and in King discussion groups online, supplemented by postcard mailings from two specialty newsletters, *The Red Letter* and *Phantasmagoria*.

In stark contrast to the production values of *Six Stories*, with its heavy interior paper stock and sewn signatures to insure the book would hold up over time, the reprint of *The Green Mile*, published in May, was little better than the previously published installments in terms of its durability. A trade paperback, on very cheap pulp paper, with a cheap glue binding guaranteed to crack its spine in time, this edition will disintegrate over time.

King fans who want durable editions would gladly have paid more for a hardback with sewn signatures, but they were happy to get what they got: all six installments under one cover.

The cost of *The Green Mile*, in the serialized edition, was approximately $19; the cost of the new edition, $14.95; too bad the book did not get a more durable showcase, like NAL's "Stephen King Collectors Editions," which used beautiful paper, with handsome type, leading, design, and sturdier binding.

For the new edition, King contributed a new introduction, supplementing his original Foreword from the serialized edition, and retained its original Afterword, as well.

On another publishing front, Doubleday—King's former publishing house—went to press with *The Speed Queen*, by Stewart O'Nan, but not under its original title—*Dear Stephen King*. A trade hardback, *The Speed Queen* got a lot of attention, including from Stephen King, whose lawyers reportedly pressured Doubleday to change the title. Whether the title caused King, his lawyers, or all of them a dose of misery, the title was discreetly changed, though not before the cover had been printed and the title on the black spine whited out and overprinted with the new title.

Stewart O'Nan, who had read and admired Gordon Lish's *Dear Truman Capote*, took a page from that book and titled his novel *Dear Stephen King*. What he hadn't counted on was King's lawyers' reaction.

What, then, *was* the connection between the title and Stephen King himself?

Publishers Weekly explained:

> The book is framed as the death-row confession of convicted murderer Marjorie Standiford, nicknamed the Speed Queen, one of the infamous Sonic Killers. Speaking into a tape recorder furnished by the author enlisted to write her story (unnamed, but presented as the author of *Misery, The Shining* and *Desperation*), Marjorie looks back at teenage life on the outskirts of Oklahoma City . . . But Stephen King's role is little more than a gimmick (it's never clear, as in Lish's novel, if the author is merely a figment of the narrator's imagination.[5]

Illustrated by Mark Geyer, who had previously illustrated King's *The Green Mile, The Speed Queen* was, according to its author, misreviewed in *Publishers Weekly* and, in a rebuttal piece published in *Phantasmagoria*, he set the reviewer straight:

> Stephen King's role in the book is that of confessor; he's the person (and persona) all of America can bring their fears and secrets to (like Truman Capote in *Dear Mr. Capote*—but Capote's dead, and why would you trust him with your story? You want the best author in America—Stephen King!). He's the one person who can show us what life is like in America, the one person who can understand all the terri-

ble things inside us and around us. He will understand and be able to tell other people Marjorie's story so they understand her. He represents Truth to Marjorie, and also possibly a judge-like figure, in that she sees her life through the lens of his fiction, continually comparing what happened to her to his characters. At this point she sees her life as a fiction, a story that she wants to find meaning in, and Stephen King is going to help her. One of the really fun things in the book is how Marjorie gives him advice on how to write certain scenes effectively. What Stephen King writes will be read by everyone and accepted as the Truth, so she's trying to put herself in the best light possible. If she can convince him to treat her like one of his sympathetic characters, she knows her memory will be safe. It's a transparent ploy: several times she asks him outright to please be nice to her.[6]

Some years ago, someone proposed the wonky idea of editing a collection of stories using Stephen King as the main character, which never got off the ground because King contacted the hopeful editor and dissuaded him from proceeding with the project.

To my mind, there's a world of difference in imagination and execution in trying to cobble together a book using King as a fictional character, and using King as the subject of the musings of a fictional character; the former strikes me as ludicrous; the latter, intriguing. Still, there's that pesky business of King's name in a commercial novel, with the hint that the name is being used to sell the book.

Regardless, it was a dead issue because *Dear Stephen King* became *The Speed Queen.* The book's dedication, however, remained unchanged: "To my dear Stephen King. . . ."

All's well that ends well, however. King read the novel and, afterward, sent Stewart O'Nan a personalized copy of *Six Stories.*

There's a big difference between fans and readers. To my mind, Anne Rice has a lot of fans, in addition to readers. These are people who don't necessarily read her books but embrace the philosophies in them, who live in a secondary universe composed of other fans who are attracted *to* Anne Rice and, incidentally, to her fiction.

In Jana Marcus's fascinating photo/text profile of Rice fans and readers, *In the Shadow of the Vampire: Reflections from the World of Anne Rice,* the range of fans, readers, and fan/readers is not surprising, considering the range of her work, from the vampire stories to the historical pieces, from the fairy tale erotica to the contemporary erotica.

Rice's fans have created "a subculture," writes Marcus in the Preface to her book, "which includes role-playing games, reading clubs, and Internet groups, all stemming from adoration for Anne and her books. These groups have, in turn, become meeting grounds for people who otherwise may never have crossed paths."[7]

Rice's fictional world and real world intertwine like a Gordian knot. And her fans—as apart from her readers—relish the various lifestyles her diverse stories showcase.

"There is an active fan club of more than eight thousand, the annual Gathering of the Coven Ball in New Orleans, movies, comic book novels, audiotapes, an Anne Rice tour company, a perfume line, a Lestat wine, T-shirts emblazoned with an MRI [magnetic resonance image] of Rice's brain, and soon a Lestat restaurant is scheduled in New Orleans," writes Marcus.[8]

What has this got to do with Stephen King? Simply this: In a world where celebrities have become public commodities, with merchandising and self-marketing to cash in on the brand name, King has repudiated that entire scene. There was an official newsletter, *Castle Rock*, but he wasn't an active participant; there is no fan club per se, though informal groups have sprung up; there's movies and audiotapes, and there was even a comic book from a movie, but there's no way in hell King would authorize anyone to run a tour company in Bangor, Maine, of King's haunts, or push a perfume line ("Buy King's Cologne, with its unmistakable scent of a freshly dug grave!"), or a burgundy wine bearing his label, or a T-shirt displaying his brain (in any form), or promote a restaurant with fare like Hot Nadine Crossed Buns, Anne Wilkes's Chicken Fricasse, or 'Salem's Lotsa Pasta.

Even so, the fans will do their own things—publish newsletters, chat on the Internet, and meet with fellow fans to celebrate King's work and fiction, which is what happened at Horrorfest, a convention held at the Stanley Hotel in 1989 that drew 325 attendees.

The Internet, however, changed the face of fandom, and instead of exchanging letters, they send e-mail, post comments in discussion groups in on-line forums, and construct web sites, with links to other web sites.

Like the rest of the world, the Kings—Stephen and Tabitha—have gone electronic; they use e-mail as a regular means of communication, monitor what's said in the news groups, and check out the web sites. (When *The Green Mile*'s web site went up, it received 1.4 million "hits"—visits from curious readers—including one from King himself.) But meeting on-line, in chat rooms (shouldn't there be one named room 217?), and receiving e-zines (electronic zines) can't substitute for meeting in person . . . so SKEMERs

(Stephen King E-Mailers) converged on Bangor, Maine, on August 8–10, for a weekend at a Holiday Inn for informal dinners, a formal presentation, trips to Bangor sites (King-related, of course), and several trips to Betts Bookstore.

King, who was out of town, would never have attended, nor did one of the staffers from King's office, who had hoped to make an appearance on Saturday when the group gathered in a meeting room in the Holiday Inn restaurant to make speeches, give its founder Michelle Rein a copy of *Six Stories* and a gift certificate to Betts Bookstore, exhibit Kingiana, and hear Stuart Tinker of Betts Bookstore give tips on collecting King. The group even managed to get a beaming creepazoid writer who signed copies of his unauthorized books on King.

That weekend also marked the official publication date of the Grant edition of *The Dark Tower IV: Wizard and Glass*, which had arrived at Betts, straight from the publisher in nearby New Hampshire.

Wizard and Glass, published six interminably long years after the previous volume, continues the epic story of Roland the Gunslinger, who, aided by Eddie, Jake, and Susannah, continues on his quest for the Dark Tower.

The previous volume ended in a cliffhanger, with Roland and his companions trapped on a sentient train, picking up speed, threatening to crash until they could talk their way out of the situation by answering Blaine the Mono's riddles and posing their own.

A beautiful edition, the $45 hardback was illustrated by Dean McKean, a British illustrator best known for his impressionistic art for Neil Gaiman's *The Sandman* comic book series.

Unlike Grant's previous editions, this one was also sold by the chain stores, including Barnes and Noble, Amazon.com (an on-line book company based in Seattle, Washington), and Waldenbooks, prompting some die-hard King fans to complain that what was once theirs—Grant's editions of King's Dark Tower novels—now belonged to everybody . . . but should that have been the case all along? Given a choice, wouldn't they have wanted to spend the extra money for the better value?

Minor complaints aside, the book's appearance everywhere, months before King's readers expected to see it, was a pleasant surprise. Even the $38 price seemed more than reasonable—King's trade books like *The Regulators* cost $24.95 and had *no* full-color illustrations, whereas *Wizard and Glass* had illustrated endpapers, numerous black-and-white decorations, and full-color, full-page illustrations.

❧27❧

It was near closing time when the Australian bookstore owner saw two tall men walk into his shop. One of them stood over six feet tall, wearing a leather jacket, sporting a heavy beard. He had gotten off his Harley motorcycle and he definitely was the kind of man you wouldn't want to mess with.

It was late at night, dark, and the store owner was understandably apprehensive, since several local retailers had been held up . . . at closing time.

The tall stranger reached into his pocket and the nervous storeowner probably gulped hard, wondering if he'd be looking at the business end of a gun. The stranger's hand cleared the pocket, not with a gun but with a fistful of bills, all hundreds.

The stranger began going through a stack of newly published fiction and said that he'd like to see that store's best-sellers for the year, since he probably had a few books on there. The store owner gave him the list, which the stranger perused.

The stranger was correct—he did have several best-sellers, including the best-selling book of the year, *The Green Mile*.

The stranger was Stephen King.

But what was he doing in the Australian Outback? And on a Harley? And what was the explosive bombshell that was set to go off back in the States, courtesy of his agent, Arthur B. Greene?

Just as large banks have swallowed up the smaller ones, large book publishers have merged, joining forces, creating a half dozen houses that among them sell the majority of best-sellers in this country.

NAL, Stephen King's publisher for two decades, was no longer a separate entity. NAL had merged with G. P. Putnam, the house that publishes Dick Francis and megaseller Tom Clancy, whose current book contract of $50 million eclipsed any deal King had gotten from his publisher.

For the last year, the rumor circulating in the King community was that King was unhappy at NAL, but only recently had he begun making his grievances public, mostly in matters of book marketing for *Desperation*, *The Regulators*, and now the six installments of *The Green Mile*. It was also well known, for instance, that King hadn't signed any new book contract with NAL, although a thousand-page manuscript, *Bag of Bones*, had been turned in to NAL in October.

The final straw: King had grumbled about his publisher's ill-advised purchase of Marcia Clark's O. J. Simpson book, which cost the company $4.2 million, a sum he knew the book could never earn out, with the glutted market of Simpson books already finding their way back to their publishers' warehouses, creating heavy returns.

These disagreements were the tip of the iceberg, but who knows what constituted the bulk of that iceberg? There was more—much more—than what King had shared with the public, but the bottom line was this: King no longer felt welcome at NAL. "Putnam brought in a very potent list. . . . I'm only speculating here, but I think I was just not that important anymore to them. It was either that or an inept negotiator. . . . I got the feeling from them, 'If you want to go, go.' "[1]

King went, no doubt surprising his publisher, wondering just what the hell was happening. NAL's Marilyn Ducksworth responded, "We wanted to continue the relationship and did everything in our power to keep him that was economically viable."[2]

From all accounts, it wasn't about the money—it was about how King was being marketed, sold, promoted as a total package, and how he felt the marketing wasn't effective, unable to reach new readers.

In a word, King's perception was that NAL had gotten complacent, and his potential sales had suffered in the process.

Part of the dissatisfaction could have been that with Clancy on the scene, King felt he'd be somewhat ignored. Clancy, after all, appeals to a mainstream audience, some of whom came to his books through his successful film adaptations, or came to his books through the extensive merchandising—spin-off computer games, collaborative nonfiction, collaborative fiction, and other Clancy-sanctioned products engineered to maximize his presence in various media.

King, on the other hand, was still perceived by the reading public as a horror writer, one whose clout in the film community had fallen sufficiently that, for the first time in years, he failed to make the annual compilation of "Power 100" in *Entertainment Weekly*, a subjective listing of who's who in the entertainment field.

Perhaps feeling like the odd man out, King had instructed his agent, Arthur B. Greene, to send out letters to a few publishing houses to allow them to bid on *Bag of Bones*. The houses included Scribner, FSG, Random House, Warner, Morrow, and Atlantic Monthly/Grove.

News of King's defection broke at Frankfurt, the international book fair, when Bookwire.com reported on the situation. At the fair itself, talks were underway, as houses began marshaling their key people to structure deals to put on the table for King.

Meanwhile, King decided it was time to get away from it all, riding a Harley motorcycle across Australia's Outback, knowing that he couldn't be reached for comment. This would be Greene's problem to deal with, not his.

Greene, however, is not a literary agent and, for whatever reasons, handled the matter quite differently from the traditional method. By publishing tradition, when a big-name author decides to jump ship, discreet inquiries are made and the prospective publisher courts the big-name author by making a personal trip to discuss possibilities. Doing so saves face for the former publisher, who wasn't looking for a divorce, and it keeps it out of the media.

Greene, King's longtime business manager and lawyer by trade, handled it as a lawyer would: He sent out letters to prospective publishers, asking for bids with stipulations attached: the size of the advance (over $17 million), a 27 percent royalty rate, and a reversions clause that would in effect give rights back to King within a specified number of years—a stark contrast to the open-ended deal in which the publisher gets to keep the book for the life of the copyright (the author's lifetime plus fifty years), with reversion only if the publisher deems the book unprofitable and decides to give it back to the author. The letter was accompanied by *Bag of Bones*, so the publishers wouldn't be bidding on a pig in a poke.

Predictably, unnamed industry sources chimed in, making their dissatisfactions known. The result: What was intended to be a private negotiation turned into a public relations nightmare for King, who found himself making the news not because of the book but because of the book deal.

Because of the politics involved, nobody would speak on record, but the consensus was clear: King had spoken out of class, and nobody was happy, least of all King.

One publisher observed, "A letter was submitted, which seemed very weird, while King was in Australia. You have a Stephen King, you pick up the phone. You don't write a letter; the publisher meets with the author."[3]

An unnamed agent chimed in: "You call a publisher and say, 'let's talk.' And by then, you've worked up the numbers. You don't just pull them out of the air. But it's not only about money; it's about editing, publishing philosophy, which psychology works the best."[4]

King agreed. "I know we did it the wrong way. Hopefully, in the end, the talk will be about the book and not about the negotiations."[5]

Unfortunately, the public dealings made King look like the disgruntled author who was abandoning the faithful publisher, which during these proceedings held its head up high and said, in so many words, that the house still considered itself in the negotiation process with King, and they were still in the running, when clearly it seemed otherwise.

The truth, at that point, was that King had left them behind permanently, but NAL had to engage in damage control, since they would soon be releasing the fourth *Dark Tower* novel in trade paperback and didn't want King's ongoing negotiations in the media to overshadow the book's release.

When King returned from Australia in early November, the hue and cry in the media about his demands had reached a fever pitch and, wanting to put an end to this embarrassing debate in the media over his book deal, he put an end to it quickly. He signed a deal with Scribner, a three-book deal that included *Bag of Bones*, an untitled collection of short stories, and *On Fiction*, King's final word on the craft of storytelling, drawing heavily on his personal experience in the trade as a scrivener.

For *Bag of Bones*, King got $2 million up front—a far cry from the $17 million he had originally asked for. He will get the bulk of his money on the back-end, as much as 50 percent of the profits. (Gross or net? As any author who has dealt with the byzantine accounting practices of the movie industry, a percentage of the profits can be worth nothing, if the numbers are manipulated to the studio's advantage.)

Though similar deals have been engineered for nonfiction books penned by celebrities, this is the first time a fiction writer has structured such a deal, bypassing the traditional advance against fixed royalties for the life of the book.

Jack Romanos, the president of the Simon & Schuster Consumer Group, was predictably enthused about this early Christmas present. "Stephen King," said Romanos, "has proven to be as creative with his deal-making as his writing. Our partnership is based on the value of the works. The actual performance of each title will determine the profit participation. The deal structure puts priority on growing the Stephen King readership to even greater levels. "[6]

Clearly, King wanted a fresh start. "I had gotten a bit stale at Viking," King said in an interview with America Online's "The Book Review," "and we had reached a point where we were a bit too comfortable with each other."[7]

Scribner—the publishing house of Ernest Hemingway and F. Scott Fitzgerald—offered the kind of literary cachet that had long eluded him; and Scribner's parent company, Simon and Schuster, had the resources to properly sell, market, and promote an author of his caliber.

The deal also underscored another important matter: Would NAL's Elaine Koster get the consolation prize and secure reprint rights in paperback for King's new books, or would NAL be shut out?

As it turned out, both Elaine Koster and NAL were shut out: Koster resigned, after twenty-five years with the firm, and NAL was not offered reprint rights on the three new books. Instead of publishing King's next horror novel, NAL found itself in its own real-world King horror story—two decades of work in building King's name and identification with the company would have to be written off.

Instead, Pocket Books, the paperback arm of Simon & Schuster, will handle the reprints in-house. In addition, King's dissatisfaction with NAL may also prompt him to take his remaining books—leased, not sold—from them, sweetening the deal with a steady-selling backlist that, over two decades, has brought millions more to NAL's coffers. (Every book King has written is in print.) *The Green Mile*—critically acclaimed and financially successful—reverts in 2000, with the rest of the titles reverting within a decade, if King wants to pull out completely.

The smart money is on King changing houses completely, putting all of his eggs in the Scribner/Simon and Schuster basket. As for NAL, they would soon be in the unenviable position that Doubleday—King's former publisher—found themselves in after the publication of *The Stand*, when King jumped ship in 1977: a king-sized hole that can't be filled except with another best-selling author.

In short, according to King, NAL appears to have done exactly what Doubleday had done: given him the perception that he was no longer welcome, at which point he simply left, without looking back. NAL, it seems, is a part of King's past, and clearly not a part of his future.

The deal done, the principals in the new deal offered their perspectives.

Stephen King: "I'm happy that the public search for a new publisher has ended so successfully. *Bag of Bones* contains everything I now know about marriage, lust and ghosts, and it was essential to me that I find the right partner to publish it."[8]

Carolyn Reidey (president of the Simon & Schuster Trade Division): "From the appearance of *Carrie* in 1974, Stephen King has demonstrated not just an ability to capture an audience of unprecedented size with more than 225 million copies of 38 books in print, but has always demonstrated a unique sensitivity to the dynamics of the publishing industry. His career has been marked by experimentation and collaboration with his various publishers."[9]

Jonathan Newcomb (president and CEO of Simon & Schuster): "Mr. King and Simon & Schuster's Consumer Group have created what may be an important new model for S&S and potentially the entire industry."[10]

Susan Moldow (publisher of Scribner): "*Bag of Bones* is the work of a writer at the peak of his powers. It combines a story of a child in jeopardy with familiar elements from King's other works such as a haunted house, an insular and isolated community, and forces no one can control. Its story of the numbing effect of grief, the endless manifestations of the creative process and the emotional richness of a April romance, introduce a host of issues and themes of interest to a very broad readership. The book offers an emotional resonance that does not take a back seat to special effects. *Bag of Bones* is a bag of treasures for a publisher's promotional effort."[11]

Gina Centrello (president of Pocket Books): "With *Bag of Bones*, Stephen King has proven he can still delight and surprise readers. It is exciting to launch King's career with Pocket with this novel. King was one of the first writers to experiment with categories and formats—as seen recently in the widely imitated serial publication of *The Green Mile*—and has a history of making deals with publishers that emphasize growth."[12]

It would be bad enough in any circumstances to have lost an author of King's caliber, but to rub salt in the wound, NAL got a reminder of King's longstanding popularity—a taste of what they would soon be missing. King's long-awaited fourth installment of the *Dark Tower*, reprinted in trade paperback, shipped out nationwide, with an estimated first printing of two million copies. A $17.95 paperback, the book got NAL's star treatment: a dedicated web site, complete with interactive discussions for its readers; a tie-in to Book-of-the-Month Club's Stephen King Library, which offered it through television and print advertising; and, most prominently, mountains of copies, supplemented by newly redesigned covers for the three previously published *Dark Tower* novels, reissued in a slipcased set, with uniformly designed covers.

Predictably, *The Dark Tower IV: Wizard and Glass* shot to the top of the best-seller lists nationwide, in addition to getting excellent reviews.

As for the fifth *Dark Tower* novel, King has little to say. In "King's comments," on the *Dark Tower* website constructed by NAL, America's best-loved boogeyman states:

> I am going to continue the Dark Tower series, mostly because I have three women who work in my office that answer the fan mail, and a lot of times they don't tell me what's going on with the fan mail, except for the stuff that I pick up myself. But they put every Dark Tower letter on my desk. This is like a silent protest saying, get these people off our backs.
>
> But my plan this time—if all goes well—is to just continue working until the cycle is done and then, that way, I can walk away from that.
>
> It's always been my intention to finish. There isn't a day that goes by that I don't think about Roland and Eddie and Detta and all the other people, even Oy, the little animal. But this book has never done what I wanted it to do. I've been living with these guys longer than the readers have, ever since college, actually, and that's a long time ago for me.
>
> I want to finish it. But there are no guarantees in this business. I can walk out of here today and get hit by a bus and that would be the end of that. Unless it came into somebody by ouija board, which is always a possibility.
>
> But the other thing is, I can try and find out that the words aren't there any more. I don't think that will happen, but you never know 'til you open the cupboard.

❧28❧

As for when *The Dark Tower V* will appear, nobody knows . . . but King *does* keep his promises and, in time, he'll honor his pact with his readers by finishing the projected seven-book series and then do what he's always done: think up another story idea and then hole up in his home office to put it on paper, after which it will appear as a book, an audiobook, and most likely, a movie as well.

In the interim, here's what King fans have in store for them in the near future: *Bag of Bones*, set in King's mythical town of Derry, Maine, promises to be prime King, to be published in September 1998. *On Fiction* will be King's second nonfiction book, and his first to examine the art and craft of writing. The untitled collection of short fiction—likely to reprint *Six Stories* and other material—will be required reading for any King fan. And, on the film front, numerous projects are in the works, according to King: *Apt Pupil* (from *Different Seasons*); a six-hour television miniseries, *Storm of the Century*; an HBO production of *Rose Madder*; New Line Cinema's *Desperation*; Frank Darabont's *The Green Mile*; and an episode for the television series *X-Files*.[1]

By all accounts, Stephen King is an ordinary-looking man. He doesn't *look* like a boogeyman; he looks normal, until he sits down at the computer and shows his true colors—he's one of the most imaginative writers in the country today, bar none. "The media," Tabitha King wrote, "are frequently disappointed to discover an ordinary Yankee, size XL, drinking beer and watching baseball while his three children throw toys and his wife stews the checkbook."[2]

That's what most deceptive about King—he *looks* normal.

He isn't.

Looking at King will tell you nothing. Just surface impressions, hardly worth mentioning.

But *reading* King will tell you everything. In a very real sense, if you want to know what King is *really* like—a question his friend Douglas E. Winter has been asked repeatedly—you'd have to read the fiction, the nonfiction, and all the other written material, because taken together the work forms a composite picture, saying: Here I am trying to make sense of my life, trying to put my obsessions in order, and here's how it looks from my unique viewpoint.

King, who turned fifty in 1997, is far from finished. Like the narrator in Robert Frost's poem, "Stopping in the Woods on a Snowy Evening," King has promises to keep and miles to go before he sleeps. Beyond the *Dark Tower* novels, there's the sense that his imagination could spin new stories as plentiful as the innumerable rooms in the New York brownstone where members of The Club gather to tell stories.

It's a testament to King's imagination that he doesn't write the same book again and again, as some of his best-selling brethren do. It's a testament to King's desire to communicate that he doesn't restrict himself to book-length fiction, but instead writes a mountain of other words in every conceivable form. It's a testament to King's talent that it's impossible to predict what he's going to write next—that's a guessing game, and a fool's game, at that. And, finally, it's a testament to King's writing skills that every once in a while, he can turn out a story as note-perfect as "The Man in the Black Suit" and hardly breathe hard as he clears that high hurdle, while other writers—including those from the world of literary fiction—look on and gasp.

Has King, as Burton Hatlen asserted, become the bridge that links popular fiction to literary fiction?

Maybe so—can *you* name another writer who sells a million copies of his latest novel *and* gets a short story selected for an *O. Henry* collection?

As for King: "I never felt a conflict in my own soul between popular fiction and so-called literary fiction; when I sit down at the word processor, I just do what I do. I am always disappointed, however, when my work or another writer's work is relentlessly ghettoized by people who would protest vehemently if blacks were excluded from their local country club."[3]

But even if King does not go across the Reach, one thing is for certain: As Norman Mailer observed, "Writers don't have lifestyles. They sit in little rooms and write."

That's what King does, has done since 1974 when *Carrie* was published.

King, who can afford to indulge himself, who obviously doesn't *have* to write for a living, does what he's done for almost a quarter-century: He gets up in the morning, takes a walk, gets a drink of water, turns on the rock music, and starts writing at his home office. Four hours a day, almost every day of the year.

He'd do it, as he said, even if he wasn't paid for it. He does it on a computer but would do it longhand in a notebook if he were 35,000 feet up and had nothing else to write on. He'd do it no matter what the critics say, and he'd do it no matter how badly the film adaptations had been made.

In the end, King writes because he doesn't have a choice. It's an agreeable vocation, an honorable profession, but most of all it's a compulsion—King, by nature and inclination, is a storyteller. That's all he's ever wanted to be and that's all that's important to him, in the end.

The fans, the fame, the celebrity, and the trappings of success—none of that really matters. What *matters* are the words, the stories, the books; and what *really* matters is making that magical link between writer and reader . . . a link that now totals 250 million books, with no end in sight.

"Time passes. King marries the wonderful Tabitha Spruce (the smartest thing he ever did in his life), King works in a laundry and teaches high-school English, King almost drowns (or maybe just thinks he does) in Sebec Lake. King publishes his first story in 1968 and by 1978 has become America's Best-Loved Boogeyman, a kind of Norman Rockwell version of Freddy Krueger, how goshdang lucky can a guy get. . . . "

—Stephen King, *Mid-Life Confidential: The Rock Bottom Remainders*

RESOURCES

I GET A GOOD BIT OF MAIL from readers, which I'm always happy to get, so this seems like a good place to recommend resources for additional reading, and discuss the most frequently asked questions posed by readers over the years.

King Books by Beahm

This is my fourth book on King, published at Andrews McMeel Publishing. In order of publication:

• *The Stephen King Companion* (Andrews and McMeel, 1989 edition), is out of print. Published as a trade paperback original, this book was the one that started me down the road writing about King.

• *The Stephen King Story* (Andrews and McMeel, 1991 and 1992). This literary profile is superseded by this book, *Stephen King: America's Best-Loved Boogeyman* (Andrews McMeel Publishing, 1998).

• *The Stephen King Companion* (Andrews and McMeel, 1995). Revised, updated, and expanded, this edition has 80 percent new material, the remainder reprinted from the original edition.

• *Stephen King Collectibles: A Price Guide* (GB Ink, Spring 1998). A privately printed, small run in hardback, annotated and photo-illustrated, intended for serious collectors who have invested in signed King books and other noteworthy collectibles. (Because of its small print run, this book will not likely be available in trade bookstores.)

Phantasmagoria: An Unofficial Stephen King Zine

Published irregularly, this thirty-two-page zine covers King's professional activities: forthcoming books, limited editions, public appearances, movie deals, along with interviews about King (and the occasional interview with King, reprinted from other sources), photographs, reprinted articles, and profiles on King that appear in magazines and newspapers, checklists, etc.

My hope is to be able to publish this quarterly, but since I publish only when sufficient news on hand warrants publication, subscribers may see as few as one or two issues a year, or five issues a year—it just depends on my schedule and what's going on in King's world.

The advantage of my zine, like all of my books on King, is that because it's not sanctioned or endorsed by King, his publishers, or his representatives, you get an objective look at what's going on in King's career. You don't get the official party line, the refined sugar put out by his publishers. You get the raw stuff.

An extension of my books on King, *Phantasmagoria* is available by subscription only. Send a first-class stamp for information to:

GB Ink
Attn: Phantasmagoria
P.O. Box 3602
Williamsburg, VA 23187

E-Mail

I welcome e-mail but, because it's a one-person operation here, please understand that I may not be able to get back to you immediately. I will, however, try to respond as soon as I can, of course.

Also, because e-mail is sometimes undeliverable, please put your name and mailing address in your e-mail, so I have an alternative method of contacting you, just in case your e-mail is returned.

I can be reached through the Internet or America Online.

AOL: Geobeahm
Internet: Geobeahm@aol.com

Web Sites

I am amazed at the amount of information available about King on web sites—the poor man's electronic printing press. Because web sites change addresses frequently, I'll not list the addresses (URLs) here. Instead, you should use your browser with the search parameters of "Stephen King" to see what turns up. You'd be surprised—there's a wealth of material on-line.

I do have my own web site, which supplements my books and my zine. Point your browser at:

http://members.aol.com/geobeahm/index.html

Frequently Asked Questions

Where can I write to Stephen King?
Stephen King c/o Philtrum Press
P.O. Box 1186
Bangor, ME 04401

Keep in mind that King gets a lot of fan mail, much of it requiring a response, which keeps his three secretaries busy. So make it easy on them by enclosing a first-class stamp or a self-addressed, stamped envelope. And don't feel offended if you get King's standard postcard, or if he doesn't respond. It's just impossible for him to answer the fan mail personally *and* write the books, so he has to allocate his time accordingly.

I'm new to King collecting. Where can I go to get King collectibles?
I recommend Betts Bookstore—your best bet for things King. Located in Bangor, Maine, the bookstore also publishes a catalog detailing new (and old) King collectibles for sale.
They can be reached via their web site at:
http://www.acadia.net/betts
They can be reached by phone at (207) 947-7052, but it's best to write and get on the mailing list.
Write to:
Stuart Tinker
Betts Bookstore
26 Main Street
Bangor, ME 04401

I'm a student and want to write about King. What secondary sources do you recommend?
Fortunately, writing about King is *much* easier these days than it was when I started in 1988, because Michael Collings has recently published an updated, revised edition of his King bibliography. Published by Borgo Press, *The Work of Stephen King: An Annotated Bibliography and Guide* can be purchased from Betts Bookstore.
For primary material—King's novels—all can be found in bookstores or at libraries. Everything King has published in book form is in print. Happy hunting!

In the 1989 edition of The Stephen King Companion, *you provided a price guide to King's books. Why wasn't that in the newer edition?*

Like insects in amber, prices for King collectibles are frozen in time, if published in a book like *The Stephen King Companion* that can't be updated on an annual basis. Besides, the sheer number of new King collectibles demanded more space than I could allocate in the new edition of *The Stephen King Companion*.

I am currently writing *Stephen King Collectibles: A Price Guide*, which will provide detailed data on every King collectible, with photos. To be published in 1998 by my small press, this price guide will be updated periodically and provide a wealth of detail that I couldn't provide in my original price guide. (Send a first-class stamp to me for more information—see address above.)

What other books do you recommend about King?

Though it's out of date, Douglas E. Winter's seminal book, *Stephen King: The Art of Darkness* is required reading. This is the book that inspired me to write about King—Doug's enthusiasm is infectious—and it inspired others, as well. Available in paperback, this authorized book, written with the consent and cooperation of Stephen King, is a fascinating read.

Also, from Citadel Press, Stephen Spignesi's *The Lost Work of Stephen King: A Guide to Unpublished Manuscripts, Story Fragments, Alternative Versions, & Oddities* covers unpublished and little-seen fiction and nonfiction. A $24.95 hardback, this book is a "must read" for anyone who wants to know about all of King's output.

I saw a hardback of The Dark Tower IV: Wizard and Glass *at Waldenbooks/Barnes & Noble/Amazon.com in the summer of 1997. It was published by Donald M. Grant, Publisher. I've never heard of them.*

Donald M. Grant, Publisher, has been one of the best-kept secrets in the King community. Founded by Donald M. Grant, a Rhode Island publisher inspired by Arkham House, which issued beautiful editions in hardback of fantasy/horror writers, Grant's books are showcase examples of how books *ought* to be made: sturdily bound, beautifully printed, handsomely designed, and sumptuously illustrated.

Grant has published several King books in limited editions—notably *Christine, The Talisman, Desperation*—and he is the hardback publisher for the Dark Tower series, for which he's issued four volumes.

For years, contractual restrictions prevented Grant from selling the Dark

Tower books into the chain stores, but that restriction has been lifted. As a result, many King fans—many of whom were unaware that such editions existed—were surprised to find a hardback of *The Dark Tower IV: Wizard and Glass* at their local chain store or through on-line sources like Amazon.com and Barnesandnoble.com, months before its publication in trade paperback from NAL.

Grant does maintain a mailing list, but my recommendation is to get on Betts Bookstore's list, since they stock Grant's King titles and collectibles from other small presses, as well.

I'm starting a King collection. Where should I start?

Start out inexpensively. Buy first editions in hardback when published, so you get them at cover price or less. Then inspect the book before you leave the store, so you don't get home with a damaged copy, which would have to be returned.

Because book jackets are very susceptible to damage, put a protective cover—a Gaylord cover or Brodart cover—on the jacket, just as your local library does, or put the book in a plastic bag.

There are several book dealers that handle King collectibles—a complete list appears in the most recent edition of *The Stephen King Companion*.

Of course, Betts Bookstore will likely have—or can get—virtually anything you want by or about King, if you've got the time and the money.

Well, folks, that's all for now, but stick around. King's going to be very active in the book and movie front in 1998 and beyond, and I'd like to keep you informed. Check in from time to time on my web site or check out *Phantasmagoria* and we'll keep the lines of communication open.

Happy hunting!

George Beahm

"Being a brand name is all right. Trying to be a writer, trying to fill the blank sheet in an honorable and truthful way, is better."

—Stephen King, "On Becoming a Brand Name," *Fear Itself*

NOTES

Abbreviations:
SK = Stephen King
GB = George Beahm
CR = *Castle Rock*
BDN = *Bangor Daily News*

Chapter 1

1. SK, *Stephen King's Danse Macabre* (New York: Everest House, 1981), p. 23.
2. Christopher Chesley, interviewed by George Beahm (Durham, Maine, October 22, 1990). [Note: All references hereafter to Chesley are to this interview.]
3. Chesley interview.
4. Brian Hall, quoted by Jeff Pert, "The Local Haunts of Stephen King," *Times Record* (Brunswick, Maine), October 29, 1990.
5. Chesley interview.
6. Douglas E. Winter, *Stephen King: The Art of Darkness* (New York: Signet, 1986). p. 21.
7. Chesley interview.
8. Ibid.
9. Ibid.
10. Ibid.
11. SK, "The Importance of Being Forry," *Mr. Monster's Movie Gold* by Forrest J. Ackerman (Norfolk, Virginia: Donning Company/Publishers, 1982), p. 9.
12. Chesley interview.
13. Ibid.
14. David King, interviewed in *The Shape Under the Sheet: The Stephen King Encyclopedia*. (Ann Arbor, Michigan: Popular Culture, Ink, 1991).
15. Chesley interview.
16. Ibid.

Chapter 2

1. Hall, quoted by Pert, in "The Local Haunts of Stephen King," October 29, 1990.
2. Chesley interview.
3. Ibid.
4. Ibid.

5. Michael R. Collings and David Engelbretson, *The Shorter Works of Stephen King* (Mercer Island, Wash.: Starmont House), p. 10.

6. Ibid., p. 13.

7. SK, "I Was a Teenage Grave Robber," in *Comics Review*, 1965.

8. SK, quoted by Richard Rothenstein, "Interview with Stephen King," *Pub* magazine May 1980, p. 33.

9. Chesley interview.

10. SK, interview, *Bare Bones* (New York: McGraw Hill), p. 90.

Chapter 3

1. SK, "King's Garbage Truck," *Maine Campus* (Orono), July 25, 1969.

2. *Chronicle of the Twentieth Century*, ed. Clifton Daniel (Mount Kisco, N.Y.: Chronicle Publications, 1987), p. 1013.

3. Ibid.

4. Sanford Phippen, "The Student King," *Maine*, Fall 1989.

5. SK, letter to Michael Collings.

6. SK, *The Bachman Books* (New York: NAL Books, 1985), p. vi.

7. SK, Introduction to "The Glass Floor," *Weird Tales* (Fall 1990), p. 37.

8. Ibid.

9. Burton Hatlen, interviewed by GB in Bangor, Maine, October 1990.

10. SK, quoted by Carroll F. Terrell, *Stephen King: Man and Artist* (Orono, Maine: Northern Lights Publishing Company, 1991), p. 44.

11. Ibid., p. 39.

12. Ibid.

13. Ibid., p. 48.

14. Ibid., pp. 52–53.

15. SK, "On Becoming a Brand Name," *Fear Itself* (New York: NAL, Plume, 1984), p. 17.

16. SK, quoted by Phippen, *Maine*, p. 20.

17. "Sniper on Tower Terrorizes Campus, Slays 12," *Chronicle of the 20th Century*, p. 952.

18. Jim Bishop, quoted by Phippen, *Maine*, p. 20.

19. David Bright, interviewed by GB in Bangor, Maine, October 25, 1990.

20. Ibid.

21. *Feast of Fear: Conversations with Stephen King*, compiled by Don Herron (San Rafael, Calif., and Novato, Pa.: Underwood-Miller, 1989), p. 2.

22. Hatlen, interviewed by GB, 1990.

23. Ibid.

24. Diane McPherson, quoted by Phippen, *Maine*, p. 20.

25. SK, "King's Garbage Truck," *Maine Campus*, February 12, 1970.

26. Tabitha King, quoted in Winter, *Stephen King: The Art of Darkness*, p. 26.
27. Ibid.
28. SK, interviewed by Rodney Labbe, "Stephen and Tabitha King," *Ubris II* (Orono, Maine), vol. 1, no. 1, 1984.
29. SK, "King's Garbage Truck," *Maine Campus*, May 7, 1970.
30. Ibid.

Chapter 4

1. *The Oxford Companion to English Literature* (New York: Oxford University Press, 1985) p. 192.
2. SK, *The Dark Tower: The Gunslinger* (New York: Plume, 1988), p. 11.
3. Chesley interview.
4. SK, *Kingdom of Fear: The World of Stephen King*, eds. Tim Underwood and Chuck Miller (New York: NAL/Plume, 1986), pp. 16–17.
5. SK, Hoyt Cinema (Bangor, Maine), October 25, 1990, on the occasion of the world premiere and press conference for *Stephen King's Graveyard Shift*.
6. Ibid.
7. Ibid.
8. Bill Thompson, "A Girl Named Carrie," *Kingdom of Fear*, Introduction, p. 31.
9. SK, "On Becoming a Brand Name," *Fear Itself*, p. 18.
10. SK, "Memo from Stephen King," *Rotten Rejections*, ed. André Bernard (Wainscott, N.Y.: Pushcart Press, 1990), p. 25.
11. Ibid., p. 19.
12. Ibid.
13. Ibid., pp. 22–23.
14. Ibid., p. 23.

Chapter 5

1. SK, *Fear Itself*, p. 24.
2. *Kingdom of Fear*, p. 32.
3. Ibid.
4. SK, *Fear Itself*, p. 25.
5. *Kingdom of Fear*, p. 31.
6. Ibid., p. 32.
7. Chesley interview.
8. NAL press release, 1977.
9. SK, *Fear Itself*, p. 28.
10. David Bright, "Hampden Teacher Hits Jackpot with New Book," *Bangor Daily News*, May 25, 1973.

11. SK, interviewed by Eric Norden, "The *Playboy* Interview: Stephen King," in *The Stephen King Companion* (1989 edition), p. 27.

12. SK, "Why I Was Bachman," *The Bachman Books* (1985), pp. ix–x.

13. William G. Thompson, letter to booksellers from Doubleday, January 1974.

14. Winter, *Stephen King: The Art of Darkness*, p. 61.

Chapter 6

1. SK, *Fear Itself*, p. 33.

2. Winter, *Stephen King: The Art of Darkness*, p. 61.

3. SK, speech in Pasadena, California.

4. Ibid.

5. Ibid.

6. Ibid.

7. Ibid.

8. Ibid.

9. Bill Thompson, quoted by SK, *Different Seasons* (New York: Viking Press, 1982), Afterword, p. 521.

10. Ibid.

11. SK, *Danse Macabre*, p. 370.

12. SK, "Night Surf," *Night Shift* (New York: Doubleday, 1978), p. 61.

13. SK, *Danse Macabre*, p. 371.

14. Al Sarrantonio, *Horror: 100 Best Books*, eds. Stephen Jones and Kim Newman (New York: Caroll & Graf, 1988), p. 162.

15. Leonard Wolf, *Dracula: The Connoisseur's Guide* (New York: Broadway Books, 1997) p. 185.

16. SK, on Thompson's reaction, "On Becoming a Brand Name," *Fear Itself*, pp. 30–31.

17. Mel Allen, "Witches and Asprin," *Writer's Digest*, June 1977, p. 27.

18. Ibid.

19. Kirby McCauley, interviewed by Christopher Spruce, "SK Literary Agent Discusses Friend and Client," *CR*, May 1986, p. 1.

Chapter 7

1. SK, interview, *Bare Bones: Conversations on Terror with Stephen King*, eds. Tim Underwood and Chuck Miller (N.Y.: McGraw Hill, 1988), p. 190.

2. SK, "On *The Shining and Other Perpetrations*," *Whispers* #17/18, August 1982.

3. Kim Foltz, with Penelope Wang, "An Unstoppable Thriller King," *Newsweek*, June 10, 1985, p. 63.

4. SK, interview, *Fear Itself*, p. 26.

5. Kirby McCauley, *CR*, p. 7.

6. SK, "On Becoming a Brand Name," *Fear Itself*, p. 40.

7. SK, "The Importance of Being Bachman," *The Bachman Books* (N.Y.: Plume, Penguin, 1996), p. vi.

8. *Fleet News* (U.K.), October 7, 1977.

9. Ibid.

10. Ibid.

11. NAL/Signet press release, December 1977.

12. SK, interview, *Bare Bones*, p. 114.

13. SK speech, Pasadena, California.

14. Ibid.

15. Peter Straub, "Meeting Stevie," *Fear Itself*, p. 11.

16. Ibid., p. 10.

17. SK, *Different Seasons* (New York: Viking Press, 1982), Afterword, p. 524.

18. SK, *Night Shift* (New York: Doubleday, 1978), Foreword, p. xvii.

Chapter 8

1. SK, interview, *Bare Bones*, p. 108.

2. *Publishers Weekly*, November 28, 1977, p. 46.

3. Hatlen interviewed by GB.

4. SK, quoted in "Novelist King Teaching Creative Writing," *News-Times* (Danbury, Connecticut), September 11, 1978.

5. SK, quoted in "Novelist to Teach," *Portsmouth Herald*, September 11, 1978.

6. SK, *Danse Macabre*, Forenote, pp. xii–xiii.

7. Ibid., p. xi.

8. Ibid., p. xii.

9. SK, quoted by John Nash, in "Orrington's *Real* Pet Sematary," *BDN*, September 13, 1988.

10. Ibid.

11. SK, *Danse Macabre*, p. 34.

12. *The Shining* (New York: Doubleday, 1977), pp. 446–47.

13. Winter, *Stephen King: The Art of Darkness*, p. 146.

14. SK, speech, Truth or Consequences, New Mexico, November 19, 1983.

15. Hatlen interview.

Chapter 9

1. Hatlen interview.

2. SK, "Why I Was Bachman," *The Bachman Books* (1985), p. x.

3. SK, interview, *Bare Bones*, p. 131.

4. Ibid.

5. Anne Rivers Siddons, Introduction, Collector's Edition, *The Dead Zone* (New York: Plume, 1994), p. xiv.

6. Fritz Leiber, "Horror Hits a High," *Fear Itself*, p. 105.

7. Ibid.

8. SK, *Silver Bullet* (New York: Signet, 1985), Foreword, p. 8.

9. Ibid., p. 10.

10. SK, quoted by Chris Palmer, "Watching *'Salem's Lot*," *BDN*, November 19, 1979.

Chapter 10

1. Jessie Horsting, *Stephen King at the Movies* (Starlog Signet, 1986), p. 6.

2. Chesley interview.

3. SK, "Special Make-Up Effects and the Writer," *DQ*, no. 52, p. 6.

4. SK, speech, Pasadena, California.

5. SK, quoted in *Stephen King Goes to Hollywood* (New York: NAL/Plume, 1987), pp. 32–33.

6. SK, interview, *Bare Bones*, p. 143.

7. SK, "A Novelist's Perspective on Bangor," *Black Magic & Music* (Bangor, Maine: Bangor Historical Society, 1983), p. 4.

8. *Feast of Fear*, p. 219.

9. Ibid.

10. *Entertainment Weekly*, article by Dana Kennedy, 1996.

11. Letter, Eric Flower to SK, March 23, 1976.

12. Letter, SK to Eric Flower, April 6, 1976.

13. Kirby McCauley, *Dark Forces* (New York: Bantam Books, 1981), Introduction, p. xiv.

14. SK, speech, Truth or Consequences, New Mexico.

15. SK, interview, *Feast of Fear*, p. 99.

16. SK, *Firestarter* (New York: Signet, 1981), Afterword, p. 402.

17. Michael Collings, *The Stephen King Companion* (1995), p. 216.

Chapter 11

1. SK, *Silver Bullet*, Foreword, p. 10.

2. Ibid., p. 11.

3. Ibid., p. 12.

4. SK, *Danse Macabre*, p. 89.

5. Ibid., p. xiii.

6. *Publishers Weekly*, February 27, 1981, p. 144.

7. SK, quoted by Winter, *Stephen King: The Art of Darkness*, p. 192.

8. Brian Ash, ed., *The Visual Encyclopedia of Science Fiction* (New York: Harmony Books, 1977), p. 241.

9. SK, *The Green Mile* (New York: Plume, 1997), Introduction, p. 6.

10. *Publishers Weekly*, February 27, 1981, p. 144.

11. SK, *Bachman Books* (New York: Plume, 1985), Introduction, p. x.

Chapter 12

1. Evelyn Waugh, *Writers on Writing*, selected and edited by Jon Winokur (Philadelphia: Running Press, 1986), p. 111.

2. SK, "On Becoming a Brand Name," *Fear Itself*, p. 19.

3. *Bachman Books*, 1996, p. vi.

4. *Different Seasons*, p. 525.

5. Ibid., p. 526.

6. Ibid., p. 522.

7. *Publishers Weekly*, June 18, 1982, p. 64.

8. Thomas Gifford, "Stephen King's Quartet," *Washington Post Book World*, August 22, 1982, p. 2.

9. *Different Seasons*, paperback edition, blurb on book cover.

10. "Apt Pupil," *Different Seasons*, p. 114.

11. Ibid., p. 124.

12. SK, interviewed by Charles Platt, *Dream Makers II* (New York: Berkley, 1983), pp. 279–80.

13. "The Body," *Different Seasons*, p. 450.

14. Ibid., p. 457.

15. Ibid., p. 517.

16. Ibid., p. 518.

17. Ibid., p. 527.

18. SK, quoted by Janet C. Beaulieu, "Gunslinger Stalks Darkness in Human Spirit," *CR*, March 1989, p. 1.

19. *The Stephen King Companion* (1989 edition), p. 220.

20. Michael Whelan, *The Art of Michael Whelan* (New York: Bantam Books, 1993), p. 118.

21. Advertising brochure from Donald M. Grant Publisher, 1982.

22. SK, "The Politics of Limiteds—Part II," *CR*, July 1985, p. 5.

23. SK, speech, Pasadena, California.

24. SK, *Feast of Fear*, p. 264.

25. *Locus*, August 1983.

26. Ibid.

27. SK, television ad produced by Ogilvey & Mather, for American Express (date unknown).

28. Source unknown.

29. Source unknown.

30. Source unknown.

31. *The Stephen King Companion* (1989 edition), p. 86.

32. Ibid.

Chapter 13

1. SK, "Why I Wrote *The Eyes of the Dragon*," *CR*, February 1987, p. 4.

2. SK, *The Eyes of the Dragon*, hardback edition, flap copy.

3. SK, quoted in "King New Book Advance — $1," *Locus*, January 1983, p. 5.

4. Richard Kobritz, quoted by R. H. Martin in "Richard Kobritz and Christine," *Fangoria*, no. 32, p. 16.

5. SK, interviewed by Marshall Blonsky, "Hooked on Horror," *Washington Post*, p. B5.

6. *Publishers Weekly*, February 25, 1983, p. 80.

7. James Charlton and Lisbeth Mark, *Writers Home Companion*, (New York: Penguin Books, 1987), pp. 32–33.

8. Waka Tsunoda, "King's 'Sematary' Unforgettable," *Sunday Portsmouth Herald*, December 4, 1983.

9. *Publishers Weekly*, September 23, 1983, pp. 61–62.

10. SK, speech, Pasadena, California.

11. SK, "The Politics of Limiteds — Part II," *CR*, July 1985, p. 1.

12. SK, letter to editor, *BDN*, June 22, 1983.

13. Letter from Ellanie Sampson to GB.

14. SK, "Entering the Rock Zone, Or, How I Happened to Marry a Rock Station from Outer Space," *CR*, October 1987, p. 5.

Chapter 14

1. Winter, *Stephen King: The Art of Darkness*, Foreword, p. xiii.

2. Ibid., p. 194.

3. Form letter distributed at the American Booksellers Convention in 1984. (The letter accompanied the advance reading copies of the novel, distributed free to booksellers.)

4. SK, "Lists That Matter (Number 8), *CR*, September 1985, p. 7.

5. SK, quoted by Gary Wood in "Firestarter," *Cinefantastique* (February 1991), p. 34.

6. Ibid.

7. SK, "King on *Firestarter:* Who's to Blame?" (letter to *Cinefantastique*), p. 35.

8. Harlan Ellison, "Harlan Ellison's Watching," *The Stephen King Companion* (1989 edition), p. 226.

9. Barney Cohen, "The Shockmeisters," *Esquire*, November 1984, p. 231.

10. SK, quoted by Winter, *Stephen King: The Art of Darkness*, p. 160.

11. *Thinner* (New York: NAL Books, 1984), p. 111.

12. Michael Alpert, "Designing *The Eyes of the Dragon*," *CR*, August 1985, p. 6.

13. SK, "The Politics of Limiteds—Part II," *CR*, July 1985, p. 5.

Chapter 15

1. Stephanie Leonard, *CR*, January 1985, p. 1.

2. Ibid.

3. Stephanie Leonard, *CR*, February 1985, p. 8.

4. SK, quoted by Stefan Kanfer, "King of Horror," *Time*, October 6, 1986, p. 78.

5. SK, quoted by Joan H. Smith, "Pseudonum Kept Five King Novels a Mystery," *BDN*, February 9, 1985.

6. Jo Koskela, "No Fair, Stephen King," letter to editor, *BDN*, 1985.

7. SK, quoted by Loukis Louka, "The Dispatch Talks with: Writer Stephen King," *Maryland Coast Dispatch*, August 8, 1986.

8. SK, "Why I Was Bachman," *The Bachman Books* (1985), p. ix.

9. Stephanie Leonard, *CR*, April 1985, p. 1.

10. Letter from Jeff Conner to GB.

11. SK, quoted by Jessie Horsting, *Stephen King at the Movies* (New York: Starlog Press, 1986), p. 70.

12. SK, quoted by Calvin Ahlgren, "King of Horror Finds Directing Unnerving," *San Francisco Chronicle*, July 22, 1986.

13. Ibid.

14. SK, "Say 'No' to the Enforcers," *CR*, August 1986, p. 7.

15. SK, *The Bachman Books* (1985), p. 7.

16. Harlan Ellison, interview, *The Stephen King Companion* (1989 edition), p. 226.

Chapter 16

1. Ray Bradbury, *War of Words* (Kansas City, Mo.: Andrews and McMeel, 1993), p. 31.

2. "Don't Make Freedom a Dirty Word," *Christian Civic League Record* (1986).

3. 112th Maine Legislature, document number 2092.

4. Jasper S. Wyman, "Another Viewpoint: Hard-core, Violent Pornography Debases and Destroys," *BDN*, February 28, 1986.

5. Ad campaign, quoted in *Locus*, 1986.

6. SK, quoted by Christopher Spruce, "Stephen King Helps Spearhead Censorship Referendum Defeat," in *The Stephen King Companion* (1989 edition), p. 143.

7. Joseph King, "Another Viewpoint: An Obscenity Law Is Obscene," *BDN*, June 5, 1986.

8. *Christian Civic League Record*, 1986.

9. SK, quoted by Christopher Spruce, *The Stephen King Companion* (1989 edition), p. 142.

10. Ibid.

11. *Christian Civic League Record*, 1986, p. 19.

12. SK, quoted in "Full Throttle with Stephen King," *New Times* (Phoenix, Arizona), July 30–August 5, 1986.

13. Robert H. Newall, "King's Film Lacks Taste," *BDN*, July 29, 1986.

14. Robert Garrett, "'Overdrive': Bodies by King," *Boston Globe*, July 26, 1986.

15. SK, press conference for *Stephen King's Graveyard Shift*, Bangor, Maine, 1986.

16. Rob Cohen, quoted by Gary Wood, "The Dark Half," *Cinefantastique*, p. 27.

17. Television listing in *USA Today*, March 2, 1990.

18. Rob Reiner, interviewed by Gary Wood, transcription of unpublished interview, 1989.

19. Richard Freeman, "Boys Will Be Boys in Refreshing 'Stand by Me,'" *Newark Star-Ledger*, August 8, 1986, p. 49.

20. David Brooks, "What Is Death, What Is Goofy?" *Insight*, September 1, 1986.

21. Rob Reiner, quoted in *Stephen King at the Movies*, p. 83.

22. SK to Michael R. Collings, "Stephen King's Comments on *It*," *CR*, July 1986, p. 1.

23. From *It*, unpaginated front matter.

24. David Gates, "The Creature That Refused to Die," *Newsweek*, September 1, 1986, p. 84.

25. *Publishers Weekly*, June 27, 1986, p. 74.

26. Walter Wagner, "More Evil Than a 15-Foot Spider," *New York Times Book Review*, August 24, 1986.

27. Ad, in Book-of-the-Month Club *News Magazine*, 1986.

Chapter 17

1. SK, *The Eyes of the Dragon*, copy on dust jacket.

2. Margi Washburn (Tucson, Arizona), letter to editor, "'Eyes' Has It," *CR*, December 1987–January 1988.

3. Ibid.

4. SK, *The Eyes of the Dragon*, copy on dust jacket.

5. *Skeleton Crew* (New York: G. P. Putnam's Sons, 1985), p. 510.

6. Harlan Ellison, *Slippage* (New York: Houghton Mifflin, 1987), p. xxii.

7. Tabitha King, "Co-miser-a-ting with Stephen King," *CR*, August 1987, p. 1.

8. SK, interview, Book-of-the-Month Club *News Magazine*, June 1987.

9. Tabitha King, "Co-misera-a-ting with Stephen King," *CR*, August 1987, p. 1.

10. Ibid.

11. British paperback, p. 11, of *SKS*.

12. SK, speech, Pasadena, California.

13. *The Ideal, Genuine Man* by Don Robertson (Bangor, Maine: Philtrum Press, dist. Putnam Publishing Group), dust jacket copy.

14. SK, in "The Ideal, Genuine Writer: A Forenote," in *The Ideal, Genuine Man*, p. ix.

15. Ibid.

16. *The Tommyknockers* (New York: G. P. Putnam's Sons, 1987), dust jacket copy.

17. SK quoted in Winter, *Stephen King: The Art of Darkness*, p.189.

18. SK, interviewed by Lynn Flewelling, "King Working on a Book He Believes Could Be His Best," *BDN*, September 11, 1990.

19. *Publishers Weekly*, October 9, 1987, p. 79.

Chapter 18

1. Waugh, *Writers on Writing*, p. 103.

2. *SKS*, p. 142.

3. SK, *Nightmares in the Sky*, p. 1.

4. Ibid., dust jacket flap copy.

5. David Streitfeld, *Washington Post Book World*, 1988.

6. Ibid.

7. Ibid.

8. *Stephen King: The First Decade, Carrie to Pet Sematary* (Boston: Twayne Publishers, 1988), Preface (no pagination).

9. SK, Christopher Spruce, interviewed by George Beahm, 1988.

10. SK, "Stephen King's WZON Rocks On," *CR*, October 1988, p. 3.

11. Stephanie Leonard, editorial comments, *CR*, September 1988, p. 2.

Chapter 19

1. Robert Diforio, quoted by Spruce, "Happy New Year . . . ," *CR*, February 1989.

2. SK, *The Dark Tower: The Gunslinger*, Afterword.

3. *Stephen King Companion* (1989 edition), p. 106.

4. Ibid., p. 108.

5. SK, *Nightmares & Dreamscapes* (New York: Viking, 1993), p. 807.

6. *The Stephen King Companion* (1989), p. 109.

7. SK, *Nightmares & Dreamscapes*, p. 801.

8. Charles C. Calhoun, *Maine* (Fodor's Travel Publications, Inc., Compass American Guides, 1994), p. 11.

9. SK, press conference, *Stephen King's Graveyard Shift*, Bangor, Maine.

10. Ibid.

11. Chris Spruce, Editor's Column, *CR*, December 1989, p. 2.

12. SK, *The Dark Half* (New York: Viking, 1989), dust jacket copy.

13. *The Bachman Books* (1996), p. v.

14. Ibid., pp. v–vi.

15. SK, *The Dark Half*, p. 108.

16. *Publishers Weekly*, September 1, 1989, p. 76.

17. Chris Spruce, "Say Goodnight, Lucy," *CR*, September 1989, p. 1.

Chapter 20

1. *Science Fiction Chronicle*, March 1990, p. 4.

2. SK, *The Stand* (1990), p. x.

3. Ibid., dedication page.

4. Ibid., p. xii.

5. Ibid.

6. Ibid.

7. *Four Past Midnight* (New York: Viking, 1990), "An Introductory Note," p. *xiii*.

8. Ibid., p. xiv.

9. Ibid., p. xv.

10. Ibid., p. 250.

11. Ibid., pp. 610–11.

12. SK, quoted by Bill Goldstein, "King of Horror," *Publishers Weekly*, January 24, 1991, p. 9.

13. *Graveyard Shift* press conference.

14. Richard Harrington, " 'Graveyard': Dead on Arrival," *Washington Post*, October 29, 1990, p. B8.

15. Rob Reiner, interviewed by Gary Wood, 1989.

16. Kathy Bates, quoted by Glenn Lovel, " 'Psycho' Jokes Aside, Actress Kathy Bates Refuses to Be Typecast," *Daily Press* (Newport News, Virginia), December 8, 1990.

17. Mike Clark, "Reiner's 'Misery' Makes Scary Company," *USA Today*, November 30, 1990.

18. Mal Vincent, "Childhood's Worst Fears Resurface When 'It' Returns to a Small Town,' " *Virginian-Pilot and Ledger-Star* (Norfolk, Virginia), November 1990, p. G3.

19. *People Weekly*, "Love Them or Loathe Them," Fall 1989, p. 45.

Chapter 21

1. "King Tells Eager Fans in Syracuse about 'Odd State of Being Famous,'" AP story in *BDN*, April 29, 1991.

2. Ibid.

3. John Ripley, "King Target of Scare," *BDN*, April 1991.

4. SK, quoted by Renee Ordway, "Kings Plan to Increase Security After Weekend Break-In," *BDN*, April 23, 1991.

5. Ibid.

6. Ibid., Tabitha King, quoted by Ordway.

7. Ibid.

8. Eric Keene, quoted by Renee Ordway, "King Home Attic Was Focus of Keene Break-In," *BDN*, April 26, 1991.

9. Ibid.

10. Ibid.

11. Ibid.

12. Ibid.

13. *BDN*, September 14, 1991.

14. Ibid.

15. Tabitha King, interviewed by Rodney Labbe, "Tabitha King: Resisting the Star-Maker Machinery," *CR*, December 87/January 88, p. 10.

16. "Woman Sues King," *Daily Press* (Newport News, Virginia), April 18, 1991.

17. John Ripley, "King Target of Scare," *BDN*, April 1991.

18. Joyce Meskis, "Sunday Book & Author Breakfast," ABA Annual Meeting, New York, June 2, 1991.

19. Ibid.

21. *The Films of Stephen King*, by Ann Lloyd, p. 91.

22. Jonathan Levin, quoted by Matt Rousch, "Stephen King Scares Up a Summer Series," *USA Today*, May 7, 1991, p. 3D.

23. Press release, *Stephen King's Golden Years,* Laurel-King, Inc., 1991.

24. Matt Rousch, "Stephen King Likes Being in the Driver's Seat," *USA Today*, August 8, 1991, p. 3D.

25. Edward Bryant, *Locus*, December 1991, pp. 21, 23.

26. SK, Press conference at ABA, Javits Convention Center, New York, June 2, 1991.

27. *Publishers Weekly*, July 25, 1991, p. 36.

28. Joe Queenan, "And Us Without Our Spoons," *New York Times Book Review*, September 29, 1991, p. 13.

29. Walter Kendrick, "Pacts with the Devil," *Washington Post Book World*, September 29, 1991, p. 9.

30. SK, "Silence of the Lambs," letter to the editor, *Washington Post Book World*, November 17, 1991.

31. Ibid.

32. *The Stephen King Companion* (1995 edition), p. 289.

33. Robert Parker, Sanders Theatre, Cambridge, Massachusetts, November 22, 1991. Public talk recorded by David Lowell.

34. Ibid., Stephen King.

Chapter 22

1. Brett Leonard, quoted by Gary Wood, "Stephen King, Computer Graphic," *Cinefantastique* (Volume 22, Number 5), April 1992, p. 6.

2. Ibid.

3. Richard Harrington, "Lawnmower: Sod Adaptation," *Washington Post*, March 7, 1992.

4. SK, quoted by Andy Marx, in "Film Clips: Stephen King Kicks Grass," *Los Angeles Times*, "Calendar" section, March 5, 1992, p. 23.

5. Ibid., Bob Shaye, quoted by Andy Marx.

6. Ibid.

7. Transcription of Gary Wood of "Columbia Pictures: 'Sleepwalkers,' " October 11, 1991.

8. SK, quoted by W. C. Stroby, *Fangoria*, June 1992, p. 28.

9. Richard Harrington, *Washington Post*, March 7, 1992.

10. Susan Wloszczyna, *USA Today*, April 1992.

11. *Entertainment Weekly*, April 1992.

12. Scott Warren Lynch, book preview of *Gerald's Game*, Book-of-the-Month Club, *Booknews Magazine*, Summer 1992.

13. *Publishers Weekly*, May 25, 1992, p. 38.

14. *The Stephen King Companion* (1995 edition), p. 297.

15. SK, "The Neighborhood of the Beast," *Mid-Life Confidential: The Rock Bottom Remainders* (New York: Viking, 1994).

16. Ibid., p. 5.

17. SK, quoted by David Streitfeld, "Hey! C.C. Writers," *Washington Post*, May 27, 1992.

18. SK, quoted by Dale McGarrigle, "King Takes Stage with Authors' Band," *BDN*, June 1992.

19. Ibid.

20. Editorial, "Read This Book," *BDN*, March 20, 1992.

21. SK, op-ed piece, *BDN*, March 20, 1992.

22. SK, *Nightmares & Dreamscapes*, p. 811.

23. Ibid., p. 812.

24. Bob Haskell, "Stephen King's Field of Dreams," from *1992 Complete Handbook of Baseball*, p. 6.

25. Ibid., SK, quoted by Haskell, p. 12.
26. Ibid., p. 10.
27. Ibid.
28. Editorial, *BDN*, June 27, 1991.
29. SK, quoted by Carroll Astbury, "King Presented Award for Service to Community," *BDN*, June 25, 1992.
30. SK, *Nightmares & Dreamscapes*, p. 6.

Chapter 23

1. Video trailer, *The Making of Stephen King's The Stand*.
2. Ibid., Molly Ringwald.
3. Michael Collings, *The Stephen King Companion* (1995), p. 288.
4. SK, *The Shooting Script: The Shawshank Redemption* (New York: Newmarket Press, 1996), Introduction, p. x.
5. Ibid.
6. Ibid., p. xii.
7. Ibid., Frank Darabont, p. 182.
8. Ibid.
9. Ibid., Gene Siskel, back-cover blurb.
10. Michael Berry, article, "The Modern Master of Horror Visits Santa Cruz, CA", on the Internet, at: http://www.sff.net.people/mberry/STCRUZ.HTM.
11. Ibid.
12. *The Stephen King Companion* (1995), p. 304.

Chapter 24

1. Book-of-the-Month Club, Summer 1995, p. 3.
2. *Entertainment Weekly* on-line, review by Mark Harris.
3. Ibid.
4. Ibid.
5. *Entertainment Weekly*, review, Ken Tucker, "Just Plane Scared" on-line.

Chapter 25

1. Burton Hatlen, *Reign of Fear* (Los Angeles and Columbia, Pa.: Underwood-Miller, 1988), p. 50.
2. *Different Seasons*, p. 518.
3. *Prize Stories 1996: The O. Henry Awards* (New York: Doubleday, Anchor, 1996), cover blurb.
4. William Abrahams, *Prize Stories*, Introduction, p. xi.
5. *Fangoria: Masters of the Dark* (New York: Harper Prism, 1997), p. 107.
6. Burton Hatlen, quoted in *Phantasmagoria* #4, p. 7.

7. Ibid., p. 8.

8. Ibid., p. 6.

9. SK, *Nightmares in the Sky*, p. 7.

10. SK, *The Green Mile* (New York: Plume, 1997), Foreword, p. xiv.

11. *Entertainment Weekly*, Dana Kennedy, "Going for Cheap Thrillers." [date not known].

12. *Entertainment Weekly*, profile by Kennedy, p. 2.

13. SK, *The Green Mile*, back cover blurb.

14. Ibid.

15. Ibid.

16. "Spectacular Fall Performance by Stephen King," Bookwire, Internet web site, 1997.

17. Ibid., Elaine Koster.

18. Ibid.

19. Ibid.

20. Ibid.

21. Ibid.

22. Ann Lloyd, *Films of Stephen King* (New York: St. Martin's Press, 1994), p. 94.

23. Ibid.

24. *Phantasmagoria* #4 (1996), p. 21.

25. Ibid.

26. Penguin USA press release, 1996.

Chapter 26

1. Winter, *Stephen King: The Art of Darkness*, p. 186.

2. "The Shining: It Lives Again," Mark Schwed, *TV Guide*, April 26–May 2, 1997 issue, p. 19.

3. *Phantasmagoria* #5 (1997), p. 14.

4. Ibid., p. 32.

5. *Publishers Weekly*, January 20, 1997.

6. "Necessary Evil" by Stewart O'Nan, *Phantasmagoria* 6 (1997), p. 23.

7. Jana Marcus, *In the Shadow of the Vampire: Reflections from the World of Anne Rice* (New York: Thunder's Mouth Press), Preface, p. ix.

8. Ibid.

Chapter 27

1. *New York Post*, November 9, 1997.

2. Ibid.

3. "Making Books: Getting Spooked by Stephen King's Tactic," by Martin Arnold, *New York Times*, November 5, 1997.

4. Ibid.
5. Ibid.
6. AOL News, PRNewswire, "Stephen King Partners with Simon & Schuster Companies," November 6, 1997.
7. AOL, "The Book Review," November 1997.
8. AOL News, "Stephen King Partners," November 6, 1997.
9. Ibid.
10. Ibid.
11. Ibid.
12. Ibid.

Chapter 28

1. AOL, "The Book Review," November 1997.
2. Tabitha King, "Living with the Boogeyman," *Murderess Ink* (New York: Workman Publishing, 1979), p. 176.
3. AOL, "The Book Review," November 1997.